CIRCUS

FANTASY UNDER THE BIG TOP

OTHER BOOKS BY THE EDITOR

Running with the Pack
Paper Cities
Bewere the Night
Bloody Fabulous
Willful Impropiety

CIRCUS

FANTASY UNDER THE BIG TOP

EKATERINA SEDIA

PRIME BOOKS

CIRCUS: FANTASY UNDER THE BIG TOP

Prime Books
www.prime-books.com

For more information, contact Prime Books:
prime@prime-books.com

ISBN: 978-1-60701-355-6

CONTENTS

INTRODUCTION

Most experiences change with age—the way adults perceive the book they loved as children is going to be quite different from the original wonderment. But few things change for us as universally and as dramatically as circuses. It's true! As children, we are delighted by the simple and the obvious, we often don't notice how depressed and depressing the animals are, how hackneyed the clowns. But as adults, we rarely managed to escape that impression—in fact, it becomes a cliche. Instead, when (and if) we go to the circuses, we are taken by the acts that require skill—trapeze and acrobats are the acts that draw the adults' attention. We look back at our childhoods, nostalgic, and realize that there's something in a child's view of the circus an adult would never recapture.

But would we want to? Childhood, idealized as it is, is often naïve. We love circuses as children with unsophisticated love—but is adult sophistication necessarily inferior? Is nostalgia superior or silly? So we write stories about circuses as conversation with ourselves, more often than not—an argument, if you will, a polemic: what have we lost? What have we gained? Can we ever set foot into the same river, and if so, is it worth trying?

There is never a single answer, of course. There is never a single story. So we have collected tales of children running away to join a circus and circuses doing the same, stories of circuses not of this world (in all senses of the word), circuses futuristic, nostalgic, filled with existential dread and/or joy. Acts mundane, and spectacular, and incomprehensible. Clowns and extinct animals. Magicians and werewolves. Acrobats and living musical instruments. But always, always arguing with ourselves—because these garish, cruel places that used to be filled with joy still have a hold on us. Because we cannot help but love them—for the sake of children we were once, or for the sake of better adults we long to become. Be it a local carnival or the most celebrated circus in the world, we will always feel that tug deep inside.

—Ekaterina Sedia, New Jersey

SOMETHING ABOUT A DEATH, SOMETHING ABOUT A FIRE

PETER STRAUB

The origin and even the nature of Bobo's Magic Taxi remain mysterious, and the Taxi is still the enigma it was when it first appeared before us on the sawdust floor. Of course it does not lack for exegetes: I possess several manila folders jammed to bursting with analyses of the Taxi and speculations on its nature and construction. "The Bobo Industry" threatens to become giant.

For many years, as you may remember, the inspection of the Taxi by expert and impartial mechanics formed an integral portion of the act. This examination, as scrupulous as the best mechanics could make it, never found any way in which the magnificent Taxi differed from other vehicles of its type. There was no special apparatus or mechanism enabling it to astonish, delight, and terrify, as it still does.

When this inspection was still in the performance—the equivalent of the magician's rolling up his twinkling sleeves—Bobo always stood near the mechanics, in a condition of visible anxiety. He scratched his head, grinned foolishly, beeped a tiny horn attached to his belt, turned cartwheels in bewilderment. His concern always sent the children into great gouts of laughter. But I felt that this apparent anxiety was a real anxiety: that Bobo feared that one night the Einstein of mechanics, the Freud of mechanics, would uncover the principle that made the Magic Taxi unique, and thereby spoil its effectiveness forever. For who remains impressed by a trick, once the mechanism is exposed? The mechanics grunted and sweated, probed the gas tank, got on their backs underneath the Taxi, bent deep into the motor, covered themselves with grease and carbon so that they too looked like comic tramps, and at the end of their time, gave up. They could not find a thing, not even registration numbers on the engine block, nor trade names on any of the engine's component parts.

In appearance it was an ordinary taxi, long, black, squat as a stone cottage, of the sort generally seen in London. Bobo sat at the wheel as the taxi entered the tent, his square behatted head flush against the Plexiglas window that opened onto the larger rear compartment. This was empty but for the upholstered backseat and the two facing chair-seats. It was the very image of the respectable, apart from the sense that Bobo is not driving the taxi but being driven by it. Yet, though nothing could look so mundane as a black taxi, from the first performance this vehicle conveyed an atmosphere of tension and unease. I have seen it happen again and again, consistently: the lights do not dim, no kettle drums roll, there is no announcement, but a curtain at the side opens, and unsmiling Bobo drives (or is driven) into the center of the great tent. At this moment, the audience falls silent, as if hypnotized. You feel uncertain, slightly on edge, as if you have forgotten something you particularly wished to remember. Then the performance begins again.

Bobo does strikingly little in the course of the performance. It is this modesty that has made us love him. He could be one of *us*—fantastically dressed and pummeling the bulb of his little horn when confused or delighted. When the performance concludes, he bows, bending his head to the torrential applause, and drives off through the curtain. Sometimes, when the Taxi has reached the point where the curtain begins to sweep up over the hood, he raises his white-gloved, three-fingered hand in a wave. The wave seems regretful, as if he wishes he could get out of the Taxi and join us up in the uncomfortable stands. So he waves. Then it is over.

There is little to say about the performance. The performance is always the same. Also, it differs slightly from viewer to viewer. Children, to judge from their chatter, see something like a fireworks display. The Taxi shoots off great exploding patterns that do not fade but persist in the air and enact some sort of drama. When pressed by adults, the children utter merely some few vague words about "The Soldier" and "The Lady" and "The Man with a Coat." When asked if the show is funny, they nod their heads, blinking, as if their questioner is moronic.

Adults rarely discuss the performance, except in the safety of print. We have found it convenient to assume a maximum of coincidence between what we have separately seen, for this allows our scholars to speak of "our community," "the community." Exegetes have divided the performance into three sections (the Great Acts), corresponding to the three great waves of emotion that overwhelm us while the Taxi is before us. We agree that everyone over the age of eighteen passes inexorably through these phases, led by the mysterious capacities of the Magic Taxi.

The first act is The Darkness. During this section, which is quite short, we seem to pass into a kind of cloud or fog, in which everything but the Taxi and its attendant becomes indistinct. The lights overhead do not lessen in intensity, they do not so much as flicker. Yet the sense of gloom is undeniable. We are separate, lost in our separation. At this point we remember our sins, our meagerness, our miseries. Some of us weep. Bobo invariably sobs, the tears crusting on his white makeup, and blats and blats his little horn. His painted figure is so akin to ours, and yet so foolish, so theatrical in its grief, that we are distracted from our own memories. We are drawn up out of unhappiness by our love for this tinted waif, Bobo the benighted, and the second act begins.

This section is known as The Falling because of the physical sensations it induces. Each of us, pinned to the rickety wooden benches, seems to fall through space. This is the most literally dreamlike of the three acts. As the sensation of falling continues, we witness a drama that seems to be projected straight from the Taxi into our eyes. This drama, the "film," is also dreamlike. The drama differs from person to person, but seems always to involve one's parents as they were before one's own birth. There is something about a death, something about a fire. Our own figure appears, radiant, on the edge of a field. Sometimes there is a battle, more often there is walking upward on a mountain path through deciduous northern trees. It is Ireland, or Germany, or Sweden. We are in the country of our great-great-great grandfathers. We belong here. At last, we are at home. It is the country that has been calling to us all our lives, in messages known only to our cells. In it we are given a brief moment to be heroic, a long lifetime to be moral. This drama elates us and prepares us for the final section of the performance, The Layers.

The beam of light from the Taxi disappears into our eyes, like a transparent wire. When our eyes have been filled by the light, the Taxi, Bobo, the sweaty lady sitting on your right, and the man in the blue turtleneck directly in front of you, all of them disappear. The first sensation is that of being on the fuzzy edge of sleep; then the layers begin. For some, they are layers of color and light through which the viewer ascends; for some, layers of stone and gravel and red sandstone; an archeologist I know once hinted to me that in this part of the performance he invariably rises through various strata of civilizations, the cave dwellers, the hut builders, the weapon makers, the iron makers, until he is ascending through towns and villages that had been packed into the earth. I, for my part, seem to rise endlessly through scenes of my own life: I see myself playing in the leaves, making snowballs, doing homework, buying a book—I cry out with happiness, seeing the littleness of my own figure and the foolishness of all my joys. For they are all so harmless! Then the external recurs again before us, Bobo waves driving through the curtain, and it is finished.

In the first years, when the Taxi was of interest to only a few, we did not worry much about meanings. We took it as spectacle, as revelation—a special added attraction, as the posters said. Then the scholars of C—— University issued their paper asserting that Bobo's Taxi was the representation of "common miracle," the sign that the world is infused with spirit. The scholars of the universities of B—— and Y—— agreed, and issued a volume of essays entitled *The Ordinary Splendor.*

G——, however, and O——disagreed. They pointed to the sordidness of the surroundings, the seedy costumes of the other acts, Bobo's little horn, his tears, the difficult benches, and the smell of cotton candy, and their volume of essays, *The Blank Day,* was much given to analogies to Darwin, Mondrian, and Beckett. Like many others, I skimmed the books, but did not feel that they had touched the real Bobo, the real Taxi: their resonant arguments, phrased with such tact and authority, battled at a great distance, like moths bumping their heavy wings against a screen door. A remark uttered by a friend of mine indicates much more accurately than they the actual quality of the Taxi's performance.

"I like to think," he told me, "of Bobo before he became famous. You must know the theory that he used to be an ordinary man with an ordinary job. He was a doctor, or an accountant, or a professor of mathematics. My sister-in-law is certain that he was the vice president of a tobacco company. 'It's in his posture,' she says. Anyhow, what I like to picture is the morning that he walked out of his house, going to work in the ordinary way, and found the Taxi waiting for him at the curb, not knowing that it was his destiny, entirely unforeseen, black and purring softly, pregnant with miracle."

SMOKE & MIRRORS

AMANDA DOWNUM

The circus was in town.

Not just any circus, either, but Carson & Kindred's Circus Fabulatoris and Menagerie of Mystical Marvels. The circus Jerusalem Morrow ran away to join when she was seventeen years old. Her family for seven years.

She laid the orange flyer on the kitchen table beside a tangle of beads and wire and finished putting away her groceries. Her smile stretched, bittersweet. She hadn't seen the troupe in five years, though she still dreamt of them. Another world, another life, before she came back to this quiet house.

Cats drifted through the shadows in the back yard as she put out food. The bottle tree—her grandmother's tree—chimed in the October breeze: no ghosts tonight. Glass gleamed cobalt and emerald, diamond and amber, jewel-bright colors among autumn-brown leaves. Awfully quiet this year, so close to Halloween.

Salem glanced at the flyer again as she boiled water for tea. Brother Ezra, Madame Aurora, Luna and Sol the acrobats—familiar names, and a few she didn't know. She wondered if Jack still had the parrots and that cantankerous monkey. The show was here until the end of the month . . .

It's the past. Over and done. She buried the paper under a stack of mail until only one orange corner showed.

Salem woke that night to the violent rattle of glass and wind keening over narrow mouths. The bottle tree had caught another ghost.

She flipped her pillow to the cool side and tried to go back to sleep, but the angry ringing wouldn't let her rest. With a sigh she rolled out of bed and tugged on a pair of jeans. Floorboards creaked a familiar rhythm as she walked to the back door.

Stars were milky pinpricks against the velvet predawn darkness. Grass crunched cool and dry beneath her feet. A cat shrieked across the yard—

they never came too near when the bottles were full. The shadows smelled of ash and bitter smoke. Goosebumps crawled up her arms, tightened her breasts.

"Stay away, witch."

Salem spun, searching for the voice. Something gleamed ghost-pale on her roof. A bird.

"Get away!" White wings flapped furiously.

The wind gusted hot and harsh and glass clashed. Salem turned, reaching for the dancing bottles.

A bottle shattered and the wind hit her like a sandstorm, like the breath of Hell. Glass stung her outstretched palm as smoke seared her lungs. She staggered back, stumbled and fell, blind against the scouring heat.

Then it was over. Salem gasped, tears trickling down her stinging cheeks. The tree shivered in the stillness, shedding singed leaves.

Cursing, she staggered to her feet. She cursed again as glass bit deep into her heel; blood dripped hot and sticky down her instep. The burning thing was gone and so was the bird.

Salem limped back to the house as quickly as she could.

For two days she watched and listened, but caught no sign of ghosts or anything else. She picked up the broken glass and replaced the shattered bottle, brushed away the soot and charred leaves. The tree was old and strong; it would survive.

At night she dreamed.

She dreamed of a lake of tears, of fire that ate the moon. She dreamed of ropes that bit her flesh, of shining chains. She dreamed of trains. She dreamed of a snake who gnawed the roots of the world.

On the third day, a bird landed on the kitchen windowsill. It watched her through the screen with one colorless round eye and fluffed ragged feathers. Salem paused, soapsuds clinging to her hands, and met its gaze. Her shoulder blades prickled.

It held a piece of orange paper crumpled in one pale talon.

"Be careful," she said after a moment. "There are a lot of cats out there."

The bird stared at her and let out a low, chuckling caw. "The circus is in town. Come see the show." White wings unfurled and it flapped away. The paper fluttered like an orange leaf as it fell.

Salem turned to see her big marmalade tomcat sitting on the kitchen table, fur all on end. He bared his teeth for a long steam-kettle hiss before circling three times and settling down with his head on his paws. She glanced through the back screen door, but the bird was gone and the bottles rattled empty in the sticky-cool October breeze.

That night she dreamed of thunder, of blood leaking through white cloth, shining black in the moonlight. No portent, just an old nightmare. She woke trembling, tears cold on her cheeks.

The next morning she wove spells and chains. She threaded links of copper and silver and bronze and hung them with shimmering glass, each bead a bottlesnare. They hung cool around her neck, a comforting weight that chimed when she moved.

As the sun vanished behind the ceiling of afternoon clouds, Salem went to see the circus.

The Circus Fabulatoris sprawled across the county fairgrounds, a glittering confusion of lights and tents and spinning rides. The wind smelled of grease and popcorn and sugar and Salem bit her lip to stop her eyes from stinging.

It had been five years; it shouldn't feel like coming home.

She didn't recognize any faces along the midway, smiled and ignored the shouts to *play a game, win a prize, step right up only a dollar*. Ezra would be preaching by now, calling unsuspecting rubes to Heaven. Jack would be in the big top—which wasn't very big at all—announcing the acrobats and sword-swallowers. He'd have a parrot or a monkey on his shoulder. It was Tuesday, so probably the monkey.

She found a little blue tent, painted with shimmering stripes of color like the northern lights. *Madame Aurora*, the sign read, *fortunes told, futures revealed*.

Candlelight rippled across the walls inside, shimmered on beaded curtains and sequined scarves. Incense hung thick in the air, dragon's blood and patchouli.

"Come in, child," a woman's French-accented voice called, hidden behind sheer draperies, "come closer. I see the future and the past. I have the answers you seek."

Salem smiled. "That accent still ain't fooling anyone."

Silence filled the tent.

"Salem?" Shadows shifted behind the curtain, and a blonde head peered around the edge. Blue eyes widened. "Salem!"

Madame Aurora rushed toward her in a flurry of scarves and bangles and crushed Salem in a tea rose-scented hug.

"Oh my god, Jerusalem! Goddamnit, honey, you said you'd write me, you said you'd call." Paris gave way to Savannah as Raylene Meadows caught Salem by the shoulders and shook her. She stopped shaking and hugged again, tight enough that her corset stays dug into Salem's ribs.

"Are you back?" Ray asked, finally letting go. "Are you going on with us?"

Salem's heart sat cold as glass in her chest. "No, sweetie. I'm just visiting. A little bird thought I should stop by." She looked around the tent, glanced at Ray out of the corner of one eye. "Has Jack started using a white crow?"

Ray stilled for an instant, eyes narrowing. "No. No, that's Jacob's bird."

"Jacob?"

"He's a conjure man. We picked him up outside of Memphis." Her lips curled in that little smile that meant she was sleeping with someone, and still enjoying it.

"Maybe I should meet him."

"Have you come back to steal another man from me?"

Salem cocked an eyebrow. "If I do, will you help me bury the body?"

Ray flinched, like she was the one who had nightmares about it. Maybe she did. Then she met Salem's eyes and smiled. "I will if you need me to."

"Where can I find Jacob?"

Ray's jaw tightened. "In his trailer, most likely. He's between acts right now. It's the red one on the far end of the row."

"Thanks. And . . . don't tell Jack or Ezra I'm here, okay? Not yet."

"You gonna see them before you disappear again?"

"Yeah. I'll try." Laughing voices approached outside. "Better put that bad accent back on." Salem ducked outside.

The wind shifted as she left the cluster of tents and booths, and she caught the tang of lightning. Magic. The real thing, not the little spells and charms she'd taught Ray so many years ago.

Jack had always wanted a real magician. But what did a carnival conjurer have to do with her dreams, or the angry thing that so easily broke free of a spelled bottle?

She followed the tire-rutted path to a trailer painted in shades of blood and rust. A pale shadow flitted through the clouds, drifted down to perch on the roof. The crow watched Salem approach, but stayed silent.

Someone hummed carelessly inside, broke off as Salem knocked. A second later the door swung open to frame a man's shadowed face and shirtless shoulder.

"Hello." He ran a hand through a shock of salt and cinnamon curls. "What can I do for you?" His voice was smoke and whiskey, rocks being worn to sand. But not the crow's voice.

"Are you Jacob?"

"Jacob Grim, magician, conjurer, and prestidigitator, at your service."

"That's an interesting bird you have there."

His stubbled face creased in a coyote's smile. "That she is. Why don't you step inside, Miss . . . "

"Jerusalem." He offered a hand and she shook it; his grip was strong, palm dry and callused. She climbed the metal stairs and stepped into the narrow warmth of the trailer.

Jacob turned away and the lamplight fell across his back. Ink covered his skin, black gone greenish with age. A tree rose against his spine, branches spreading across his shoulders and neck, roots disappearing below the waist of his pants.

He caught her staring and grinned. "Excuse my *dishabille*. I'm just getting ready for my next act." He shrugged on a white shirt and did up the buttons with nimble fingers. The hair on his chest was nearly black, spotted with red and grey—calico colors. Ray usually liked them younger and prettier, but Salem could see the appeal.

"How may I help you, Miss Jerusalem?"

She cocked her head, studied him with *otherwise* eyes. His left eye gleamed with witchlight and magic sparked through the swirling dark colors of his aura. The real thing, all right.

"Your bird invited me to see the show."

"And see it you certainly should. It's a marvelous display of magic and legerdemain, if I do say so myself." He put on a black vest and jacket, slipping cards and scarves into pockets and sleeves.

"Actually, I was hoping you might have an answer or two for me."

He smiled. Not a coyote—something bigger. A wolf's smile. "I have as many answers as you have questions, my dear. Some of them may even be true." He smoothed back his curls and pulled on a black hat with a red feather in the band.

The door swung open on a cold draft before Salem could press. A young girl stood outside, maybe nine or ten. Albino-pale in the grey afternoon light, the hair streaming over her shoulders nearly as white as her dress. Salem shivered as the breeze rushed past her, much colder than the day had been.

"Time to go," she said to Jacob. Her voice was low for a child's and rough. She turned and walked away before he could answer.

"Your daughter?" Salem asked.

"Not mine in blood or flesh, but I look after her. Memory is my assistant." He laid a hand on her arm, steering her gently toward the door. "Come watch the show, Jerusalem, and afterwards perhaps I'll invent some answers for you."

So she sat in the front row in the big top and watched Jacob's show. He pulled scarves from his sleeves and birds from his hat—Jack's parrots, not the white crow. He conjured flowers for the ladies, read men's minds. He pulled a blooming rose from behind Salem's ear and presented it with a wink and a flourish. Velvet-soft and fragrant when she took it, but when she looked again it was made of bronze, tight-whorled petals warming slowly to her hand.

He tossed knives at Memory and sawed her in half. She never spoke, never blinked. It was hard to tell in the dizzying lights, but Salem was fairly sure the girl didn't cast a shadow.

She watched the crowd, saw the delight on their faces. Jack had wanted an act like this for years.

But not all the spectators were so amused. A man lingered in the shadows, face hidden beneath the brim of a battered hat. Salem tried to read his aura, but a rush of heat made her eyes water, leaking tears down tingling cheeks. The smell of char filled her nose, ashes and hot metal. When her vision cleared, he was gone.

After the show, she caught up with Jacob at his trailer. Ray was with him, giggling and leaning on his arm. She sobered when she saw Salem. The two of them had given up on jealousy a long time ago; Salem wondered what made the other woman's eyes narrow so warily.

"Excuse me, my dear," Jacob said to Ray, detaching himself gently from her grip. "I promised Jerusalem a conversation."

Ray paused to brush a kiss across Salem's cheek before she opened the trailer door. "Try not to shoot this one," she whispered.

"I'm not making any promises," Salem replied with a smile.

She and Jacob walked in silence, away from the lights and noise to the edge of the fairgrounds, where the ground sloped down through a tangle of brush and trees toward the shore of White Bear Lake. The water sprawled toward the horizon, a black mirror in the darkness. She made out a bone-pale spire on the edge of the water—a ruined church, the only building left of the ghost town the lake had swallowed.

Jacob pulled out a cigarette case, offered Salem one. She took it, though she hadn't smoked in years. Circuses, cigarettes, strange men—she was relearning all sorts of bad habits today. He cupped his hands around a match and she leaned close; he smelled of musk and clean salt sweat. Orange light traced the bones of his face as he lit his own.

"So, witch, ask your questions."

She took a drag and watched the paper sear. "Who is the burning man?"

"Ah." Smoke shimmered as he exhaled. "An excellent question, and one deserving of an interesting answer." He turned away, broken-nosed profile silhouetted against the fairground lights.

"These days he's a train man—conductor and fireman and engineer, all in one. He runs an underground railroad, but not the kind that sets men free." His left eye glinted as he glanced at her. "Have you, perchance, noticed a dearth of spirits in these parts?"

Salem shivered, wished she'd thought to wear a coat. Jacob shrugged his jacket off and handed it to her. "This train man is taking the ghosts? Taking them where?"

"Below. Some he'll use to stoke the furnace, others to quench his thirst. And any that are left when he reaches the station he'll give to his masters."

"What are they?"

"Nothing pleasant, my dear, nothing pleasant at all."

"What do you have to do with this?"

"I've been tracking him. I nearly had him in Mississippi, but our paths parted—he follows the rails, and the Circus keeps to the freeways."

"So it was just bad luck he got caught in my bottle tree?"

"Your good luck that he left you in peace. He hunts ghosts, but I doubt he'd scruple to make one if he could."

"So why the invitation?"

He smiled. "A witch whose spells can trap the Conductor, even for a moment, is a powerful witch indeed. You could be of no little help to me."

"I'm not in the business of hunting demons, or ghosts."

"You keep a bottle tree."

"It was my grandmother's. And it keeps them away. I like my privacy."

"He'll be going back soon with his load. The end of the month."

"Halloween."

He nodded. "That's all the time those souls have left, before they're lost."

"I'm sorry for them." She dropped her cigarette, crushed the ember beneath her boot. "I really am. And I wish you luck. But it's not my business."

"He takes children."

Salem laughed, short and sharp, and tossed his jacket back to him. "You don't know my buttons to press them."

He grinned and stepped closer, his warmth lapping against her. "I'd like to find them."

"I bet you would. Good night, Jacob. I enjoyed the show." And she turned and walked away.

That night Salem drifted in and out of restless sleep. No dreams to keep her up tonight, only the wind through the window, light as a thief, and the hollowness behind her chest. A dog howled somewhere in the distance and she tossed in her cold bed.

Six years this winter since she'd come back to nurse her grandmother through the illnesses of age that not even their witchery could cure, until Eliza finally died, and left Salem her house, her bottle tree, and all the spells she knew. Years of sleeping alone, of selling bottles and beads and charms and seeing living folk twice a month at best.

We'll always work best alone, her grandmother had said. Salem had been willing to believe it. She'd had her fill of people—circus lights and card tricks, grifting and busking. The treachery of the living, the pleas and the threats of the dead. Dangerous men and their smiles. Living alone seemed so much easier, if it meant she never had to scrub blood and gunpowder from her hands again, never had to dig a shallow grave at the edge of town.

But she wasn't sure she wanted to spend another six years alone.

October wore on and the leaves of the bottle tree rattled and drifted across the yard. Salem carved pumpkins and set them to guard her porch, though no children ever came so far trick-or-treating. She wove metal and glass and silk to sell in town. She wove spells.

The moon swelled, and by its milksilver light she scried the rain barrel. The water showed her smoke and flame and church bells and her own pale reflection.

A week after she'd visited the circus, someone knocked on her door. Salem looked up from her beads and spools of wire and shook her head.

Jacob stood on her front step, holding his hat in his hands. His boots were dusty, jacket slung over one shoulder. He grinned his wolf's grin. "Good afternoon, ma'am. I wondered if I might trouble you for a drink of water."

Salem's eyes narrowed as she fought a smile. "Did you walk all this way?"

"I was in the mood for a stroll, and a little bird told me you lived hereabouts." He raised ginger brows. "Does your privacy preclude hospitality, or are you going to ask me in?"

She sighed. "Come inside."

The bone charm over the door shivered just a little as he stepped inside, but that might have been the wind. She led him to the kitchen, aware of his eyes on her back as they crossed the dim and creaking hall.

The cat stood up on the table as they entered, orange hackles rising. Salem tensed, wondered if she'd made a mistake after all. But Jacob held out one hand and the tom walked toward him, pausing at the edge of the table to sniff the outstretched fingers. After a moment his fur settled and he deigned to let the man scratch his ears.

"What's his name?" Jacob asked.

"Vengeance Is Mine Sayeth the Lord. You can call him Vengeance, though I'm pretty sure he thinks of himself as the Lord."

Jacob smiled, creasing the corners of autumn-grey eyes; his smile made her shiver, not unpleasantly.

"Sit down," she said. "Would you like some coffee, or tea?"

"No, thank you. Water is fine."

She filled a glass and set the water pitcher on the table amidst all her bottles and beads. Vengeance sniffed it and decided he'd rather have what was in his bowl. Jacob drained half the glass in one swallow.

"Nice tree." He tilted his stubbled chin toward the backyard, where glass gleamed in the tarnished light. He picked up a strand of opalite beads from the table; they shimmered like tears between his blunt fingers. "Very pretty. Are you a jeweler too?"

She shrugged, leaning one hip against the counter. "I like to make things. Pretty things, useful things."

"Things that are pretty and useful are best." He ran a hand down the curve of the sweating pitcher and traced a design on the nicked tabletop. Salem shuddered at a cold touch on the small of her back.

Her lips tightened. Vengeance looked up from his bowl and rumbled like an engine. He leapt back on the table, light for his size, and sauntered toward Jacob. Big orange paws walked right through the damp design and Salem felt the charm break.

"Did you think you could come into my house and 'witch me?"

"I could try."

"You'll have to try harder than that."

"I will, won't I."

He stood and stepped toward her. Salem stiffened, palms tingling, but she didn't move, even when he leaned into her, hands braced against the counter on either side. His lips brushed hers, cold at first but warming fast. The salt-sweet taste of him flooded her mouth and her skin tightened.

After a long moment he pulled away, but Salem still felt his pulse in her lips. Her blood pounded like surf in her ears.

His scarred hands brushed the bottom of her shirt. "You said something about buttons . . . "

"Will you help me?" he asked later, in the darkness of her bedroom. The smell of him clung to her skin, her sheets, filled her head till it was hard to think of anything else.

Salem chuckled, her head pillowed on his shoulder. "You think that's all it takes to change my mind?"

"All? You want more?"

She ran her fingers over his stomach; scars spiderwebbed across his abdomen, back and front, like something had torn him open. Older, fainter scars cross-hatched his arms. Nearly every inch of him was covered in cicatrices and ink.

"Is prestidigitation such dangerous work?"

"It is indeed." He slid a hand down the curve of her hip, tracing idle patterns on her thigh. "But not unrewarding."

"What will you do if you catch this demon of yours?"

He shrugged. "Find another one. The world is full of thieves and predators and dangerous things."

"Things like you?"

"Yes." His arms tightened around her, pressing her close. "And like you, my dear." She stiffened, but his fingers brushed her mouth before she could speak. "Tell me you're not a grifter, Jerusalem."

"I gave it up," she said at last.

"And you miss it. You're alone out here, cold and empty as those bottles."

She snorted. "And you think you're the one to fill me?"

His chuckle rumbled through her. "I wouldn't presume. Raylene misses you, you know. The others do too. Wouldn't you be happier if you came back to the show?"

The glass in her chest cracked, a razorline fracture of pain. "You don't know what would make me happy," she whispered.

Callused fingers trailed up the inside of her thigh. "I can learn."

He rose from her bed at the first bruise of dawn. "Will you think about it, if nothing else?" Cloth rustled and rasped as he dressed in the darkness.

"I'll think about it." She doubted she'd be able to do anything else.

"We're here through Sunday. The circus and the train." He stamped his boots on and leaned over the bed, a darker shadow in the gloom.

"I know." She stretched up to kiss him, stubble scratching her already-raw lips.

Her bed was cold when he was gone. She lay in the dark, listening to hollow chimes.

Salem spent the day setting the house in order, sweeping and dusting and checking all the wards. Trying not to think about her choices.

She'd promised her grandmother that she'd stay, settle down and look after the house. No more running off chasing midway lights, no more trouble. It had been an easy promise as Eliza lay dying, Salem's heart still sore with guns and graves, with the daughter she'd lost in a rush of blood on a motel bathroom floor.

She didn't want to go through that again. But she didn't want to live alone and hollow, either.

The bird came after sundown, drifting silent from the darkening sky. The cat stared and hissed as she settled on the back step, his ears flat against his skull.

"Come with me, witch. We need you."

"Hello, Memory. I thought I had until Sunday."

"We were wrong." The girl lifted a bone-white hand, but couldn't cross the threshold. "We're out of time."

Salem stared at the ghost girl. Older than her daughter would have been. Probably a blessing for the lost child anyway—she had a witch's heart, not a mother's.

The child vanished, replaced by a fluttering crow. "There's no time, witch. Please."

Vengeance pressed against her leg, rumbling deep in his chest. Salem leaned down to scratch his ears. "Stay here and watch the house."

As she stepped through the door, the world shivered and slipped sideways. She walked down the steps under a seething black sky. The tree glowed against the shadows, a shining thing of ghostlight and jewels. Beyond the edge of her yard the hills rolled sere and red.

"Where are we going?" she asked Memory.

"Into the Badlands. Follow me, and mind you don't get lost." The bird took to the sky, flying low against heavy clouds. Salem fought the urge to look back, kept her eyes on the white-feathered shape as it led her north.

The wind keened across the hills and Salem shivered through her light coat. The trees swayed and clattered, stunted bone-pale things shedding leaves like ashes.

The moon rose slowly behind the clouds, swollen and rust-colored. Something strange about its light tonight, too heavy and almost sharp as it poured over Salem's skin. Then she saw the shadow nibbling at one edge and understood—eclipse. She lengthened her stride across the dry red rock.

Time passed strange in the deadlands, and they reached the end of the desert well before Salem could ever have walked to town. She paused on the crest of a ridge, the ground sloping into shadow below her. On the far side of the valley she saw the circus, shimmering bright enough to bridge the divide.

"No," Memory cawed as she started toward the lights. "We go down."

Salem followed the bird down the steep slope, boots slipping in red dust. A third of the moon had been eaten by the rust-colored shadow.

Halfway down she saw the buildings, whitewashed walls like ivory in the darkness. A church bell tolled the hour as they reached the edge of town and Memory croaked along with the sour notes.

Shutters rattled over blind-dark windows and paint peeled in shriveled strips. The bird led her to a nameless bar beside the train tracks. Jacob waited inside, leaning against the dust-shrouded counter.

Salem crossed her arms below her breasts. "You said Sunday."

"I was wrong. It's the burning moon he wants, not Hallow's Eve." Witchlight burned cold in the lamps, glittering against cobwebbed glass. His eyes were different colors in the unsteady glow.

"Where is he now?"

"On his last hunt. He'll be back soon."

"What do you need me for?"

He touched the chain around her throat; links rattled softly. "Distraction. Bait. Whatever's needed."

She snorted. "That's what Memory's for too, isn't she? That's why he was watching your act. You're a real bastard, aren't you?"

"You have no idea."

She reached up and brushed the faint web of scars on his left cheek. "How'd you lose your eye?"

He grinned. "I didn't lose it. I know exactly where it is."

Memory drifted through the door. "He's coming."

Jacob's smile fell away and he nodded. "Wait by the train station. Be sure he sees you."

"What's the plan?"

"I had a plan, when I thought we had until Sunday. It was a good plan,

I'm sure you would have appreciated it. Now I have something more akin to a half-assed idea."

Salem fought a smile and lost. "So what's the half-assed idea?"

"Memory distracts him at the train station. We ambush him, tie him up, and set the trapped ghosts free."

"Except for the part where my charms won't hold him for more than a few minutes, that's a great idea."

"We won't mention that part. Come on."

A train sprawled beside the station platform, quiet as a sleeping snake. Its cars were black and tarnished silver, streaked with bloody rust, and the cowcatcher gleamed fang-sharp in the red light.

The platform was empty and Jacob and Salem waited in the shadows. She could barely make out the words White Bear on the cracked and mildewed sign.

"They built this town for the train," she whispered, her face close enough to Jacob's to feel his breath. "But the Texas and Pacific never came, and the town dried up and blew away."

"This is a hard country. Even gods go begging here."

Footsteps echoed through the silent station; a moment later Salem heard a child's sniffling tears. Then the Conductor came into view.

A tall man, dressed like his name, black hat pulled low over his face. Even across the platform Salem felt the angry heat of him, smelled ash and coal. A sack was slung over one broad shoulder, and his other hand prisoned Memory's tiny wrist.

Salem swallowed, her throat gone dry, and undid the clasp around her neck. The chain slithered cold into her hand. Jacob's hand tightened on her shoulder once, then he stepped into the moonlight.

"Trading in dead children now?" His growl carried through the still air. "You called yourself a warrior once."

The Conductor whirled, swinging Memory around like a doll. His face was dark in the shadow of his hat, but his eyes gleamed red.

Jacob took a step closer, bootheels thumping on warped boards. "You fought gods once, and heroes. Now you steal the unworthy dead." He cocked his head. "And didn't you used to be taller?"

"You!" The Conductor's voice was a dry-bone rasp; Salem shuddered at the sound. "You died! I saw you fall. The wolf ripped you open."

Jacob laughed. "It's harder than that to kill me."

"We'll see about that." He released Memory and dropped the bag as he lunged for Jacob.

Memory crawled away, cradling her wrist to her chest. The chain rattled in Salem's hand as she moved; Jacob and the Conductor grappled near the edge of the platform and she had no clear shot.

Then Jacob fell, sprawling hard on the floor. The Conductor laughed as he stood over him. "I'll take you and the witch as well as the dead. The things below will be more than pleased."

Salem darted in, the chain lashing like a whip. It coiled around his throat and he gasped. His heat engulfed her, but she hung on.

"You can't trap me in a bottle, little witch." His eyes burned red as embers. Char-black skin cracked as he moved, flashing molten gold beneath. A glass bead shattered against his skin; another melted and ran like a tear.

She pulled the chain tighter—it wouldn't hold much longer. The Conductor caught her arm in one huge black hand and she screamed as her flesh seared.

"Didn't the old man tell you, woman? His companions always die. Crows will eat your eyes—if I don't boil them first."

A fury of white feathers struck him, knocking off his hat as talons raked his face. The Conductor cursed, batting the bird aside, and Salem drove a boot into his knee.

He staggered on the edge for one dizzying instant, then fell, taking Salem with him. Breath rushed out of her as they landed, his molten heat burning through her clothes. Her vision blurred and White Bear Valley spun around in a chiaroscuro swirl.

"Jerusalem!" She glanced up, still clinging to the chain. Jacob leapt off the platform, landing lightly in a puff of dust. "Hold your breath!"

She realized what was coming as he stuck his fingers into the ground and pulled the world open.

White Bear Lake crashed in to fill the void.

"Wake up, witch. You're no use to me drowned."

She came to with a shudder, Jacob's mouth pressed over hers, his breath inside her. She gasped, choked, rolled over in time to vomit up a bellyful of bitter lake water. Her vision swam red and black, and she collapsed onto weed-choked mud. Cold saturated her, icy needles tingling through her fingers.

"Did he drown?" she asked, voice cracking.

"His kind don't like to swim." He turned her over, propping her head on his soaking knees. "I could say it destroyed him, if that's how you'd like this to end." Above them the shadow eased, the moon washing clean and white again.

"What could you say if I wanted the truth?"

Jacob's glass eye gleamed as he smiled. "That it weakened him, shattered that shape. He lost the train and its cargo. That's enough for me tonight."

"Not too bad, for a half-assed idea." She tried to sit up and thought better of it. The cold retreated, letting her feel the burns on her arm and hands. "Are you going to thank me?"

He laughed and scooped her into his arms. "I might." And he carried her up the hill, toward the circus lights.

Halloween dawned cool and grey. Glass chimed in the breeze as Salem untied the bottles one by one, wrapping them in silk and laying them in boxes. The tree looked naked without them.

The wind gusted over the empty hills, whistled past the eaves of the house. The tree shook, and the only sound was the scrape and rustle of dry leaves.

"Sorry, Grandma," she whispered as she wrapped the last bottle. Light and hollow, glass cold in her hands. "I'll come back to visit."

When she was done, Jerusalem Morrow packed a bag and packed her cat, and ran away to join the circus.

CALLIOPE: A STEAM ROMANCE

ANDREW J. McKIERNAN

Her voice is of a host angelic, but fallen. Her every breath breeds melodious paeans that pull and tear at my soul—in ways both tender and cruel—and I weep with pain and joy to hear them. For, as surely as Eros struck Apollo and Daphne, am I so sorely wounded by her song. But be that barb of gold or lead? Ah, now therein lies the tale.

I saw her first down at the Quay or, more rightly should I say, I heard her. I was returning from my place of work at the Patents Office, on George Street, and was anxious to make the five o'clock ferry. My wife had invited guests for tea and, as was my usual form, I was running late.

As I rounded onto Alfred Street, I saw a big four-master had pulled in to dock between two steamers. Men were in her rigging, clambering up masts and tying sails to yardarms with much agility and speed. Her cargo was being unloaded and a stack of crates, trunks and tarpaulin-covered boxes were gathering on the dock.

A number of carts were already lined up along the street, anxious to get the best of whatever cargo the barque carried.

The steam-horses that drew the carts were enormous machines, almost twice the size of a natural horse. They stamped at the ground, iron hooves striking sparks from the cobbles in what seemed bored frustration. I knew, having seen the blueprints, that this was but a mechanical twitching of internal gears and push-rods, a spasm of built up torque, and not any sort of emotional reaction at all. Through the haze of steam venting from their nostrils I could see they stood four deep across the road, barring the way. Slowly and carefully I made my way through, ducking under one magnificently polished beast and almost scalding the nape of my neck on the hot boiler-tank of its belly as I went.

When I reached the wharf for the North Shore ferry there was barely a line at the ticket booth. The ferry had not even docked. Frankly, I could not believe my luck. Luck is a most unusual occurrence for me, and rarely do I find myself in a situation where the worst is *not* the inevitable.

So, in order to ensure my luck was real, I fumbled in my pocket for a penny. I pulled the first coin my fingers encountered and looked down at it; a penny. I stared out at the approaching ferry and at the green shore awaiting me just across the harbour. I would be home for tea, just as I'd promised—and I knew how happy that would make my wife.

I stepped up to the line with a new spring in my step, three from the booth and plenty of time. I clutched the penny in my hand and thought of hot tea and scones, and probably some cake. Oh, yes, most definitely, some cake.

Two from the booth. I thought of the smile I would bring to my wife's face when I walked in the door. Maybe I would buy some flowers to brighten up the table. The ferry was docking, its passengers stepping out across a plank and onto the wharf.

From somewhere behind me came a gentle melody, carried upon a breeze unto my ear. It came softly at first and the tune, though unfamiliar, caught my attention. It was gay and uplifting, with a lively step that gave mind of parades and summer days. There was something of the seaside and of circuses in that tune, and of the joy of being young and full of life.

One from the booth. I turned for a moment to discover the music's origin and saw, further down the quay, a gathering had formed like a tight knot around something I could not quite see. In the centre of the crowd, rising just above their heads, I could discern a splash of red, a hint of sunlight glinting off polished brass, and a great wreath of steam rising into the air like a cloud. With that great, billowing cloud the music suddenly rose up in volume, stunning everybody on the quay. It was a bone shaking sound and the crowd-knot loosened. It was so loud I was sure it could be heard all the way up Macquarie Street.

The music drowned out everything around me, like a hundred tuned train-whistles played by a god. And, though there were no cathedral walls to echo that mellifluous song, the surrounding harbour was quite adequate in its acoustics. Every note was felt in the flesh, rising up through the wooden boards of the quay, entering through the feet, filling the soul. A low bass drone sent shivers through my spine, taking control of my legs, moving me inexorably closer to that euphonious epicentre.

I thought not of the ferry nor of my wife in our home across the harbour.

I thought nothing of my promise to her, or of the guests who would soon be arriving. I thought nothing at all as I walked across the quay, entranced by a song.

I pushed my way through what remained of the crowd, heeding not their indignant vituperation as I passed. There were not so many there now and I could not understand how some, so unaffected by the music, could have felt the desire to leave. Such a thought was incomprehensible to me as I stepped into the front row and beheld the originator of that heavenly choir.

Before me was a carriage, garish and red, ornamented along its wide panels with gold-leaf scrolls and fleur-de-lys. Across the side in large white letters was written *McKenzie's Universal Circus & Museum of the Bizarre*.

One side of the carriage was open to the crowd and I could see within an arrangement of polished brass pipes stretching up and out through the ceiling. In front of the pipes but within the carriage were set two tiers of polished ivory and ebony keys, like those of an organ. A calliope, I remembered. The instrument was called a calliope.

At the keyboard, playing the music that affected me so greatly, sat the most beautiful woman I had ever encountered in my life.

She wore a skirt of mandarin that flared gracefully across her hips, falling in neat pleats to the floor of the carriage. Her blouse was of white merino, cinched tight at the waist and trimmed with purple braid on epaulettes and leg-o-mutton sleeves. Her hair was dark, drawn up and back into a twist of curls that fell like a waterfall down the nape of her long neck, revealing ears as fine as porcelain. Her profile was as perfect a collection of curves and lines as Nature could produce. Face smooth and white as if it had been powdered; lips and cheeks aglow with the touch of petals of geranium or poppy; eyes hidden behind long, dark lashes.

She did not turn her beautiful head or swerve in any way from the playing of her instrument. Only her fingers and hands moved, running deft and sure from key to key. It was the most pleasing scene my mind had ever the fortune to behold.

Then, as I stared, watching her play, she parted her angelic lips and started to sing.

Never would I have imagined a voice that could rise above the gay and thunderous melody of the steam organ. But rise it did; louder and louder, smoother than silk. It soared and swooped, over and around the counterpoint her fingers coaxed from the keyboards. For a moment her voice would disappear amongst the notes of the organ, flittering here and there, only to appear again, ascending glissando, to flutter ever higher. Then, from a tremolo sustained until its buzz settled in the marrow, it would dive like a bird a'hunt for a note to pierce the heart. Time and time again she found that note until, with every quaver and semiquaver, my love did flow for her.

There was, at some stage, a man who came to stand before me. I barely noticed his presence bar the fact that he partly obscured my view. I would have stood there oblivious had he not rattled a red wooden box at me in a most annoying manner. Each time the box rattled, metal upon metal, the sound would intrude upon my pleasure. Every shake produced a clangorous cacophony of coins that perturbed my mind from the beauty of the steam organ and its wondrous vocal accompaniment. With little thought but for removing this distraction I reached into my pocket and withdrew a coin, barely looking as I placed it into the box.

Then the man was gone, moving on to the next person in the crowd. I'm sure that, just for a moment, I saw the calliope player tilt her head towards me in acknowledgement, and smile. My heart seemed to stop, and time stood still beneath that beatific face and the light that shone in her eyes. Looking back now, I feel that I am starting to understand a little of Einstein's Relativity.

I don't know how long I stood watching and listening, or for how long she played and sang, but when she stopped a curtain dropped across the side of the carriage, hiding her from view. A final gust of steam exhausted itself from the pipes with a high, piercing wheeze and the crowd dispersed.

I stood there, numbed by too many emotions. The joy of the music—its melody and rhythm—still lingered in my mind, but it was rapidly giving way to a great sense of loss. I knew the music would fade, my memory of her dissolve over time like a badly developed heliotype.

I saw a man, dressed in suit of black, trimmed at collar and cuff with braid of gold in a mock-military fashion. He carried the red box in his hands as he moved towards the back of the carriage. It was not until he had disappeared behind the Calliope that I realised his connection and decided to follow.

"Excuse me, sir," I said, finding him turning a series of valves jutting from a boiler tank fastened to the carriage's rear end. He looked up and scowled.

"I was wondering about the calliope player," I said, "and if it might be possible to know her name? I found her performance most gratifying and would like to thank her with a note."

The circus man stared at me for a moment and then laughed. "So y'want to send a note of thanks to our Kally, eh? Yes, I'm sure she'd value a note from you, kind sir."

He stood up from his task, wiping his dirty hands on a rag, and tapped the side of the carriage with his fist.

"She works hard, our Kally. Always appreciates a bit of appreciation, she does," he said and thrust his right hand out at me. I took it, shaking gently as his firm grip encompassed my smaller hand.

"My name's McKenzie," he said. "Why don't y'come back tomorrow night, on me, and deliver your note in person? I'm sure Miss Kally would love to meet you. We'll be up at Moore Park the next three nights, and then we'll be movin' on."

McKenzie released my hand and bent back to his task. I stood there, expecting Kally to exit the trailer at any moment. "I don't think she'll be coming out too soon, sir," McKenzie said, intuiting the reason for my hesitation. "I *will* tell her to expect you tomorrow night though."

His tone was a little harder now and when he didn't look up again, I took our conversation to be over. I knew I would return tomorrow night. I had, after all, been invited and it would be impolite to refuse. Of course Miss Kally would like her admirers to deliver their thanks in person. It was only sensible.

I turned back towards the wharf and had only taken two steps when a horn blared from across the water. The ferry was already three quarters of the way across the harbour. There wouldn't be another for almost an hour. And I'd donated my last penny to *McKenzie's Universal Circus & Museum of the Bizarre*.

There had long been talk of bridging the north and south sides of the harbour. Francis Greenway first proposed the idea of a bridge in 1815 and, despite some enthusiasm, work was never commenced. It's an engineering feat I would have liked to have seen—a bridge of iron stretching from shore to shore—but Mr. Beach's Pneumatic Rail System proved so successful in New York that the City of Sydney commissioned one too and all talk of a harbour bridge was soon forgotten.

Begun in 1888, the *Pneumatic Cross-Harbour Subway*, or the *Tube* as it is commonly known, was a daring enterprise. Many died during its eight year construction, but it has been hailed internationally as a marvel of modern construction. I don't like it. I don't like the closeness, or the thought of so much water pressing down upon me from above. I don't like the stale air. The smell of sweat and of lavender oil applied so liberally by well-to-do women that it fills the cramped cars like a miasma. I don't like the feeling of being alternately blown and sucked along a sealed tube by enormous, whirring fans at either end. What if the car didn't stop and ran into the fan? What if the fans were to stop while we were still in the tunnel? What if the tube were to spring a leak, releasing the pressure that gave us motion, letting in the harbour to drown, or crush, us under its weight?

No, I do not like the Tube at all. But I caught it home that afternoon and paid a farthing for the pleasure.

When I returned home late my wife was, understandably, in a state of great agitation. I'd not thought of an excuse for my lateness and stammered something about crowded streets and long lines at the ferry. She huffed and puffed and I could tell she didn't believe a word of it. I knew she suspected me of having met the boys for a drink at the *Fortune of War*. It was a plausible notion that I saw no reward in dispelling.

My wife's guests were already chatting in the drawing room and I made myself scarce, retiring to my study to avoid the prolonged tongue-lashing I was most certainly due. Things would quiet down eventually, I knew, but I would also need a reason for being out the following night, for I fully intended on seeing Kally again and extending my admiration of her skills.

I could think of nothing else. My head was constantly distracted by the memory of her voice, her face, the beauty of her music. I could say an emergency Lodge meeting had been called . . . and yet, my wife need only speak to one of the other wives at the Teashop on Lavender Street for my ruse to be revealed. If it rained—which was unlikely—I could say the ferries were cancelled, but the rain would have to be especially heavy, harbour swells especially high . . . why then wouldn't I just catch the Tube as I had tonight?

In the end I decided to claim the need to work back late, it not being inconceivable given the projects I frequently worked on. My wife would not be happy—she seldom was when I came home late—but at least it was an excuse that might ring true.

I left for work early the next morning, sneaking around the house like a thief as I made my breakfast and packed a lunch. I scrawled a hasty note informing of my intention to work late and signed it with my undying love. At that moment I hesitated—pricked at heart by my deceit, my guilt—and nearly threw the note in the furnace, fully intending to make my way home on time that night. But I didn't. I left the note on the kitchen bench and stepped out into the cool, pre-dawn air, silently closing the door behind me.

Work was an extended exercise in tedium. The blueprints I was reviewing for a patent application were complex and it was difficult for me to assess the device's overall safety. I understood the concept, which was a simple one: a variation on the common steam engine, but without need of a constant supply of combustible material such as coal. Instead, a pellet of refined Uranium dioxide would sit at the centre, heating a boiler of heavy-water to steam with its own radiant emanations. It was an ingenious design but the plans were vague on the amount of heat generated and I was unsure of the boiler's ability to handle the pressures produced.

I glanced at my wall clock frequently, making only occasional notes, tapping my pencil on the desk to mark off the seconds. The Radioactive Sciences were relatively new, and I knew little, certainly not enough to make a valid call on the device. I knew of the fortuitous (but doomed) meeting of Maria Sklodowska and Nicola Tesla in Paris in 1892. That two years of research under Becquerel had led them to an entirely new branch of science, and that the announcement of their findings at the *Exposition Internationale et Coloniale* in 1894 had sent scientists the world over scampering to understand this new source of wonder. The bitter feud that eventually tore the Tesla-Sklodowska research team apart was well publicised, appearing front-page of all the major newspapers. Behind all the name-calling and back-stabbing, Sklodowska and Becquerel urged caution and a drive towards scientific investigation of Radium's peculiar properties, whilst Tesla looked only for ways to exploit its energy in any way possible. For a time, scientists were as popular and gossiped about as Oscar Wilde and Queen Victoria, but it was Tesla's showmanship that ruled the media circus. In the end, Sklodowska's concerns were practically ignored and the future commercialisation of Radium was assured.

But this trivia was of no use to me. I was sure someone in the office would know more on the details and less on the gossip, or at least have a resource I could consult. By the time I'd decided to seek assistance it was after five o'clock and so I packed my work away and headed off to the circus.

Moore Park has always been a refuge for leisurely activity. The Zoological Gardens are well stocked with exotic—although often sickly—fauna, including a pair of elephants donated by the King of Siam. There is always a game of some description in progress on the long, dry fields of the park: rugby, cricket, Australian Football, and once I even witnessed a game of baseball played by a team of travelling Americans. But on that day the park was different.

It was as if, overnight, a strange and colourful city had sprung up across the field. Bright striped canopies rose up like giant mushroom caps and people moved among them like ants. At the very centre, higher and larger than all the other tents, was the Big Top.

I moved down the midway, through dust and the eager cries of concessionaires, looking always for the bright-red carriage of the Calliope and its player. I could not see it anywhere and so made my way to the ticket wagon.

"Mr. McKenzie told me to come," I said when I reached the front of the line. "I'm here to see the Calliope player."

The young ticketing girl looked at me for a moment as if weighing my worth for some unknown task. Her eyes were filled with all the innocence of a street whore.

"Mr. McKenzie told you, did he?" she said and smiled. "Well then, shouldn't keep Miss Kally waiting, should we, if Mr. McKenzie says so? Nice gent like you, I'm sure she'll be happy to make your acquaintance. Won't be 'til after the show though, I'm 'fraid. It's just about to start and Miss Kally provides all the music. Star of the show, she is."

I took the ticket she proffered and made my way to the Big Top. I was now a little unsure of whether I was truly expected.

The tent was already crowded with people who filled the stands, tiered six high, that circumscribed the inside wall. In the very centre were three white rings laid out upon the ground, the middle ring almost twice as large as the other two. Great poles stood at the intersection of the circles, holding up the roof, heavily guyed with wires and ropes stretched from canopy to floor. I found a seat as near to the front as I could and settled in, breathing not too deeply the hot and unwholesome atmosphere of dust and sweat, greasepaint and animal dung. The man beside me took up more than a fair share of his own seat and looked to rest himself on a share of mine as well. I shuffled and squirmed, hoping he would get the message that my seat was for my behind alone.

On the far side of the main ring, directly opposite where I sat, there was a raised platform upon which I could see the red wagon of the Calliope. The curtain in its side was closed but gas footlights on the platform shone up, illuminating the carriage and its fine wrought scroll-work like a jewel.

I barely noticed McKenzie as he stepped into the main ring. My eyes were otherwise focused on the curtain. I heard his introduction though as it rang out deep and loud among the people and canvas.

"Roll up! Roll up! Welcome, one and all, to McKenzie's Universal Circus and Museum of the Bizarre! The greatest show you will ever see in this, or any other, world! Sights that will dazzle, sights that will amaze, sights that you will find nowhere else, ladies and gentlemen. Nowhere! They are all here for your delectation and delight. But! In order to endure the wonder of those sights we must first have sound! Ladies and Gentlemen, I give you the rapturous rhapsodies of our very own Musical Muse . . . Kally Maelzel!"

The curtain dropped to reveal her, dressed as she had been the previous day, seated at the Calliope's keyboard. There was a great puff of steam from the pipes and the first note resounded through the tent like the rumble of thunder. Her fingers danced and a melody grew out of the bass, a brisk and merry tune that lifted the spirits in an instant. Kally's voice joined the Calliope's mad and festive waltz, singing not words but pure notes which like as not could break glass, but were as pleasing as a bluebird's song. There was movement in the ring, a troupe of clowns, I think, but I paid little attention. I was taken again by the music of the Muse and knew no more until it was all over, the crowd moving out, stepping over and around me as I sat still and quiet in my seat.

When the tent was empty and I sat alone, McKenzie came out from behind some curtains and approached me.

"Enjoy our show, sir?" he asked and I think I managed a nod. "I spoke to Miss Kally and she was most grateful for your kind attention. I hope you enjoyed her playing enough to convey your admiration in person?"

He cocked an eyebrow at me and held out his hand to lead me from my seat.

"Why yes. Thank you, Mr. McKenzie," I said, rising slowly, half in a dream, almost stepping on a discarded apple core. I allowed him to lead, watching my step amongst the carpet of detritus, until we stepped into the ring. Even then, he did not let go of my arm but led me across the great circle to the raised platform.

The footlights burned brightly still but the curtains of the carriage were closed once more. We stepped up onto the platform and made for the back.

"This way, sir," McKenzie said, stopping at the door in the rear of the carriage, knocking loudly on its frame.

From inside I heard her speak, a sound as melodious as her song. "Come in, I've been expecting you, sir," she said. "I have heard that my music pleases you." And McKenzie opened the door.

The interior of the carriage was lit by the gentle flicker of a single gas-lamp resting on a small table in the corner. Kally sat at her keyboard as if she had not moved an inch in the long moments since the performance. She turned her head to face me as I stepped up and through the door.

And there I stopped.

Her eyes were an unearthly blue, an azure glow that did more than reflect the light of the gas-lamp. They seemed to shed their own soft light, piercing me with a glance. She blinked, a rapid and sharp down-up of her eyelids. Flick-flick, like the shutter of a camera.

"Please, have a seat," she said, motioning with a nod to a small stool at her side. Her voice evinced a German or Austrian accent and I could barely match the movement of her lips with the words she spoke, as if my eyes and ears had become detached in time, one from the other.

I sat on the stool and stared at her for a moment. She was beautiful. More beautiful up close than she'd been from afar. Her complexion so smooth. The lines of her face so graceful. The shallow curve of her neck a parabola of perfection.

But I'd heard the music in her voice; read the movement of her lips and the flutter of her eyelids; noticed the smooth efficiency of her movements. In the sudden silence of the moment I could even hear the turning of delicate gears and the gentle huff-puff of pistons moving inside cylinders. I knew now. I was not looking at a woman, but at an automaton.

"Ahh, I see that I am not who you thought I would be," Kally said, each letter a tone manipulated by some internal mechanism—tones blending to form words and sentences, phrases, thoughts. Were they thoughts? Were they *her* thoughts? I did not think it possible.

"I won't be far, Kally," McKenzie said from the doorway. "Just give me a holler if you need me," and he was gone, the door closed.

I was not exactly shocked. Automatons are not unusual in this new and modern age. From steam-horses to calculating-machines, simple automata have been making our life easier since not long after Watt perfected the steam engine. But automatons could not talk. They did not express opinions or sing and play with passion. They could not! Their actions were mechanical, programmed, a symptom of turning gears and cams, pistons and rods. No, I was not shocked, but I was most certainly confused.

I'd heard, of course, of von Kempelen's fraudulent Chess Player. How everyone, even Napoleon, had been duped until a young New York author named Poe exposed the hoax in an article. A man concealed inside the workings to make the moves where the mechanism could not. I would not be so easily fooled.

I looked her up and down, trying to discover where a human operator might be hidden. Her torso and waist were too slender to fit even a small child but her skirts pooled around the stool on which she sat and anyone could have hidden therein. I was of half a mind to reach down, right there and then, and lift her skirts to uncover the scoundrel behind this charade . . . but, despite what I knew, it felt unseemly to even contemplate looking beneath a woman's skirt.

"I am no trick, dear sir," she said after a while, clearly interpreting my gaze correctly. "I am, exactly as you have guessed, no more a woman than this old steam organ is a man."

"But how?" I asked. "I mean, you play! You sing and, unless Mr. McKenzie has slipped me an awfully strong dose of opium, I am conversing with you right now! How could that be if you were . . . if you were . . . an automaton?" The word itself seemed impolite, considering the company, but I could think of no other.

Her eyes slipped then, looking down towards the floor, and I could almost see the corners of her mouth turn down in sorrow.

"You are right to question," she said, her voice soft and mournful. "I *am* an automaton. All gears and clockwork. Steam pumping through my veins instead of blood, offered up to me through a tube." Here she turned and did lift the back of her skirts to indicate a pipe that came out of the floor and disappeared into the small of her back. There was a valve there too, at the juncture of pipe and lumbar, and I wondered what would happen to Kally if I turned it.

She lowered her skirts quickly and continued, "It might as well be a chain, this pipe that feeds me and moves me and gives me life. I might as well be a prisoner, or a slave, or . . . or . . . a machine! Whilst McKenzie controls my boiler I am no better than that! A machine to be switched on and off as needed."

I reached out my hand in sympathy, half expecting the automaton to cry.

"But I still don't understand how!" I said. "If you are a machine how can we be having a sensible conversation? If you're just a machine how can you feel that way at all? I'm sorry, my Lady, if I seem insensitive, but you are a marvel to me. You were beautiful before I knew, but now . . . but *now.*"

"My kind sir, you are so wonderful to say so."

She turned and adjusted a few stops on the keyboard. I could see now that her movements were not exactly natural. They were smooth and precise and all too graceful to be those of a real person.

"I will tell you then," she said, her fingers settling on the keyboard, tinkering at a soft and simple melody.

"You know, I am sure," she said, "of von Kempelen's Turk, the player of chess, and how it was discovered to be a fraud. My creator, after whom I am named, was its owner at the time and, even though he knew it to be a trick, he paraded the device throughout the Americas. When evidence of the deception became public he fled back to England, taking the Turk with him. At the time, Mr. Maelzel had full intentions of throwing the thing overboard and into the Atlantic, but Fate chose otherwise.

"On board was the British mathematician Charles Babbage, returning from Massachusetts where he'd been spruiking the plans for his Analytical Engine with hopes of obtaining the funding the Royal Society had been loathe to provide. Babbage had also heard of the fraud but, nevertheless, the Turk was of sufficient internal complexity to interest him. He suggested changes, and improvements, and the introduction of one of his own Analytical Engines whereby the need for a deceptive *human* chess-player might be removed.

"Upon returning to England Maelzel and Babbage began work on their project. They soon decided that the plan to convert the Turk was unworkable and resolved on a new project . . . I am the result of that project, kind sir. Maelzel created my body, Babbage my mind—although Babbage himself loathed almost all kinds of music. My playing and voice are based somewhat on that of Lady Byron herself . . . although the vocal mechanism itself was developed by Faber. But, I am more than the sum of my parts, as I hope you can see. And more than a mere machine. *Cogito ergo sum*, dear sir, or at least *I* like to think so."

And here she laughed, a real laugh, although her jest seemed melancholy to me. Her fingers started pecking at a brighter tune but I heard a sadness even there.

"And so, here I am," she said, her voice bouncing between notes. "A monster no less than Frankenstein's own. A creature fought over by my creators. Later, lost by Maelzel in a bout of drunken gambling to McKenzie's devious carnival wiles. A machine, a possession. Yet, I *feel* myself a slave. Has a machine the right to feel that way? If a machine feels that way, is it a machine?"

She turned to me, her eyes imploring, asking me to assay the very truth of her existence. I realised her playing had stopped and in the silence my heart sank.

"You are, Madame, a Lady of intelligence, charm, wit and beauty," I said, as nervous as a schoolboy courting. "It sickens my heart to see you this way. You must leave at once! Sever your contract. Pay off your owner's debt. I will speak to the man myself. I'm sure he will see the folly of the way he has been keeping you." It came out all of a sudden and I meant every word, but again she laughed and this time it was at me.

"Oh no, you are too kind, but I cannot *leave*! I am not an employee but an attraction! And where would I go? *How* would I go? The pipe that binds me to the boiler is as strong a shackle as you will find in any prison, sir."

I looked again to her skirts, at the floor, imagining the pipe running underneath the floorboards and out to the stoked boiler attached to the rear of the carriage.

"But steam-horses," I said, "*they* carry their own boiler and furnace around with them. You could have a smaller engine developed, maybe contained in a wheeled palanquin so you could move around?"

The very idea excited me, but again she laughed and played, and sang a piece from *The Beggar's Opera*:

"The Modes of the Court so common are grown,
That a true Friend can hardly be met;
Friendship for Interest is but a Loan,
Which they let out for what they can get.
'Tis true, you find
Some Friends so kind,
Who will give you good Counsel themselves to defend.
In sorrowful Ditty,
They promise, they pity,
But shift you for Money, from Friend to Friend."

"Are you saying my words mean nothing?" I asked, offended, feeling a sudden anger arise. "That I should be putting my money where my mouth is? Is that all this is? A ruse to empty my pocket? If that is the case then I . . . "

"No, no, not at all," she said demurely. "You take my song too literally, sir. I meant only that your Counsel is sage, but the ideas contained therein would cost more money than I can ever hope to lay claim."

She turned to face me then, her entire torso swivelling smoothly on well-oiled bearings. In the flickering light of the gas-lamp her shadow writhed across the carriage curtain, wreathing her in a halo of darkness.

"I have thought on this long, dear sir, do not think I have not," she said. "I have little time for mental reckoning—my steam supply is cut off almost immediately after a performance—but even while I play I am able to spare a small portion of my thoughts to the dream of leaving this mobile cell, this endless parading before the world, this life of performance but nothing else. Ten years. For ten years I have had these thoughts."

She stopped and her head cocked slightly to one side, as if she were listening carefully. When she next spoke it was in the tiniest whisper, like a flute played softly somewhere far away.

"I've made the acquaintance of an engineer, in Belgium," she said and I had to strain forward to hear. "He has been very kind to me, dear indeed, and has promised to help me if he can. He assures me he is near to perfecting a suitable engine, just as you described but . . . our funds are lacking. He is a most wondrous man, so generous and gallant to help, but it will take time. It will take time and I have only the thought of him to keep me hoping . . . it might be years before we return to the Continent though, years!"

My heart seemed to shrivel in my chest. Who was this Belgian engineer? How long had they been acquainted? Irrationally, I disliked the man instantly. Jealousy welled up in me, bitter and confusing. I was a married man. I'd only known Kally for a few minutes; had not known of her at all a day ago. She was not even a *real* woman! An automaton, a machine! And yet, I could not deny the way her music, her voice, made me feel. Could not deny the beauty of her face, nor the travesty of the life-line that bound her to that circus as a slave.

"I want to help you, Kally," I said, using her name aloud for the first time, tasting the sweetness of it in my mouth. "I am not a man of wealth but I will find a way. I have some funds—not much, but some. I will give it all to you. I don't want you trapped in this carriage and I don't want you waiting for some chap in Belgium to get you out. There are engineers here, in Australia, who can help. I know many of them. I'll introduce you. *I'll* fund the research. *I'll* get you out of here."

It all came out in a rush with no thought for how I was going to accomplish *anything*. I had no money with which to fund research. No connections, no experience. I was a Patent Office Clerk. Any money in the family was my wife's; her inheritance, held in tight reign against my spending. I had no way of freeing Kally from her cage. None of this occurred to me until I was on my way home. None of it mattered at the time.

Our hushed conversation was interrupted by a knock at the door and the loud voice of McKenzie on the other side. "You okay in there, Kally? Hope you're not talkin' a load'a hot air to your admirer now," and he laughed. "We really should be shuttin' up for the night. 'Tis getting late and coal costs money, ya know."

"Yes, Mr. McKenzie," Kally said and then, softly to me, "Thank you, sir, thank you, but you really should go now. Mr. McKenzie has let me talk far longer than usual but I fear his patience will soon end."

I stood quickly, almost knocking over the stool, and put my hand on her arm. It was hard and cold through the material of her dress and didn't feel at all human. I don't know why I was surprised. I assumed padding, I suppose, some attempt at making her feel as realistic as she looked. But then she was not designed to be touched. Somehow this revelation made her life seem all the more tragic.

"I will help you, Kally," I said, whispering, reaching for the door handle. "I will be back tomorrow night. I'll bring some money—to help the Belgian if he is your only hope—but I'll think of something else. Something to get you away sooner."

She smiled at me then, subtle gears turning, working her mouth into a perfect bow. Her eyes glowed with what I imagined was new hope, steeling me for the promises I'd made.

"Tomorrow night, be ready," I said and stepped out the door.

The lights were off and my wife was already asleep when I returned home around ten o'clock that night. I crept through the house and climbed into bed as quietly, and as carefully, as I could. My wife did not stir but continued snoring softly as I lay staring at the ceiling.

Sleep did not come. Answers did not come.

Calliope music and Kally's beatific voice played constantly in the back of my mind. Her face formed out of shadows like angels seen in the chance shape of a cloud but darker, more beautiful than any angel could be. A Muse caged for the entertainment of the masses. I had to help her. I had to free her. I could not think how.

Eventually the first grey light of dawn filtered through the curtains. I arose and moved silently to the credenza in the corner of the room, mindful of loose floorboards as I went. The credenza's cover was down and as stiff and creaky as a crone. With cautious deliberation I was able to raise it and hunt around for our financials. I found them where I expected; a bundle of papers bound with string, tucked at the back of the top drawer.

I took the bundle and a pile of clothes and dressed in the hall. I did not take breakfast nor leave a note. I left with as much stealth as a middle-aged man is able, feeling excited and guilty, and as naughty as a schoolboy.

The office was still locked when I arrived. I let myself in with my key, locking the door behind me, knowing I had a couple of hours before anyone else was likely to arrive.

I went straight to Archives and pulled every registered patent on steam-engines I could find. I searched for variations on Sterling's thermal-engine, and even found a rejected patent for a dangerous sounding "internal-combustion" engine. I piled them all on my desk and started to read.

My problem was one that had plagued the best engineering minds for a generation. How to build a smaller, lighter, more portable engine? A steam-engine that did not need continual stoking and feeding? I was a patents clerk! How could I hope to find an answer where other, greater minds had failed?

None of the patents before me could answer the questions either.

But were they the questions Kally needed answering? As the morning wore towards lunch I realised that they were not. She had her Belgian engineer. She didn't need me to build a vehicle for her escape. But I wanted to be the one to emancipate her; I wanted to be the hero, to earn her gratitude and adulation.

I was being selfish and not thinking of Kally at all.

I felt in my jacket pocket for the bundle of paper I'd stowed there earlier. There were the details of our accounts at the Bank of New South Wales. A small pile of Gold and Wool Bonds, already browned and torn at the edges. Our Mortgage.

I took two of the Wool Bonds and one of the Gold and stuffed the rest into the bottom drawer of my desk. The pile of patents, useless to me, I placed onto a trolley for someone else to file.

The Bank was in Macquarie Place and I chanced through the doors at a time of relative quiet. I was able to walk right up to the cashier and present my Bonds without waiting. The cashier took them without a word and stalked off through a side door, returning after a short while with a ridiculously large pile of banknotes.

I did not hear the amount and I do not remember signing whatever was presented for me to sign. I was too busy looking at the money before me: five pound notes stacked an inch thick. Surely that was enough to buy Kally her freedom?

With renewed enthusiasm I bounded back to the office, every stride a joyful step closer to Kally.

The afternoon passed quickly as I leapt around the office annoying everyone, not accomplishing a scrap of work. I joked and danced and sung merry tunes. I waxed lyrical on the beauty of women, of music, and of freedom. When they'd endured enough of me I tidied my desk and shuffled papers, humming to myself, cheeks sore from grinning.

As I rearranged the desktop for the fifth or sixth time my grin widened further, widened until it burst open with a laugh I'd no chance of containing. Everyone in the office looked up, wondering if I'd lost my mind, but no, I most definitely had not! Before me was the very patent I'd been examining all week: a radium powered steam-engine, scalable, without the need for coal, and with a fuel supply that could theoretically last many, many years.

I waited until the rest of the office had returned to their work and folded the blueprints into a tight square. With barely controlled glee I slipped them into my jacket pocket beside the money.

For the rest of the afternoon I twiddled my thumbs, grinning my painful grin at all who looked my way.

Five o'clock came and I was out the door, hat in hand, before the bell had even finished ringing. I skipped the streets to Surry Hills and through Chippendale, whistling as I went, the distant sounds of the circus my beacon.

The girl at the ticket-carriage passed me a ticket without a word. At the Big Top I did not even need to produce it, the usher letting me pass with a nod of recognition and a smile.

Kally's performance was both ecstasy and agony. The ecstasy of her playing, her voice. The agony of waiting, of knowing that her salvation resided in my coat pocket. I closed my eyes and soared with her, shutting out the clowns and jugglers, the acrobats and animals. I heard only her sorrow, and a longing to be free, and knew that tonight I would deliver her dream.

When the show was over I moved immediately towards her gilded carriage, bold and full of purpose. McKenzie saw me and wandered across the ring.

"Ah, you've returned," he said. "I was wonderin' if our Kally'd entranced y'enough to warrant a second visit."

He took me by the elbow and led me towards the back of the carriage. A young roustabout was there, pulling on rigging and tightening knots. He glared at me as McKenzie led me to Kally's door and I felt his jealousy like a baleful fire. Kally's grace and sophistication would never be for the likes of him and he knew it, hating me for being someone he could not. McKenzie gestured for me to step up to the door and knock and so I did.

"Come in, dear sir," came Kally's voice from inside, as sweet as honey poured over sadness.

She sat as she would always sit if she remained in that place: fingers resting lightly on keyboard, skirts arranged around her in a bell of pleats and folds. The gas-lamp lit her face with soft, warm light, flickering shadows across the walls of the carriage.

I closed the door and took the stool beside her, not daring to say a word until I'd given McKenzie a chance to leave. We sat like that for a while, in silence, me simply staring into her eyes and waiting for the right moment to speak.

"Kally," I said eventually, never taking my eyes from hers. "You don't need to stay here any more. I've found a way."

A twitch of gears, and a smile appeared on her face. Her eyes glowed with a fresh light: *hope*, I thought, *hope is what I see in her eyes.*

"I knew you could help me," she said, one hand reaching out to rest on my knee. A hot flush rose through me at her touch. I could not speak, only nod and smile the same grin I'd worn all afternoon. "You, sir, are my knight in shining armour, my Galahad. With your help my Belgian friend's tasks will be so much shorter, my release so much swifter. Maybe years instead of never. I don't know how to thank you, sir."

I found my voice then, spurred forward by my desire to make her even happier than I'd already made her.

"No, Kally. It's so much better than that. You won't need your Belgian friend anymore. I have something better! The plans for a new engine. A smaller steam-engine that doesn't need coal. Doesn't need anything except water and some radium and it will run for decades!"

She looked at me curiously then, as if this was not at all what she had been expecting. On a woman I would have called that expression "concealed disappointment." On Kally, it marred the perfection of her features so severely that I sat back, startled and confused, and took a very deep breath.

"This is a way out for you, Kally," I said. "I thought . . . I thought it would please you."

"I'm sorry," she said, her hand leaving my knee, voice filling with sorrow. "I do not mean to seem ungrateful. You have done so much for me, and your plans sound wonderful, but I have no money to build an engine. Those plans would only be a false hope to me. To know they exist . . . to not have the means of making them a reality . . . it would be too cruel to me, sir."

She had turned again to face the Calliope's keyboard. Her hands rested lightly on the keys, head downcast, eyes closed. I sat there for a moment in the silence, wondering if McKenzie had turned off her boiler. *Not yet, not yet,* I thought. *Please not yet! I haven't told you everything yet.*

"Kally?" I said softly. "Kally, are you still there?" I reached out and touched my fingers to her cheek, caressing its contours gently, slowly. I sensed movement beneath the surface, machinery turning, ticking away like the workings of a clock. If she were real I believe she would have been crying.

"I have money. Enough money to build the engine. Enough money to get you out of here," I said and her eyes opened. Her head turned to me on well oiled bearings, slowly, and a smile returned to her face.

"You do?" she asked and I reached into my jacket pocket. I first laid the plans out on the keyboard and placed the bundle of notes atop.

"I do. I haven't counted it, but I guess there's five hundred pounds there. That's more than enough for someone to build an engine from those plans, Kally."

She stared down at the money: more, I was sure, than she had ever seen. It was more than I had ever seen.

"You must tell me your itinerary," I said. "I'll organise an engineer while you're away. Get things started."

Kally laughed, a sound like a tree full of twittering birds.

"Yes, yes, it's wonderful," I said. "By the time you return to Sydney it will be done. You will be free of McKenzie. Free of all this . . . all this . . . " and I gestured around the carriage, unable to find the words to describe the horror she had lived.

She laughed again and I laughed too, with her and for her, happy that I'd fulfilled my promise. Happy that I was truly her knight.

"I knew it," she said between laughs. "You had me worried for a moment there. Plans indeed! But in the end you came through. I knew it the minute I laid eyes on you. I can always spot a dupe."

Her words did not register with me at first. I was too caught up in her laughter, in my own puffed pride. I saw only her smile. Heard only the trill of her laugh. It was not until her hands came down hard on the keyboard, a roar erupting from the Calliope's pipes, that the words finally registered in my mind. By then it was much too late.

The door behind me burst open at her signal, its edge catching me in the small of the back. I toppled forward off the stool, Kally still laughing as I fell beside her. The curtains parted and the grimy roustabout and a companion dived through. They landed on top of me, forcing the air from my lungs. My face crunched into the rough floorboards of the carriage and I felt my nose break, warm wetness spreading down my chin, soaking the carriage floor.

I stayed that way, unable to move, unable to talk, two fat ruffians sitting on my back. Pain raced up my spine and throbbed across my face. Kally sat motionless on her stool above me and I heard a third person moving around near the door.

"You alright, Kally?" I heard McKenzie ask.

"Fine, Boss," Kally's sweet voice curdling to poison in my mind. "Just like the rest of them in the end. Turns out he had money after all. Told you I can pick them. You worry too much."

"Must be five hundred pounds here," McKenzie said. "That's a damn good haul, Kally. Better than California by far. You've outdone yourself this time, me girl."

"You taught me well, Boss," Kally said and they both laughed. The roustabouts on top of me laughed too, squeezing more pain through my body. Finally I must have managed a sound because their attention turned to me.

"May as well dump him somewhere, boys," McKenzie said.

Dump me? I was sure then that they meant to kill me. I tried to struggle, thrashing frantically in a vain attempt to unseat my unwelcome passengers. Every movement brought fresh pain searing through my lungs, pounding in my back, hammering in my head.

"Get him out of here," McKenzie said and something hard came down on the nape of my neck, shooting darkness up into my brain, stopping the pain.

I awoke with my face resting in a bed of moss, cool and moist. My body ached from crown to toe. My dignity hurt more.

I crawled, though with some difficulty, from beneath a bush that grew against a large fig tree. Early morning sunlight stabbed through the green canopy overhead, blinding me until my eyes adjusted. I heard the horn of a steamer in the harbour, close by. I could hear a voice in the distance calling to allow women the Vote. Another voice cried of Daniel and the lion's den. The Domain, they had dumped me in the Domain.

My wallet was gone, as was my watch. My shirt was stained brown with blood. I covered the stains as best I could by buttoning up my jacket, which was still relatively clean, and headed slowly, painfully, in the direction of Moore Park.

By the time I arrived, *McKenzie's Universal Circus & Museum of the Bizarre* had gone. The grounds where they had been were a dry and trampled mess. Only piles of horse and camel dung, ticket stubs and peanut shells, remained to mark their passing.

I found the blueprints, scuffed and torn and covered with dirt, between the wheel ruts where the Calliope had stood. I stared at the plans for a while, opening them up and spreading them across the ground. She could have taken them. She could have hidden them from McKenzie and found a way to use them. A way to escape.

A part of me knew, knew I'd been taken for a fool, knew that Kally had never wanted to escape. And yet, the memory of her music played on inside my mind. The wonder of what she was—a marvellous thinking, feeling machine—would not leave. I loved her and despised myself for my weakness. Love and hate, lust and loathing, gold and lead transmuted within my soul until I ached with a pain born of their union. Ah, Eros, you are a capricious child!

I had no idea of where the Circus was headed next. North or South? Inland to Parramatta and settlements west? Whichever way they had gone, they had a half-day start on me. And who was I trying to fool anyway? The walk from the Domain had nearly killed me. I could go no further.

I folded the blueprints and placed them carefully in my jacket pocket. I would keep them, just in case.

For the rest of the afternoon I sat there, under a tree, watching children play cricket in the fields. The children ran, and laughed, and their competition was fierce but, even above the crack of the bat and their raucous cheers, the haunting strains of Calliope music still pricked at my heart.

WELCOME TO THE GREATEST SHOW IN THE UNIVERSE

DEBORAH WALKER

The flexible metal wallings shrouding the Circosphere wavered as the shuttle craft drew too close. In the control booth, Jinkers Morrell sighed. "Shuttle craft . . . " She checked on her computer for the name of the vehicle and sighed again. "Shuttle craft *Coco the Clown*. You are in violation of the space boundary of this facility. A repeat offence will result in immediate cancellation of your free circus passes."

The space craft's communications array activated. Jinkers saw the faces of two teenage boys.

"Whatever happened to the famous *Amazing Galaxy Show* welcome?" asked the young pilot. He was wearing an illuminated clown nose. It was flashing.

"You've been notified," said Jinkers. She switched off the array and turned to Mr Barrie who ran the external protocols for the station. "Does that happen a lot?" she asked.

Mr Barrie was monitoring the craft on his computer, making sure that it did indeed return to the proscribed space runs. "Yes, Gaffer. A couple of times a day."

Jinkers looked over his shoulder. She was glad to see that those clowns were able to follow the route inside. "Any significance to the pattern?" she asked.

"No, Gaffer. Kids from all over the colonies like to push the boundaries."

Jinkers Morrell ran the Circosphere. She was a fine administrator. As part of her duties she ensured that she did every job on the station at least once a year. Today she'd been monitoring the arrival of the punters, over-seeing the integrity of the outer Circosphere.

"Thank you, Mr Barrie, I can see that you've got everything running smoothly here—as usual."

"Thank you, Gaffer."

Jinkers could see that he wanted to say something more. She smiled at him, giving him an opportunity to ask, "Is everything all right, Gaffer?"

To most people she would have answered, "Sure, everything's great." But this was Mr Barrie. Jinkers had started her circus career here, in this control booth. So instead, she said, "No, sir. I'm afraid not, something is wrong with my circus. I can feel it. I just don't know what it is yet."

"Aye, I thought so. I'll let you get on then."

Just telling someone made her feel better. Jinkers said her goodbyes and headed back to her office.

Jinkers walked past the Theatre of Laughter where the clowns played out the soap-opera dramas which were televised and transmitted to the colonies. The clowns wore only tokens of their traditional dress, perhaps bright buttons on a spacesuit or white make-up for the lead actresses. But they were still clowns attuned to the humour and pathos of the human condition. The punters packed the stalls. These actors were superstars in the colonies. She walked past the Theatre of Culture where the art works of Earth were displayed. Distinguished academics waited to discuss and argue the merits of each piece. She walked past the covered Theatre of Erotica where the performers danced their lavish spectacles. Jinkers smiled at the queue of youngsters waiting outside. Only those who were eighteen could enter. Nobody had ever beaten the retinal scan. From the Theatre of Nature she heard the sounds of Earth's animals. To the punters they were legendary beasts, seen only once in a lifetime. She listened for a moment to the roars and to the gasps of the audience. The big cats were in the theatre today.

There was so much to see here in the Circosphere, a wealth of imagination geared to every taste and desire. The best performers of Earth and her colonies were here. It was a palace of merging cultures and lavish wealth.

In the distance, a flash of colour caught Jinker's eye. She saw a jewelled tower rising high towards the electronic sky. It was the Theatre of History. Babylon had come to the Circosphere again. She remembered visiting Babylon twenty years ago, when she had first come to the Circosphere. How she'd marvelled at the sight. She had to see this again. Jinkers walked quickly to the theatre. She pushed through the punters standing at the ornate gates. The golden mosaic lions and the mushussu dragons looked down upon her.

She breathed in the aroma of the replicated Babylon: aged spice and dry sand. The costumed circus people acted out the roles of ancient Babylonians. Here were a group of Ishtar's handmaidens laughing with the punters. Here were the stern faced soldiers, their eyes barely flickering as Jinkers nodded to them.

Jinkers entered the lapis lazuli palace of Nebuchadnezzar. She remembered the sense of awe that had struck her, the majesty of the spectacle had overwhelmed her twenty years ago. There was nothing like this on her colony home world, where all resources were geared towards survival. But here on the Circosphere there was magic. Jinkers had felt part of it. The history of Earth belonged to her and to every other human.

But now, as Jinkers walked through the palace, she didn't feel the same. She watched the punters stare in wonder at the spectacle of their collective past. She wanted to share their experience, to recapture the emotion she'd felt all those years ago. But all she could see was a facsimile of reality. When she looked at the throne, she didn't marvel at the luxury of wealth, instead she saw the cost of the gold plating and remembered the builders' overpriced estimates.

She listened to David interpreting Nebuchadnezzar's famous dreams, the dreams written into the Old Testament and passed through thousands of years of history. She saw the punters listening intently to David's words. They believed. But Jinkers only saw an actor nervously playing his first major role.

She saw through the illusion of history. Her administrator's eye had spoiled the magic and the fantasy.

The Theatre of History team had worked hard. She made a mental note to send them a memo acknowledging their efforts. Then Jinkers left Babylon and walked slowly back to her office.

Her office was located at the heart of the Circosphere. The Theatres of Entertainment ran in all directions from this core. Jinkers was responsible for this massive space station, ensuring that the punters had the most marvellous time of their lives—so that the real business of the Circosphere could be achieved.

A myriad messages awaited her. It was surprising how many messages could be accumulated in a few short hours away from her office. She ran them through the A.I. programme to select for importance.

"Every day the circus balances on the tightrope," that's what Barnabus Mcfee, her predecessor, used to say. But lately, Jinkers had been unsure of her footing. She felt as if her next steps could see the edifice of the circus crashing to the ground.

The computer finished analysing the messages, prioritising a message from Brent Atwoods as the most important. She issued an e-call for him to join her immediately.

She opened the screens to her office window and took in the view. She refreshed herself in the view of the stars. Yes, it still re-energized her, even after all these years.

She took out a bowl of kibble for her pet tortoise, Horatio. She liked Horatio. *He* never did anything unexpected. And he never wandered off. He was, in fact, the perfect pet for the Circosphere administrator.

A knock on the door and Brent entered her office. He looked excited.

"Hello, Brent, what can I do for you?"

"Jinkers, you're looking well."

She wasn't, but she was grateful for his courtesy. Jinkers shared a common bond with Brent. They'd arrived at the Circosphere from the same colony world, at about the same time, both desperate to shed off the ennui of their farming colony world. They'd both risen through the ranks. They had yearned for glamour and excitement. They hadn't found it. Instead, they'd found science and administration. But dreams change as you grow older and they were both content with their current roles. It was important work, the most important work in the galaxy.

"How's the family?" Brent was happily married to Bella, a lovely woman and a contortionist. Jinkers smiled to herself.

"Great. Great. Joshua's obsessed with the tigers at the moment."

"Wants to be an animal trainer?"

"Of course, but I'm trying to persuade him to consider veterinary science, instead."

Jinkers would have loved to have a proper conversation with Brent. It seemed that she had little time for her friends, lately. But, she thought of the all the messages on her computer and said, "Shall we get down to business? You sent me a message about some anomalous readings . . . "

Brent led a team of psychologists. Science and research were the real business of the Circosphere. The punters would be surprised to know that there were more scientists here than performers.

"Of course, Gaffer. There are some very interesting results from the audiences in the Theatre of Laughter."

Jinkers took the e-notepad Brent offered her. The technical data made no sense to her. "Talk me through it, please."

"It was the clowns who first noticed it. They'd been reporting for weeks that the audience 'wasn't right' but we ignored them. You know how they complain." Brent scowled—a sign of his embarrassment.

"But this time . . . " prompted Jinkers.

"Well, they insisted. So, to humour them, we upgraded our analysis. And you know what? They were right. A significant percentage of the audience were reacting too quickly, in some cases before joke resolution."

"They were laughing before the joke? It wasn't just randomised humour?"

"No, we factored that out. There is definite evidence of pre-laughter."

"And what world has it come from?"

"It's randomised across all the colonies."

"And you interpret the data as . . . ?"

"Some of the audience have developed precognitive ability."

"But it's randomised, right? Across all the colonies?"

Earth Central funded the Circosphere, and Earth Central feared diversity. Who could tell what strange effects the different colony biospheres might have? A different sun, strange radiation, a variation in elemental chemistry, anything might initiate physical or mental changes in the colonists. The Circosphere has two functions. To unite the colonists through a central culture, reminding them of their shared heritage; and to monitor the colonists, to check that they weren't growing away from the common core of humanity.

"I think that you can anticipate a very large increase in your research grant when Earth Central hears about this," said Jinkers. Was this the source of her strange worries? Was she sensing this change in the punters' abilities?

"Thanks, Jinkers," said Brent. He looked pleased, as well he might. This was an immeasurably significant piece of research. It certainly justified the astronomical expense of running the Circosphere. Resources and prestige would follow in the wake of this discovery.

"Bella wants to know if you want to come to dinner tonight."

"Great. Set it up with my secretary."

Jinkers worked through the rest of the reports. There were changes in the food preferences in sector six. That needed to be monitored, changes in colony preferences was important information for Earth Central's massive distribution centres. But she couldn't concentrate on her work. Her mind kept returning to Brent's discovery. Precognitive development in the punters? She felt dizzy. She was the edge of a precipice. She wrote out her report and e-posted it to Earth Central. Who would have dreamed that humanity stood on the threshold of such an amazing development?

Dreams—Jinkers had been remembering some strange dreams lately. Dreams of wandering down long tunnels, looking through glass walls to see a spiral stairway reaching to the stars. She pulled up a report from the dream scientist team. Yes, there *had* been changes in the frequency and quality of the dreams in both staff and the punters. But instead of calling in the scientists for a detailed report, Jinkers decided upon a somewhat less orthodox approach.

"Got to look my best for this visit," she said to Horatio, as she pulled out a mirror from her desk drawer. She applied some skin brightening moisturiser and a natural coloured lipstick. "Not that I can compete with her. Say, Horatio, how do I look?"

But aesthetic judgements were not within the ken of her pet, and he only responded to her question with his reptilian gaze, before returning his attention to view of the stars.

"You're not much help." Judging for herself in the mirror, Jinkers announced "You'll do," before striding out of her office to seek out the mystery of dreams within the tent of Madam Zelda.

Zelda had the kind of beauty that made men sigh and women grimace in despair. She wasn't young, but she was youthful, growing inexplicably more attractive with age. And, rather annoyingly, she was a lovely person, too.

Zelda was a dream reader and fortune teller. Brent told Jinkers that she merely read the body language of the punters. And Jinkers believed that, but in the presence of Zelda that knowledge seemed to fade. Zelda commanded you to believe in her magic.

"Jinkers, how lovely to see you. It's been too long. How's Horatio?" Zelda invariably asked after her pet.

"It's lovely to see you, too, Zelda. Horatio's okay. He's been off his food, lately."

"He senses the trouble in the Circosphere. Wise creatures, the reptiles, old creatures."

Jinkers raised an eyebrow. "What do you know, Zelda?"

"There have many strange dreams lately. Sit down, my dear. Let me read your fortune for you."

Jinkers reached for the pack of cards that rested on the table between them.

Zelda, put her hand over the cards. "No, not those. I think the situation calls for something different." She reached for a different, older pack of cards. "These were my grandmother's cards."

"What's wrong with the other ones?" asked Jinkers.

"Choose three cards, my dear."

Jinkers moved her hand over the old, worn cards, then she quickly laid three cards on the table. She had selected, The Stranger, The Sideshow and The Void.

Zelda stared at the cards. She had lost some of her poise. For the first time Jinkers could see age resting in her friend's face.

"What's wrong, Zelda?"

"Dreams have been touching many minds lately. It betokens something, something extraordinary." Zelda smiled. "The cards are unclear, as they always are, my dear. But I will say this to you: look underneath the surface of your problems. There are unseen layers in our universe."

"I'd hoped for something a little more specific, Zelda."

"Don't worry, Jinkers. The answers will come to you soon. Use the motif of the circus to unwind them."

It was time to go to dinner with Brent and his family. Jinkers noticed that Horatio had still not finished his kibble. "What's a matter, Horatio? Do you sense it too? Zelda said that you're wise. Can you help me?"

But Horatio only stared at the window and at the distant stars.

"Something's wrong in the Circosphere, Horatio. What is it?"

Jinkers should have felt invigorated by the news of Brent's discovery. But . . . But . . . Perhaps she had been here too long. She was a thirty-five-

-year-old woman talking to a tortoise. She realised, with some surprise, that she was unhappy. She had friends; she had important work: the most important work in the galaxy. So why did the Circosphere feel so dull and routine? Even in the midst of this latest crisis, time felt dead to her. The magic of the circus had faded for Jinkers. It was something she'd thought would never happen.

"I'm going to put on some lipstick, and I'm going to have a good time. Paint on a smile, eh, Horatio?"

"Do you still want to be an animal trainer, Josh?" Jinkers asked. Sometimes the old tricks worked, she was enjoying herself, a home-cooked meal, the company of Brent and Bella and their irrepressible son, Josh.

"No way, Aunty Jinkers, I want to be a scientist."

"He had the revelations programme at school this week," said Bella. When the circus children turned fourteen, certain realities of the Circosphere were explained.

"Yep. I want to spy on the punters, the suckers."

"I'm not sure that's what we do here," said Jinkers, smiling. That was pretty much her own response when she had learnt about the evaluation programmes.

"It's not spying, you know that," said Bella. "There's no secret that we gather data here."

Joshua scowled. *He looks so much like his father,* thought Jinkers.

"We just don't advertise the fact. People come here to enjoy themselves and if we gather some useful information at the same time, well, that's all to the good."

"Aww, Mum . . ."

"But a scientist is a fine career choice," said Brent.

"Better paid than a lion tamer," said Jinkers.

"Well, I don't just want to be a scientist. I want to be a super scientist."

"What do you mean, Josh?"

"I want to spy on the observers, make sure that they're doing their job properly."

Jinkers laughed. "A super spy! Marvellous! Did you think that up by yourself? I wouldn't be surprised if Earth Central did have some spies, as you put it, observing the us. Who watches the watchers? What's the harm if . . . ?" She stopped, suddenly. "Excuse me. I'm so sorry, Bella, I need to get to my office immediately." Jinkers ran out of the room and sprinted to her office. She sat at her desk, panting, out of breath.

Before she did anything she needed to think. She needed to think carefully.

Jinkers believed in the ethos of the Circosphere, it was imperative to pull the colony worlds together. The Circosphere created the cohesions humanity needed to prevent fragmentation and division. Jinkers believed in science, she believed that the colonies needed to be observed and monitored.

But she also believed in the life of the circus. She pulled together all the strands of entertainment. She was the ring-master. She was in control of this enormous, multi-stranded palace of observation, of science, of cohesion, of entertainment and of magic. This was her circus. She was the circus. And she knew then, that somebody had got in under the canvas.

Jinkers Morrell said in a clear, distinct voice, "I know you're there—show yourself."

Nothing happened.

"Okay then." She activated her computer. "Have it your own way. I'm reporting this to Earth Central."

"Wait." A figure materialised in front of her: a humanoid figure: an alien figure.

"Who the hell are you? How long have you been in my circus?" This was big. This was massive.

"Apologies, Madam Morrell. We are representatives. We have been in your establishment for a few weeks."

"Where are you from?"

The alien walked around her office. He looked almost human, but not quite. There was an indefinable essence of strangeness cast over his entire countenance. "We inhabit another galaxy, Madam Morrell."

Another galaxy! Earth Central had dismissed the possibility of sentient alien life in the universe.

The alien continued to traverse her office. Jinkers' mind was racing. He didn't *seem* belligerent. Jinkers was riding along her instincts. They had always served her well.

"We are impressed that you identified us so quickly." The alien picked up a handful of Horatio's kibble. "There are always a few inconsistencies, no matter how hard we try to blend in. I'm afraid we've caused some false readings in your data. Were you expecting us? We were under the belief that your species had dismissed alternative sentience as an implausible possibility."

"This is my circus," said Jinkers. "I know what goes on here. Why are you here?"

"We do the same as you, Madam. We observe. What did you say, earlier?" he smiled, an unfortunate occurrence revealing a mouthful of teeth. "Who watches the watchers? Well, we do." He held out his hand to Horatio, who stretched his neck out and began to nibble the food in the alien's outstretched palm. "And Madam Morrell, to extend your metaphor: I have a free pass to an outstanding show."

"A universal spectacular?"asked Jinkers

"Indeed. Madam Morrell, welcome to the greatest show of your life: the Universal Federations of Sentience." Horatio continued to feed. "We thought that you might like to be the one to announce the news to the rest of humanity."

The universe just got interesting, thought Jinkers, as she put the call through to Earth Central.

VANISHING ACT

E. CATHERINE TOBLER

Jackson's Unreal Circus and Mobile Marmalade picked her up a day outside Denver. Jackson wouldn't stop for a cow on the tracks, but he stopped for this little thing, with her pale hair and paler eyes. Brought the entire train to a stop to scoop her from the tracks with his long arms.

She huddled against his chest, her small body nearly folded in on itself, and we all watched, in confusion and fascination both. The long hem of her dirty shift caught the cow catcher and the remains of said beast.

She was none of my concern, but Jackson placed her in my car and made her just that. He laid her down in the corner, in my favorite chair, my only chair. She looked all the more pale against the blue and gold stripes. Their brilliance had long since faded, but looked new against her washed out skin. Her bare feet were crusted with dirt and muck and I didn't look much beyond that.

I was working with the quarters when she began to wail, rolling them across my fingers before trying to turn them into nickels. The steam whistle crowed as we crossed the state line, Colorado into New Mexico, and she came alive as though submerged in hot water.

The quarters tumbled off my fingers, onto the floor where they lay as she shrieked, curled her hands over her ears, and moaned. Her face was creased with pain; for a moment, she looked like she'd been raked with hot metal.

After listening to her, I wanted to do the same; curl into a ball and moan. Instead, I went to her. Crouched before the chair and tried to get her to lower her hands.

First thing I noticed was that her hands didn't feel like hands. She was soft, as though her bones hadn't yet firmed up. A baby in the guise of a ten year old. Second thing I noticed was the way she went quiet when I touched her.

I thought she would twist away, scream, holler, anything but what she did, which was melt into me, against my chest. Her soft hand curled its way into my shirtfront, her thumb working over the nearest dirty button.

"Stop that."

Tried to push her out of my arms, I did, but she wouldn't go. She took to purring like a cat, like the big lions Jackson kept caged in the car behind mine. To keep me in line, he said, but I could make them vanish with a thought. Still, I didn't like the idea of where they might end up, so I left them alone, and they did the same for me.

The girl's purring took up residence inside my head, worked some kind of magic and made me tumble toward the mattress Opal had snickered at, but had still come to. And where did that memory come from, I wondered as I drowned inside that rumbling sound. I was lost inside it as though it was a maze. Couldn't find my way out, so I just gave in and eventually it bled into a familiar dark quiet I recognized as sleep.

Woke to the train slowing again and I wondered if Jackson was stopping for another sprite on the tracks. Stars painted the sky overhead and the air smelled like manure. We'd reached our destination then.

I untangled myself from the boneless girl. She lay as though dead and I moved away as quick as I could. Before she could latch on again. Before she thought to hold me and purr and make me a lost thing.

The air outside was cool, smelled like snow would be on the ground come morning. I pulled my coat around me, rubbed my hands together, and approached the first of the weird sisters as they emerged from their own car. I offered up one hand; Gemma took it, but Sombra's hand was just as quickly there. It seemed one hand around mine, though I knew there to be two.

The sisters were two halves of the same thing, one light and one dark. Where one was concave, the other was convex. Where one was sharp rocks, the other was smooth water. Sombra's hair was the night sky while Gemma's was the stars. And sometimes, they were exactly backwards from that.

Why, I wondered, couldn't Jackson have placed the little girl in with them? They were women, they'd had children, countless children or so they said. I'd had plenty of women, but no children. Never would. Didn't need or want them. Would be all too easy to wish them gone and have them vanish.

Sombra and Gemma moved like fog across the ground. Their feet never touched the ground as they drifted away. They wouldn't help with the unloading; they never did and no one ever expected they would. They floated into the night and dissolved into fireflies against the blackness as they swept and blessed the campsite.

Five long and pale fingers wrapped around my half-warmed hand and I started at the touch. Looked down and found the little girl clutching me, her fingers warmed, water barely contained by skin. She looked up at me and her mouth curled in a crescent moon smile.

I could see now that her pale hair was drawn into disorganized ropes, like the jumble you'd find on the dusty ground after the tents came down, messy on the ends like they hadn't been tended in a few years. Her mouth was as pale as her skin; her smile slipped away, but her grip tightened and she looked around, as if to ask where and why we were.

"Performin' here," I said and tried to loose my hand from hers, but she was having none of it. I walked and she fell into easy step beside me, though her little legs shouldn't have been able to keep up.

Silas and Lawrence were already unloading the tents. I finally shook the girl's hand off of mine, swung up into the car, and helped Hunter roll another of the striped cylinders to the door. We maneuvered it around, gave it a swift kick down, and the boys carried it off.

There were twenty-four tents in all. The girl watched me the whole time, perched like an owl on the fence across from the door. Her eyes were almost blue, but as the last tent came down I decided the color was only from the nearest light. She would move away and her eyes would change, no doubt.

"Got a name?" I asked her as I came out of the car and headed back toward mine. She watched me as I took a rumpled cigarette from my coat and placed flame against its tip. Drew deep and exhaled once before she answered.

"You?"

"Ladies first," I insisted. She was tiny and odd, but a lady nonetheless. Her colorless eyes skimmed over me, then met mine again.

"Rabi," she said and I choked on the smoke that rolled down my throat.

She snatched the cigarette from my hand, tossed it to the ground and mashed it under her pale toes. I thought I might cough up my stomach, but she brushed her fingers down my arm and I calmed. Instantly, like my mother touching me after a nightmare. I looked at her through the fall of my hair.

"At's *my* name." My voice was hoarse. I turned and thumped the side of my car. Painted in silver by Gemma, trimmed in black by Sombra, was my name and my claim to fame. Rabi, Vanquisher and Vanisher Extraordinaire.

The little girl's mouth twisted and she looked around, searching for another name. Any would do, any name, any word. She looked like a snowflake standing there, eyes flitting from thing to thing, the dirty hem of her shift lifting in the cold breeze. Her skin should have been puckered from the cold, her toes burned from the cigarette, but she showed no discomfort.

Finally she shook her head.

I shrugged. Didn't matter. She wasn't mine to name. I'd be damned if I was going to do it.

Work continued through the night. The little girl didn't seem to tire; she helped where she thought she could, with small things, and took to following the weird sisters when they returned. She was the reverse of a shadow, but the very shadow Sombra should have had right then; as pale as she was dark. And when it was Gemma's turn to darken, the child could flutter in her wake.

I hauled a rope, helped pull a tent upright. The red and white striped fabric soared against the pre-dawn sky, snapped as the ropes pulled it taut. That cloth shuddered as inner supports were placed thus and so, ribs and organs and muscles to give the beast a chance of standing.

The marmalade stand was up before the sun, which wasn't saying much as snow had begun to fall. Too many clouds for there to be sun. I crossed the stubble grass, drawn by the scent of Beth's fresh rolls and marmalade. I bought a small jar of the orange and a bundle of rolls, kissed her cheek and let her squeeze my backside before I walked back to my car.

Found the little girl there, wrapped in the blue blanket with its purple stars. She looked like a ghost and I told her as much.

"Not a ghost," she said and I saw that she had one of my books. I didn't have many. It was the atlas she had spread in her lap, and she pointed to a small town. "We are here."

I nodded as I punched a hole in the bag of rolls. Drew one out, cracked open the jar of marmalade. I tore the roll open next and two fingers sufficed as knife to spread the marmalade. The girl's attention was drawn away from the book; she watched me spread the marmalade, lift, and eat the roll. Marmalade clung to my lips; I licked them clean and she mimicked the motion.

"Gemma says you make things vanish," she said as I finished the roll in three more bites. The rolls were so hot, they'd steamed the bag. I took another one out and tossed it to her. Her watery fingers caught it without hesitation. She broke it open, inhaled the fragrant steam, and stretched her hand toward the marmalade.

Her long fingers were better suited to working as knives. She spread the marmalade smooth and even and took a cautious bite, then another, then made the roll disappear in the cavern of her mouth. With a swallow it was gone.

"You make things vanish," she repeated.

And I knew she didn't mean the roll I'd just eaten. "That's what I do." I nodded and tore open my second roll. She came closer and took another from the bag. She went slower with her second, as I did with mine.

"Really vanish, not magic vanish."

I nodded again, and I never liked where this conversation was going. It was classic, as though she'd pressed her ear against the side of my car a few weeks ago and listened while Anne begged me to do it, to make him vanish and stop beating on her and how could I say no, why wouldn't I do it, couldn't I understand? She wailed—wailed like the girl did when we crossed the state line—and I knew what was coming.

Except it didn't. Not yet.

We sat, in companionable calm, eating rolls and marmalade, while the snow fell silently beyond the open car door.

Ritual and tradition play a big part in Jackson's life and so it was on the first evening that he gathered us performers together. A meal, not lavish but steaming and generous, had been spread atop the ancient wood table Jackson claimed to have carted from one side of Europe and back again before the war. And at this table we all took our places, under the softly flowing fabric of the big top.

Seeing as how the little girl didn't have a place, she made herself one. A round full moon resting in Sombra's lap, that's how she looked. She didn't help herself to much that night; she took a biscuit and some water, but little else, though Sombra tried to get her interested in the beans. Nope, she was determined not to have any.

I sat between Foster and Jackson and Jackson seemed genuinely happy about the stay we would have in this little town. These folk were dying for some good entertainment. Kids had seen the posters, he said, and no matter the dirt and rips, they'd run home. Foster could picture them digging out cans of pennies. They'd be back and he'd be counting those pennies. Foster always smelled like money, like old paper and metal.

Denver had been good to us, but this little place would be better. New Mexico was a fine state, and the little girl turned her attention to us as Jackson and Foster talked about the buttes and scrub brush and the way storms seemed to roll right down the mountains and explode on the plains. The little girl shook at that.

Her whole body trembled. Sombra tried to comfort her, but the girl rolled out of her lap, under the table. Soon enough I felt her curled against my boots. I resisted the urge to reach down and touch her hair. Jackson and Foster changed the subject—back to money—and she calmed.

Almost forgot she was there. As I made to get up, I felt her weight against me. My movement woke her and sleepily she emerged from the table, covered here and there with crumbs and dirt. They didn't seem to bother her none. She lifted her hand and I took it in mine and together we walked back to my train car.

"Going to be here long?" she asked as she climbed under the blue blanket.

"Seven days at the most." Jackson had never stayed in a place longer than that. This town was a speck, a speck that didn't have a name anyone knew, and while the people might be hungry for what we could give, they wouldn't have much money. Santa Fe would be better, but Jackson had his mind set on heading farther west, toward the coast if possible.

She was restless in her sleep, kept kicking and shoving me. Finally I moved away from her, sat in my chair and smoked a cigarette. It was cold, but the snow had stopped for the moment.

Where had she come from? What had she been doing out on that track? Most things we saw on the tracks were either there by mistake or looking to end their lives. Two years ago, Jackson obliged a young man by the name of Coleman Bean. After that, Jackson didn't stop his train for anyone. Till a few days ago.

She twisted and turned and finally sat up, her hair in a big clump on the left side.

"Could sleep better if the clouds would stop."

I crumpled my cigarette in the tin tray and stood. Above the mattress, there was a cargo door and I unlatched the squeaky hook and rolled it open. Above the mattress now, the sky was that soft pink that comes before a snow. The girl shivered, but not from the cold.

Making things disappear is easy if you think about it, but most folks don't think. I couldn't make the clouds disappear; I hadn't fully mastered clouds or water or flowers. But, I could move them along, so I did. Willed them to move on toward Texas. The little girl stopped shivering once the pink sky turned black and the stars made themselves known. She relaxed back into the blankets and I got under with her.

"There's Jupiter," she whispered and extended a long arm beyond the covers. I swear she almost touched that planet with her pointer finger. She sure did blot it out for a moment or two.

"And Mars, but you know, I think I like Saturn the best."

Her little voice broke apart as she ended that sentence and she began to tremble again, like she'd done at the dinner table. I reached for her forehead, thinking to soothe her fear away, but she slapped my hand away, scooted to the other side of the mattress.

"Don't take it away," she said. "It's all I have left."

I did not question her, for it made sense to me. Fear could be a good friend. Lord knows fear had kept me alive during some pretty long nights. It was keeping me awake right now, wondering what the thing beside me was, for though it looked like a young girl, I knew it was not. It was something else, but I still had no name for it.

She slept then and I left the mattress, tossing the warmed blanket over her before I walked away. I went to my table and picked up the quarters and made them dance over my fingers before making them vanish entirely. They didn't slide up my sleeves and they didn't go through the cracks in the table.

Without the clouds, the air outside was bitter. I turned up the collar of my coat and buttoned it. The ground crunched under my feet and laughter carried to me in the frosty night.

The Doshenkos were practicing in the main tent, flying through the air with the greatest of intentions. They never seemed to get it quite right.

Pasha slipped from Oleg's hands and plummeted to the netting where she somersaulted. Oleg laughed and so did Pasha. Perhaps one day, he said and she echoed it while climbing back up to try again.

Away from their circle of laughter, it seemed colder and I hurried my steps, to the weird sisters' tent with purple and gold stripes. I kneeled before the flap and listened, listened so hard that I could hear them breathing inside. The air was spiced with incense here, sandalwood and lavender, and I took a deep breath.

It merged with their own and for a moment we breathed together. It felt as though I were inside the tent, snuggled between ample breast and small, and then as abruptly as I'd been there, I was here again, kneeling in dirt.

I didn't have to dig deep; the quarters were not buried far. All six of them were right where I'd sent them and this time none of them melted. They weren't a lost thing to me. Not this time. I gripped them hard, till their edges pressed into my fingers.

Things were easy to lose; hanging on to them took talent. Making things vanish was easy, if you knew where to send them. Knew the exact place as well as you know your own hands.

And I knew this place, this dark and spicy doorway, for many men had kneeled and gone through—this one included—but not tonight. I took my quarters and whispered goodbye to the sisters before taking my leave.

The little girl was sitting in the doorway to my car when I returned. Her thin legs swung restlessly. She wanted to run, but didn't know where to go. Wanted to vanish, but didn't know where to put herself.

"We go west from here?" she asked. Her hands plucked at her shift. "I heard the man, Jackson, say west. We can't go west."

I pocketed my quarters and looked at her, wondering exactly how she meant to stop this train and its people from going west. I waited for an answer and she only grew more agitated. The shift was shredding under her fingers; she was plucking hard enough to tear the thin fabric.

"I can't go west." And she was firm about that. "Not even if there's more hot rolls and marmalade. East," she said finally giving me a clue. "And a little south. Would that be so hard? Won't Jackson reconsider?"

"There's nothing that way. Jackson goes where the people are, where the money is. Has his mind fixed on San Francisco eventually. I think he's got family there." Did she notice the way my voice caught on that word, family? Her sharp eyes didn't miss much; they were narrow now, as though she meant to study me the way I'd been studying her. Don't do that, little girl, I thought and she sat straighter.

"East."

She turned her face up to the stars, but Saturn didn't lie in the east so I didn't figure it was a star she was following. "What's east?" I asked and she didn't look at me. Didn't turn away from the stars. Didn't even answer me.

And before long, it was too cold to just stand there, so I had to go inside. I started a fire in the small grate, warmed my hands and my feet, and made sure the smoke wouldn't roll back on us during the night.

It didn't roll back on us, just on me, for when I woke she was still out there looking at the stars. I saw her point to one and heard her say, "I am there."

But she wasn't there—she was here—and that was her entire problem.

She hadn't meant to come to Earth, she told me. It was all one big mistake. She'd been running from her family, had to get away, and this is where she ended up. She had to stop running because her ship stopped. Caught something in the engine and when she was about to get it right, a New Mexican storm slapped her down. Two years, that's how long she'd been here, trying to figure a way back home.

Two years ago, Jackson had stopped the train for a young man named Coleman Bean. A lot could happen in two years.

Couldn't find any of her own kind. Seemed she was the only one, and that thought filled her with an agony that tasted like metal in the back of her throat. She'd climbed onto the tracks to kill herself, but damn Jackson had to go and stop. Had to find that shred of soul within himself and put it to use that night.

"You was glowing like some firefly," I said. "I think that might have caught his attention. Maybe he thought you was a diamond." I grinned and she shoved me. She didn't look like a diamond or a firefly.

I didn't mean to come to this place, either, I finally told her, though it wasn't Earth I was meaning. This circus train. But I'd been running, too, and yes away from family. Sombra and Gemma spotted me in a track-side bar, performing card and coin tricks for a little cash. They told me they had a better deal, both in and out of their tent. They were right, so I came to the tracks and watched the train slow as they said it would. Anything was better than going back.

"Going back is the only thing," she countered as she stuck her bare feet toward the flames. "Until you do, you're in limbo. Fancy Earth word. Why'd you run?"

"Why did you?"

She didn't answer me and I didn't answer her and the night blurred into morning as we warmed our feet beside the darkened grate.

The first night of the show is perhaps the best. Mistakes happen, but that's part of the fun. Like Manny and his lions; surely he didn't mean for the male to eat his red coat, but it happened. Buttons and all, down the hatch and the audience applauded while the big cat licked his lips.

We didn't have many animals in the show. The monkeys seemed to be the favorites, but Miss Victoria Solace didn't appreciate the way they stole her hat and wore it around the ring. They pranced and chattered and the men roared and pointed. I made the hat vanish from the monkey's paws and reappear on her head, much to her delight.

Mrs. Isabel Tompkins had the kind of mind I liked, clear and warm like a summer pond. I could see everything that lay under the surface and when she handed me her handkerchief and bade me "vanish it!" it was easy enough to do so. In her mind I could see her orderly kitchen, though her husband Harry was always fussing with the bread box and tinkering under the sink and she wished he would stop.

I couldn't make him stop, but I took her handkerchief, and folded it in half. In half again, and once more. I folded until I couldn't fold anymore, until the fabric had no more to give. And then I pinched the fabric between my fingers and it vanished. Isabel's eyes flew wide and the entire audience applauded and roared.

She expected me to pull the fabric from my sleeve. They always do. But I could only lift my hands and tumble away toward the next thing to vanish. She would find her handkerchief, folded between the kitchen table leg and the golden but scarred wood flooring. The table would have stopped its rocking, but it wouldn't occur to her to look for two months.

The little girl watched the entire show through the legs of an enormously fat man. She was pressed under the bleachers, and though she could have had a much better seat, she didn't seem to want one. I could understand the need to hide; coming to Jackson's had been a way of hiding. Couldn't live with Sherri Lynn anymore. Just couldn't.

Her mind was like Mrs. Tompkins, so clear I could see every thought and know them as if they were my own. I could see Sherri Lynn's past, could know how she felt about her daddy and how she wished he would vanish. And it was all too easy after knowing that darkness.

All too easy to pluck him from the hardware store where he worked and bury him in the worm-rich mud beneath the shed of a house he had lived in twenty years before. Sherri Lynn hated that shed, but knew every corner of it. I took that memory, made it my own, and sent him there. The disappearance of Ralph Moody was never explained, though no one seemed to mourn him.

Still, it was that kind of thing that bothered me. I pictured that man, slowly suffocating in that dirt, and just couldn't live with the fact that I'd done it. Didn't matter that he'd touched Sherri Lynn wrong. Didn't matter that he hit his wife and called her names you wouldn't call a dog.

I couldn't pull him back out of the ground; once he was gone, he was gone. I tried, but couldn't budge him. Once a thing vanished, it was gone to me. Someone else could come upon him. He could be a found thing then, but to me he was a lost thing. Vanished. Except the quarters, I reminded myself. I was getting better. Maybe in time, things wouldn't have to be so lost.

"Rabi," the little girl said after the show. She slipped her long fingers into mine and handed me a stone. She had picked it from beneath the bleachers; I could feel the very depression it had made in the ground. Shallow and as cool as the night air.

In her mind, she showed me where she wanted the rock to go. The desert plain was lit by only starlight; the brush and cactus made strange shadows over the ground. In the ground, buried beneath rock and mud, was a piece of a lost thing. Metallic and not something I could fully understand. I tried to, but I felt the same murk I did when I tried to look into the little girl. She was giving me this, allowing me to see, but I couldn't understand.

The rock vanished from my palm and the breath went out of her. It was like wind moving through trees, that soft whooshing sound the leaves make. She made this sound, her hand relaxed in mine, and we continued on toward my train car, without another word spoken between us.

Come morning, Jackson was more excited than I'd seen him in days. He interrupted everyone's practice and called us all to the main tent. Pasha Doshenko stayed on her trapeze, swaying above us as Jackson talked.

"It's a good deal," he kept saying while he rubbed his hands together and paced before the crowd of us. It's like he was trying to convince us, something he'd never done. He'd always told us where we were going and those who wanted to follow did. A few had been lost along the way, but what better show was there than Jackson and his unreal circus and marmalade?

"There's a man, you see," he said and I did see, a round man with round glasses and thick hands, and this man offered Jackson more money than he'd ever been offered for a performance. "Food and real shelters included," Jackson continued and I saw in his mind a hotel with a swimming pool and everything. I saw warm baths and soft beds. "We'd stay for the winter, till things get warm again."

That part of the deal was important, I realized, and I felt the pain in Jackson's hands as though it was my own. He was young, but his bones had already started to rub together, causing him pain no matter how he moved. Jackson wanted to bed down somewhere warm for a few weeks and move on when spring came.

"Dallas," he finally said. Which was backwards from where we were going. It would delay San Francisco, he said and I got a flash of a beautiful young girl in his mind. Not his lover, but his mother as he remembered her from his childhood. Jackson wanted to get home, wanted it badly, but didn't know if he could stand the winter ride to get there.

This was agreeable for the little girl who began to purr against my side. I'd forgotten she was there, but traveling east was fine with her and when Jackson took his vote, her long pale arm was one of the first to rise.

Didn't matter to me where we went, really, but Dallas was a little too close for my comfort. Close to Sherri Lynn, close to the little house that had been ours. She was still there; she wouldn't leave her roses nor her turtles for anything in the world. She liked her teaching, liked being far from her family.

"Limbo," the little girl whispered and I wondered then if my mind were clear to her like Sherri Lynn's had been to me. "Goin' east, goin' east." She couldn't contain her excitement.

"What is it you want me to make vanish?" I asked, wanting this over. Once I did the trick, she would go. Wouldn't she?

But she shook her head and her pale hair rubbed her shoulders and then my coat as she nuzzled up to me. I froze under her touch. I didn't need this, didn't need her telling me I was in limbo. I wasn't. I'd moved on with my life, did what was best for me and Sherri Lynn both.

The little girl didn't answer, and I found out later that night that Gemma, now as dark as Sombra, and Sombra, now as light as Gemma, had named her Vara. Vara curled herself up at my grate once more and slept through the show, while I danced and performed until exhaustion claimed me and I made a man's vanished coin appear in a woman's all-too visible cleavage. He chuckled, she shrieked, but the play went on.

The train moved at a steady pace through the New Mexico desert. It was strange to see snow across cactus and scrub brush, over the red and taupe earth, but there it was and it looked pretty.

Vara didn't move from the small window much. She stayed huddled in the blanket and her breath made small puffs of fog on the pane. Every now and then she pressed her fingers against the glass, as if trying to measure distance. Once, she got excited about a landmark, but we passed it and she realized it wasn't the mountain she'd been thinking about.

She started wailing the next day, as the train drew closer to the state line. She woke me with her crying and there was nothing I could do to calm her. Her cries rose until the window shattered and the train ground to a sudden halt. Froze up on the tracks, as though it was caught in ice. Vara wrenched herself from my arms, scrambled out of the car, and across the frozen desert.

I watched her go, the tail of her shift flipping up and down like an antelope tail. She'd refused all offer of other clothing; didn't want anything that made her look human, she told Gemma. There was no danger of that, I thought, but kept my opinion to myself. She was too small and too pale to be human, but running away . . . she had that down pat.

With the train stuck on the tracks, we weren't going anywhere for a while. Jackson's hot cursing should have melted the frozen wheels, but they remained wedged against the track, unmoving.

Gemma, back to her stardust self, shoved me and I stumbled into the brush. "Go after her," she demanded, and Gemma never demanded. Those hands coaxed and that voice tempted, but now they demanded and I went, following the trail Vara had left in the snow.

It was a wide trail, clumsy and crooked. Her feet must be frozen, I thought, but told myself they weren't human feet at all and maybe she didn't even feel the cold. The cloudy sky above me began to darken, though it couldn't be much past mid-day. My own feet were cold, legs stiff, and I didn't want to go much further.

Vara was sprawled on the ground ahead of me, one hand stretching toward the eastern horizon. I touched my hand to her back and found her like a block of ice. No matter that she wasn't human, she was cold and I picked her up and cuddled her into my coat. She was passive against me, maybe too cold to react, but when I turned away and headed back toward the train, she whimpered.

In my mind I saw a picture of what "east" meant to her, and I fell to my knees. They cracked against stone, but I couldn't feel any pain as I went down. Could only see and feel what Vara showed me then and there.

The metal was curved, the smooth edge of a ship meant for the stars. Her ship once upon a time, but now it was broken, most of it carried away. She couldn't get home, couldn't find her people, but wanted to get back to that one remaining piece of ship. And if she couldn't get there, she wanted to disappear.

It would be easy, I found myself thinking. Easy to make her vanish, into that bit of ground, nestled against the metal of her ship. But no, no, God I just wouldn't do it. She was living and breathing and I wouldn't end that.

She felt my refusal, but was too cold and weak to move away from me. She pushed against my chest, made me feel all that she was missing—the touch of her mother's hand, the nuzzle of her lover, the familiar dirt of her homeworld—but still I refused.

Vara reached up and grabbed a handful of my hair. She yanked, tried to make me feel pain, any pain that would equal her own, but she couldn't and that only made hers more keen. She touched me again, this time deeper, and unlocked my own pain. Made me touch Sherri Lynn and the desolation she had known after I vanished. I had closed that off long ago, but Vara opened it as easy as she might a door.

Left that morning and didn't tell Sherri Lynn, couldn't tell her, and she woke alone in the bed. My things were neat in the closets and drawers, but I was gone. Gone like the fairies came and took me in the night.

Sherri Lynn was broken, like Vara's ship. Submerged in cold ground, buried so no one could find her. She was dying there, cold and alone, and here I was, playing in the circus without a care in the world. Accepting Beth's warm smile, finding comfort in Gemma and Sombra's bed. Taking time with ladies like Anne who came to visit and wanted something to vanish in exchange for a little roll and tumble. Pretending Sherri Lynn didn't exist.

It was easier than going back, but going back we were and if I wouldn't press Vara into her ground, she would press me into mine.

When Vara was ready to go, she released the train from its slumber. The wheels slowly turned and steam rolled back over the cars. Merrily we roll along, Jackson whispered and refused to look at Vara.

"Shouldn't have ever stopped for her," he said.

"She'd be dead then."

"Blown to bits like that cow," Jackson agreed and I knew he meant it.

The cow had been a spectacular thing, standing there one minute, flying in a thousand pieces the next. The train only slowed briefly. I could have moved it before we hit. But I hadn't. Why? Sometimes the simplest answers are the truth. I didn't want to. I wanted to see what happened. That was why any of us did anything. Just wanted to see what happened.

Making the cow disappear was easy, moving it just off the tracks to the lazy stretch of grass beyond. It would chew grass for a few more years, but it was stupid and would wander onto the tracks again sooner or later.

To Jackson, Vara was a stupid thing. A thing that would wander onto another track sooner or later.

She didn't move when I laid her down on the mattress. Her knees were still drawn to her chest. I covered her with the blanket and watched her, and wondered if I was wrong.

"You could find a life here," I finally said. "It could be a good one."

She roused at that. Sat up and turned toward me, stretching toes toward the fire I'd made. Vara shook her head. "I don't want to be something unreal, something people pay money to see. I just want to go home. And can't."

She picked up the thing nearest her hand, a discarded shoe, and threw it at me. I was so startled I didn't react and the shoe hit me in my chest. It fell to the floor as she yelled at me.

"And you can. Your home is there and you don't go."

"My home is here."

"This is no home." She pounded the mattress and gestured around her. There was little here that would make this a home; the room itself never existed in one place for more than a few nights. There was no yard, no flowers, no real bed with sheets and pillows. No photographs on the wall and no mail in a mailbox. No Sherri Lynn.

"I had to come here," I said as I reached for the shoe Vara had thrown. I picked it up, held it in my hands, used it as a focal point. Anything so I wouldn't have to look into Vara's eyes. "I did it to a man once, made him vanish, and it's too easy to do it again. I can't do it again, I won't. Not even for the best of reasons, don't you see?"

I think she did see, because she turned away from me. I dropped the shoe and crouched behind her, wrapped my arms around her small shoulders and pressed a hand over her heart. Or whatever it was that fluttered inside of her like a caught fish.

"Right here and now you are alive. It don't matter that you're different. It don't matter where you came from. No one is goin' to care about those things."

"But I care." Her voice was small, so small I could have held it in my palm and had room for a bird, a shoe, and maybe a jar of marmalade. "I am those things. And you, you have this wonderful gift and all you do is make coins roll down women's dresses. You could help me—I've shown you the place."

There would be no arguing. I'd known that all along.

"Then let's go, you and me. Let's go now." She turned in my arms and her eyes brightened. Her watery fingers squeezed my arms. She was ready now. She had nothing to pack.

And neither did I really, so when the train stopped for the night, we stole into the car of horses and took One Eye, who Jackson was always threatening to shoot. Grabbed some rolls and marmalade, and vanished into the night.

We weren't alone right away; Sombra and Gemma followed us, in shadows and bits of starlight, but they didn't talk so we didn't acknowledge them. When eventually they left us, the air grew cool and damp. Vara looked back, as though she felt them go.

We rode that whole long night through and through the next day; we stopped only long enough to eat. Vara was too excited about getting to the place she'd shown me in her mind. Her mind was more clear now, she was showing me more things. Things I didn't really want to see, but couldn't help but noticing.

She had one thing on her world that she missed as much as she missed familiar faces. Smashed berries was all she could think to call it in her head. Like the marmalade, I thought as her pale finger slid into the jar to scrape the final sweet bits from the bottom.

Next twilight brought us to the place Vara had shown me in her mind. It wasn't a pretty place, barren and deeply scarred. Vara slipped out of my loose hold and ran across the snowy ground, light as a fleck of lint. She went over a small ridge and I rode One Eye down after her.

Vara kneeled in the dirt, took up handfuls of it and scrubbed it over her skin. This was the place, she'd lived here for a month before she'd found the courage to leave and look for her own kind. But there were none, only tall, dark strangers who didn't speak her language and so she'd had to learn.

"I want to go, will you make me vanish?"

I got off One Eye, slow because I could feel the ground vibrating with her excitement. Came to her side and kneeled down there, touching the dirt that covered her and then the ground itself.

That metallic thing was under there, the piece of her ship, and I could feel the small remains of another of her kind. Not much left, maybe a finger or toe. Whatever else had been taken away with shovels. I could still feel the deep grooves they'd made that day in the dirt.

"Rabi."

"You didn't show me the other before."

She showed me now, this other being, her lover, her Sherri Lynn. Color blinded me, while a sensation like hair being brushed backwards made my skin go bumpy. I wanted to throw up and I wanted to cry, because this feeling was familiar. I tasted Vara's longing—bitter. She wanted to be taken away in shovels as this one had been.

Vara's dirty fingers curled into my shirt sleeve and I shook my head. "Can't put you in this ground," I whispered. "You'll die."

She knew exactly what she was asking here. There was no hesitation in her eyes or her mind. Her hand tightened in my sleeve and she bent to her knees, as if they'd grown too watery to hold her.

"Not going home is already like death."

The truth in that hit me hard, so hard that I saw it then—a clean green orb hanging in the heavens. The cool of an alien wind brushed over my arms, made my hair stand at attention. An alien sun sank into a topaz sea and all around me, birds that were not birds whirled and cried. I tried to breathe, but could not. Couldn't take breath until Vara stopped touching me.

I breathed, but the image of the place did not leave me. I could see the flowers and the pollen on the flowers, and the small bugs embedded in the stems. I could see a structure, not like any house I knew, but it smelled friendly and tasted like love. I opened my mouth and took it whole and as I swallowed, Vara's excitement rippled over me and tasted like smashed berries.

I focused on that small house and its taste. With Vara's small hand in mine, I could nearly feel the door, and it seemed to move under my fingers. Swinging inward, it revealed to me a room with a fire and a tall, tall figure, and I knew this was Vara's family. Felt it as though it was my own.

When I looked at Vara, her face was smooth, like someone had pulled a sheet of pale plastic from chin to forehead, sticking a finger in to leave a mouth hole. Vara's hand wasn't a hand, either; no hand like I knew. Under her vaguely human cloak, she was nothing I understood, nothing I could understand without a hundred lifetimes to do so.

But I could understand the things in my head. Family and warmth and water and bright skies lit by a shining star. I thought about those things, about those things through Vara. I thought about Vara, about her under that bright sky, pale toes in the golden water. I pictured her there and she giggled as though she already were.

She began to melt in my hands, pale sugar water running into the red dirt. Her mouth was still open in a dark O, her eyes wide with surprise—was it surprise or fear? Oh, it was fear. It stabbed me hard in the chest and I tried right then, tried so hard, to stop her from vanishing. Was it going wrong? I didn't know. Couldn't know.

"Vara," I whispered, but that had never been her name and her alien mind did not recognize it.

Once a thing goes, it goes. She was becoming a lost thing to me and no matter how I tried to hold her together, she still slipped through my fingers. She was going somewhere I could no longer find her, a place I could not even imagine without her guidance. She was cold and wet and then nothing at all. I felt an indistinct, lingering sense of her, a shimmer of warmth wrapped up in smashed berries. Then, nothing at all.

The cold began to seep through my trousers and I became aware of the light across the horizon. It had stopped snowing and the sun was coming up.

I guided One Eye out of the small depression and we kept moving east. Would have been easy to ride back to the train, but I couldn't go back, not now. Not going home is already like death.

Sherri Lynn was shoveling snow from her walk when I saw her two days later, her nose reddened from the cold, a green hat mashed over her pale hair. She looked up at the sound of horse hooves on the cold ground, stiffened when she saw it was me. I got down, but didn't come any nearer.

She extended her hand, slow and shaking, and I placed my own within it. Sherri Lynn's mind was now dark and cloudy. It was a blessed darkness and I loved the things I could not see.

"Coleman," she whispered, disbelieving.

That voice was familiar, warm with an uneven edge. I squeezed her hand and she whispered once more. I vanished into her voice, into the memories that flooded her, that flooded me. Familiar, haunting places, that tasted like love and marmalade.

QUIN'S SHANGHAI CIRCUS

JEFF VANDERMEER

Let me tell you why I wished to buy a meerkat at Quin's Shanghai Circus. Let me tell you about the city: *The city is sharp, the city is a cliche performed with cardboard and painted sparkly colors to disguise the empty center—the hole.*

(That's mine—*the words.* I specialize in holo art, but every once in a chemical moon I'll do the slang jockey thing *on paper.*)

Let me tell you what the city means to me. So you'll understand about the meerkat, because it's important. Very important: Back a decade, when the social planners ruled, we called it Dayton Central. Then, when the central government choked flat and the police all went freelance, we started calling it Ven*iss*—like an adder's hiss, deadly and unpredictable. Art was Dead here until Ven*iss*. Art before Ven*iss* was just Whore Hole stuff, street mimes with flexi-faces and *flat media.*

That's what the Social Revolutions meant to me—not all the redrum riots and the twisted girders and the flourishing free trade markets and the hundred-meter-high ad signs sprouting on every street corner. Not the garbage zones, not the ocean junks, not the underlevel coups, nor even the smell of glandular drugs, musty yet sharp. No, Veniss brought Old Art to an end, made me dream of *suck-cess*, with my omni-present, omni-everything holovision.

Almost brought *me* to an end as well one day, for in the absence of those policing elements of society (except for pay-for-hire), two malicious thieves—nay, call them what they were: Pick Dicks—well, these two pick dicks stole all my old-style ceramics and new style holosculpture and, after mashing me on the head with a force that split my brains all over the floor, split too. Even my friend Shadrach Begolem showed concern when he found me. (A brooding sort, my friend Begolem: no blinks: no twitches: no tics. All economy of motion, of energy, of time. Eyee, the opposite of me.) But we managed to rouse an autodoc from its wetwork slumber and got me patched up (Boy, did that hurt!).

Afterwards, I sat alone in my apartment/studio, crying as I watched nuevo-westerns on a holo Shadrach lent me. All that work gone! The faces of the city, the scenes of the city, that had torn their way from my mind to the holo, forever lost—never even shown at a galleria, and not likely to have been, either. Ven*iss*, huh! The adder defanged. The snake slithering away. When did anyone care about the real artists until after they were dead? And I was as close to Dead as any Living Artist ever was. I had no supplies. My money had all run out on me—plastic rats deserting a paper ship. I was a Goner, all those Artistic Dreams so many arthritic flickers in a holoscreen. (You don't have a cup of water on you, by any chance? Or a pill or two?)

I think I always had Artistic Dreams.

When we were little, my twinned sister Nicola and I made up these fabric creatures we called cold pricklies and, to balance the equation, some warm fuzzies. All through the sizzling summers of ozone rings and water conservation and baking metal, we'd be indoors with our make-believe world of sharp-hard edges and diffuse-soft curves, forslaking the thirst of veldt and jungle on the video monitors.

We were both into the Living Art then—the art you can touch and squeeze and hold to your chest, not the dead, flat-screen scrawled stuff. Pseudo-Mom and Pseudo-Dad thought us wonky, but that was okay, because we'd always do our chores, and because later we found out they weren't our real parents. Besides, we had true morals, true integrity. We knew who was evil and who was good. The warm fuzzies always won out in the end.

Later, we moved on to genetic playdoh, child gods creating creatures that moved, breathed, required attention for their mewling, crying tongues. Creatures we could destroy if it suited our temperament. Not that any of them lived very long.

My sister moved away from the Living Art when she got older, just as she moved away from me. She processes the free market now.

So, since Shadrach certainly wouldn't move in to protect me and my art from the cold pricklies of destruction—I mean, I couldn't go it alone; I had this horrible vision of sacrificing my ceramics, throwing them at future Pick Dicks because the holo stuff wouldn't do any harm of a *physical nature* (which made me think, hey, maybe this holo stuff is Dead Art, too, if it doesn't impact on the world when you throw it)—since that was Dead Idea, I was determined to go down to Quin's Shanghai Circus (wherever *that* was) and "git me a meerkat," as those hokey nuevo westerns say. A meerkat for me, I'd say, tall as you please. Make it a double. In a dirty glass cage. (Oh, I'd crack myself up if the Pick Dicks hadn't already. Tricky, tricky pick dicks.)

But you're probably asking how a Living Artist such as myself—a gaunt, relatively unknown, and alone artiste—could pull the strings and yank the chains that get you an audience with the mysterious Quin.

Well, I admit to connections. I admit to Shadrach. I admit to tracking Shadrach down in the Canal District.

Canal District—Shadrach. They go together, like *Volodya* and *Sirin*, like Ozzie and Elliot, Romeo and Juliard. You could probably find Shadrach down there now, though I hardly see him any more on account of my sister Nicola. That's how I met Shadrach, through Nicola when they shared an apartment.

You see, Shadrach lived below-level for his first twenty-five years, and when he came up he came up in the Canal District. "A wall of light," he called it, and framed against this light, my sister Nicola, who served as an orientation officer back then for peoples coming above ground. A wall of light and my sweet sister Nicola, and Shadrach ate them both up. Imagine: living in a world of darkness and neon for all of your life and coming to the surface and there she is, an angel dressed in white to guide you, to comfort you, to love you. If you had time, I'd tell you about them, because it was a thing to covet, their love, a thing of beauty to mock the cosmetics ads and the lingerie holos . . .

Anyway, ever since the space freighters stopped their old splash 'n' crash in the cool down canals, the Canal District has been the hippest place in town. Go there sometime and think of me, because I don't think I'll be going there again. Half the shops float on the water, so when the ocean-going ships come in with their catch and off-load after decon, the eateries get the first pick. All the Biggest Wigs eat there. You can order pseudo-whale, fiddler, sunfish, the works. Most places overlook the water and you can find *anything* there—mechanicals and Living Art and sensual pleasures that will leave you quivering and unconscious. All done up in a pallet of Colors-Sure-To-Please. Sunsets courtesy of Holo Ink, so you don't have to see the glow of pollution, the haze of smog-shit-muck. Whenever I was down, there I would go, just to sit and watch the Giants of Bioindustry and the Arts walk by, sipping from their carafes of alkie (which I don't envy them, rot-gut seaweed never having been a favorite of mine).

And so I was down, real down (more down than now, sitting in a garbage zone and spieling to you), and I wanted a talk with Shadrach because I knew he worked for Quin and he might relent, relinquish and *tell me* what I wanted to know.

It so happened that I bumped into Shadrach in a quiet corner, away from the carousing and watchful eye of the Canal Police, who are experts at keeping Order, but can never decide exactly *which* Order, if you know what I mean, and you probably don't.

We still weren't alone, though—parts merchants and debauched jewelried concierge wives and stodgy autodocs, gleaming with a hint of self-repair, all sped or sauntered by, each self-absorbed, self-absorbing.

Shadrach played it cool, cooler, coolest, listening to the sea beyond, visible from a crack in our tall falling walls.

"Hi," I said. "Haven't seen you since those lousey pick dicks did their evil work. You saved my skin, you did."

"Hello, Nick," Shadrach replied, looking out at the canals.

("Hello, Nick," he says, after all the compli- and condi-ments I'd given him!)

Shadrach is a tall, muscular man with a tan, a flattened nose from his days as courier between city states—the funny people gave him that—and a dour mouth. His clothes are all out of date, his sandals positively reeking of antiquity. Still thinks he's a Twenty-Seventh Century Man, if you know what I mean, and, again, you probably don't. (After all, you *are* sitting here in a garbage zone with me.)

"So how're things with you?" I said, anticipating that I'd have to drag him kicking and screaming to my point.

"Fine," he said. "You look bad, though." No smile.

I suppose I did look bad. I suppose I must have, still bandaged up and a swell on my head that a geosurfer would want to ride.

"Thanks," I said, wondering why all my words, once smartly deployed for battle, had left me.

"No problem," he said.

I could tell Shadrach wasn't in a talking mood. More like a Dead Art mood as he watched the canals.

And then the miracle: he roused himself from his canal contemplation long enough to say, "I could get you protection," all the while staring at me like I was a dead man, which is the self-same stare he always has. But here was my chance.

"Like what, you shiller," I said. "A whole friggin' police unit all decked out in alkie and shiny new bribes?"

He shrugged and said, "I'm trying to help. The bigger the big fish, the more the small fish need a hook."

"Not a bad turn of phrase," I said, lying. "You get that from looking into the water all damn day? What I need is Quin."

Shadrach snorted, said, "You *are* desperate. An invite to Quin?" He wouldn't meet my gaze directly, but edged around it, edged in between it. "Maybe in a million years you'd build up the contacts," he said, "the raw money and influence."

I turned away, because that stung. The robbery stung, the not-being-able-to-sell-the-art stung. *Life* stung. And stunk.

"Easy for you, Shadrach," I said. "You're not a Living Artist. I don't need an invite. Just give me the address and I'll go myself to beg a meerkat. Anything extra I do on my own."

Shadrach frowned, put on a more serious face, said, "You do not know what you are asking for, Nicholas." I thought I saw fear in him—fear and an uncharacteristic glimpse of compassion. "You *will* get hurt. I know you—and I know Quin. Quin isn't in it for the Living Art. He's in it for other reasons entirely. Things *I* don't even know."

By now I'd begun to break out in the sweats and a moist heat was creeping up my throat, and, hey, maybe I'd had too much on the drug-side on the way down, so I put a hand on his arm, as much to keep my balance as anything.

"For a friend," I said. "For Nicola. I need a break or I'm going to have to go below level and live out my days in a garbage zone." (And look where I am today? In a garbage zone. Talking to you.)

Bringing up my sister was low—especially because I owed her so much money—but bringing up below level was lower still. Shadrach still had nightmares about living underground with the mutties and the funny people, and the drip-drip-drip of water constantly invading the system.

He stared at me, white-faced, the knuckles of his hands losing color where they clutched the rail. Did he, I hoped, see enough of my sister in me?

But I'm not heartless—when I saw him like that, the hurt showing as surely as if they'd broken up a day ago, I recanted. I said, "Forget it, my friend. Forget it. I'll work something else out. You know me. It's okay-dokey."

Shadrach held me a moment longer with his gray, unyielding eyes and then he sighed and exhaled so that his shoulders sagged and his head bowed. He examined his stick-on sandals with the seriousness of a podiatect.

"You want Quin," he said, "you first have to promise me this is a secret—for life, god help you. If it gets out Quin's seeing someone like you, there'll be a whole bunch of loonies digging up the city to find him."

Someone like you hurt, but I just said, "Who am I going to tell? Me, who's always borrowing for the next holo? People avoid me. I am alone in the world. Quin's could get me close to people."

"I know," he said, a bit sadly, I thought.

"So tell me," I said. "Where is it?"

"You have to tell Quin I sent you," he said, and pointed a finger at me, "and all you want is to buy a meerkat."

"You that budsky-budsky with Quin," I said, incredulous—and a little loud, so a brace of Canal policemen gave me a look like *I* was luny-o.

"Keep your voice down," Shadrach said. Then: "Go west down the canal-side escalators until you see the Mercado street light. There's an alley just before that. Go down the alley. At the end, it looks like a dead-ender because there are recycling bins and other debris from the last ten centuries. But don't be fooled. Just close your eyes—it's a holo, and when you're through, there's Quin's, right in front of you. Just walk right in."

"Thank U, Shadrach," I said, heart beating triple-time fast. "I'll tell Nicola that you gave her the time of day."

His eyes widened and brightened, and a smile crossed his face, fading quickly. But I knew, and he knew I knew.

"Be careful," he said, his voice so odd that shivers spiraled up my vertebrae. He shook my hand. "Quin's a strange . . . man," he said. "When it's over, come and see me. And remember, Nicholas—don't—don't dicker with him over the price to be paid."

Then he was gone, taking long, ground-eating strides away from me down the docks, without even a goodbye or a chance to thank him, as if *I* was somehow tainted, somehow no good. It made me sad. It made me mad. Because I've always said Shadrach was Off, even when Nicola dated him.

Shadrach and Nicola. I've had relationships, but never the Big One. Those loving young lovers strolling down by the drug-free zones, those couples coupling in the shadow of the canals, they don't know what it is to be desperately in love, and perhaps even Nicola didn't know. But I thought Shadrach would die when she left him. I thought he would curl up and die. He should have died, except that he found Quin, and somehow Quin raised him up from the dead.

What does Quin do, you ask? (As if *you* have the right to ask questions knee-deep in garbage. But you've asked so I'll tell you:) Quin makes critters. He makes critters that once existed but don't now (tigers, sheep, bats, elephants, dolphins, albatrosses, seagulls, armadillos, dusky seaside sparrows) or critters that never existed except in myth, *flat media*, or holos (Jabberwocks, Grinches, Ganeshas, Puppeteers, Gobblesnorts, Snarks) or critters that just never existed at all until Quin created them (beetleworms, eelgoats, camelapes).

But the *best* thing he does—the Liveliest Art of all, for my purposes—is to improve on existing critters. Like meerkats with opposable thumbs. His meerkats are like the old, old Stradi-various violins, each perfect and each perfectly different. Only the rich could procure them, through influence mostly, not money, because Quin didn't work for money, it was said, but for *favors*. Though no one could guess *what* favors, and at what cost. Rumor had it Quin had started out assisting state-sponsored artificial pregnancies, before the fall of government, but no one knew anything concrete about Quin's past.

So I daydreamed about meerkats after Shadrach left me. I imagined wonderful, four-foot tall meerkats with shiny button eyes and carrot noses and cool bipedal movement and can-I-help-you smiles. Meerkats that could do kitchen work or mow the atrophiturf in your favorite downtown garden plot. Even wash clothes. Or, most importantly, cold cock a pick dick and bite his silly weiner off.

This is the principal image of revenge I had branded into my mind quite as violently as those awful neuvo westerns which, as you have no doubt already guessed, are my one weakness: "Ah, yessirree, Bob, gonna rope me a meerkat, right after I defend my lady's honor and wrassle with this here polar bear." I mean, come on! No wonder it was so hard to sell my holo art before the pick dicks stole it.

But as I headed down the alley which looked quite dead-endish later that night—having just had a bout of almost-fisticuffs (more cuffs than fisties) with a Canal District barkeep—I admit to nervousness. I admit to sweat and trembling palms. The night was darker than dark—wait, listen: *the end of the world is night*; that's mine, a single-cell haiku—and the sounds from the distant bright streets only faintly echoed down from the loom 'n' doom buildings. (Stink of garbage, too, much like this place.)

As I stepped through the holograph—a perfect rendition that spooked me good—and came under the watchful "I"s in the purple-lit sign, Q U I N ' S S H A N G H A I C I R C U S, I did the thrill-in-the-spine bit. It reminded me of when I was a kid (again) and I saw an honest-to-greatness *circus*, with a *real* sparrow doing tricks on a highwire, even a regular dog all done up in bows. I remember embarrassing my dad by pointing when the dog shat on the circus ring floor and saying, "Look, Dad, look! Something's coming out the back end!" Like a prize, maybe? I didn't know better. (Hell, I didn't even know my own Dad wasn't real.) Even then the genetic toys I played with—Ruff the Rooster with the cold eyes I thought stared maliciously at me during the night; Goof the Gopher, who told the dumbest stories about his good friends the echinoderms—all produced waste in a nice solid block through the navel.

But I have let my story run away without me, as Shadrach might say but has never said, and into *nast*algia, and we wouldn't want that.

So: as soon as I stepped into the blue velvet darkness, the doors sliding shut with a *hiss* behind me, the prickly feeling in my spine intensified, and all the sounds from the alley, all the garbage odors and tastes were replaced with the hum of conditioners, the stench of sterility. This was high class. This was *atmosphere*.

This was *exactly* what I had expected from Quin.

To both sides, glass cages embedded in the walls glowed with an emerald light, illuminating a bizarre bunch of critters: things with no eyes, things with too many eyes, things with too many limbs, things with too many teeth, things with too many *things*. Now I could detect an odor, only partially masked by the cleanliness: the odor of the circus I had seen as a kid—the bitter-dry combination of urine and hay, the musky smell of animal sweat, of animal presence.

The cages, the smell, made me none too curious—made me look straight ahead, down to the room's end, some 30 yards away, where Quin waited for me.

It had to be Quin. If it wasn't Quin, Quin couldn't be.

He sat behind a counter display: a rectangular desk-like contraption within which were embedded two glass cases, the contents of which I could not I.D. Quin's head was half in dark, half in the glow of an overhead light, but the surrounding gloom was so great that I had no choice but to move forward, if only to glimpse Quin in the flesh, in his seat of power.

When I was close enough to spit in Quin's face, I gulped like an oxygen-choked fishee, because I realized then that not only did Quin lean over the counter, he *was* the counter. I stopped and stared, mine eyes as buggee as that self-same fishee. I'd heard of Don Daly's Self Portrait Mixed Media on Pavement—which consisted of Darling Dan's splatted remains—but Quin had taken an entirely different slant that reeked of genius. (It also reeked of squirrels in the brain, but so what?)

Portrait of the Artist as a slab of flesh. The counter itself had a yellowish-tan hue to it, like a skin transplant before it heals and it was dotted with eyes—eyes which blinked and eyes which did not, eyes which winked, all watching me, watching them.

Every now and again, I swear on my slang jockey grave, the counter undulated, as if breathing. The counter stood some three meters high and twenty long, five wide. In the center, the flesh parted to include the two glass cages. Within the cages sat twin orangutans, tiny but perfectly formed, grooming themselves atop bonzai trees. Each had a woman's face, with drawn cheekbones and eyes that dripped despair and hopelessness.

Atop the counter, like a tree trunk rising out of the ground, Quin's torso rose, followed by the neck and the narrow, somehow serpentine head. Quin's face looked almost Oriental, the cheekbones pinched and sharp, the mouth slight, the eyes lidless.

The animal musk, the bitter-sweetness, came from Quin, for I could smell it on him, pungent and fresh. Was he rotting? Did the Prince of Genetic Recreation rot?

The eyes—a deep blue without hope of reflection—stared down at the hands; filaments running from each of the twelve fingers dangled spiders out onto the counter. The spiders sparkled like purple jewels in the dim light. Quin made them do undulating dances on the countertop which was his lap, twelve spiders in a row doing an antique cabaret revue. Another display of Living Art. I actually clapped at that one, despite the gob of fear deep in my stomach. The fear had driven the slang right out of me, given me the normals, so to speak, so I felt as if my tongue had been ripped from me.

With the sound of the clap—a naked sound in that place—his head snapped toward me and a smile broke his face in two. A flick of his wrist and the spiders wound themselves around his arm. He brought his hands together as if in prayer.

"Hello, sir," he said in a sing-song voice oddly frozen.

"I came for a meerkat," I said, my own voice an octave higher than normal. "Shadrach sent me."

"You came alone?" Quin asked, his blue eyes boring into me.

My mouth was dry. It felt painful to swallow.

"Yes," I said, and with the utterance of that word—that single, tiny word with entire worlds of agreement coiled within it—I heard the glass cages open behind me, heard the tread of many feet, felt the presence of a hundred hundred creatures at my back. Smelled the piss-hay smell, clotted in my nostrils, making me cough.

What could I do but plunge ahead?

"I came for a meerkat," I said. "I came to work for you. I'm a holo artist. I know Shadrach."

The eyes stared lazily, glassily, and I heard the chorus from behind me, in deep and high voices, in voices like reeds and voices like knives: "You came alone."

And I was thinking then, dear Yahwah, dear Allah, dear God, and I was remembering the warm fuzzies and the cold pricklies of my youth, and I was thinking that I had fallen in with the cold pricklies and I could not play omnipotent now, not with the Liveliest of the Living Arts.

And because I was desperate and because I was foolish, and most of all, because I was a mediocre artist of the holo, I said again, "I want to work with you."

In front of me, Quin had gone dead, like a puppet, as much as the spiders on his fingers had been puppets. Behind me, the creatures stepped forward on cloven hooves, spiked feet, sharp claws, the smell overpowering. I shut my eyes against the feel of their paws, their hands—clammy and soft, cruel and hot, as they held me down. As the needles entered my arms, my legs, and filled me with the little death of sleep, I remember seeing the orangutans weeping on their bonzai branches and wondering why they wept for me.

Let me tell you about the city, sir. Like an adder's kiss, sharp and deadly. It's important. Very important. Let me tell you about Quin and his meerkats. I work for Quin now, and that's bad business. I've done terrible. I've done terrible things—the deadest and deadliest of the Dead Arts, the cold pricklies of the soul. I've killed the Living Art. I've killed the living. And I know. I know it. Only. Only the flesh comes off me and the flesh goes on like a new suit. Only the needle goes in and the needle comes out and I don't care, though I try with all my strength to think of Shadrach and Nicola.

But the needle goes in and . . .

Let me tell you about the city . . .

SCREAM ANGEL

DOUGLAS SMITH

They stopped beating Trelayne when they saw that he enjoyed it. The thugs that passed as cops in that town on Long Shot backed away from where he lay curled on the dirt floor, as if he was something dead or dangerous. He watched them lock the door of his cold little cell again. Disgust and something like fear showed in their eyes. The taste of their contempt for him mixed with the sharpness of his own blood in his mouth. And the *Scream* in that blood shot another stab of pleasure through him.

He expected their reaction. The Merged Corporate Entity guarded its secrets well, and Scream was its most precious. Long Shot lay far from any Entity project world and well off the jump route linking Earth and the frontier. No one on this backwater planet would know of the drug, let alone have encountered a Screamer or an Angel. That was why he had picked it.

Their footsteps receded, and the outer door of the plasteel storage hut that served as the town jail clanged shut. Alone, he rolled onto his side on the floor, relishing the agony the movement brought. He tried to recall how he came to be there, but the Scream in him turned each attempt into an emotional sideshow. Finally he remembered something burning, something . . .

. . . *falling.*

It had been one of their better shows.

He remembered now. Remembered last night, standing in the ring of their makeshift circus dome, announcing the performers to an uncaring crowd, crying out the names of the damned, the conquered. Each member of his refugee band emerged from behind torn red curtains and propelled themselves in the manner of their species into or above the ring, depending on their chosen act.

He knew the acts meant little. The crowd came not to see feats of acrobatics or strength, but to gawk at otherworldly strangeness, to watch aliens bow in submission before the mighty human. Trelayne's circus consisted of the remnants of the subjugated races of a score of worlds, victims to the Entity's resource extraction or terraforming projects: the Stone Puppies, lumbering silica beasts of slate-sided bulk—Guppert the Strong, squat bulbous-limbed refugee from the crushing gravity and equally crushing mining of Mendlos II—Feran the fox-child, his people hunted down like animals on Fandor IV.

And the Angels. Always the Angels.

But curled in the dirt in the cold cell, recalling last night, Trelayne pushed away any thoughts of the Angels. And of *her*.

Yes, it had been a fine show. Until the Ta'lona died, exploding in blood and brilliance high above the ring, after floating too near a torch. Trelayne had bought the gas bag creature's freedom a week before from an *ip* slaver, knowing that its species had been nearly wiped out.

As pieces of the fat alien had fallen flaming into the crowd, Trelayne's grip on reality had shattered like a funhouse mirror struck by a hammer. He could now recall only flashes of what had followed last night: people burning—screaming—panic—a stampede to the exits—his arrest.

Nor could he remember doing any Scream. He usually stayed clean before a show. But he knew what he felt now lying in the cell—the joy of the beating, the ecstasy of humiliation. He must have done a hit when the chaos began and the smell of burnt flesh reached him. To escape the horror.

Or to enter it. For with Scream, horror opened a door to heaven.

Someone cleared their throat in the cell. Trelayne jumped, then shivered at the thrill of surprise. Moaning, he rolled onto his back on the floor and opened his eyes, struggling to orient himself again.

A man now sat on the cot in the cell. A man with a lean face and eyes that reminded Trelayne of his own. He wore a long grey cloak with a major's rank and a small insignia on which a red "RIP" hovered over a green planet split by a lightning bolt.

The uniform of RIP Force. A uniform that Trelayne had worn a lifetime ago. Grey meant Special Services: this man was RIP, but not a Screamer. RIP kept senior officers and the SS clean.

The man studied a PerComm unit held in a black-gloved hand, then looked down at Trelayne and smiled. "Hello, Captain Trelayne," he said softly, as if he were addressing a child.

Trelayne swallowed. He was shaking and realized he had been since he had recognized the uniform. "My name is not Trelayne."

"I am Weitz," the man said. The PerComm disappeared inside his cloak. "And the blood sample I took from you confirms that you are Jason Lewiston Trelayne, former captain and wing commander in the Entity's Forces for the Relocation of Indigenous Peoples, commonly known as RIP Force. Convicted of treason in absentia three years ago, 2056-12-05 AD. Presumed dead in the MCE raid on the rebel base on Darcon III in 2057-08-26."

Trelayne licked his lips, savoring the flavor of his fear.

"You're a wanted man, Trelayne." Weitz's voice was soft. "Or would be, if the Entity knew you were still alive."

The Scream in Trelayne turned the threat in those words into a thrilling chill up his spine. He giggled.

Weitz sighed. "I've never seen a Screamer alive three years after RIP. Dead by their own hand inside a month more likely. But then, most don't have their own source, do they?"

The implication of those words broke through the walls of Scream in Trelayne's mind. Weitz represented real danger—to him, to those in the circus that depended on him. To *her*. Trelayne struggled to focus on the man's words.

" . . . good choice," Weitz was saying. "Not a spot the Entity has any interest in now. You'd never see Rippers here—" Weitz smiled. "—unless they had ship trouble. I was in the next town waiting for repairs when I heard of a riot at a circus of *ips*."

Ips—I.P.'s—Indigenous Peoples. A Ripper slur for aliens.

Weitz stood up. "You have an Angel breeding pair, Captain, and I need them." He pushed open the cell door and walked out, leaving the door open. "I've arranged for your release. You're free to go. Not that you can go far. We'll talk again soon." Looking back to where Trelayne lay shivering, Weitz shook his head. "Jeezus, Trelayne. You used to be my hero."

Trelayne slumped back down on the floor, smiling as the smell of dirt and stale urine stung his throat. "I used to be a lot of things," he said, as much to himself as to Weitz.

Weitz shook his head again. "We'll talk soon, Captain." He turned and left the hut.

Think of human emotional response as a sine wave function.
Peaks and valleys. The peaks represent pleasure, and the valleys
pain. The greater your joy, the higher the peak; the greater your
pain, the deeper the valley.

*Imagine a drug that takes the valleys and flips them, makes them
peaks, too. You react now to an event based not on the pleasure or
pain inherent in it, but solely on the intensity of the emotion created.
Pain brings pleasure, grief gives joy, horror renders ecstasy.*

*Now give this drug to one who must perform an unpleasant task.
No. Worse than that. An immoral deed. Still worse. A nightmare
act of chilling terminal brutality. Give it to a soldier. Tell them
to kill. Not in the historically acceptable murder we call war, but
in a systematic corporate strategy—planned, scheduled, and
budgeted—of xenocide.*

They will kill. And they will revel in it.

Welcome to the world of Scream.

> —Extract from propaganda data bomb launched on
> Fandor IV CommCon by rebel forces, 2056-10-05 AD.
> Attributed to Capt. Jason L. Trelayne during
> his subsequent trial in absentia for treason.

Feran thought tonight's show was their finest since the marvelous Ta'lona
had died, now a five-day ago. From behind the red curtains that hid the
performers' entrance, the young kit watched the two Angels, Philomela and
Procne, plummet from the top of the dome to swoop over the man-people
crowd. Remembering how wonderfully the fat alien had burnt, Feran
also recalled the Captain explaining to him how that night had been
bad. The Captain had been forced to give much power-stuff for the burnt
man-people and other things that Feran did not understand.

The Angels completed a complicated spiral dive, interweaving their
descents. Linking arms just above the main ring, they finished with
a dizzying spin like the top the Captain had made him. They bowed to
the applauding crowd, folding and unfolding diaphanous wings so the
spotlights sparkled on the colors.

Feran clapped his furred hands together as Mojo had taught him, closing his ear folds to shut out the painful noise of the man-people. As the performers filed out for the closing procession around the center ring, Feran ran to take his spot behind the Stone Puppies. Guppert the Strong lifted Feran gently to place him on the slate-grey back of the nearest silica beast.

"Good show, little friend!" Guppert cried. His squat form waddled beside Feran. Guppert liked Long Shot because it did not hold him to the ground as did his home of Mendlos. "Of course, Guppert never go home now," he had told Feran once, his skin color darkening to show sadness. "Off-planet too long. Mendlos crush Guppert, as if Stone Puppy step on Feran. But with Earth soldiers there in mecha-suits, now Mendlos not home anyway."

Waving to the crowd, the performers disappeared one by one through the red curtains. Feran leapt from the Stone Puppy, shouted a goodbye to Guppert, and scurried off to search for Philomela. Outside the show dome, he sniffed the cool night air for her scent, found it, then turned and ran into the Cutter.

"Whoa, Red! What's the rush?" The tall thin man scowled down at Feran like an angry mantis. The Cutter was the healer for the circus. "Helpin' us die in easy stages, s'more like it," was how the Cutter had introduced himself when Feran had arrived.

"I seek the Bird Queen, Cutter," Feran replied.

Sighing, the Cutter jerked a thumb toward a cluster of small dome pods where the performers lived. Feran thought of it as the den area. "Don't let him take too much, you hear?"

Feran nodded and ran off again, until a voice like wind in crystal trees halted him. "You did well tonight, sharp ears."

Feran turned. Philomela smiled down at him, white hair and pale skin, tall and thin like an earth woman stretched to something alien in a trick mirror. Even walking, she made Feran think of birds in flight. Philomela was beautiful. The Captain had told him so many times. He would likely tell Feran again tonight, once he had breathed her dust that Feran brought him.

"Thank you, Bird Queen," Feran replied, bowing low with a sweep of his hand as the Captain had taught him. Philomela laughed, and Feran bared his teeth in joy. He had made the beautiful bird lady laugh. The Captain would be pleased.

Procne came to stand behind Philomela, his spider-fingered hand circling her slim waist. "Where do you go now, Feran? Does Mojo still have chores for you?" He looked much like her, taller, heavier, but features still delicate, almost feminine. His stomach pouch skin rippled where the brood moved inside him.

"He goes to the Captain's pod," Philomela said. "They talk—about the times when the Captain flew in the ships. Don't you?"

Feran nodded. Procne's eyelids slid in from each side, leaving only a vertical slit. "The times when those ships flew over our homes, you mean? Your home, too, Feran." Procne spun and stalked away, his wings pulled tight against his back.

Feran stared after him, then up at Philomela. "Did I do wrong, Bird Queen?"

Philomela folded and unfolded her wings. "No, little one, no. My mate remembers too much, yet forgets much, too." She paused. "As does the Captain." She stroked Feran's fur where it lay red and soft between his large ears, then handed him a small pouch. "Feran, tonight don't let the Captain breath too much of my dust. Get him to sleep early. He looks so ... tired."

Feran took the pouch and nodded. He decided he would not tell the Captain of Philomela's face as she walked away.

Merged Corporate Entity, Inc.
Project Search Request
Search Date: 2059-06-02
Requestor: *Weitz, David R., Major, RIP Special Services*
Search Criteria:
Project World: *All*
Division: *PharmaCorps*
Product: *Scream*
Context: *Field Ops / Post-Imp*
Clearance Required: *AAA*
Your Clearance: *AAA*

Access Granted. Search results follow.
Scream mimics several classes of psychotropics, including psychomotor stimulants, antidepressants, and narcotic

analgesics. It acts on both stimulatory *and* inhibitory neurotransmitters, but avoids hallucinogenic effects by maintaining neurotransmitter balance. It enhances sensory ability, speeds muscular reaction, and lessens nerve response to pain. It affects all three opiate receptors, inducing intense euphoria without narcotic drowsiness.

Physical addiction is achieved by four to six ingestions at dosage prescribed in Field Ops release 2.21.7.1. Treated personnel exhibit significantly lowered resistance to violence. Secondary benefits for field operations include decreased fatigue, delayed sleep on-set, and enhanced mental capacity.

Negative side effects include uncontrolled masochistic or sadistic tendencies, such as self-mutilation or attacks on fellow soldiers. Scream is therefore not administered until military discipline and obedience programming is completed in boot camp. Long-term complications include paranoid psychoses and suicidal depression. Withdrawal is characterized by hallucinations, delirium, and seizures, terminating with strokes or heart attacks.

Attempts to synthesize continue, but at present our sole source remains extraction from females of the dominant humanoids on Lania II, *Xeno sapiens lania var. angelus* (colloq.: Scream Angel). The liquid produced crystallizes into powder form. Since the drug is tied to reproduction (see Xenobiology: Lania: Life Forms: 1275), ensuring supply requires an inventory of breeding pairs with brood delivery dates spread evenly over—

*** *File Transfer Request Acknowledged* ***
Xenobiology File: Lania: Life Forms: 1275

The adult female produces the drug from mammary glands at all times but at higher levels in the reproductive cycle. Sexual coupling occurs at both the start and end of the cycle. The first act impregnates the female. The brood develops in her until delivery after thirty weeks in what the original Teplosky journal called the "larval form," transferring then to the male's pouch via orifices in his abdominal wall. For the next nineteen weeks, they feed from the male, who ingests large quantities of Scream from the female.

The brood's impending release as mature nestlings prompts the
male to initiate the final coupling—

Trelayne lay in his sleep pod at the circus waiting for Feran and the hit of
Scream that the kit brought each night. The meeting with Weitz had burst
a dam of times past, flooding him with memories. He closed his eyes, his
face wet with delicious tears. Though all his dreams were nightmares, he
did not fear them. Terror was now but another form of pleasure. Sleep at
least freed him from the tyranny of decision.

*Twenty again. My first action. I remember . . . Remember? I'd give my
soul to forget, if my soul remains for me to barter.*

Bodies falling against a slate-grey sky . . .

The RIP transports on Fandor IV were huge oblate spheroids, flattened
and wider in the middle than at the ends. Trelayne and almost one
hundred other Rippers occupied the jump seats that lined the perimeter
of the main bay, facing in, officers near the cockpit. Before them, maybe
a hundred Fandor natives huddled on the metal floor, eyes downcast but
constantly darting around the hold and over their captors. The adults were
about five feet tall and humanoid, but their soft red facial hair, pointed
snouts and ears gave them a feral look. The children reminded Trelayne of
a stuffed toy he had as a child.

Fresh from RIP boot camp, this was to be his first action. These Fandorae
came from a village located over rich mineral deposits soon to be an Entity
mining operation. They were to be "relocated" to an island off the west coast.
He added the quotes in response to a growing suspicion, fed by overheard
jokes shared by RIP veterans. He also recalled arriving on Fandor, scanning
the ocean on the approach to the RIP base on the west shore.

There were no islands off the coast.

The other Rippers shifted and fidgeted, waiting for their first hit of the
day. The life support system of their field suits released Scream directly into
their blood, once each suit's computer received the transmitted command
from the RIP Force unit leader. If you wanted your Scream, you suited up
and followed orders. And god, you wanted your Scream.

His unit had been on Scream since the end of boot camp. Trelayne knew
he was addicted. He knew that RIP wanted him and all his unit addicted. He
just didn't know why. He had also noticed that no one in his unit had family.
No one would miss any of them. Another reason to follow orders.

Twenty minutes out from the coast, a major unbuckled his boost harness and nodded to a captain to his right. Every Ripper watched as the captain hit a button on his wrist pad.

The Scream came like the remembered sting of an old wound, a friend that you hadn't seen in years and once reunited, you wondered why you had missed them.

The captain's voice barked in their headsets, ordering them out of their harnesses. Trelayne rose as one with the other Rippers, StAB rod charged and ready, the Scream in him twisting his growing horror into the anticipation of ecstasy. The Fandorae huddled closer together in the middle of the bay.

The captain punched another button. Trelayne felt the deck thrumming through his boots as the center bay doors split open. The Fandorae leapt up, grabbing their young and skittering back from the widening hole, only to face an advancing wall of Rippers with lowered StAB rods.

Some of the Fandorae chose to leap. Some were pushed by their own people in the panic. Others fell on the StAB rods or died huddled over their young.

Trelayne pulled a kit, no more than a year, from under a dead female. He held the child in his arms, waiting his turn as the Rippers in front of him lifted or pushed the remaining bodies through the bay doors. When he reached the edge, Trelayne lifted the kit from his shoulder and held it over the opening. It did not squirm or cry, only stared a mute accusation. Trelayne let go, then knelt to peer over the edge.

A salt wind stung sharp and cold where it crept under his helmet. He watched the kit fall to hit the rough grey sea a hundred feet below. Most of the bodies had already slipped beneath the waves. The kit disappeared to join them.

A nausea that even Scream could not deflect seized Trelayne. Pushing back from the edge, he wrenched his visor up to gasp in air. A Ripper beside him turned to him, and for a brief moment Trelayne caught his own reflection in the man's mirrored visor. The image burned into his memory as he fought to reconcile the horror engulfing him with the grinning mask of his own face . . .

Dreaming still . . . falling still . . . falling in love . . .

Trelayne made captain in a year, as high as Screamers could rise in RIP. He took no pride in it. When the Scream ran low in him, his guilt rose black and bottomless. But his addiction was now complete. Withdrawal for a Screamer meant weeks of agony, without the filter of Scream, then death. The Entity was his only source. He did what he was told.

Rippers burnt out fast on project worlds, so the Entity rotated them off relo work every six months for a four-week tour on a "processed" world. Trelayne's first tour after making captain was on Lania, the Angel home planet, arranging transport of Angel breeding pairs from Lania to project worlds with RIP Force units. The Entity had found that, with Angels on-planet, concerns over Scream delivery could be put aside for that world.

Sex with an Angel, said RIP veterans, was the ultimate high. But upon arrival, Trelayne had found them too alien, too thin and wraith-like. He decided that their reputation was due more to ingesting uncut Scream during sex than to their ethereal beauty.

Then he saw *her*.

She was one of a hundred Angels being herded into a cargo shuttle that would dock with an orbiting jump ship. Angels staggered by Trelayne, their eyes downcast. He started to turn away when he saw her: striding with head held high, glaring at the guards. She turned as she passed him. Their eyes locked.

He ordered her removed from the shipment. That is how he met her. As her captor. Then her liberator. Then her lover.

The Earth name she had taken was Philomela. Her Angel name could not be produced by a human throat. She brought him joy and pain. He was never sure what he brought her. She gave herself willingly, and her pleasure in their lovemaking seemed so sincere that he sometimes let himself believe—believe that she clung to *him* in those moments, not to a desperate hope for freedom. That she did not hate him for what RIP had done to her people.

That she loved him.

But Scream strangled such moments. Though not on combat doses, he still needed it for physical dependency. On low doses, depression clouded life in a grey mist. Could she love him when he doubted his own love for her? Why was he drawn to her? Sex? His private source of Scream? To wash his hands clean by saving one of his victims? And always between them loomed an impassable chasm: they were separate species who could never be truly mated.

The news reached him one rare afternoon as they lay together in his quarters. His PerComm unit, hanging on the wall above them, began to buzz like an angry insect. He pulled it down and read the message from the Cutter, the medic in his unit.

She watched him as he read. "Jase, is something wrong?"

He had come to expect her empathy. Whether she could now read his human expressions or sense his mood, he didn't know. He threw the unit away as if it had stung him and covered his face with a hand. "Mojo. One of my men, a friend. He's *fallen*."

"Is he—"

"He's alive. No serious injuries." As if that mattered.

"Do you think he tried to take his life?"

"No," he said, though the drug in him screamed yes.

"Many do—"

"No! Not Mojo." But he knew she was right. Suicide was common with Screamers, and "joining the Fallen" was a favored method—a dive that you never came out of. The Entity punished any survivors brutally. Screamers were easily replaced, but one LASh jet could cut the return on a project world by a full point.

"Now comes the judging your people do?" she asked.

"Court martial. Two weeks." If they found Mojo guilty they would discharge him. No source of Scream. *Better to have died in the crash*, he thought. He got out of bed and began dressing. "I have to leave Lania, return to my base. Try to help him."

"They will judge against him. You will not change that."

"I know. But I have to try. He has no one else."

She turned away. "We have few moments together."

She was shaking, and he realized that she was crying. He misunderstood. "I'll be back soon. It'll be better then."

She shook her head and looked up at him. "I mean that we have few moments *left*. It is my time."

He stood there staring down at her. "What do you mean?"

"I must produce a brood." She turned away again.

"You mean you will take a mate. One of your own kind."

"His name is Procne," she said, still not looking at him.

He didn't know what to do or say, so he kept dressing.

She turned to him. "I love you," she said quietly.

He stopped. She waited. He said nothing. She lay down, sobbing. He swallowed and formed the thought in his mind, opened his mouth to tell her that he loved her, too, when she spoke again. "What will become of me?" she asked.

All his doubts about her rushed in to drown the words in his mouth. He was but a way of escape to her. She did not love him. She would give herself to one of her own. She was alien. The Angels hated RIP for what they had done. She hated him.

He pulled on his jacket and turned away . . .

The trial. I tried, Mojo—but nothing can save us when we fall, and we were falling the moment they put it in our blood . . .

The day after Mojo's trial, Trelayne entered the RIP barracks pod. The Cutter and two other Rippers sat on drop-bunks watching Mojo stuff his few possessions into a canister pack. Mojo wore his old civvies, now at least a size too small. He still had a Medistim on his arm, and he moved with a limp.

The others jumped to attention when they saw their visitor. Cutter just nodded. Trelayne returned the salutes then motioned toward the door. After a few words and half-hearted slaps on Mojo's back, they filed out, leaving Trelayne and Mojo alone.

Mojo sat down on his bunk. "Thanks, Cap. Hell of a try."

Trelayne sat, forcing a smile. "You forget we lost?"

Mojo shrugged. "Never had a chance. You know that. None of us do. Just a matter of time. If the Scream don't get you, they will. No way out for the likes of us."

Trelayne searched Mojo's broad face. *I have to try,* he thought. *We won't get another chance.* "Maybe there is a way."

Narrowing his eyes, Mojo glanced at the door and back again. He looked grim. "I'm with you, Cap. Whatever, wherever."

Trelayne shook his head. "They'll kill us if we're caught."

"I'm a dead man already. We all are."

Trelayne sighed and started talking . . .

And so the fallen dreamed of rising again, eh Mojo? What fools we were. But we gave them a run for a while, didn't we?

Trelayne returned to Lania. In his absence, Philomela had taken Procne as her mate. She refused to see Trelayne. He added her and Procne to the next cargo of Angels being shipped to the project worlds, with himself as the ship's captain.

He did not see her until after their ship had made the first jump. Philomela was summoned to the captain's cabin, to be told to which planet she and her mate had been consigned.

She stiffened when she entered and saw him. "You."

He nodded and waited.

"Sending us into slavery to be bred and milked like animals, this was not enough? You had to be here to see it happen, did you, Jason?" She looked around. "Where is the captain?"

"I am the captain on this trip."

She looked confused. "But you have never gone on these . . . "

He sighed. "Please sit. I have much to say . . . "

Why did I risk everything to save her? Love? Guilt? As penance? For her Scream? In a desperate hope that one day she would turn to me again? Or as I fell, was I willing to grasp at anything, even if I pulled those I loved down with me?

From the ship's observation deck, Trelayne and Philomela watched a shuttle depart, carrying a "shipment" of twenty pairs of Angels for the project world below.

"Do you know why I chose my Earth name?" she asked.

Her voice was flat, dead, but he heard the pain that each of these worlds brought her as more of her people were torn away, while she remained safe, protected. "No. Tell me," he said.

"In a legend of your planet, Philomela was a girl turned into a nightingale by the gods. That image pleased me, to be chosen by the gods, elevated to the heavens. Only later did I learn that the nightingale is also a symbol of death."

Trelayne bowed his head. "Phi, there's nothing—"

"No, but allow me at least my bitterness. And guilt."

Guilty of being spared. By him. She and Procne spared, only because an addict and xenocide and soon-to-be traitor needed his drug source close. He had stopped trying to examine his motives beyond that. The Scream would mock the small voice in him that spoke of a last remnant of honor and noble intent.

"My sister is on that shuttle," Philomela said quietly.

Trelayne said nothing for there was nothing to say. They watched the tiny ship fall toward the planet below . . .

At each planet on that trip, we gathered to us the castoffs, the unwanted,

*the remnants of a dozen races, together with the Fallen. And then, suddenly,
there was no turning back . . .*

Trelayne's first officer, a young lieutenant-commander named Glandis,
confronted him on the bridge. She wasn't backing down this time.
"Captain, I must again register my concern over continued irregularities
in your command of this mission."

Trelayne glanced at the monitor by his chair. Mojo and eleven other
ex-Rippers were disembarking from a shuttle in the ship's docking bay.
In two minutes, they would be on the bridge. He tapped a command,
deactivating all internal communications and alarms. He turned to
Glandis. "Irregularities?"

"The ip *cargo* we have acquired at each of our stops."

"Those *people* are to be transported to the Entity's Product R&D center
on Earth," Trelayne responded.

Glandis snorted. "What research could the Entity conduct with—" She
read from her PerComm. "—a Mendlos subject?"

"Physiological adaptation to high-grav," Trelayne replied.

"A Fandorae kit? A Fanarucci viper egg?"

"Biotech aural receptor design, and neural poison mutagenics
development." *One minute more*, he thought.

Glandis hesitated, some of the confidence leaving her face. "You have
also protected one specific breeding pair of Angels for purposes that have
yet to be made clear to me."

"They, too, are slated for Entity research." Trelayne rose. *Thirty seconds.*
"Synthesization of Scream."

"What about this stop? It was not on our filed flight plan."

"Late orders from RIP Force command." *Fifteen seconds.*

"I was not informed."

"You just were."

Glandis reddened. "And what purpose will a dozen disgraced
ex-members of RIP Force serve?"

Now, thought Trelayne. The door to the bridge slid open. Mojo and four
other ex-Rippers burst in, Tanzer rifles charged and pointed at Glandis and
the bridge crew. Glandis turned to Trelayne with mouth open then froze.

Trelayne had his own weapon leveled at Glandis. "Their purpose, I'm
afraid, is to replace the crew of this ship."

And so the Fallen rose again, to scale a precipice from which there was no retreat, and each new height we gained only made the final fall that much farther . . .

After leaving the Bird Queen, Feran ran past the closed tubes of the barkers, the games of chance, and the sleep pods of the performers. The kit moved easily among the ropes, refuse, and equipment, his path clear to him even in the dim light of sputtering torches and an occasional hovering glow-globe.

The show used fewer glow-globes than when Feran had first arrived. The Captain said the globes cost too much now. Feran didn't mind. He needed little light to see, and liked the smell of the torches and the crackle they made.

Turning a corner, Feran froze. Weasel Man stood outside the Captain's pod. The Captain said that the man's name was Weitz, but he reminded Feran of the animals the kit hunted in the woods outside the circus. The door opened. Weasel Man stepped inside.

Feran crept to the open window at the pod's side. He could hear voices. His nose twitched. His ears snapped up and opened wide, adjusting until the sound was the sharpest.

Trelayne lay on his sleep pod bunk, shaking from withdrawal. Feran was late bringing his nightly hit. Weitz lounged in a chair, staring at him. It had been five days since their meeting in the jail. "Where've you been, Weitz?" Trelayne wheezed.

"Had some arrangements to make. Need a hit, don't you?"

"It's coming," Trelayne mumbled. "What do you want?"

Weitz shrugged. "I told you. The Angels."

"But not to hand them back to the Entity, or you'd have done it by now," Trelayne said. But if Weitz wanted the Angels, why didn't he just take them? He had his own men and a ship.

Weitz smiled. "Do you know there are rebels on Fandor IV?"

"Rebels? What are you talking about?" Where was Feran?

"Ex-RIP rebels like you, or rather, like you once were."

"Like me? God, then I pity the rebels on Fandor IV."

Weitz leaned forward in his chair. "I'm one of them."

Trelayne laughed. "You're RIP SS."

"I assist from the *inside*. I supply them with Scream."

Trelayne stared at Weitz. This man was far more dangerous than he had first appeared. "You've managed to surprise me, Major. Why would you risk your life for a bunch of rebels?"

Weitz shrugged. "I said you were my hero. The man who defied an empire. I want to do my part, too."

Trelayne snorted. "Out of the goodness of your heart."

Weitz reddened. "I cover my costs. No more."

I'll bet, Trelayne thought. "Where do you get Scream?"

"I . . . acquired a store doing an SS audit of a RIP warehouse."

"You stole it. A store? Since when can you store Scream?"

Weitz smiled. "A result of intense research prompted by your escape with the Angels. You made the Entity realize the risk of transporting breeding pairs. Angels are now kept in secure facilities on Lania and two other worlds, producing Scream that's shipped to project worlds with RIP forces. Angels live and die without *ever* leaving the facility they were born into."

Trelayne shuddered. Because of him. But the Scream in him ran too low to find any joy in this new horror.

They fell silent. Finally Weitz spoke. "So what happened, Trelayne? To the Great Rebel Leader? To the one man who stood up to the Entity? How'd it all go to hell?"

"Screamers are in hell already. We were trying to get out."

"You got out, in a stolen Entity cruiser. Then what?"

Shivering, Trelayne struggled to sit up. Where was Feran? "We jumped to a system the Entity had already rejected. Only one habitable planet. No resources worth the extraction cost."

"And set up a base for a guerrilla war on the Entity."

"No. A colony. A home for the dispossessed races."

"You attacked Entity project worlds," Weitz said.

"We sent messages. There was never any physical assault."

"Your data bombs flooded Comm systems for entire planets."

"We tried to make people aware of what the Entity was doing. Almost worked." Trelayne fought withdrawal, trying to focus on Weitz. The man was afraid of something. But what?

"I'll say. You cost them trillions hushing it up, flushing systems. But then what? The reports just end."

"The Entity still has a file on us?" That pleased Trelayne.

"On you," Weitz corrected. "You've got your own entire file sequence. Special clearance needed to get at them. Well?"

Trelayne fell silent, remembering the day, remembering his guilt. "I got careless. They tracked us through a jump somehow, found the colony, T-beamed it from orbit."

"An entire planet? My god!" Weitz whispered.

"A few of us escaped." But not Phi's children, her first brood. More guilt, though she had never blamed him.

"In a heavily armed cruiser with a crew of ex-Rippers."

He looked at Weitz. *That* was it. Even through the haze of withdrawal, he knew he had his answer: Weitz thought Trelayne still had a band of ex-Rippers at hand, battle-proven trained killers with super-human reflexes and their own Scream supply. Something like hope tried to fight through the black despair of his withdrawal. Weitz would try to deal first.

"And this?" Weitz took in the circus with a wave of a hand.

"After we lost the base, we had to keep moving. As a cover story to clear immigration on each world, I concocted a circus of aliens. Then I ran out of money, had to do it for real."

"What if someone had recognized you? Or knew about Angels?"

Trelayne struggled to speak. "We avoided anywhere with an Entity presence, stayed off the main jump routes." He started to shiver. "Why do you want Angels if you have a store of Scream?"

"My supply'll run out, and I can't count on stealing more."

Trelayne stared at Weitz. "So what's the deal?"

Weitz smiled. "Why do you think I won't just take them?"

"Against a crew of ex-Rippers pumped on Scream?"

Weitz's smile faded. He studied Trelayne. "Okay. Let's assess your position. One: I gave your ship's beacon signature to Long Shot's space defense. If you run, you'll be caught."

Trelayne said nothing.

"Two: if you're caught, your ip pals get sent back to their home worlds. And you know what that means."

Trelayne stayed silent, but his skin went cold.

"Three: you, Mojo, and the medic get executed for treason."

"Like I said, what's the deal?"

Weitz studied Trelayne again, then finally spoke. "Both Angels for my store of Scream—a lifetime supply for you and your men. I lift the order on your ship and turn my back as you and your band jump. Your life goes on, with Scream but no Angels."

Life goes on, if you called this life. That much Scream was worth a fortune. But nowhere near the value of a breeding pair.

So there it was. Betray his love or die. What choice did he have? Refuse, and Weitz would turn them over to the Entity, and all would die. Run, and be killed or caught by the planetary fleet. Give her up, along with Procne, and at least the others would be free. Besides, she had turned from him, taken one of her own. She had only used him to escape, had always used him. She was an alien and hated him for what he had done to her race.

She had never really loved him.

All that stood against this were the remnants of his love for her, and a phantom memory of the man he once had been.

Outside, Feran waited for the Captain's reply to Weasel Man. He didn't know what the Captain would do but he knew it would be brave and noble. Feran listened for the sound of the Captain leaping to his feet and striking Weasel Man to the floor. But when a sound came, it was only the Captain's voice, small and hoarse. "All right," was all he said.

"You'll do it?" That was Weasel Man. Feran did not hear a reply. "Tomorrow morning." Weasel Man again. The door opened, and Feran scooted under the pod. Weasel Man stepped out smiling. Feran had seen sand babies smile like that on Fandor just before they spit their venom in your eyes.

As he watched the man walk away, fading into the darkness, something inside Feran faded away as well. He stood staring into the shadows for a long time, then turned and entered the pod. The Captain lay in his sleeping place. He seemed not to notice Feran. The kit put the pouch from the Bird Queen on the table, then left without a word. The Captain did not call after him.

How long Feran wandered the grounds, he did not know. Some time later, he found the Cutter and Mojo sitting in front of a fire burning on an old heat shield panel from the ship.

"Seen the Captain, Feran?" asked Mojo. Feran just nodded.

"He's had his bottle? All tucked in for the night?" the Cutter asked. Feran nodded again as Mojo scowled at the Cutter.

They sat silently for a while. "Does it hurt when you lose someone you love?" Feran asked, ashamed of the fear in his voice, the fear that he felt for Philomela.

The Cutter spoke. "Hurts even more to lose 'em slowly. Watch 'em disappear bit by bit 'til nothing's left you remember."

Feran knew the Cutter meant the Captain. "Shut up, Cutter," Mojo growled. "You've never been there. Only a Screamer knows what he lives with." He patted Feran's head. "Never mind, kid."

The Cutter shook his head but spoke no more. Feran rose and walked slowly away to once again wander the Circus grounds. This time, however, something resolved itself inside his young mind so that when he found himself outside the sleep pod of the Angels he interpreted this as a sign that his plan was pure.

The Bird Queen was alone. She spoke little as he told his tale, a question here or there when the words he chose were poor. She thanked him, then sat in silence, her strange eyes staring out the small round window of the pod.

Feran left the Angel then, not knowing whether he had done good or evil, yet somehow aware that his world was a much different place than it had been an hour before.

*** *Search Results Continued* ***

Xenobiology File: Lania: Life Forms: 1275

The impending release of a brood of mature nestlings prompts the male Angel to initiate final coupling. This act triggers the female's production of higher concentrations of Scream. Scream is the sole nourishment that the young can ingest upon emergence, and also relieves the agony of the male after the brood bursts from him. The female must receive the nestlings within hours of the final coupling, or she will die from the higher Scream level in her blood, which the nestlings cleanse from her system.

The evolutionary advantage of this reproductive approach appears to stem from the increased survival expectations of a brood carried by the stronger male, and the ensured presence of both parents at birth. Although Teplosky drew parallels to the Thendotae on Thendos IV, we feel . . .

Unable to sleep, Feran rose early the next day. A chill mist hung from a grey sky. For an hour, he wandered outside the big dome, worrying how to tell the Captain what he had done and why. He stopped. Toward him strode the Captain, with Mojo at his side. Both wore their old long black cloaks, thrown back to reveal weapons strapped to each leg. The gun metal glinted blue and cold, matching the look in the Captain's eyes.

Feran felt all his fears of the previous night vanish like grass swimmers into the brush. The Captain *was* going to fight. He would beat Weasel Man, and all would be well.

The Cutter stepped out of the dome as the Captain and Mojo stopped beside Feran. The Captain reached down to ruffle the fur on Feran's head, then glanced toward the dome. "Ready?"

The Cutter nodded. "Just get him inside."

A cry made them turn. Procne ran toward them, stumbling with the bulging weight of the brood inside him. "She's gone! She's gone!" he cried. He fell gasping into the Cutter's arms. Feran went cold inside.

The talking box on the Captain's belt beeped. He lifted it to his face. "It's from Phi. Time delayed delivery from last night." They waited as he read. When he spoke, his voice was raspy, like when he took too much dust. "She's given herself to Weitz. She knows that I won't surrender her and Pro, that I'll fight. She doesn't wish me or any of us to die." He dropped the device in the dirt. "She knows me better than I know myself, it would seem," he whispered.

"Our brood—" Procne began.

"She says she would rather her children die than live as slaves, kept only to feed monsters that destroy races."

"No! Our final coupling was last night. The brood comes!" He placed a thin hand on his pouch. "The essence they must feed on is rising in her blood. If she is not here when they emerge, they will die. If they die without cleansing her . . . "

"She will die, too," the Captain finished. "She knew this."

Mojo frowned. "How'd she know about Weitz? You only told me and Cutter, and just this morning." The Captain shook his head. Cutter shrugged.

Feran felt as if he were outside his body watching this scene but not part of it, unable to act. Well, he *had* acted, and this was what had come of it. He heard a voice saying "I told her." It seemed to be coming from somewhere else, and only when they all turned to look at him did he realize he had spoken.

Silence fell. The Captain knelt down before him, and all the words that Feran had tried to find before came pouring out. He turned his head, baring his throat to the Captain, offering his life. Instead, warm arms encircled him and held him tight. Feran knew that this was a "hug" and found it oddly comforting. The Captain whispered "Oh, Feran," and Feran began to sob.

"So now what?" the Cutter growled as the Captain stood.

They waited. Then the Captain spoke, his voice as calm as when he told Feran a story. "Same plan, with one change. We need Pro with us." He turned to Procne, and Feran felt a stillness settle, like before two alpha males fought. "You and I, we've never quite got it straight between us. Just knew that she somehow needed us both. You never forgave, never trusted me. Can't say I ever blamed you. Well, I'm asking you to trust me now. If only because you know I wouldn't hurt her."

Procne stared at the Captain for several of Feran's heart beats, then nodded. The Captain turned to the Cutter. "Take Pro inside. Make it look like his hands are tied." He spoke then to all of them. "Nobody moves till I do, and I won't move until I know where he's got Phi. And remember: we need Weitz alive."

Muttering under his breath, the Cutter pulled Feran into the dome. Feran looked back. The Captain and Mojo strode toward the main entrance, their long cloaks closed, hiding their weapons and shutting out the rain that began to fall hard and cold.

Inside, Feran saw Guppert standing beside two Stone Puppies. He scampered over to them, glad to leave the morose Cutter, then stopped. Weapons were strapped to one side of the great silica beasts, the side hidden from the door. The Puppies lay on the ground, and Guppert's shoulder came to the top of their backs.

Guppert grinned and rapped a fat fist on the slate side of the nearest one. "Puppies make good fort, Guppert thinks." He pointed to the ground. "This where you come, little one, with Guppert, when I give word." He waddled around to the other side of the Puppies where water buckets and scrub brushes lay. "Now, we get busy looking not dangerous." He and Feran began scrubbing the Puppies. The Cutter stood with Procne between them and the entrance, Procne's hands bound behind him.

Feran heard them first. "They are here," he whispered.

Cutter nodded. A few seconds later, two men in RIP SS uniforms entered with guns. They looked around, then one called outside. "All clear." Weasel Man came in, then the Captain and Mojo, and more men in SS uniforms. Feran counted, his hope fading as each one entered. Ten, plus the first two, and Weasel Man. Four carried a metal case, their guns slung.

"Thirteen. Damn, I hate thirteen," muttered the Cutter as he left Procne and sauntered toward a Puppy. Still scrubbing, Guppert moved to the hidden side of his beast. Feran followed.

Weasel Man looked around. "Where's the rest of your crew?"

The Captain shrugged. "Dead or deserted."

Weasel Man raised an eyebrow and glanced at his men. The Captain nodded at the case. "That our stuff?" he asked, pulling back a sleeve to reveal a Medistim pack. He hit a button on it. Feran knew that he had just taken a "hit." Mojo did the same.

Weasel Man wrinkled his brow. "It was going to be."

The Captain smiled. "But you've reconsidered."

"We have the female already—" Weasel Man said.

"Her name is Philomela," the Captain said.

"And you're outnumbered—"

The Captain nodded. "Just a bunch of old derelicts."

"—so now I think we'll just take this one, too."

"His name is Procne." The Captain hit the stim pack again. So did Mojo. Feran had never seen the Captain take two hits. "So you'll leave me and Mojo to die in slow agony?"

Weasel Man shifted on his feet. Feran smelt his fear. The man nodded at the case. "That's worth a fortune—"

"And you have to cover your costs, don't you? Where is she?" the Captain said, taking a third hit.

"On my ship, hovering above us waiting for my call." Weasel Man patted his talking device. "Now, why don't—"

Being a predator, Feran was the first other than the Captain to know that the moment had arrived. The killing moment. And in that moment, for the first time, Feran realized something.

The Captain was a predator, too.

Weasel Man was still talking, "—this over with—"

The Captain and Mojo, moving faster than Feran thought men could move, threw back their cloaks and pulled their guns. The Captain shot Weasel Man twice, once through his gun arm and once through his leg. The air sizzled as Mojo fired, killing three before they could even raise their weapons. The Captain shot three more before Weasel Man hit the ground screaming. Feran closed his ear flaps to shut out the screams, his nose stinging from the burnt-air smell. The Cutter and Guppert shot one Ripper each from behind the Puppies. The last four, who had kept their guns slung, died still reaching for their weapons.

As he watched, Feran felt only fear. Not of the killing, for he knew killing, but fear of the look on the Captain's face.

The Captain stepped over the bodies to where Weasel Man lay like a trapped animal. "Call your ship. Tell them to land outside this dome to pick up the other Angel."

Weasel Man spat blood. "Screw you."

The Captain put his gun against Weasel Man's forehead. The man swallowed, but shook his head. "You wouldn't kill an unarmed man in cold blood, Trelayne. You aren't capable of it."

But for the twitching of one eye, the Captain seemed carved from stone. Then he laughed. He laughed and laughed until Feran felt fear again— fear that he did not really know this man. Suddenly the Captain reached down and with one hand lifted Weasel Man by the throat and held him off the ground. Feran had no words for what he saw in the Captain's eyes as his voice boomed inside the dome. "I HAVE RIPPED BABIES FROM MOTHER'S ARMS. I HAVE KILLED THOUSANDS AND LAUGHED WHILE THEY DIED. I HAVE ENDED RACES. LITTLE MAN, I AM CAPABLE OF THINGS YOU COULD NEVER IMAGINE." The Captain dropped him then and looked down at the man, and Feran heard the sadness in the Captain's voice as he almost whispered, "I am capable of *anything.*"

Weasel Man lay gasping in the dirt. Then he looked up, and Feran knew the Captain had won. Weasel Man was baring his belly and neck, showing submission. He took his talking device with a shaking hand and spoke into it. Feran couldn't hear the words, but the Captain nodded to the others.

Feran relaxed. Guppert and the Cutter were slapping each other on their backs. Mojo sat slumped on the ground, his head between his knees, sobbing but apparently unhurt.

A cry cut the air. Feran spun, teeth bared. High above, Procne hovered, wings beating, head thrown back, face contorted in agony. His pouch bulged, then split as a cloud of bloody winged things burst from him and fell screeching toward them.

The brood had arrived.

Trelayne had not taken combat doses of Scream for over two years. The killing, and the joy it had brought, had shaken him. Now as the brood rained down bloody chaos from above, he felt his tenuous grip on reality slipping away. Knowing that the brood must live or Phi would die, he tried to follow what they were doing, but the Scream kept drawing him to the bloody corpses. He realized then that the brood was also being drawn to them.

Resembling winged toads with humanoid faces, grey and slick, the brood swarmed over the bodies, driving a long tendril that protruded from their abdomen into any open wound. But they stayed only a second at each spot, and with each attempt became more frenzied. *Scream*, he thought, *they need blood with Scream.*

"Trelayne!"

The cry spun Trelayne around. Weitz knelt, Tanzer held in a shaking hand. Blood soaked an arm and leg, and flowed from his forehead. Weitz leveled the gun at Trelayne.

The brood found Weitz before he could fire, swarming him, plunging their tendrils into each wound, into his eyes where the blood had run down from his forehead, probing, searching. Screaming, he clawed at them, then stiffened and fell forward.

The nestlings leapt up from his corpse to form a shrieking, swirling mass above the ring. They were tiring. *They are dying*, Trelayne thought. *Blood with Scream. Blood with Scream.*

He tore open his shirt. Pulling a knife from his belt, he slashed at his chest and upper arms. He dropped the knife and stood with arms outspread, blood streaming down him, waiting for the smell of the Scream in his blood to reach the brood.

They swooped down from above the ring, swarming him like bees on honey, driving their tendrils into his flesh wherever he bled. The pain surpassed even what Scream let him endure. A dark chasm yawned below him, and he felt himself falling.

Trelayne awoke on his back, pale green light illuminating a bulkhead above him. The weight pressing him into the bed and the throb of engines told him he was on a ship under acceleration.

Something was wrong. No. Something was right. Finally he felt right. He felt human. He felt . . .

Pain. Real pain. Pain that hurt. He tried to rise.

"The Captain has returned to us." It was Feran's voice.

"In more ways than one, fox boy, in more ways than one." The Cutter's face appeared above him. "Lie still for chrissakes. You'll open the wounds again."

Trelayne lay back gasping. "What happened?"

"We won. We took Weitz's ship."

"Mojo? Procne? Phi—where's Phi?" he wheezed.

Her voice came from across the room. "All your family is safe. Guppert, the Puppies. All are here with us."

Trelayne twisted his head. She lay on another bunk, Procne asleep beside her. "Didn't know I had a family," he said weakly.

"We knew, Jason Trelayne. All along we were your family."

The Cutter moved aside, and Trelayne could see the brood clinging to her. She smiled. "Yes. You saved my children."

"I haven't seen that smile in a long time, Phi."

"I have not had reason for a long time."

"I feel . . . I feel . . . "

"You feel true pain. And you wonder why." Her gaze dropped to something at his side. Only then did Trelayne realize that one of the brood lay beside him, and that the tiny creature still had its tendril inside him. He tried to move away.

"Lie still, dammit," the Cutter snapped. "This ugly little vacuum cleaner hasn't got you quite cleaned up yet."

"What are you talking about?"

The Cutter checked a monitor on the wall above the bunk. "The brood's feeding's reduced the Scream in your blood to almost nil. The big bonus is zero withdrawal signs. Remember when you tried to kick it when we started the colony?"

Trelayne nodded, shuddering at the memory.

The Cutter rubbed his chin. "These little suckers must leave somethin' behind in the blood, lets the body adjust to lower levels of Scream. Angels'd need the same thing when the brood feeds from 'em." He looked at Trelayne. "You just bought a new life for every Screamer the Entity ever got hooked."

As the implication of that sank in, Mojo's face appeared at the door. One of the brood clung to him as well. "We're nearing the jump insertion point. Where're we headed, Cap?"

Silence fell, and Trelayne could sense them waiting for his answer. He remembered something Weitz had said and smiled through his pain. "I hear there are still rebels on Fandor IV."

Mojo grinned and disappeared toward the bridge with Cutter. Trelayne turned to Feran. The kit moved away. Trelayne's smile faded as he understood. He stared at the kit then spoke very quietly. "Feran, the Captain Trelayne that you saw in the dome today . . . he died with all those other men. Do you understand?"

An eternity passed. Then Feran ran to him and hugged him far too hard, and it hurt. His wounds hurt. The nestling at his side hurt. God, it all hurt, and it was wonderful to hurt again and to want it to stop.

Later, the ship slowed for the jump, and weightlessness took him. But to Trelayne, the sensation this time was not of falling. Instead, he felt himself rising, rising above something he was finally leaving behind.

THE VOSTRASOVITCH CLOCKWORK ANIMAL AND TRAVELING FOREST SHOW AT THE END OF THE WORLD

JESSICA REISMAN

Grey patted Franche the polar bear on her broad back, leaning against her side as he ran a diagnostic between a handscan and his internal link; he then shot the record through that internal link to the bear's permanent file. The bear's coarse, thick ruff of white-wine colored fur glistened under the glow of the show's biolumes, strung about the counterfeit forest of the fairway.

When the Vostrasovitch Clockwork Animal and Traveling Forest Show shut down for the night, they partially rolled up the forest and did maintenance on the clockworks and the rest of the aging operation.

Clockwork, of course, was misnomer, nostalgic anachronism. All the creatures in the show were biomechanical, masterpieces of art, technology, and science.

Rare few real animals still lived in the world, and most of those were human. The few bio-preserves, where efforts were made at preserving and recreating something of the lost wealth of nature, were heavily guarded strongholds that few humans ever entered. World government controlled the work strictly; speciation not sanctioned by the government was illegal. Too many powerful interests had agendas dictating what flora and fauna to focus on developing, agendas based on who would profit most from that development.

The only purely biological fauna Grey had ever seen were insects: the locusts that had overrun the last wheat fields in his childhood, the perpetual gnats, and cockroaches.

He figured their clockworks were better than the legendary real things anyway. Franche would never try to eat him, or hurt him with her great clawed paws and teeth. She didn't need much in the way of energy, and put no strain on their very limited food supplies.

"Grey." Rubov stopped beside him, carrying a toolbox. "Going to run some tests on the ambients. Tell your mother, when she comes by for her closing check," Rubov squinted at the time through his internal link, "in a few ticks, that I'll get to the tank problem next."

Grey peered over Franche's back toward the offside of the forested fairway, where the rolling tank garden that grew most of their supply of fresh food sat, along with the show's trucks and spot-habs. There were always tank problems. He shivered a little in the chill, stomach grumbling around the usual end-of-the-day hollow. "What do you think is wrong with the ambients?"

Grey was so used to the breeze in trees, bird song, and animal sounds that made up the background ambient of the show that he was rarely aware of it on or off, but it had cut out several times that day and their customers—townies, rover cabals, and nomads—had definitely noticed.

Rubov grunted, shifting the toolbox and wiping a hand over his face, grime set into the creases of his age in a delicate tattoo mapping. He stomped away with only the grunt for answer.

Franche ran through her system maintenance checks as she did every night after a show, accompanied by a low grumbling. Grey listened with half an ear. The grumbles were part of the system check function set into all their biomechs; changes in tone or frequency indicated potential issues before they made it into primary systems. A good handler knew the sound of each biomech's check vocalization better than the sound of their own breath, a language repeated over and over. Even with the occasional warning signals, it was a limited vocabulary. Raised with Franche, Grey had known the entire repertoire of her vocalizations before he fully mastered speaking in complete sentences himself.

Franche offered no surprises—down to the rip in her hide at right shoulder haunch that he'd mended five times. He checked it now, fingers sifting down through thick fur to find it still holding from the last patch-up. The bear finished her grumbling check with a click of blunted teeth and went into shut down: the illusion of breath, of life and volition in muscle and eye all stilled. Franche became a statue, like one of the taxidermy animals in museums and roadside galleries. Grey found this routine comforting, as known and trusted as his mother's frowns. He crumpled the handscan and shoved it in a pocket of his coveralls as his mother came toward him from among the trucks and spot-habs.

"All right with Franche?" She opened with this question as she reached their little pavilion. She always opened with this question at the end of a show. She put the same question to each of the five handlers responsible for the show's main attractions: a leopard, two wolves, a long-eared, long-legged black tail jackrabbit, a red lemur, and a polar bear. She always started with Grey and Franche.

"All good," Grey gave the answer she most liked to hear. While there was no variation in his mother's question, in his answers, of course, there was—more and more as the years went by and time wore away at the great white bear, just as it might have at the genuine article, Grey liked to think. "Rubov says he'll get to the tanks soon as he has a go at the ambients."

She frowned, the lines of her face falling into the expression familiarly, and nodded. Her dark hair was tied up in a green scarf; hard muscles showed in her arms, age and work in her hands. Something surfaced in her eyes, like a turn of light in brown water.

"I wish you could have heard the real thing," she said, looking up into what was left of the holomech forest, a convincing illusion of holographic bark and leaf on a springy, collapsible scaffold framework of trunk and branch.

Grey followed her gaze. "What?"

She gestured with one hand and then snapped the hand into a fist. "Real life. A mourning dove call, song birds, wind in the leaves of a real wood, the creaking of tree branches, crickets. Real life that doesn't flicker on and off at the whim of an old generator powered by photovoltaic paint and spit. Actual birds, Grey . . . " She shook her head. The show had no flighted birds; biomech birds had a shorter operational duration than the mammals, the mechanism of flight a source of endless malfunction.

Grey leaned back against Franche, squinting up at the night sky beyond holomech leaves. "The world's still real, mom—the sky, the earth. We're real. Anyway, I've heard wind plenty, and there are for damn sure lots of insects left."

"Our animals aren't—there's a difference, Grey. You don't understand, don't know what you've missed."

He shrugged. "I know the real things could be dangerous and needed more land and resources than we could spare them. And anyway, since they're gone, or as good as, isn't it better if I don't know what I've missed?"

His mother's gaze strayed over the still polar bear and she shook her head again, her eyes tired. " . . . but can they suffer?" she said softly.

"What?"

"It's a quote. Look it up," she said, moving on to check with the other handlers in their pavilions.

As she went, the ambients came on, a susurrus of breeze shifting leaves, spiked by the occasional bird song, rose, fell, rose again, then cut off abruptly. Grey found himself more than usually aware of the sound of the empty night that remained.

In the deep of the night the wind picked up into a hard driving rush that scoured earth and anything in its path with dust and debris. It scratched and clattered and whined at the outside of the pavilion, the structure's side panels, raised during the day to gather power through their photovoltaic-painted surfaces, sealed down for the night. Grey, waking, listened to the wind that sounded like it was punishing the earth. Franche was a reassuring bulk beside him, still and breathless, but warm from soaking power through the conduits to the pavilion's solar cells.

He lay awake for a long time, listening to the wind.

In the early morning, the predawn light a solemn husk already cleaving from the day, Grey stretched and rubbed at dry eyes. He remembered the wind in the night and knew there would be cleanup before the show opened.

He cracked the pavilion's door and a coating of dust sifted to the ground. Gritty dunes and eddies covered everything.

A light went on in the canteen tent by the tank truck, a small square of light in the dust-smudged dawn. Still rubbing at his eyes, Grey headed for breakfast.

Hours later, gritty from cleaning up the wind's leavings but without time for more than a quick sluice with tepid recyc water, Grey opened the pavilion, raising all six sides. Franche stood as he'd left her. Disconnecting the bear from the power conduits and stowing them, he brought her out of downcycle as crew unrolled the fairway and the forest sprang into life around them. Franche's servos warmed up and the bear stretched front and back, growling and roaring.

All the animals did their warm-ups: the wolves howled; the leopard leapt from ground to pavilion roof and back; the red lemur tossed a ball back and forth with his handler; the jackrabbit's ears turned as she leapt and ran, the morning light making blush-veined hollows of long black-edged ears.

Custom was slow, people from the nearby town with their children, a few lone nomads. The day was already hot, the sky beyond the holomech trees a dingy glare, and the landscape to be glimpsed beyond the show's boundaries dry and barren. The ambients kept up their cocoon of breeze in trees, bird song, and occasional rain sounds. Franche roared and stood on her hind legs, towering over children and then bowing down to let them pet her. The older adults, those old enough to mourn the real thing, touched the bear with a sorry reverence that had always annoyed Grey. He preferred the children—they found only joy in Franche.

As the afternoon sloughed into dusk and the biolumes glowed to life among the trees, the tenor of the custom changed, families replaced by more nomads, rover cabals, and adult townies in groups. The show sold alcohol at night, pouring it from the barrels in which they fermented it into patrons' personal cups or, for an extra fee, crude starch cups that began disintegrating after one drink. The lights picked out the bony white of birches and silver-brown of larch trees. Franche's coat glowed under the spectral illumination.

The bear rumbled as Grey rubbed her energetically about the neck and ears.

"How do you make her nose wet?" The question came from a little girl in clean, patchy clothes.

Grey glanced around for a parent. There were few other children left on the fairway and those were all accompanied. The little girl touched Franche's broad black nose with one finger, and then reached a small hand to the fur above one of the bear's liquid dark eyes.

"She's built that way," Grey said.

"I held a real bear once," the girl said. She looked around, lips pursed worriedly. Grey followed her glance to a tall man speaking with Grey's mother. The girl lowered her voice and continued, "A black bear cub. Its nose was wet and cold. Your bear is very good, but the real one was squirmy and . . . " She rubbed her nose. "He licked my face and smelled good; his claws scratched my arm and he cried out when he got hurt."

"A real bear cub?"

The girl nodded at the dubious tone in Grey's voice. "He died, though. He wasn't made quite right."

The man who'd been speaking to Grey's mother called, "Anna!" crooking an arm, and the girl ran to join him.

The man and little girl disappeared among the trees and other groups of people. A little while later, as Franche sat on her great hind quarters and licked a plate-sized front paw, Grey's mother joined him with a preoccupied frown on her face.

She touched Grey's hand. "Here, after we close tonight, go into the town, this location. That man you saw me with—?" Grey nodded, "will meet you. He may have something for the show." The location came through his link at her touch and Grey nodded again. "Just check it out and let me know. I'm not sure it's anything we can use—he may be a bit of a crank, but you never know. It's a public place, and though Chernitown's a pit, it should be safe."

"What does he have?"

"Something—real, he says."

"That's illegal."

His mother nodded, but didn't say anything.

"Mom, we don't need a 'real,' illegal animal—one that could hurt someone, carry disease, that would need food and water!"

"Just go check it out."

"For fuck's sake—why?"

"Because, Grey," she snapped, angry and tired and intense, "there might be some worthwhile—some *real*—work to be done." Her anger subsided on a breath. "Just go and see what he has; it's probably nothing but a con. He probably has some biomech programmed for pain response or something sick like that."

Chernitown huddled gloomy in the night, its only illumination that of floating biolume globes here and there and the day's stored sunlight glowing in photovoltaic paint on old buildings and roofs. Like most such towns, this one was the remnants of the past with several tank gardens at its center, the water reclamation system a spiraling hedge of pipeline and machinery around it. The rest was a gallimaufry of buildings giving into the badlands rolling away in all directions. That was much of the world now, humans gathered in enclaves scattered like stars in a light-bleached sky. Satellites connected them all through the world link, but travel was hard, sometimes brutal and deadly, and only nomads, rover cabals, and groups like the Vostrasovitch show did it at all, and then only among clusters of tank towns.

Grey found the meet location through link: a stillery at the outer edge of one of the reclamation arms. The bar banked up against a towering elbow of copper pipe, the distilling works parasited into the pipes' seams and bolts. Colored biolumes hung from grids of smaller pipe and a hodgepodge of tables and chairs surrounded a space for dancing. Music came from cheap interface speakers hooked into the world link.

He ordered vodka—distilled from corn grown in the tanks—at the bar and leaned against it. The festive atmosphere and warm, frankly sexual glances from a young man down the bar and a woman dancing nearby made him wish he was here on his own, rather than on his mother's business. Mostly he stayed away from the towns they set up near, because it was safer. He'd gone into a few, to meet his needs as he got older, but found the roving cabals offered easier options.

Now he regretfully turned down the subtle invitations with a smile and shake of his head, focusing instead on the vodka—harsh but warming—and a piece of art hanging above the bar, a set of holoboxes cobbled together out of spare bits and parts. It depicted, in an infinity frame-within-frame that drew the gaze ever deeper, a rich, painted jungle scene with a tiger crouched in thick foliage, its jaws clamped over the neck of a water buffalo. The water buffalo's one visible eye was wide, the tiger's snarl fierce, blood staining crimson on the fur of both animals. It was beautiful and horrible. Grey shivered, looking at it, an uncomfortable feeling ticking over like a clock within him. In his head, he heard again his mother's words from the day before: . . . *but can they suffer?*

He'd just taken the last swallow of biting, clear liquor when he caught a glimpse of the man he'd seen talking to his mother earlier. The man haunted the edges of the biolume light, in the shadows of a rough alcove, but when Grey reached the alcove, the man was gone.

Grey scanned the area. The man didn't reappear and he felt an odd disappointment—given that he didn't believe the man had anything, and, if he did, that they should have anything to do with it.

He considered his options. Back to the bar and a possible hook-up or back to the show grounds to let his mother know the guy had skipped.

With a rueful glance back to the pool of colored light and bodies, Grey made for the exit.

He kept to the main track through the town, retracing his steps along the packed dirt thoroughfare. Quiet took the place of the stillery's friendly noise, the dark between hulking buildings barely leavened by the occasional floating biolumes that showed him ruts in the track and steps up or down to doorways.

A flicker of movement caught his eye as he passed an alley. Grey paused, peering into the dark. The back of his neck prickled.

He made out just the edge of a fire escape. A fleck of shadow moved and then the man stepped out of the shadows. He had a hand tucked inside his loose vest, cradling something at chest level. He was very tall, only appearing to be thin because of that height, with shaven head and beard at the same stage of dark stubble. He crooked one finger of his free hand to Grey, coming no further out of the alley himself.

When Grey hesitated, he pulled his hand out of his vest slowly. A smudge of something sat on his palm; then he threw the hand up and the smudge became a blurred, hovering movement of wings with a tiny body at its nexus. Grey wasn't sure if he was looking at a monstrous insect or a tiny bird. Suddenly it darted close to Grey, making him duck back. Whatever it was hovered at eye level and the buzz of its wings thrilled over his skin briefly before it darted away to hover elsewhere. He lost sight of it until the man, squeezing several drops of something onto his hand, held his palm up in the air again and the creature darted back to land.

Grey found he'd stepped into the alley, his gaze on the bird. "It's biological?"

"Entirely."

Grey glanced around. No wonder the man was so furtive; the tiny bird, if truly pure biological, was illegal enough to get him locked away for years.

"They usually go into partial hibernation in the night," he said, stroking the tiny bundle of feathers with one finger before slipping it back into his vest. "So this one's sleepy."

Questions crowded Grey's mind. Before he could ask any of them, the man turned, saying, "Follow me."

Grey shook his head. Not safe. But he recalled that hovering, darting form, the breeze of its wings as it hovered close, buzzing the air, barely glimpsed details of needle beak and iridescence in the feathers. The sense of fragility and . . . something he didn't know how to name.

Even if it wasn't pure biological, he thought, shying from the feeling he couldn't name, it was remarkable—he'd never seen a flighted biomech bird of such artistry.

He followed.

The man stayed several steps ahead, moving quickly down one narrow track and then another. Grey set his link to map the way and hurried to keep up. They didn't go far before the man stopped at a metal door. He palmed the chemical lock and pushed the door open, slipping quickly inside and almost shutting the door on Grey in his hurry to close it.

Inside, Grey followed him through a dingy kitchen into an open room with a sagging couch and a low table, a curtained doorway through which Grey glimpsed the little girl, an abandoned sprawl of skinny limbs. He thought she was asleep, but then caught the gleam of her eyes, watching him pass.

The man disappeared through another doorway. Following, Grey stumbled to a halt as he crossed into a space that opened up two or three stories above, a kind of silo filled with vegetation, reaching toward the simulated sunlight of a kind of lighting Grey had never seen. The air was a fug of green and rot, warm and dank like the inside of a tank garden. The heavy vegetation hung over makeshift lab tables, grimy scientific equipment, and the grisly artifacts of failed speciation work. The remains of dissected creatures of flesh and blood, strange, twisted things of paw and tail, floated in jars. The carcass of something was draped over a row of cryo storage units.

But up in the riot of tree and vine leaves, among gouts of flowers—red trumpets and spurts of little blue blossoms trailing from wedges of soil suspended on wire ledges in the trees—there, several tiny birds hovered and darted, filling the air with their buzz and whirr.

Watching them, Grey swayed, dizzy in the heat of the place. This slice of contained jungle overwhelmed him in a way their tank garden never had. It pulled at Grey. It confused him, tugging at something inside that was unfamiliar, alarming.

A buzz in the air and one of the tiny brown birds hovered just beyond his reach, at eye level, needle beak and seed eye black and keen, its wings a blur of motion. It darted up, zipping through the air too fast to trace until it came to a whirring hover at a trailing vine of the red trumpets, inserting its long, slender black beak deftly into one blossom after another. It had a white frill and bronzy green iridescence distinguished its brown feathers.

"They're used to coming to humans—the sugar scent I put on my hands earlier, that's how I train them, as much as they can be trained."

"But, why would you . . . " Grey gestured.

"Why what? Risk prosecution and imprisonment?" He rubbed a long hand over his stubbled head. "Or, perhaps, why bother with such messy work at all?" He gestured to the jars, the carcass on the storage units. "It's fraught with failure and disappointment, after all. And pain . . . theirs and mine."

There was a pad of feet behind him and Grey turned to see the little girl. Her name, he remembered, was Anna. She climbed up onto the table next to a line of jars with twisted things floating in them. She took a scanbook from under one arm and unrolled it, dragging a finger down the slick surface. Then she read from it, as if at a school lesson, something read often, though she tripped over some words, lisping others. Grey recognized it as a passage from a book his mother sometimes read to him when he was a child.

"The animals were lost. The largest to the smallest, the cats, the dogs, the bears, the pa . . . pachy-derms; gazelle, giraffe, hippo, hyena, hare; the apes and lemurs, marsupials and rodentia; the reptilian, lizard, crocodile, snake, and their cousins, the birds, kestrel, plover, swan, robin, owl, and heron; the frogs, that wore mutation like port—portent—for generations before they left the world for good; coral, crustacean, mollusk, plankton. A slow motion catast . . . ropy—"

"Catast*rophe*," her father interrupted.

"—catastrophe took the world. The species surviving wrought havoc on the world; famine and plague winnowed the humans to a fragment of their former numbers.

"The animals were lost and one night a woman, in hungry dream, found their representative in a wood—"

"That's very good, Anna, but that's enough for now."

"Okay, Da." She let the scan roll back up and crossed her legs under her nightshirt, looking at Grey. "It says why," she said to him, as if confidentially, "why my Da does this."

Her father continued. "Yes, scientists are at work in other places, under government auspice, bringing back what they can of all we lost in the collapse. In clean, controlled environments, regulated by arbiters of policy who argue endlessly, and have vested interests in what fauna, what flora, and when and who will benefit from it."

He spoke gently, despite the tenor of his words, and his hands and arms traced gestures on the air, intense gaze holding Grey.

"In clean white labs and controlled preserves, they work to bring back our lost biodiversity, strictly regulating the work. But it's work that belongs to all of us. What I do is illegal, yes. But what they do in their labs is no more real than the counterfeit life of the things in your show."

Grey flinched, thinking of Franche, then of the diorama in the stillery.

"Life," the man turned, arms out, "life is dirty, painful, *bloody*— invention can be marvelous—like biomech creatures—but it isn't life." He looked up at the darting birds. "They're so fragile when first born; they can be hurt, they can die so easily. Making a place for them to live, to grow, to flourish . . . how can you ask why?" His voice had gotten very soft, and Grey strained to hear him, stepping closer.

He was unsure what to say to the man's ardent words, the expectant expression on his face. "Why did you talk to my mother?"

"I need help in spreading the work. Your show travels. Under cover of your clockwork beasts, your ersatz forest, my real creatures and seeds can be taken far. There are people waiting for them, with gardens and habitats in the wastes. We have a network. Your mother, I think, is sympathetic to this cause."

Thinking about it, about his mother, Grey had to agree. His gaze was drawn back to the birds.

"What are they?" he asked, watching one hover at a flower, dipping its needle slender beak within, an unlikely, thrilling piece of theater.

"Flower kissers!" Anna said.

"Hummingbirds," the man said. "Brown Incas, mostly, with some other bits."

Grey watched them, just tiny brown birds—startling, living things of aerodynamic wonder.

"Here." The man took Grey's hand in his own and squeezed several drops of clear liquid onto his hand out of a small vial. He mimed holding the hand flat, palm up.

Grey watched one of the hummingbirds drop from the air, straight down to land on his open palm: a tiny, near weightless puff of warm feathers, flight muscle, and fragile bone. Its tiny claws pricked his skin. It hit him like sudden rain into desert, soaking down to wake a long-dormant seed; the seed's carapace cracking to that touch was pain, the pale, blind shoot of life threading forth, wonder.

One black eye looked at Grey as he looked at it.

Looked at him, and saw him.

As Franche never had, never would.

STUDY, FOR SOLO PIANO

GENEVIEVE VALENTINE

This is how it might have gone:

The Circus Tresaulti spent the winter on the road, Ayar the strong man knocking the stakes into the ground when it was frozen over.

They bartered for liquor to keep warm, and when spring came they pushed the trucks through the mud to save oil, and everything went on as before, and nothing broke.

But that was the winter they found the house.

The mansion stands more than two miles from the city walls, far enough that the looters have given up, and it's been left to rot so long that the city's children wouldn't understand it's a house.

The windows go first, from enemy fire and bad frosts. Then the moss and ivy move in, and the birds, and the rain. At last, the brick begins to crumble.

By the time the Circus comes, it will be a ruin.

But by the time the Circus comes, the storm has been raging for days, and the house rises up from the road, and Boss thinks, We must rest here, there's no way to go on.

"Stop," says Boss, and the Circus stops.

The Circus waits in leaking trailers while Boss takes her lieutenants through the house.

Then, her lieutenants are Elena from the trapeze, and Panadrome the music man, who presses his accordion bellows tight to his side to keep it from sharp edges, and Alec, their final act, who folds his gleaming wings tight against his back so he can fit through the hole in the wall.

Inside, the ceiling is waterlogged and sagging, but when Alec opens his wings even the nails sing for him.

Alec laughs, and the birds in the rafters scatter as if he's called them down.

(Alec will be dead in a year; these are the last birds he sees.)

They split up to cover ground; the house was grand, before it went to seed.

What Boss sees: five rooms with floors that haven't rotted through; a ballroom with a chandelier still hanging; three bathrooms with copper pipes intact behind the stone. (She can see metal right through walls, by now.)

What Boss does not see: Alec in a dining room with only a sideboard left, silhouetted against wallpaper that was green once. He faces a painting of a banquet, but his head is lowered. His wings are folded; he is still.

Elena stands behind him. Her forehead rests on his bare back, in the cradle between the wings. Her eyes are closed; her skin becomes pinker, as if she's waking from a long sleep.

(His wings are tall. They swallow her.)

Panadrome is beside the piano when Boss finds him.

One of the legs has collapsed, dropping the higher registers to the ground, and a few keys sank with the impact, but otherwise it's pristine.

He holds a blanket in his skeleton fingers, and the piano is free of dust; long ago someone, in their terror, still risked a kindness to a beautiful thing.

"We'll stay here," Boss says.

He doesn't think it's a good idea. He thinks the Circus might fall apart if it stops.

After too long he says, "As you like."

"You think it's not safe?"

Alec comes in, and Elena a few moments later.

"If you want us to live in an obstacle course," Elena says, "you've found the right place."

Boss says, "They can use the mess to shore up the holes, then. Call them."

Elena scowls and goes.

Alec smiles at Boss, holds out a hand. "Did you see the dining hall? There's a painting of a banquet, in case you forget what room you're in."

A moment later Panadrome is alone, one hand on the piano, pulling in breath he doesn't need.

Boss has a knack for skeletons.

Panadrome has never asked to have his silver hands covered over (though more than once Boss brought back someone's hands, still bleeding, and asked, "You need a pair of gloves?").

He is proud of the slender phalanges, the slightly curved metatarsals, the wrist joints always dark with oil. It is a testament to her art, and he would never dream of covering it.

But it is not a hand.

(A painting of a banquet may be beautiful, but you're no less hungry.)

They gave him oranges to carry, palm down. It strained very particular muscles so you could hold your hands aloft for the length of a concert.

(You cannot rest your weight in your fingertips when you play; your fingers are puppets, and the palms of your hands are the framework that holds them aloft.)

Now, he can play the accordion just as well as he ever could, though he thinks it's not as though anyone plays the accordion so much as cajoles a song from it.

But in the crumbling house, he stands beside the piano without moving to the bench.

(Panadrome's hands are pipes and gears. He does not have the spread between fingers that you need—the spread you could achieve if you practiced hard enough, if you held enough oranges, if you were born with the necessary reach. He could cover thirteen notes, in his prime.)

He has not seen a piano in a long time; winters are hard, and their wood burns as well as any other.

He is the last piano player in the world, the very last, and in the crumbling house he stands beside the instrument and trembles.

The Circus makes a home.

They drag stones to patch up the holes, and bolster the ceilings where they can, and come to blows over who gets the driest rooms, and Ayar the strong man reaches through the brick walls like they're made of cheese and pulls away long strands of copper. He takes it all; Boss wants it for the things she builds, and there's no knowing the next time they'll have a store like this.

"You look like a snake charmer," says Little George, when Ayar brings them to the workshop trailer for safekeeping.

(Not a drop of rain has gotten into the workshop. The workshop is sealed tight as the grave.)

Elena fights to keep the aerialists in their trailer and out of the house ("Just what I need, one of them breaking and me having to start from scratch."), but Boss allows no mutinies.

So Elena turns her battle to getting them the driest room, and they all crowd their pallets in, laughing, alongside Ayar and Jonah, whose clockwork lungs are susceptible to damp.

Elena lasts two hours before she moves her things to the third story.

The next day Boss says, "The floors up there are rotted through. You'll fall and snap your head off."

"I'll take my chances," Elena says.

Panadrome comes back to the piano room, often, and pulls the blanket away like a magician mid-trick.

He thought he was used to knowing that there would be no music that did not come from him, from the brass barrel of his body and the spindly silver lengths of his arms, from the bellows on one side and the keys on the other that make him useless for work.

He thought it would please him, to have power like that. (You think a lot of strange things, before the truth sinks in.)

If he tried, he might be able to play the final duet from *Heynan and Bello*. If he tried.

The melodies are layered, but the range is not large; it's an *opera expressiva*, and those rely on depth over breadth.

It's a pleasure to conduct. It lacks the classic majesty of *Queen Tresaulta*, but *Heynan and Bello* has its own appeal for the musician: every theme (the bold brother Bello, the clever sister Heynan, the court families, the castle) can be played over any of the others.

During the siege, when all the themes are played at once, the wall of sound is transporting, and even from his harbor on the conductor's podium there was a sense that the music could break free and swallow them.

The finale is softer. Only Heynan and Bello are onstage, and their separate notes move quietly forward into the end. When they're about to be discovered, they clasp hands and pitch themselves over the edge of the tower into the sea, to keep their love from becoming known.

After they fall, the love theme plays. It has appeared only once before, in the moment of their first kiss, two bars of music between their own songs like a dream they only remember after it's too late.

He found himself bent almost double at the end of every performance, as if he could pull every bow over the strings himself.

But he has never understood it.

The music is beautiful enough that he should be able to understand (he's a musician, that's his work), but it's the reverse; their themes are so sad that every time he conducts it, he thinks that this time they will face whoever enters, and triumph, and walk out free.

(If you can make something so beautiful, why would you ever stop?)

This is what he thinks about every time Boss is going to bring someone into the circus.

She takes his hand, pulls him aside (she never hesitates to touch him, the only one of them who does).

Then she asks, "What did you think of that?", and behind her eyes the performer is already taking shape.

"I vote yes," he says, because if you can make something beautiful, why would you ever stop?

(Her hands are always warm; he doesn't know how he knows.)

"No fires," Boss says, the first night.

The house is far from the city, but she knows by now that the kind of city that grows from a prison is the kind that doesn't like neighbors moving in.

She and Alec make their bed in a room with no windows, just in case. His wings catch any light they can find.

"It's charming," he says the first night, as they listen to what might be birds fighting over their heads. "Reminds me of camping."

(It's a joke. He was born after the war started; that kind of leisure doesn't exist any more. But she tells him what the world was like, and he pretends, because it pleases her.)

"Go to sleep," she says, smiling, and he settles onto his stomach, his wings along his back.

They each face away from the other, pretending to sleep, for a long time.

He is listening to the little bird-sounds above them that he knows are Elena.

Boss is listening as hard as she can, right through the walls, for the sound of the city coming for them.

For a while, everything is quiet.

The crew sleeps, recovering from the winter. The aerialists sleep, recovering from Elena.

The floors start to fall in, and the Grimaldi Brothers practice by balancing on each other in the weakest points, and leaping away when the boards give in. (Little George stands in the doorways, judges how impressive the tumbling is, and declares winners.)

Ayar and Jonah find a few books under a pile of rubble, read them until the paper starts to flake.

Elena strings up a trapeze in the attic.

"The birds won't be happy," says Alec, at dinner.

(Elena still comes down to dinner with the rest; Boss gave the order.)

Elena seems not to hear, and it's Little George who says under his breath, "She's probably eating them," and gets a box on his ears from Boss.

Panadrome watches from his corner for a while before he disappears.

(He's long ago given up the pretense of food. He tried for a while, to be part of the family, but some things aren't worth pretending over.)

The house is enormous, but they seem to fill it more as days pass, until it's a trick to find a room that won't eventually be hosting the Grimaldis as they play.

There are two exceptions.

The music room they leave alone. Boss gave the order.

The attic is Elena's, and that's all it takes to keep them out. Not worth the trouble; she holds a grudge.

No one gives that one a second thought. No one even glances at the attic stairs, growing from a servants' staircase at the end of some hallway they gutted of pipes.

(No one sees the second set of footprints marking passage, flanked with little sharp cuts in the dust where his feathers have been.)

The city sees them.

When the militia comes, Boss meets them with Little George beside her, and two of the crew in their work clothes, and one of the crew dressed up in bangles and veils. The others arrange themselves inside the house to hide their numbers and look as sweet as possible.

Alec, Panadrome, Ayar, and Jonah crowd into the windowless room where Boss and Alec sleep. Elena stands guard at the door, in case the city people make it that far. (She was a good soldier, in her day.)

Little George comes up to relieve them.

"She said we were happy to put on a week of free shows," he says, still panting from the sprint upstairs. "They didn't want any of it. They said we have until nightfall to leave town, or they're going to burn us out."

"What did Boss say?" Panadrome frowns.

"She said, Yes of course, no harm meant, we didn't realize it was city property, thank you for the warning, we'll start packing right now, and then they left."

Alec is smiling. "And what does Boss *really* say?"

Little George grins so hard his ears move up his head.

"She says if they're going to be rude, so can we. We're heading to the woods to harvest what we can."

Jonah and Ayar and Alec walk out smiling.

Panadrome doesn't move. He stands where he is, and reminds himself over and over that the piano is just another beautiful thing.

They've all said goodbye to beautiful things; it's the nature of the business.

Still, he stands where he is a long time.

(What Panadrome does not see: Elena standing in the attic, looking at Alec's footprints in the dust, reminding herself it's the nature of the business.)

Jonah comes back with an armful of potatoes.

"There are more," he says, "it's just that the ground cover is so thick, and I can't reach."

(His lungs are housed in a gold beetle-dome; he has to be careful.)

Boss organizes a hunting party, and under cover of dusk they slink into the trees to shore up enough food to keep the crew from dropping dead around them.

Panadrome takes the time to look over the house, now that people's boots have left a trail where the floor is sound. He'd never been beyond the ground floor before; he's not an adventurer, by nature.

He's on the second story when the music starts, and he thinks his mind is playing tricks on him.

But there are too many mistakes his imagination would never make, and he creeps downstairs wishing there was a weapon left for him to wield.

Instead he creeps to the doorway, glances inside.

Elena is kneeling, playing a song they use in children's primers, pausing every few chords to frown and adjust her fingering.

Her hands are strong enough (a lifetime on trapeze), but her fingers are stiff. She had a poor teacher. The piano's out of tune, which doesn't help.

But still he rests his temple on the wall, and listens to the first notes in ages that haven't come from him.

Then she pauses mid-phrase, and he realizes after too long that she's standing. It's not absence of mind—she's given up. The notes are hanging, dissonant.

"You have to finish," he says, moving into sight.

If she's startled, it doesn't show. "I don't remember."

"I'll teach you," he says.

He must sound too desperate, too eager, because she levels a look at him he's rarely seen. Cruel, yes, and angry, yes, and terrified, but not this.

"Play it yourself," she says.

He raises and drops his hands a few inches (it passes as a shrug), says, "I can't."

She watches his fingers, glances out the window.

(He can see her thinking, *You still could, if you had any courage*, but she's known him long enough to try not to be cruel.)

"Please, just to the end," he says. "Only ten measures."

(Before Boss gets back, he thinks. He would never let her see him this way; he would never seem so ungrateful.)

"We'll have to leave," she says. "You can't keep this."

He doesn't answer. (He's asked for so little, in all this time. There must be a way.)

When he doesn't meet her eye, she says, "This house was a mistake. Don't let this ruin you, too."

He doesn't understand her. He nods to her—manners, always—and goes.

In the kitchen he breathes so deeply that the brass strains against the bolts.

This is what he can't admit: his body forgets.

The music he remembers; he remembers things he said and did. But he has forgotten the taste of wine, and the pinch of the baton between his fingers, and the itch at his throat from his tie. Thinking back is like watching film, knowing it happened but sensing nothing.

He learned accordion after; for the Circus, he can play.

But the rest was so long ago, he might kneel in front of the piano and not have one note left in him.

(The first thing he sensed was the warmth of the sun rising, and when he opened his eyes Boss was in front of him, standing watch.)

The music comes back after a very long time. It's halting, and off-key, and she needs an orange under her palm—her fingers will wear out, this way.

But you don't examine a gift (manners, always), so he stays where he is, closes his eyes, listens until the song is over.

What Panadrome does not see:

The others coming back from the forest in the deep night, with enough plants to survive on. Alec leads the way, wings loose, carrying a blanket filled to bursting.

When he sees Elena in the doorway, he smiles like a crowd is watching.

But then he reaches her.

Then his face softens, and his wings tremble, and she reaches out over his shoulder to touch them.

For a moment they stand in the hall as if on the edge of the castle tower.

Then she pulls back her hand. (Boss is coming, and they don't dare be seen, and by morning they'll be on the road and have to leave this behind; it's the nature of the business.)

She walks alone up to the attic, and Alec stands and waits for Boss and the others bringing in the harvest.

What Panadrome does not see: notes moving quietly forward, into the end.

What no one sees:

Alec emerging from the forest as the clouds thin across the moon, and light flickers off his wings like a signal beacon across the hills to the city.

Little George is on the deep-night watch; he's the one who comes running inside.

"They're coming!" he shouts.

The house riots.

The crew knock each other awake and scramble. The Grimaldi Brothers drop through the hole in their floor.

It takes less than five minutes for the Circus to run, when it has to. They've made an art of vanishing when the takings go cold.

Panadrome has nothing to gather, but still he cannot leave.

He's standing beside the piano when Elena finds him.

"We can't leave it," he says. "Not for them."

"Burn it yourself, then," says Elena.

She's holding a match; her voice is the kindest it's ever been.

"What?" he says. "No."

"Better you than them," she says. "A funeral or a butchering."

He looks at her. His face has turned to stone.

"It might be the last one," he says. His mouth is dry, somehow. "The very last."

She looks him in the eye. She says, "I know."

She rests it in the plate of his palm, vanishes.

He closes his eyes, feeling the piano behind him as though it's moving closer, swallowing him.

Then he opens them, and Boss fills his vision.

(Every time he looks at her is a little like that first time; waking, and knowing he is bound.)

"We can take it with us," he says. "Please. Ayar can carry it."

"No time to be careful," she says. "No spare fuel to carry it."

Panadrome feels his body is falling to pieces.

"But *look* at it!"

There are tears in her eyes.

"They're coming," Boss says. "We have to go."

But she doesn't move.

Even Elena has turned in the doorway to watch, Elena who has never waited.

He looks at the piano as if he could lay hands on it and bring it to life.

Far away come the familiar sounds of a mob.

In another lifetime, someone might come to this house to take refuge from the winter. They might find the piano, and kneel, and play.

But someone is coming now, axe in hand and looking for kindling, and they might not even take the blanket off before they start their work.

Boss hasn't moved. He realizes this is the illusion of choice; Boss has given her order.

(He doesn't look at Elena. She gave him the match; there is no question what she would do at the castle precipice, on the verge of being found out.)

When he strikes the match against his palm, his silver fingers do not tremble; he does not feel the fire.

The whole house has caught by the time the last truck is on the road.

Panadrome looks out the grimy window as the fire snakes the ivy, races across the rafters.

He imagines he can see the piano through a gaping window, long past the point he knows it's gone.

(He ran as soon as he dropped the match inside, and the fire caught. Some things he can, barely, stand; the sound of piano wires snapping is not one.)

Boss sits beside him without speaking.

In their view, the house turns into a hearth, into a lit match, into nothing.

They pass the thin, pale lamp of some other city, far away, but Boss doesn't give the signal, and so no one turns. The trucks rattle over the rocky ground.

It's almost a metronome, he thinks as if from some other life; phantom oranges rest in the upturned nests of his palms as he presses his fingers to the keys as long as he can before they fall.

Finally they escape the very last of the city light, and there's nothing left but the sky, silent and cold and spotted with stars.

(Panadrome hasn't missed the stars; he's not an adventurer, by nature.)

"Stop," says Boss, and the Circus stops.

MAKING MY ENTRANCE AGAIN WITH MY USUAL FLAIR

KEN SCHOLES

No one ever asks a clown at the end of his life what he *really* wanted to be when he grew up. It's fairly obvious. No one gets hijacked into the circus. We race to it, the smell of hotdogs leading us in, our fingers aching for the sticky pull of taffy, the electric shock of pink cotton on our tongue. Ask a lawyer and he'll say when he was a kid he wanted to be an astronaut. Ask an accountant; he'll say he wanted to be fireman.

I am a clown. I have always wanted to be a clown. And I will die a clown if I have my way.

My name is Merton D. Kamal.

The Kamal comes from my father. I never met the man so I have no idea how he came by it. Mom got the Merton bit from some monk she used to read who wrote something like this: We learn humility by being humiliated often. Given how easily (and how frequently) Kamal is pronounced Camel, and given how the D just stands for D, you can see that she wanted her only child to be absolutely filled to the brim with humility.

My Mom is a deeply spiritual woman.

But enough about her. This is my story.

"Merton," the ringmaster and owner Rufus P. Stowell said, "it's just not working out."

I was pushing forty. I'd lost some weight and everyone knows kids love a chubby clown. I'd also taken up drinking, which didn't go over well right before a show. So suddenly, I found myself without prospects and I turned myself towards home, riding into Seattle by bus on a cold November night.

Mom met me at the bus stop. She had no business driving but she came out anyway. She was standing on the sidewalk next to the station wagon when she saw me. We hugged.

"I'm glad you're home," she said.

I lifted my bag into the back. "Thanks."

"Are you hungry?"

"Not really."

We went to Denny's anyway. Whenever my Mom wanted to talk, we went to Denny's. It's where she took me to tell me about boys and girls, it's where she took me to tell me that my dog had been hit by a car.

"So what are you going to do now?" She cut and speared a chunk of meatloaf, then dipped it into her mashed potatoes and gravy before raising it to her mouth.

"I don't know," I said. "I guess I'll fatten up, quit drinking, get back into the business." I watched her left eyebrow twitch—a sure sign of disapproval. I hefted my double bacon cheeseburger, then paused. "Why? What do *you* think I should do?"

She leaned forward. She brought her wrinkled hand up and cupped my cheek with it. Then she smiled. "I think you've already tried the clown thing, Merton. Why don't you try something different?"

I grinned. "I always wanted to be a sword-swallower but you wouldn't let me."

"What about . . . insurance?"

"Well, it gets steep. The swords are real, Mom."

The eyebrow twitched again. "I'm being serious. Remember Nancy Keller?"

Of course I did. I'd lost my virginity with her back in eleventh grade. It was my second most defining moment that year. Three days later, Rufus P. Stowell's Traveling Big Top rolled into town and my first most defining moment occurred. They said I was a natural, I had the look and the girth. Would I be interested in an internship? I left a note for Nancy in her mailbox thanking her for everything in great detail, hugged my Mom goodbye and dropped out of high school to join the circus.

Mom was still waiting for me to answer. "Yes, I remember her."

"Well, she's some big mucky-muck now at CARECO."

"And?" I took a bite of the cheeseburger.

"And I told her you were coming home and asked her if she'd interview you."

I nearly choked. "You did *what*?"

"I asked her if she'd interview you. For a job."

I had no idea what to say.

So the next morning, Mom took me down to J.C. Penney's and bought me my first suit in thirty years. That afternoon, she dropped me downtown in front of the CARECO building, waved goodbye and drove away.

The CARECO building was new. I'd visited a few times over the years, had watched buildings come and buildings go. But I had never seen anything like this. It looked like a glass Rubik's Cube tilted precariously in a martini glass full of green jello. Inside, each floor took on the color coding of the various policies they offered. Life insurance was green. Auto, a deep blue. I can't remember what color Long-Term Disability was. Each color had been painfully worked out, according to a plaque near the door, by a team of eminent European corporate psychologists. Supposedly, it would enhance productivity by reducing the depression inherent within the insurance industry.

While I was reading the plaque, a man stepped up to me. He was as tan as a Californian, wearing sunglasses and a Hawaiian shirt despite impending rain. I went back to reading. "Excuse me," he said.

"Yes?"

"Have you seen a monkey around here?"

I shook my head, not really paying attention to the question. "Sorry."

He smiled. "Thanks anyway."

I went inside. I rode three escalators, two elevators and talked to seven receptionists. I sat in a chair that looked like plastic but was really made of foam. I filled out long and complicated application forms.

An hour later, someone took me up into an office at the top of the highest point of the inside of the glass Rubik's Cube.

Nancy Keller looked up. She smiled until my escort closed the door on her way out.

"Merton D. *Camel*," she said, stretching each syllable.

"Kamal. Hi, Nancy." The view from her office was spectacular. The walls were glass framed in steel and I could see the city spread out around me in a wide view that pulled at my stomach. The office had a modern-looking desk in the middle of it, a few chairs and some potted plants.

"I'm surprised to see you after so long. Back from clowning around?"

"I am." I smiled. "You look good." And she did. Her legs were still long but her hair was short and she'd traded her Van Halen tank top for a crisp blue suit.

She ignored my compliment and pointed to another of those foam chairs. "Let's get this over with."

I sat. She sat. I waited, trying to ignore the places where my wool suit created urgent itching.

She studied my application, then she studied me. I kept waiting. Finally, she spoke. "This interview," she said, "consists of two questions." She leaned forward and I realized the button on her suit coat had popped open to reveal more cleavage than I remembered her having. "First question. Do you remember the day you left for the circus, three days after our . . . *special* moment." She made little quote marks in the air when she said "special."

I nodded. "I do. I left you a note." I grinned. "I think I even said thank you. In some detail."

She nodded, too. "Second question. Did you ever stop to think that maybe . . . just maybe . . . my *father* would be the one getting the mail?" She stood and pushed a button on her desk. I stood, too. "Thank you for coming, Mr. Camel. Patrice will see you out." She extended her hand. I shook it and it was cold.

Later, I was working on my third bowl of ice cream and looking over the Twelve Steps when her assistant called with the offer.

"It's easy," Nancy Keller said again. I wasn't sure I'd heard her right. "I want you to drive a monkey to our branch office in New Mexico."

"That's my job?"

She nodded. "If you don't futz it up, there'll be another."

"Another monkey?"

"No," she said. "Another job. This monkey's one of a kind."

"And you're sure you don't want me to just take him to the airport and put him on a plane?"

"I'm sure."

I should've asked why but didn't. "Okay. When do I leave?"

"As soon as you get your Mom's car." She noticed my open mouth. "This monkey," she said, "needs as much anonymity as possible."

"I'm traveling with an incognito monkey in a twenty-year-old station wagon?"

"Yes. You'd better get changed."

"Changed?" I knew I'd worn the suit two days in a row but I figured the first day didn't really count.

"You can't be seen like that. What would a guy in a suit need with a monkey? I need a clown for this one."

I was opening my mouth to question all of this when Patrice came in with a thick envelope. Nancy took it, opened it, and started ruffling through the hundred-dollar bills.

"I'll get changed, get the car, be back in an hour," I said.

Nancy smiled. It was a sweet smile, one that reminded me of eighties music and her parents' ratty couch. "Thanks, Merton."

The monkey and I drove southeast, zigzagging highways across Washington, crossing over the Cascades into dryer, colder parts of the state. There was little snow on the pass and the miles went by quickly.

The monkey was in an aluminum crate with little round holes in it. They'd loaded him into the back in their underground parking garage. Two men in suits stood by the door, watching.

"You shouldn't need anything else, Merton," Nancy said. "He's pretty heavily sedated. He ought to sleep all the way through."

I looked at the map, tracing my finger along the route she'd marked in blue highlighter. "That's . . . around seventeen hundred miles, Nancy." I did some math in my head. "At least two days . . . and that's if I really push it."

"Just bring his crate into your hotel room. Discreetly, Merton." She smiled again. "You'll be fine. He'll be fine, too."

Naturally, I'd said okay, climbed into the car and set out for Roswell, New Mexico.

When we crossed into Oregon, the monkey woke up.

I knew this because he asked me for a cigarette.

I swerved onto the shoulder, mashing the brakes with one clown-shoed foot while hyperventilating.

"Just one," he said. "Please?"

I couldn't get out of the car fast enough. After a few minutes of pacing by the side of the road, convincing myself that it was the result of quitting the booze cold turkey, I poked my head back into the car.

"Did you say something?" I asked, holding my breath.

Silence.

Releasing my breath, I climbed back into the car. "I didn't think so." I started the car back up, eased it onto the road. I laughed at myself. "Talking monkeys," I said, shaking my head.

"Monkeys can't talk," the monkey said. Then he yawned loudly.

I braked again.

He chuckled. "Look pal, I'm no monkey. I just play one on TV."

I glanced up into the rearview mirror. A single dark eye blinked through one of the holes. "Really?"

He snorted. "No. I don't. Where are we supposed to be going?"

"Roswell, New Mexico."

"And what does *that* tell you?"

I shrugged. "You got me."

"Let's just say I'm not from around here."

"Where *are* you from?" But it was sinking in. Of course, I didn't believe it. I had laid aside the cold turkey alcohol withdrawal theory at this point and was wondering now if maybe I was tilting more towards a psychotic break theory.

"Unimportant. But I'm not a monkey."

"Okay then. Why don't you go back to sleep?"

"I'm not tired. I just woke up. Why don't you let me out of this box and give me a cigarette?"

"I don't smoke."

"Let's stop somewhere, then. A gas station."

I looked back at him in the rearview mirror. "For someone that's not from around here, you sure know an awful lot." More suspicion followed. "And you speak English pretty good, too."

"Well," the monkey said. "I speak it *well*. And I may not be *from* here but I've certainly spent enough time on this little rock you call home."

"Really?" Definitely a psychotic break. I needed medication. Maybe cognitive therapy, too. "What brings you out this way?"

"I'm a spy."

"A monkey spy?"

"I thought we'd already established that I'm *not* a monkey."

"So you just look like one?" I gradually gave the car some gas and we slipped back onto the highway.

"Exactly."

"Why?"

"I have no idea. You'd have to ask my boss."

I pushed the station wagon back up to seventy-five, watching for road signs and wondering if any of the little towns out here would have a psychiatrist. "Where's your boss?"

"Don't know," the monkey said. "I gave him the slip when I defected."

"You defected?"

"Of course I defected."

"Why?"

"Got a better offer."

It went on like that. We made small talk and Oregon turned into Idaho. I never asked his name; he never offered. I found a Super Eight outside Boise and after paying, hauled his crate into the room.

"So are you going to let me out?"

"I don't think that'd be such a good idea," I told him.

"Well, can you at least get us a pizza? And some beer?"

"Pizza, yes," I said. "Beer, no." I called it in and channel-surfed until it arrived.

The holes presented a problem. And I couldn't just eat in front of him. I went to open the crate.

It was locked. One of those high powered combination jobs.

"Odd, isn't it?"

"Yeah," I said. "A bit."

He sighed. "I'm sure it's for my own protection."

"Or mine," I said.

He chuckled. "Yeah, I'm quite the badass as you can see."

That's when I picked up the phone and called Nancy. She'd given me her home number. "Hey," I said.

"Merton. What's up?"

"Well, I'm in Boise."

"How's the package?"

"Fine. But . . . " I wasn't sure what to say.

"But what?"

"Well, I went to check on the monkey and the crate's locked. What's the combination?"

"Is the monkey awake?" Her voice sounded alarmed.

I looked at the crate, at the eye peeking out. "Uh. No. I don't *think* so."

"Has anything—" she paused, choosing her word carefully, "—*unusual* happened?"

I nearly said you mean like a talking space alien disguised as a monkey? Instead, I said, "No. Not at all. Not really." I knew I needed more or she wouldn't believe me. "Well, the guy at the front desk looked at me a bit funny."

"What did he look like?"

"Old. Bored. Like he didn't expect to see a clown in his lobby."

"I'm sure he's fine."

I nodded, even though she couldn't see me. "So, about that combination?"

"You don't need it, Merton. Call me when you get to Roswell." The phone clicked and she was gone.

In the morning, I loaded the monkey back into the car and we pointed ourselves towards Utah.

We picked up our earlier conversation.

"So you defected? To an insurance company?" But I knew what he was going to say.

"That's no insurance company."

"Government?"

"You'd know better than I would," he said. "I was asleep through most of that bit."

"But you're the one who defected."

He laughed. "I didn't defect to *them*."

"You *didn't*?"

"No. Of course not. Do you think I *want* to be locked in a metal box in the back of a station wagon on my way to Roswell, New Mexico, with an underweight clown who doesn't smoke?"

I shrugged. "Then what?"

"There was a guy. He was supposed to meet me in Seattle before your wacky friends got me with the old tag and bag routine. He represents certain *other* interested parties. He'd worked up a bit of an incognito gig for me in exchange for some information on my previous employers."

I felt my eyebrows furrow. "*Other* interested parties?"

"Let's just say your little rock is pretty popular these days. Did you really think the cattle mutilations, abductions, anal probes and crop circles were all done by the same little green men?"

"I'd never thought about it before."

"Space is pretty big. And everyone has their schtick."

I nodded. "Okay. That makes sense, I guess." Except for the part where I was still talking to a monkey and he was talking back. It was quiet now. The car rolled easy on the highway.

"Sure could use a cigarette."

"They're bad for you. They'll kill you."

"Jury's still out on that," the monkey said. "I'm not exactly part of your collective gene pool." He paused. "Besides, I'm pretty sure it doesn't matter."

"It doesn't?"

"What do you really think they're going to do to me in Roswell?"

The monkey had a point. The next truck stop, I pulled off and went inside. I came out with a pack of Marlboros and pushed one through the little hole. He reversed it, pointing an end out to me so I could light it. He took a long drag. "That's nice," he said. "Thanks."

"You're welcome." Suddenly my shoulders felt heavy. As much as I knew that there was something dreadfully wrong with me, some wire that had to be burned out in my head, I felt sad. Something bad, something *experimental* was probably going to happen to this monkey. And whether or not he deserved it, I had a role in it. I didn't like that at all.

"Have you seen a monkey around here?" the California Tan Man had asked me two days ago in front of the CARECO building.

I looked up. "Hey. I saw that guy. The one in Seattle. What was the gig he had for you? Witness protection type-thing?"

"Sort of. Lay low, stay under everyone's radar."

Where would a monkey lay low, I asked myself. "Like what?" I said. "A zoo?"

"Screw zoos. Concrete cage and a tire swing. Who wants that?"

"What then?"

Cigarette smoke trailed out of the holes in his crate. "It's not important. Really."

"Come on. Tell me." But I knew now. Of course I knew. How could I not? But I waited for him to say it.

"Well," the monkey said, "ever since I landed on this rock I've wanted to join the circus."

Exactly, I thought, and I knew what I had to do.

"I'll be back," I said. I got out of the car and walked around the truck stop. It didn't take long to find what I was looking for. The guy had a mullet and a pickup truck. In the back of the pickup truck's window was a rifle rack. And in the rifle rack, a rifle. Hunting season or not, this was Idaho.

I pulled that wad of bills from my wallet and his eyes went wide. He'd probably never seen a clown with so much determination in his stride and cash in his fist. I bought that rifle from him, drove out into the middle of nowhere, and shot the lock off that crate.

When the door opened, a small, hairy hand reached out, followed by a slender, hairy arm, hairy torso, hairy face. He didn't quite look like a monkey but he was close enough. He smiled, his three black eyes shining like pools of oil. Then, the third eye puckered in on itself and disappeared. "I should at least try to fit in," he said.

"Do you want me to drop you anywhere?" I asked him.

"I think I'll walk. Stretch my legs a bit."

"Suit yourself."

We shook hands. I gave him the pack of the cigarettes, the lighter and all but one of the remaining hundred dollar bills.

"I'll see you around," I said.

I didn't call Nancy until I got back to Seattle. When I did, I told her what happened. Well, *my* version about what happened. And I didn't feel bad about it, either. She'd tried to use me in her plot against a fellow circus aficionado.

"I've never seen anything like it," I said. "We were just outside of Boise, early in the morning, and there was this light in the sky." I threw in a bit about missing time and how I thought something invasive and wrong might've happened to me.

I told her they also took the monkey.

She insisted that I come over right away. She and her husband had a big house on the lake and when I got there, she was already pretty drunk. I'm a weak man. I joined her and we polished off a bottle of tequila. Her husband was out of town on business and somehow we ended up having sex on the leather couch in his den. It was better than the last time but still nothing compared to a high wire trapeze act or a lion tamer or an elephant that can dance.

Still, I didn't complain. At the time, it was nice.

Three days later, my phone rang.

"Merton D. Kamal?" a familiar voice asked.

"Yes?"

"I need a clown for my act."

"Does it involve talking monkeys?" I asked with a grin.

"Monkeys can't talk," the monkey said.

So I wrote Nancy a note, thanking her in great detail for the other night. After putting it in her mailbox, I took a leisurely stroll down to the Greyhound Station.

When the man at the ticket counter asked me where I was headed, I smiled.

"The greatest show on earth," I said. And I know he understood because he smiled back.

THE QUEST

BARRY B. LONGYEAR

On the planet Momus, south of the Town of Tarzak, lies the village of Sina nestled between the Fake Foot river delta and the glittering expanses of the Sea of Baraboo, named in honor of the ship that stranded the original circus on Momus two centuries before. The sun, just peeking over the edge of the sea, bathed the rooftops of Sina in red, while tufts of idle clouds warmed themselves in the glow above the water. Far below them, two figures dressed in hooded robes of purple stood upon a rotting wharf. The taller of the two scratched, then pulled, at a long white beard as he stared out across the Sea of Baraboo. He turned and looked at the scowling face of his corpulent companion. "Please, Durki. Try to understand."

Durki raised one thick black eyebrow and settled the scowl on his face more deeply. "You will kill yourself, you old fool!" His voice, high and nasal, grated on the ear. "You will drop dead from age, if you escape the storms, the exiles, and monsters. I say it again, Pulsit, you are an old fool!" Durki folded his arms.

Pulsit raised his brows. "Now, Durki, that is no manner in which to address your master. You are a terrible apprentice."

Durki snorted. "I might say a thing or two about your qualities as a master, Pulsit. I am over forty years old, yet I am *still* an apprentice!"

Pulsit winced. "Ah, Durki, please keep your screeching voice to a bearable volume." He shook his head. "How can I turn you loose on an audience with that voice? That's why no other master storyteller would take you on. But, I took you on, Durki. You owe me something for that."

Durki turned down the comers of his mouth, raised his eyebrows and nodded. "True." He reached within his robe and extracted a small copper bead. He held it between thumb and forefinger and dropped it into Pulsit's hand. "I trust this squares our accounts?"

"One movill? That's what you figure your debt is after eight years as my apprentice?"

Durki shrugged. "I may have been too generous, but keep the change. It helps ease my mind for allowing you to go off and kill yourself."

Pulsit turned his gaze back out over the sea. "Bah! What concern is it of yours, you disrespectful wretch?"

"I have plans on becoming a storyteller, Pulsit, not your partner in suicide. You've never been off the central continent; I doubt you've even been as far as Kuumic—"

"I have too!"

"—and now you want to travel the girth of the entire planet Momus! You know nothing of the dangers! Nothing!"

"Keep your screeching down!" Pulsit looked up the wharf toward the houses along the shore. "Everyone in Sina will be demanding coppers from us for driving them out of bed at this hour. Where is that fisher?"

Durki looked up the wharf, then back out over the ocean.

"Perhaps Raster thought better about it. Perhaps he would feel responsible for your suicide."

Pulsit frowned and turned toward his apprentice. "You must stop saying that! I have no intention of killing myself. I am a storyteller, Durki, and I must have experiences to draw upon. All the priests have to do is record history; the newstellers relate events; a storyteller," Pulsit tapped the side of his head, "must have imagination."

Durki shook his head. "You have been a storyteller for many years without having to leave the continent to fuel your imagination."

"My fires—"

"Which were none too hot to begin with."

"My fires . . . are cold. It is only a great adventure such as I have planned that can replenish them." Pulsit looked back up the wharf. "Ah, at last. Here is Raster now."

Durki turned and watched as an enormous hulk, garbed in the yellow-and-green stripes of the freaks, reeled out from between two buildings and staggered onto the wharf. Under the fellow's left arm were two large jugs, while a third hung from a finger. He grasped a fourth jug with his massive right hand, taking gulps of the contents every few steps. Between gulps, he would wipe dry his black beard with the sleeve of his none too clean robe. Durki shook his head and looked at Pulsit. "To whom should I send your belongings?"

The freak pulled up next to the two storytellers and looked down upon them as he belched out a great cloud of sapwine fumes. Durki waved his arms and backed off. Raster smiled, exposing teeth that might more properly be called "slabs." "I apologize, Pulsit, for making you wait." He sloshed the jug in his right hand. "It took me considerable time to convince Fungarat the merchant to leave his bed and sell me this medicine." Raster raised an eyebrow and leaned toward Durki. "To keep off the sea's chill."

Pulsit held up a hand. "No apology is necessary, Raster. Which boat is yours?" Pulsit waved his hand in the direction of the many sleek sailing vessels belonging to the fishers of Sina. Raster squinted his bleary eyes in the indicated direction, then shook his head. He took a step toward the edge of the wharf, bent over and pointed, jug still in hand. "There." Pulsit and Durki looked down and observed the craft Raster indicated. The single-masted wooden craft wallowed next to the pilings amongst the garbage discarded by the other ships. If it had ever been painted, the paint was gone. Tatters of ropes hung from mast and railings, while coils and tangles of rope littered the few places on the deck not occupied with piles of empty brown jugs. On the boat's stern, lettered in fading yellow paint, was her name, *Queen of Sina.*

Durki took in the sight and nodded. "You spoke the truth, Pulsit. It will not be suicide; it will be murder!"

Raster jumped from the wharf onto the *Queen's* deck, and the two storytellers held their breaths while the small boat rocked under the force of the freak's landing. Raster kept his feet and walked forward to the tiny cabin to store his medicine. Pulsit stood and placed a hand on Durki's shoulder. "You will not join me in my adventure, then?"

"I am only an apprentice storyteller, Pulsit. It would take the great magician Fyx, himself, to survive a voyage in that leaking tub."

Pulsit dropped his hand. "Very well. Good-bye, Durki, and I hope you can find another master before too long." The master storyteller went to a ladder and began climbing down to the boat.

Durki leaned over the edge of the wharf. "Another master? Pulsit, where am I to find a master with this voice of mine? Come back, you old fool! The fish will eat you, you know that?"

Pulsit reached the level of the *Queen of Sina* and jumped over the side, stumbled and fell on the deck. He stood and arranged his robe. Raster stumbled out of the cabin and began pulling on a rope. A once-white sail, now decorated in black and grey-green mildew, commenced its halting journey to the top of the mast. Pulsit waved, then turned and went into the cabin. Still holding the rope, Raster looked up at Durki and threw a few coppers up on the wharf. "Release the lines, will you?"

"You would make me an accomplice to murder?" Durki snorted, stooped over and picked up the coppers. After he had stuffed them into his purse, he went to the pilings fore and aft, lifted the frayed rope ends and let them splash into the water. As the sail reached the top of the mast, its triangle filled with a gentle breeze and began drawing the boat away from the wharf. Durki looked up at the clear sky, muttered either an oath or a prayer, then scampered down the ladder and jumped onto the deck of the *Queen of Sina*.

Raster secured the mast line and weaved over to where Durki kept a wistful eye on the shrinking houses of Sina. "If you are coming, Durki, it will cost you fifty coppers, the same as your master."

Durki turned and glowered at the freak. "You get my coppers, Raster, when I reach my destination alive!"

Raster shrugged. "Fair enough." The freak went back to secure the tiller.

Durki looked back toward Sina, sickeningly confident that his fifty coppers were as safe as if they were on loan to a cashier from Tarzak.

That night, the Town of Sina long gone from view, the *Queen of Sina* pitched and plowed through the dark, shrieking outrages of a summer storm at sea. Durki, his face a delicate hue of yellow-green, turned from the tiny glassed-in porthole and watched Raster take a gulp from a jug. The three adventurers sat upon built-in benches surrounding a rough plank table that occupied most of the cabin. A fishoil lamp swung and sputtered above the table, emitting an evil smell. Raster belched, and Durki's shade changed to green-yellow. Durki pointed aft with a shaking finger. "Raster . . . who is steering this misbegotten thing?"

"Steering?" Raster scratched his head, then shrugged. "I know not, Durki." Raster pointed at Pulsit, Durki, and himself, in turn. "One, two, three. We are all here; then no one should be steering."

The apprentice storyteller plunked his elbows on the table and gently lowered his face into his hands. "Tell me, oh great man of the sea, what is to keep us from swamping or piling up on some rocks?"

Raster shook his head. "It is a good question, Durki."

The freak smiled and held out his hands. "But, I have never been one for intellectual talk—"

"By the crossed eyes of the Jumbo!" Durki lowered his hands. "Raster, why aren't *you* out there steering?"

Raster grinned and slapped the table top, causing everything upon it, including Durki's elbows, to leap in the air a hand's breadth. "Hah! By my coppers, that's one I can answer! I would get wet."

"Wet? *Wet!*"

Pulsit placed a gentle hand upon Durki's shoulder. "Calm yourself. I believe Raster has secured the tiller. This fine ship can steer itself, you see?"

"See?"

Pulsit nodded and held out his other hand toward Raster. "Our captain says we are days away from any land or rocks—"

"Days?" Durki grabbed his mouth with both hands, swung his feet over his bench plank and rushed through the cabin door, out onto the deck. Raster stood, reached out a long arm, and pulled the cabin door shut. He seated himself, hefted his jug and took a long pull.

Pulsit stretched his arms, clasped his hands behind his head, and leaned back against the cabin wall. "Ah, my captain, I can feel my storyteller's blood stirring already. This will be a fine adventure." He brought his hands down and cocked his head. "Listen!" A long, low moan could be heard. "Listen to it wail. Is it a sea dragon? The ghosts of a stricken ship?"

Raster lowered his jug and pointed an ear in the direction of the sound. "It's Durki. He's got the shipslops."

Pulsit sighed. "Of course, Raster, of course. But the mournfulness of it—doesn't it stoke up your imagination?"

Raster took another pull from his own brand of fuel, lowered the jug and listened to the apprentice retching, cursing, and wailing at the wind. The freak nodded. "Now that you point it out, Pulsit, it does sound . . . well, the way I always thought of the slave souls sounding."

Pulsit raised his brows. "Slave souls?"

Raster shook his head. "Only a myth of the fishers in these parts. The slave souls were victims the sorcerer pirate Bloody Buckets enchanted, then strapped to his mainmast to keep watch."

Pulsit rubbed his hands as Durki gave out with another moan. "Bloody Buckets! Excellent!" A dreamy look came into the storyteller's eyes. He spread his arms. "The tormented souls of Bloody Bucket's victims howled a warning, that wind and storm driven night, as the . . ." Pulsit lowered his hands and looked at Raster. "What was the ship's name?"

"Ship?"

"Bloody Bucket's ship."

Raster wrinkled up his face in confusion. "I told you, Pulsit; it's only a myth."

"I know, but I am a storyteller. I must let my imagination run free. Here we can take myth, coat it with belief, and make a story—no, *live* a story!" Pulsit reached out and picked up Raster's jug and took a gulp. He replaced the jug, shook his head and held up a finger. "The ship."

Raster warmed to the task and rubbed his hands together. "The *Black Tide* is his ship; the foulest most evil barge upon the water."

"A great name." Durki issued another moan. "Captain! Captain Buckets! What does the watch say?" Pulsit nodded toward Raster. "You shall be Bloody Buckets."

Raster grinned. "Then, mate, call me 'Bloody.' I lay bare the guts of any swab what calls me 'Buckets.' " Raster took another pull from his jug as Durki howled again. The jug dropped to the table as Raster held his hand to his ear. "Avast! Mate, avast there!"

Pulsit finished another gulp at the jug. "Aye, Bloody, what be it?"

Raster waved his hand above his head. "The wretches up there signal us of an approaching prize. Call out the hands!"

"Aye, Bloody." Pulsit pushed open a porthole glass and shouted. "All hands on deck! Bloody has need of your evil hands and steel blades." Above the port, a scream, then a whimper evidenced that Durki had not yet been washed overboard. "The crew is assembled, Bloody."

Raster glared at the wall. "Aye, and a scurvy lot they are too." The freak looked around the cabin, and pulled loose two narrow planks that served as trim between the wall and overhead. He handed one to Pulsit. "Your blade, mate."

Pulsit stood and swung the plank around his head. "It shall be always in your evil service, Bloody."

Raster swung his own plank, tried to stand, but staggered back against the wall. "Avast, ye swabs! On the horizon sails a fat merchantman. Helmsman, aim the *Black Tide* down her gullet, and you line monkeys—up top! Stay the mainsheets, matten down the batch covers and mizzle the fizzenmast! Har! There shall be rapine, loot, and killing for all before the sun sets—" Raster stabbed a thumb into his own chest. "Or my name ain't Bloody Buckets."

They both dropped down on the benches and refueled on sapwine. After an impressive pull, Raster placed the jug on the table. "What now?"

Pulsit nodded. "The other ship—what shall we call it?"

Raster rubbed his chin. "Should it be a special name?"

"Yes. The *Black Tide* is evil. To fight evil, we must have good. The name of the merchantman must reflect good."

Raster nodded. "The *Honor Bright,* carrying a cargo of . . . " His bleary eyes fell upon his jug. "Medicine to ease the sufferings of a stricken city."

Pulsit clapped his hands and missed. "Excellent, and I shall captain the *Honor Bright.* Captain John Fine is my name."

Raster weaved to his feet, shielded his eyes from an imaginary sun with one hand and pointed with another. "Captain Fine! Captain Fine! Abaft the bort peam, there!"

"Aye, Mister Trueheart? What is it?"

"Captain, bearing down on us is a pirate ship." Raster fell back against the wall and held his hand to his neck. "The *Black Tide!*"

Pulsit stood next to Raster and placed an arm around his huge shoulders. A hint of a smile played on the storyteller's lips. "Have courage, Mister Trueheart. Our ship is fast, and our crew is the finest to be found in any port."

"But, Captain, it is Bloody Buckets!" Durki issued a drawn-out howl. "Listen! Hear his ghost watch!" The sound diminished to a moan, then to a whimper.

Pulsit nodded gravely. "The poor souls. But stiffen your spine, Mister, else we shall fail and a city will die."

Raster pushed himself away from the wall, held his plank before him and nodded. "Aye, Captain. I am all right now."

Pulsit looked at his own plank and turned to Raster. "We must have blood. What do you have?"

Raster turned to a locker next to the cabin door, stooped and opened it. With both hands he emptied the locker of odd bits of line, empty brown jugs, a half-bolt of sailcloth, paint-caked brushes, and finally a large closed bucket of paint. "Here it is. I must use this to mark my trapbuoys."

"What color is it?"

Raster opened the wooden top, and stood out of the way. The paint was bright scarlet. "And, there is your blood."

Pulsit closed his eyes and held out his hands. "Although the *Honor Bright* was swift, the *Black Tide* quickly closed the distance, driven by Bloody Bucket's sorcery. Grappling hooks flew from the pirate ship, and in moments, the two ships were bound together. Bloody's crew swarmed over the side." Pulsit dipped his plank into the paint and jumped up on one of the benches. "Defend yourself, Bloody!"

Raster dipped his plank and mounted the bench on the opposite side of the table. "Hah, Captain Fine! I'll have yer soul strapped to my mizzenmast, or me name ain't Bloody Buckets!" The freak lunged at the storyteller, slapping his arm with the plank. "First blood!"

Pulsit diverted the next blow, but Raster's onslaught drove the storyteller to the door of the cabin. As he narrowly avoided a killing blow, Pulsit drove in and poked Raster in the stomach. "Hah, Bloody! Take that!"

Raster picked up the paint and sloshed it down his front.

"Curses, Fine! Ye have marked me, that's true. But, I am Bloody Buckets, with the strength of ten!"

"Then, up with your blade, pirate, and have at it!" Pulsit swung, knocking the bucket across the cabin, splattering them both, as well as the cabin, with paint. As Raster stepped into a large puddle of paint, he slipped and came crashing down on the deck. Pulsit leaped to the fallen freak's side, lifted his plank, and brought it down next to Raster's neck in a mock beheading. "And, die, Bloody Buckets! Die!" Pulsit stood and looked in the direction of the overhead. "And Captain Fine, wounded and bleeding, stood atop the deck of the *Honor Bright,* his victory sweet on his tongue, while the flesh of the evil pirate grew cold." Pulsit listened and could hear nothing but the creaks of the ship, the shrieks of the wind and the snores of Raster. "And, at last, poor souls, you are free!" The storyteller backed up against a wall, slid down, and passed out.

Durki opened the cabin door, stepped inside and saw both his master and the fisher on the deck, soaked in red. More red covered the walls, table and overhead. "Whoops!" Durki covered his mouth and staggered back on deck. In moments the moans of the slave souls once more stole across the waters.

The next morning, the waves of the night before calmed to gentle swells, Durki pushed himself up from the railing and placed his hands gently against his aching ribs. He thought upon it for a moment, then concluded that his stomach had finally given in to its fate. He looked around the deck, found a canvas bucket attached to a rope, then picked it up and drew some sea water. He splashed it over his head, rubbed his face and dried it in the gentle wind coming from the northwest. "Perhaps," he said to the fingernail of new sun coming over the horizon, "perhaps this will not be so bad after all." He turned and walked forward of the cabin, coming to a halt at the ship's prow. The *Queen of Sina* dipped into the gentle swells ever so slightly, and Durki was delighted at the lack of response from his bowels. "An adventure will do much to fuel my own storyteller's imagination. I now understand torment."

Durki clasped his hands behind his back, assumed a deep frown, and began pacing back and forth in front of the cabin. "This is a king's man of war, Ponsonberry, not a pleasure ship! I *said* fifty lashes, and I *meant* fifty lashes! Now, strip that wretch to the bones, and be quick about it lest you find yourself touched by the cat!"

Durki stopped, turned, and held out his hands. "Captain Cruel, I would rather stand the lashes myself, than subject an innocent man to them."

"You would, eh, Ponsonberry! Then order back the master at arms. It would never do to have a common seaman lay bare the back of a king's officer. *I will swing the cat myself!*"

A thumping came from the deck. "Have mercy, Durki, and still your mouth!"

Durki squatted next to one of the cabin ports. "Ah, Raster, you besotted freak. You are up then?"

"Of course I'm up, and with a head the size of the universe!"

Durki snorted. "You must pay the price for your ways, Raster." He heard a scuffle from inside the cabin, then Raster speaking Pulsit's name. "Raster, what is it?"

The freak's face, eyes as red as the paint splashed on his skin, appeared in the porthole. "Come down quick, Durki. I think your master is dying."

Durki and Raster sat on opposite sides of the table, while on the third bench, his face drawn and grey, Pulsit lay prone, covered with sailcloth up to his neck. His grizzled head rocked from side to side with the motion of the ship. Durki turned away and closed his eyes. *Amar looked down at the broken body of the great flyer Danto, then up at the trapeze, still swaying against the canvas of the big top. He looked one more time at Danto, then begin climbing the ladder, ignoring the pain from his crippled left leg. "The crowd was told they'd see the backwards quadruple tonight, and if it takes my last breath, they will!"*

"Durki, what are you mumbling about?" Raster gulped from his jug and slammed the container on the table.

Durki shrugged. "I was thinking. The deathwatch is an old story."

"Too depressing. I like stories with action, glitter, and pretty girls." Raster belched.

"Aren't you soaking up the sapwine a little early?"

Raster shrugged. "A scale from the dragon that bit me." The freak cocked his head at Pulsit's quiet form. "Your master, do you think he will be all right?"

Durki shook his head. "I don't know. He is an old man."

They gathered like vultures around the old man's deathbed, rubbing their hands, smiling to each other in secret, counting their inheritances before the body grew cold . . . " Durki reached for the jug, took a gulp, and replaced the container on the table. "You are right, Raster. This is too depressing. What would you like to talk about?"

Raster rubbed his chin and raised his eyebrows. "What do you think about the new ambassador to Momus—the one from the Tenth Quadrant?"

Durki shrugged. "I am a storyteller, Raster, not a newsteller. I do not follow politics."

Raster laughed. "Neither am I a newsteller, but I take an interest in whether or not I will become a slave."

"What are you talking about?"

"The ambassador—a Vorilian, lnak by name—is in Tarzak right now. He would get the Great Ring to vote away the defenders from the Ninth Quadrant and accept those from the Tenth."

Durki rubbed his chin. "What do the defenders from the Ninth Quadrant defend us from?"

"Why, from the Tenth Quadrant, of course."

Durki shrugged. "Then, if we were defended by the Tenth, we would be safe, wouldn't we?"

Raster frowned, held up a finger, then dropped it. He shook his head. "Our statesman, Allenby, doesn't see it that way. He thinks we must keep the Vorilians away from Momus. I agree."

Durki waved his hand impatiently. "Let's talk of other things, Raster. This holds no interest for me."

"No interest?" Raster held out his hands, his eyebrows arched in wonder. "Things are happening that will change the courses of planets—of quadrants, or perhaps the entire galaxy! Your storyteller's blood is thin indeed if it cannot draw inspiration from such events."

"As I said, I am no newsteller." Durki reached for the jug.

"You mean to say that the idea of a great war—perhaps one in space—is of no interest to a storyteller?"

Durki put down the jug, turned his face to the overhead and closed his eyes. *Tadja jetted to one side as the Vorilian glop fiend's bolt sped past. The vapor trail from a passing ship obscured his vision as he tried to sight his weapon on the Vorilian* . . . Durki looked back at the jug, then shrugged. "Stories like that might interest some, but I don't think you'll find them among the better sorts of people."

Raster frowned, then stabbed himself in his chest with his thumb. "*I* like stories like that!"

Durki nodded. "I rest my case. You see, Raster, most of the listeners we storytellers have at fires along the road, or in the squares of the large towns, don't happen to be wine soaked, overmuscled, frustrated freaks." Durki raised his eyebrows. "No offense."

Raster grabbed the jug, stood and stomped to the cabin door. "I must go on deck."

The door slammed behind the freak, and Durki turned toward Pulsit as his master began mumbling and moaning. "Pulsit?"

"Durki . . . is that you?" The old man's voice was weak.

"Yes. Are you all right? How do you feel?"

Pulsit reached out a hand and grasped the front of Durki's robe. "Did you see him? Where's the body?"

"Him? See who?"

"Bloody Buckets. We fought all night." Pulsit relaxed his grip and fell back onto the bench. "Ah, it was glorious!"

Durki stared. "*Humor him, doctor, otherwise the maniac will kill us all!*"

"Did, uh, Mister Buckets fight well, Pulsit?"

The old man cackled. "Did he fight well? Look at me, you fool! Anyone who could put Captain John Fine on his back fights well!" Pulsit's eyes rolled up, then the old man relaxed and fell asleep.

Durki shook his head. *"You lock me behind these doors, thou cowering knave in white! But, who is to judge the sane? Are you locking me away from the sane? Or, are you keeping me safe from all those out there? That is it, isn't it? I am the last sane man in the world—ha, ha, ha, ha, ha . . . "*

For the next few days, Pulsit raved, Raster swilled, and Durki wretched their collective way across the Sea of Baraboo until they came in sight of the continent of Midway. Actually, it was the *Queen of Sino* that came in sight of Midway, rather than her passengers, since Raster's state of constant blindness relieved itself only for as long as it took to find more medicine. Pulsit, of course, lay on his bench in the cabin, traveling the bruised reaches of his mind, while Durki hung from the railing, praying for death. The continent of Midway was named in honor of the collection of sideshows that filled the hold of the lone shuttle stranded there in the disaster of the circus ship *Baraboo.* It was isolated from the rest of the planet Momus. Few ships came to its shores, which caused the inhabitants of the coastal village of Mbwebwe to gather on the beach as the *Queen* came into view. Since the original inhabitants of Midway were comprised of a troupe of Ubangi Savages who also did seconds as Wild Men Of Borneo, and another troupe of acrobatic midgets, it was a curious lot that stood upon the beach examining the *Queen.* After a time, Azongo, the village headman, came to the obvious conclusion. He looked down at Myte, the meter-tall village priest, and held out his arm toward the approaching ship. "It is obvious, Myte. That unfortunate vessel has been attacked by sea pirates. Look at its tatters of rope and sail, and the rotting bodies draped over railings and deck."

In the cabin, Pulsit sat on his bench, peered through one of the front portholes, and also came to the obvious conclusions. *Cannibals!* His eyes went from the dark savages with their great shaggy heads, to the lighter-skinned midgets that stood beside them. *Giant cannibals!*

Pulsit leaned against the cabin wall and held a hand against his forehead. *What am I doing here? My crew depends upon me—and that city! We haven't delivered the medicine for that city . . . city—why can't I remember its name?* The old man's hand dropped to his lap, he turned his head and looked out of the porthole. The inhabitants of Mbwebwe were moving closer to the water. *The cannibals are attacking, and my crew without a leader!* Pulsit weaved to his feet, pushed his way across the cabin, and picked up a paint-smeared plank leaning in the corner. He hefted it and swung it about his head. *As long as I have breath in my body and a blade in my hand, John Fine is not defeated. I'll not have my crew garnished for a savage's gullet!*

Pulsit opened the cabin door, pulled himself up the four steps to the deck, then swooned against the roof of the cabin. "Mister Trueheart! Where be you, man? Call the hands on deck! Stand by to repel boarders!"

Raster pushed from his face the pile of rags and ropes he had covered himself with the night before, opened his eyes, and saw a gaunt visage standing over him shouting and swinging a bloody blade. His eyes opened wide, and he pushed himself back in fear. His mouth worked a silent scream as he saw the tangle of ropes on his legs and feet. "Snakes! Oh, merciful Momus, God of Ridicule, spare me!" Raster bounded off the deck, throwing the ropes aside, then ran to the railing and flung himself over the side.

"Mister Trueheart!" Pulsit staggered to the railing and watched Raster swim toward the shore. "Trueheart, you coward! Come back and stand your ground, man!" The bottom of the *Queen* grounded, knocking Pulsit off his feet.

As he pulled himself up, he looked over the railing to see the inhabitants of Mbwebwe wading toward the ship. He backed up against the cabin, then turned and ran to the other side of the ship. *More cannibals! Waves of them!* He saw Durki hung over the railing and swatted the apprentice across the buttocks with the plank. "Awake, there, crewman! Arm yourself!"

Durki moaned, opened his eyes and saw the golden beach and trees of the village. "Land! Dry, hard, solid land!" He smiled, pulled himself over the railing, and fell into the shallow water with a smack. Pulsit looked down to see Durki wading toward shore.

What is this? Do I command nothing but cowards? Do the gods test my courage with these things? First one brown hand, then another and another grasped the railing. Pulsit smacked one with his plank, heard a curse, followed immediately by a splash. "Hah! Defend your heathen selves!" Pulsit ran up and down the railing, smacking hands with the plank and glorying in the curses and sounds of bodies falling into the drink. "If he need must, John Fine shall take on your entire cannibal nation!" For a moment, no new hands appeared on the railing, and Pulsit leaned over the side to see the last of the dark natives wading away from the *Queen*. The old man raised a fist toward the shore and shook it. "I am Captain John

Fine, commander of the *Honor Bright!* I cannot be defeated! I say this to you: Send me *more* cannibals!"

He tossed his head back to laugh, then felt strong arms grasp him from behind. He turned his head to see dark faces and shaggy heads swarming over the deck. *I am captured!* The plank was taken from his hand, and he felt himself being moved to the other side of the ship, lifted over the railing, and lowered into waiting brown arms. *Still, I am John Fine!* "Hear me, you heathen devils!"

"I beg your pardon!" answered one.

"Do not trust your mouths when they water for this body! You shall choke on John Fine!" Pulsit laughed, then became quiet as a great darkness came over him. Those who carried him exchanged puzzled looks, then shrugged and headed toward the beach.

Even though he eyed the food suspiciously and had developed the habit of jumping at the slightest sound, Pulsit appeared well enough by that evening to join his companions at Azongo's table. Coppers were exchanged for the repast, and Durki felt blessed as he enjoyed the packed feeling of the first solid food he had been able to hold down for days. But, recalling his own screech of a voice, he listened with envy as Azongo conversed in rich resonant tones. As a pause in the conversation came, Durki nodded toward the headman. "I would give much to have been born with a voice such as yours, Azongo."

The headman laughed, exposing a glare of teeth filed to needle points. "So would I, storyteller. But, I was not born with this sound. It came only after long practice for my wild man act."

Durki looked around the table, then turned back to Azongo. "Since we are finished eating, I would lay a few coppers in your palm to see your act."

Raster waved his hand and shook his head. "I've seen several wild man acts, and they are good sleeping aids, but nothing for an evening's entertainment. They couldn't scare a child."

Azongo raised his eyebrows. "And, freak, would you care to wager your coppers on that?"

"No, but I'll stake a jug of sapwine against a jug of this cobit brew of yours." Raster held up his cup.

Azongo rubbed his chin, then nodded. "Done." He reached forward and extinguished the oil lamp in the center of the table, leaving only a single lamp on the wall to illuminate the room. He stood, turned his back on his dinner guests, and removed his robe. "Hhuurrraaaaggh!" Azongo leaped about in a crouch, his body scarred and tattooed in bright, fantastic patterns, his face contorted such that his eyes and filed teeth seemed larger than life. In the flickering half-light of the lamp, there was little doubt that the creature before them was a primitive, unreasoning machine of blood lust, coiled and ready to strike. Azongo leaped over the low table and landed next to Raster with his hands held forward, claws extended. "Aarrrgggh!"

Raster backed up against the adobe wall of the room. "Very well, Azongo! Enough!"

The headman relit the table lamp, collected his coppers and sapwine, then returned to his place. Pulsit watched all of this, but kept his silence. *The natives are restless. When the time is ripe, I must try to convince them that I am a god.*

Raster shook his head. "Even the wild man act of the Tarzak freaks does not compare to your performance, Azongo. If you came back with us to the Central Continent, you could gather coppers by the sackful."

"Indeed."

Raster nodded. "But the act is only better, not very different." He rubbed his chin. "What you need is a victim. Play out a drama of life-and-death." Raster nodded again. "Yes, that would put the act in the Great Square in Tarzak."

Azongo sipped at his cup, mulling over Raster's words.

"It would do me good to make my living with an act again." He held out his hands. "Since we are mostly all wild men, there is little demand for such an act here. And, there are others better than I. Being headman of this village is the only way I can keep a roof over my head." Azongo lowered his hands and shrugged. "But, where *would* I find such a victim?"

Raster stuck his thumb in his chest. "Me." He leaned forward. "I am a strongman with the Sina freaks, but there are many who are stronger, and with better acts. My pitiful performance as a fisher is all that allows me to keep myself in sapwine. But, together we shall become rich." Raster turned toward Durki. "Durki, do you think your master would devise a story for Azongo and I to act out?"

Durki turned his head and looked at Pulsit. The old storyteller stared with unseeing eyes at the lamp on the table. Durki looked back at Raster and shrugged. "Pulsit is still in the grip of his imagination. If he were well, he could devise a fine story."

Azongo scratched his head, then pointed a finger at Durki. "There is talk of a doctor two day's ride from here."

"Will he treat my master?"

Azongo nodded. "It is said that the doctor treats those who come to him in exchange for plants and animals. It is also said that he has seven fingers on each hand."

Raster shrugged. "That is nothing. Vorub of the Tarzak freaks has sixteen fingers, yet he cannot make a living at it. "

"You do not understand, Raster." Azongo lowered his voice. "The talk is that the doctor does not come from the planet Momus."

"Is he a Vorilian?"

Azongo shrugged. "It is all talk. Still, he may be able to help your master. If Pulsit becomes well and writes Raster and I a story, we can put together a great act."

Durki nodded. "Perhaps the doctor can do something for my voice as well."

Azongo laughed. "That I can do. You must exercise your voice by forcing the air out of your body sharply, and growling with your throat, like this." Azongo took a deep breath, then forced it out. "Hhhoooowaughhhh!" the headman nodded. "It will thicken up your voice if you practice it every chance you get. Try it."

Durki took a deep breath. "Hoowah."

Pulsit's eyes came to life, darting between Durki and Azongo. *What is this? What heathen ritual?*

Azongo shook his head. "You must force the air out faster. Hhhoooowaughhhh!"

"Hhoowahh!"

"Hhhoooowaughhhh!"

"Hhooowaugh!"

"Much better." He nodded toward Raster. "If you are to be my victim, you will need a good scream. Try this." Azongo took another breath. "Aaaaaah!"

Raster nodded. "Aye, it chills the bones." He took a deep breath. "Aaaaaaah!"

As the three screamed and growled, a tear trickled down Pulsit's cheek. *The peasants of the field—listen to them suffer the tortures of the damned! Look. beyond! A dragon! What horror!*

"Hhhoooowaughhhh!"

"Aaaaaaaaah!"

Pulsit weaved to his feet and placed a hand on Raster's shoulder. His other hand held an imaginary lance in Azongo's direction. "Fear not, sweet maiden, for I, the Golden Knight, shall slay yon dragon and lay its carcass at your feet!"

Azongo leaned forward and spoke to Durki. "Is your master well enough to tell us a story?"

Durki sighed. "This is no story to Pulsit's troubled mind, but reality. He sees the dragon—" He nodded toward Raster. "And the maiden."

Azongo shook his head. "With the morning's light, then, we shall set off to find this strange doctor."

Two days ride from Mbwebwe, deep in the Donniker Basin, stood a compound surrounded by tall, vine-hung saptrees. Surrounding the compound were tall metal fences, the enclosed area being divided again and again into smaller areas containing representatives of Momus's peculiar life forms. In its center stood a blue metal building from which curious apparatus bristled, giving the structure the appearance of a bowl-cut porcupine. Inside, Doctor Shart clasped his seven-fingered hands together and groveled before an image on his laboratory's telescreen.

"All I need is a little more time, Ambassador Inak. If I can have just a little more time—"

"Enough!" The image scowled, then pointed a couple of fingers at Shart. "I don't know what halfwit approved the funding for your project, Shart, but when the Council of Warlords receives my report, someone is in for a roasting!"

Shart wrung his hands together. "Inak, the experiments are very complicated, and I am the only one at the station. If you could see your way clear to approving my request for an assistant—"

The image raised its thin yellow brows. "You astound me! You expect the Tenth Quadrant to expend *more* monies in support of your demented theories? Fantasy. Utter and complete fantasy!"

"Inak, just think of the benefits to the government if I am successful.

Think of being able to control the entire animal population of a planet. Think of it—being able to spread diseases at will using specially adapted carriers—"

"Think of it?" Inak's brows dropped into a frown. "That's all we can do, Shart, is think about it. We certainly haven't seen any results."

Shart smiled and held his hands out at his sides. "If the Ambassador will remember, the Warlords looked favorably upon my project. It would place a great weapon in their hands, and—"

"Only if you begin getting results, Shart. No more of this—when will you have something positive that I can report?"

Shart shrugged. "Perhaps . . . thirty days. My experiment on the virus is almost completed. After that, it's just a matter of tuning and adjusting the control banks."

Ambassador Inak rubbed his pointed chin, then nodded toward Shart. "Perhaps, then, we will be able to send a very glowing report to the Warlords. Yes, that will be just about right."

"If I might inquire, Inak, right for what?"

"The commission from the United Quadrants will be here soon, and then there will be a long period of investigation and negotiation. Allenby, the puppet of the Ninth Quadrant, refuses to consider our proposal . . . " Inak leaned forward. "But, if I can show the Great Statesman of Momus that not accepting our proposal would bring disaster to his people . . . Do you get my meaning?"

"I will do my best, Inak—"

"No, Shart! You will succeed!" The image faded and the screen went blank.

Shart placed the thumb of his right hand against the tip of his nose and wiggled the remaining six fingers in the direction of the screen. "Yaaaaaaaah!" He dropped his hand and half turned away when the automatic sensor alarm began to buzz. "What now?" He sighed, then switched the function selector on the screen control. Four figures, riding in one of the clumsy Moman lizard carts, were approaching the station. "Not another patient." Shart shook his head, then remembered toying with the idea of training a Moman to handle the multitude of simple tasks around the laboratory that ate up his time. Now that Inak had turned down his latest request for an assistant, and had stepped up the timetable, what choice had he?

Shart deenergized his screen, then turned and entered a corridor leading to the side of the compound facing the road. At the end of the corridor, he opened the door and stepped outside. Immediately, his sense of hearing was assaulted by screams and growls. He narrowed his eyes and examined the travelers. In the rear of the cart, one of the local wild men, a large man in yellow-and-green stripes and a short, fat man in purple, screamed and growled at each other. Off to one side, a quiet old man, also in purple, seemed to be nodding off. Shart rubbed his hands together. "Excellent!"

The cart pulled to a stop in front of the doctor, and the huge lizard that provided the vehicle's motive power sat down and held out its right front foot, palm up. "Anow here. Payup."

The wild man jumped from the cart, then caught a sack thrown to him by the large man in green and yellow. The sack was handed to the lizard, and Shart watched as the lizard reached into the sack and began stuffing fat cobit roots into its mouth. The wild man kicked the lizard. "Look, you wait. Understand?"

The lizard nodded without looking up from the sack. " 'Stand."

The wild man walked around the lizard and came to a stop in front of the Vorilian. "Doctor? I understand that you will treat patients for a fee."

Shart looked from the wild man to the pair screaming and growling in the cart, then back to the wild man. "What seems to be their trouble?"

The wild man looked confused, then he laughed. "There is nothing wrong with them, doctor. They practice their acts. Your patient is the old one. His name is Pulsit. The two in the back are Durki and Raster, and I am Azongo of the Mbwebwe wild men, also headman of that village."

Shart frowned, then nodded. "What is the old one's trouble?"

Azongo whirled a finger next to his head. "He sees things."

Shart waved a hand at the cart. "Bring him down from there, and let me look at him."

Azongo held up a hand. "One moment, doctor. What is your charge? We were told by the villagers at the base of the plateau that you desire plants and animals."

Shart shrugged. "I have no need of such things now. But, I will look at him all the same."

Azongo frowned. "You mean you will treat him for *nothing?*"

Shart remembered that, in the curious reaches of the Moman mind, a service not charged for is worthless. If he charged nothing, he would lose his patient—and, possibly, his head. "Of course not. I must have money—those little copper things."

"How many?"

Shart rubbed his narrow chin. "Twenty-five."

On the cart, the one called Durki reached into the old one's robe and withdrew a small sack. He turned to Azongo. "Pulsit has only twenty-three coppers on him."

Shart nodded. "That will do."

Azongo backed up and rubbed his own chin. "Well, Doctor, what *is* your price? I expect such haggling in the market, but from a doctor, I expect a firm price for a specific service."

Shart sighed. "Of course. My price is twenty-five, but surely between the three of you, another two coppers can be produced."

Azongo shook his head. "Buying roots for the lizard cleaned us out. Can Pulsit owe you the remaining two coppers?"

"Of course."

"At what rate of interest?"

"N-n-n . . . " Shart stopped himself from saying "none."

"What was that, Doctor?"

"Nine."

"Nine! Nine percent!" Azongo pulled on his lower lip, then shrugged. "Very well." The wild man motioned to the others in the cart. "Lower him down."

Shart and the wild man steadied Pulsit as he came down, and immediately the doctor began examining Pulsit's head. Well above the old man's hairline, he found a large, dark bruise. Azongo folded his arms. "How long will it take? Should we wait?"

"No. It will take some time. You and your friends go back. I'll send him along when he is well."

Azongo shook his head. "How will he pay for the return trip?"

Shart's black eyes bugged. "By the spirits!" He turned toward Azongo. "By then he will be well enough to negotiate his own loan!"

The wild man nodded and held out his hand. "Here."

"What's that?"

"Your coppers."

Shart held out his hand, took the coppers and watched while the wild man climbed back up into the cart, picked up a plank, and swatted the lizard. "On to Mbwebwe!"

The lizard lifted an eyebrow, checked the sack to make sure it was empty, then tossed it aside and began moving the cart around. As the cart pulled out of sight, Shart threw the twenty-three coppers into the grass, then led the old man into the corridor.

Pulsit awakened and found himself in a small room containing only a cot and a small table cluttered with medical-looking things. Images of pirates, cannibals, and dragons flashed through his mind, but he could distinguish them from the world of fact. He assigned the images to his story mill, sighed at his new feeling of well-being, then swung his legs to the floor and sat up.

"Ah! I see you are awake."

Pulsit's eyes widened as he looked around at the empty room. *The ghost of Harvey Marpole leered at the new victim, seated helpless, alone—trapped. Cold, rotting, unseen hands reached for William's throat. Fingers of ice closed around vessels of pulsing blood, stemming their flow. They pressed against the path that air must take to feed William's lungs, ending it . . .*

Pulsit jumped as the door opened and Doctor Shart entered. "It is good that you are better. Come, we have much work to do."

Pulsit frowned. "Eh?"

Shart pushed seven-fingered hands into the pockets of his lab coat and looked down his pointed nose at the Moman. "It is my fee for making you well. You are to work for me."

"Work for you? I agreed to this?"

"Yes."

The storyteller frowned, then nodded. "Well, if I agreed." He looked up at the Vorilian. "What kind of work is it?"

Shart pulled a hand from his pocket and motioned toward the door. "Come."

After being brought to the laboratory, Pulsit was introduced to his tasks, which consisted of operating the automatic glassware cleanser, changing and cleaning the complex's air filters, monitoring the vector-escape alarm system, laundry, and assorted tasks from filing to emptying the trash. Pulsit observed, listened, then nodded at the Vorilian. "Doctor, I can see that you are a great scientist with many important responsibilities. How is it that you have no assistants to perform these insignificant tasks?"

Shart shook his head, then nodded. "Even a Moman can understand, where the Warlords do not." The Vorilian sighed. "You must understand, Pulsit, that no one is more loyal to the Warlords of the Tenth Quadrant than I. But . . . " Shart shrugged, then held out his hands to indicate his laboratory. "This is the work of a lifetime—a lifetime of too little appreciated struggle and privation." The Vorilian walked to a rack of clear tubes that towered from the floor to the overhead. The tubes were coiled with dark wires and were filled with a pink, cloudy vapor. "Do you know what this is?"

Pulsit walked to the rack, stopped next to it, and shook his head. "I know not, Doctor."

Shart placed a hand on one of the braces supporting the tubes, and caressed it as he answered. "This . . . this is the work of thirty years—much of it financed out of my own meager resources. No one had my insight—my *vision!* As only a mere student at the Vorilian Academy of Total Warfare, I formed the theories that made all this possible." Shart made two fists and shook them. "But it took all these years to acquire for my effort the limited attention I now have. This station and myself for an assistant!"

Pulsit frowned and nodded. "Excellent."

Shart raised his brows. "Excellent?"

"I mean, your life—its circumstances—make excellent material for a storyteller."

"A what?"

Pulsit bowed. "I am Pulsit of the Sina storytellers." The old man stood up and rubbed his bearded chin. "I also do biographies." The storyteller held out a hand toward the rack. "What is this? To do your life and play it before the crowds on Momus, I should be familiar with your work."

Shart smiled, exposing his triple rows of pointed teeth.

"My life?"

"Certainly. The lives of great heroes are very popular. Your struggle, your achievement—these are the things of heroics."

Shart looked at the rack, then placed a hand on his cheek. "That's true, old Moman. A hero. Yes, that *is* true!" The Vorilian held out his hands toward the rack. "This is my work—a virus, each one for the infection of a different life form." Shart rubbed his hands together. "Once a life form is infected I can control it—make it do what I want, or go anywhere I choose. And, once a life form is infected, it will spread the virus among others of its kind. By directing the movements of just a few infected creatures, in time I will be able to control all the life forms on this planet—with the exception of the humans."

Pulsit raised his brows. "Quite an accomplishment! Indeed, yes. Quite an accomplishment. But, what could you do with such a power?"

Shart held out his hands. "If one controls the animal life on a planet, one controls the planet. Plagues can be directed to any part of the globe's surface, ecological balances disrupted, causing crop failures, great masses of predatory creatures can be used as an army to lay waste vast populations—Just think of the weapon it would make!"

Pulsit nodded. "It would have even more uses of a peaceful nature, Doctor."

Shart shrugged. "Yes, I suppose so, but the Warlords are interested in my work only as a weapon. Still, its success as a weapon will make my name. Then, perhaps, it can be incorporated into plans of a peaceful nature."

Pulsit held out his hands. "Doctor, as important and impressive as this work is, why do you not have at least one assistant?"

"Hah! The Warlords have no idea of the complications. This is why my work does not include the control of humans—the complications are too vast to untangle by myself. Each strain of the virus must be suited to each life form, which is difficult even for the simple creatures. My experiments take time, and the Warlords want results now." Shart shook his head. "They are skeptical of my work, and plan to cut off my funds if I can't show them . . . well, you understand."

Pulsit nodded. "Doctor Shart, I would like to tell the story of your life to the people along the roadside fires. To do this, I must know all about you."

Shart rubbed his hands together. "No one knows more than I that my story needs telling, Pulsit, but there is so much to do, and the Warlords—"

"Tut, tut, Doctor. These few tasks I am to do to work off my debt will not take up all of my time. I can work on your biography in my spare time."

Shart nodded, then grinned. "I have kept a daily journal since the Academy, and I have my old yearbooks—would they be of any assistance?"

Pulsit clapped his hands together. "Wonderful! Do you have them here?"

"Yes. One moment, and I'll get them." Shart turned and all but ran from the laboratory.

Pulsit walked once around the lab, his mind trying out bits and snatches of narrative. *Almost from his first day, the young Shart knew he was destined for greatness. What the brilliant Vorilian scientist did not know was how he would have to fight, claw, and struggle to achieve his due . . .* Pulsit nodded as he decided that the bio would find many willing listeners at the fires. "It will definitely play."

Pulsit stopped before a bank of dials, readouts, meters, and switches. The console had a swept panel that enabled an operator seated before it to reach and see all the controls easily. Mounted above the console was a large screen. "Hmmm." Pulsit stepped before the chair and lowered himself to the seat. *Captain Nova seated himself before the ship's controls, set his square-cut jaw, then placed a thick-knuckled hand on the override switches to the ship's reactors. He waited until the enemy formation swung, presenting its side to his ship, then he jammed the switches, throwing power to his engines. "Now, you'll see this possum come to life!" His hand flew among the controls, turning dials, flicking switches, forcing the ship to seek and destroy the enemy ships. Smoke filled the cockpit, and Captain Nova saw, almost too late, the enemy ship that had opened fire on him. Flicking another row of switches, Nova launched a salvo of torpedoes at the enemy, held his breath, then laughed as the rogue ship vaporized . . .*

"Wha . . . what are you doing?"

Pulsit turned to see Shart standing in a doorway with his arms loaded with books. The Vorilian was looking around at the laboratory, which Pulsit noticed was filled with a grey-yellow haze of smoke. The storyteller turned back to the console, then removed his fingers from it as though they had been burned. "I apologize, Doctor. I must have been carried away with a new kind of story I was thinking—"

Shart dropped the journals and yearbooks with a crash. "You . . . you tripped the vector purge!" He walked to the rack of tubes. The vapor inside was no longer pink; it was now grey. Shart shook his head, placed a hand on the rack brace, then leaned his weight against it. "The work of thirty years . . . gone. All gone."

Pulsit stood, walked over to the rack and placed a gentle hand upon Shart's shoulder. "I am very sorry, Doctor. Had I the coppers, I would lay a handsome apology in your hand."

"Gone. All gone."

"But, Doctor—" Pulsit rubbed his hands together, then slapped Shart's back. "Just think how this will help your biography."

Shart looked at Pulsit, a dazed expression on his face. "Help?"

"Indeed!" Pulsit held out his hands. "So close to success, only to have victory snatched from you. The determined scientist, however, is not defeated. He gathers himself together and begins again the task." Pulsit patted the Vorilian on the back. "It does much to strengthen the hero's character, don't you think?"

Shart pushed himself away from the rack, stared at Pulsit with ever-widening eyes, then began patting his pockets. "My gun! Where is it? Where's my gun?"

Pulsit looked around the laboratory. "I don't know, Doctor. Where did you have it last?" The storyteller turned and began looking in the vicinity of the swept control console. "When we have a spare moment, Doctor, I have a new kind of story I'd like to discuss with you. As a scientist, your opinion would be very useful." Pulsit took a last look, shrugged, then turned around. "I don't see your gun over here, Doc—" The old man saw Shart, gun in hand, taking aim between the storyteller's eyes.

"All gone. All my work—*gone!*"

Pulsit held up his hands. "Now, Doctor . . . "

Shart fired, but anger shook the hand that held the gun, causing the weapon to ignite the magnesium front panel on the control console. The thick white smoke, intense heat, and blinding light—more than the gun—caused Pulsit to pull up his robe and head for the nearest door. "I'll *kill* you, you old maniac!"

Pulsed beams deflected off the walls and deck as the old storyteller sped through the door, then closed it behind him. Pulsit leaned against the door, took several deep breaths, then noticed that he was in one of the animal compounds. Through the door, he heard Shart crashing in his direction. The old man pushed himself away from the door, then ran for the fence. Squawks, hisses, and growls assaulted his hearing as feathered, furred, and scaled creatures ran to get out of his way. The fence around the compound was double his own height, and he knew he could never climb it. He heard a snoring, looked in the direction of the sound, and saw one of the great lizards of Arcadia sleeping next to the fence. He ran over to it, stopped and kicked the huge lizard in the shoulder. "Wake up!"

The lizard opened one slitted eye and observed the human. "Uf?"

More squawks and growls told Pulsit that Shart was close on his heels. "Quick. Lift me over the fence."

The lizard sat up. "'Ow much?"

"Two sacks of roots, and another of tung berry cakes." The lizard smiled and held out his palm. "Payup." Pulsit looked around the lizard's shoulder and saw Shart dashing around the compound, weapon in hand. He pointed at the Vorilian. "He'll pay for both of us."

The lizard nodded, grabbed Pulsit by the back of his robe, and hoisted him over the fence. The storyteller's feet were running before they touched the ground.

The lizard turned and looked back into the compound at Shart. "Doc'or." Shart looked at the lizard, then looked to where the reptile was pointing. Through the fence he could see Pulsit running down the road. He turned to head toward a gate, but stopped short as a great green foot grabbed his shoulder.

"Wawk! What are you doing? Let me go!"

The lizard shook its head. "You payup. Two sack roots, sack tungarry cake."

Pulsit came to a turn in the road, slowed, then stopped. "This . . . too much . . . old man." He saw a rock, sat down and took several deep breaths. When his vision cleared, Pulsit looked back toward the station. The lizard had Shart by both ankles and was shaking the Vorilian. He could barely make out the lizard demanding "You payup! Payup!"

The storyteller nodded. "As well he should, too!" Still puffing, Pulsit pushed himself to his feet and began the long trek back to Mbwebwe.

Four days later, Pulsit sat at Azongo's table, waiting for his companions' reaction to his tale. Raster shook his head. "The doctor doesn't seemed to have helped much."

Azongo nodded. "Pulsit, I don't know if you'll ever chase the devils from your mind."

Pulsit frowned, then held up his hands. "Wait! I am not seeing things—"

"Oh!" Raster smiled, then laughed. "Then, it was a fine story, Pulsit. A fine story."

Azongo nodded. "It is good that you are well." The wild man shrugged. "But, as a story . . . " He shook his head.

Pulsit turned toward Durki. "What do you think?" Durki grimaced, then shook his head. "It was a terrible story, Pulsit. Just terrible!"

The old storyteller's eyebrows went up a notch. "And, just what is so terrible about it?"

The apprentice shook his head. "Such a tale; it's awful. First, it's too . . . technical—all those knobs, tubes, coils, and such. Then, a being from another planet! That's story fare for the likes of Raster."

Pulsit frowned. "Doctor Shart *is* from another planet!"

Durki shook his head. "Which still doesn't make it a story worth telling." Durki clasped his hands together and spoke as though he were the master lecturing a none-too-bright apprentice. "The people only want to hear the classic tales: the circus, fights between white and black magic, great fortune tellers solving mysteries. This kind of stuff—this technical fantasy story—will never be popular."

Pulsit rubbed his chin, then shrugged. "Nevertheless, Durki, this is the story I shall tell when we get back to the fires."

Durki looked down. "Then, that decides me, Pulsit."

"In what?"

"My screaming and growling are coming along so well that Raster and Azongo have asked me to join their act. Azongo will be the wild man, Raster the hero, and I shall be the victim."

Pulsit thought a moment, then nodded. "I suppose you are all ready to head back to Sina."

Durki shrugged. "I have had enough adventure, and we are anxious to take our act on the road. Will you devise a story for our act?"

Pulsit nodded. "Certainly."

"How much?"

Pulsit stood, walked to the door, and turned back. "We can discuss that later. I would be alone for a while."

Raster stood. "Pulsit?"

"Yes?"

"I thought it was a fine story."

Pulsit nodded. "Thank you."

"Even though you had no pretty girls in it. Perhaps, next time, you could add one or two?"

"Perhaps." The old storyteller lifted the door curtain and left.

It is, of course, well-known that the new act of Azongo, Raster, and Durki became an overnight success in Tarzak, where it first played the Great Square, and was then commissioned to play the Great Ring as part of the circus there.

Less known is the old storyteller who brought a new kind of tale to the fires along the road from Kuumic to Tarzak. He spoke his tales of space, strange beings, and high adventure, and all listened in wonder. Few appreciated his tales at the beginning, but soon a following began to grow—small, but enough to keep the old fellow in coppers. It is said that he told his stories as though he actually lived them, but little heed should be paid to such things, for that is only part of the storyteller's art. And, Pulsit of the Sina storytellers was an artist.

26 MONKEYS, ALSO THE ABYSS

KIJ JOHNSON

1.

Aimee's big trick is that she makes twenty-six monkeys vanish onstage.

2.

She pushes out a claw-foot bathtub and asks audience members to come up and inspect it. The people climb in and look underneath, touch the white enamel, run their hands along the little lions' feet. When they're done, four chains are lowered from the stage's fly space. Aimee secures them to holes drilled along the tub's lip, gives a signal, and the bathtub is hoisted ten feet into the air.

She sets a stepladder next to it. She claps her hands and the twenty-six monkeys onstage run up the ladder one after the other and jump into the bathtub. The bathtub shakes as each monkey thuds in among the others. The audience can see heads, legs, tails; but eventually every monkey settles and the bathtub is still again. Zeb is always the last monkey up the ladder. As he climbs into the bathtub, he makes a humming boom deep in his chest. It fills the stage.

And then there's a flash of light, two of the chains fall off, and the bathtub swings down to expose its interior.

Empty.

3.

They turn up later, back at the tour bus. There's a smallish dog door, and in the hours before morning the monkeys let themselves in, alone or in small groups, and get themselves glasses of water from the tap. If more than one returns at the same time, they murmur a bit among themselves like college students meeting in the dorm halls after bar time. A few sleep on the sofa and at least one likes to be on the bed, but most of them wander back to their cages. There's a little grunting as they rearrange their blankets and soft toys, and then sighs and snoring. Aimee doesn't really sleep until she hears them all come in.

Aimee has no idea what happens to them in the bathtub, or where they go, or what they do before the soft click of the dog door opening. This bothers her a lot.

4.

Aimee has had the act for three years now. She was living in a month-by-month furnished apartment under a flight path for the Salt Lake City airport. She was hollow, as if something had chewed a hole in her body and the hole had grown infected.

There was a monkey act at the Utah State Fair. She felt a sudden and totally out of character urge to see it. Afterward, with no idea why, she walked up to the owner and said, "I have to buy this."

He nodded. He sold it to her for a dollar, which he told her was the price he had paid four years before.

Later, when the paperwork was filled out, she asked him, "How can you leave them? Won't they miss you?"

"You'll see, they're pretty autonomous," he said. "Yeah, they'll miss me and I'll miss them. But it's time, they know that."

He smiled at his new wife, a small woman with laugh lines and a vervet hanging from one hand. "We're ready to have a garden," she said.

He was right. The monkeys missed him. But they also welcomed her, each monkey politely shaking her hand as she walked into what was now her bus.

5.

Aimee has: a nineteen-year-old tour bus packed with cages that range in size from parrot-sized (for the vervets) to something about the size of a pickup bed (for all the macaques); a stack of books on monkeys ranging from *All About Monkeys!* to *Evolution and Ecology of Baboon Societies*; some sequined show costumes, a sewing machine, and a bunch of Carhartts and tees; a stack of show posters from a few years back that say **24 Monkeys! Face The Abyss**; a battered sofa in a virulent green plaid; and a boyfriend who helps with the monkeys.

She cannot tell you why she has any of these, not even the boyfriend, whose name is Geof, whom she met in Billings seven months ago. Aimee has no idea where anything comes from any more. She no longer believes that anything makes sense, even though she can't stop hoping.

The bus smells about as you'd expect a bus full of monkeys to smell, though after a show, after the bathtub trick but before the monkeys all return, it also smells of cinnamon, which is the tea Aimee sometimes drinks.

6.

For the act, the monkeys do tricks or dress up in outfits and act out hit movies—*The Matrix* is very popular, as is anything where the monkeys dress up like little orcs. The maned monkeys, the lion-tails and the colobuses, have a lion-tamer act with the old capuchin female, Pango, dressed in a red jacket and carrying a whip and a small chair. The chimpanzee (whose name is Mimi, and no, she is not a monkey) can do actual sleight of hand; she's not very good, but she's the best Chimp Pulling A Coin From Someone's Ear in the world.

The monkeys also can build a suspension bridge out of wooden chairs and rope, make a four-tier champagne fountain, and write their names on a whiteboard.

The monkey show is very popular, with a schedule of 127 shows this year at fairs and festivals across the Midwest and Great Plains. Aimee could do more, but she likes to let everyone have a couple months off at Christmas.

7.

This is the bathtub act:

Aimee wears a glittering purple-black dress designed to look like a scanty magician's robe. She stands in front of a scrim lit deep blue and scattered with stars. The monkeys are ranged in front of her. As she speaks they undress and fold their clothes into neat piles. Zeb sits on his stool to one side, a white spotlight shining straight down to give him a shadowed look. She raises her hands.

"These monkeys have made you laugh, and made you gasp. They have created wonders for you and performed mysteries. But there is a final mystery they offer you—the strangest, the greatest of all."

She parts her hands suddenly, and the scrim goes transparent and is lifted away, revealing the bathtub on a raised dais. She walks around it, running her hand along the tub's curves.

"It's a simple thing, this bathtub. Ordinary in every way, mundane as breakfast. In a moment I will invite members of the audience up to let you see this for yourselves.

"But for the monkeys it is also a magical object. It allows them to travel—no one can say where. Not even I—" she pauses; "—can tell you this. Only the monkeys know, and they share no secrets.

"Where do they go? Into heaven, foreign lands, other worlds—or some dark abyss? We cannot follow. They will vanish before our eyes, vanish from this most ordinary of things."

And after the bathtub is inspected and she has told the audience that there will be no final spectacle in the show—"It will be hours before they return from their secret travels"—and called for applause for them, she gives the cue.

8.

Aimee's monkeys:
- two siamangs, a mated couple
- two squirrel monkeys, though they're so active they might as well be twice as many
- two vervets
- a guenon, who is probably pregnant though it's still too early to tell for sure. Aimee has no idea how this happened
- three rhesus monkeys. They juggle a little
- an older capuchin female named Pango
- a crested macaque, three Japanese snow monkeys (one quite young), and a Java macaque. Despite the differences, they have formed a small troop and like to sleep together
- a chimpanzee, who is not actually a monkey
- a surly gibbon
- two marmosets
- a golden tamarin; a cotton-top tamarin
- a proboscis monkey
- red and black colobuses
- Zeb

9.

Aimee thinks Zeb might be a de Brazza's guenon, except that he's so old that he's lost almost all his hair. She worries about his health but he insists on staying in the act. By now all he's really up for is the final rush to the bathtub, and for him it is more of a stroll. The rest of the time, he sits on a stool that is painted orange and silver and watches the other monkeys, looking like an aging impresario viewing his *Swan Lake* from the wings. Sometimes she gives him things to hold, such as a silver hoop through which the squirrel monkeys jump.

10.

No one seems to know how the monkeys vanish or where they go. Sometimes they return holding foreign coins or durian fruit, or wearing pointed Moroccan slippers. Every so often one returns pregnant or leading an unfamiliar monkey by the hand. The number of monkeys is not constant.

"I just don't get it," Aimee keeps asking Geof, as if he has any idea. Aimee never knows anything any more. She's been living without any certainties, and this one thing—well, the whole thing, the fact the monkeys get along so well and know how to do card tricks and just turned up in her life and vanish from the bathtub; *everything*—she coasts with that most of the time, but every so often, when she feels her life is wheeling without brakes down a long hill, she starts poking at this again.

Geof trusts the universe a lot more than Aimee does. "You could ask them," he says.

11.

Aimee's boyfriend:

Geof is not at all what Aimee expected from a boyfriend. For one thing, he's fifteen years younger than Aimee, twenty-eight to her forty-three. For another, he's sort of quiet. For a third, he's gorgeous, silky thick hair pulled into a shoulder-length ponytail, shaved sides showing off his strong jaw line. He smiles a lot, but he doesn't laugh very often.

Geof has a degree in creative writing, which means that he was working in a bike-repair shop when she met him at the Montana Fair. Aimee never has much to do right after the show, so when he offered to buy her a beer she said yes. And then it was four A.M. and they were kissing in the bus, monkeys letting themselves in and getting ready for bed; and Aimee and Geof made love.

In the morning over breakfast, the monkeys came up one by one and shook his hand solemnly, and then he was with the band, so to speak. She helped him pick up his cameras and clothes and the surfboard his sister had painted for him one year as a Christmas present. There's no room for the surfboard so it's suspended from the ceiling. Sometimes the squirrel monkeys hang out there and peek over the side.

Aimee and Geof never talk about love.

Geof has a Class C driver's license, but this is just lagniappe.

12.

Zeb is dying.

Generally speaking, the monkeys are remarkably healthy and Aimee can handle their occasional sinus infections and gastrointestinal ailments. For anything more difficult, she's found a couple of communities online and some helpful specialists.

But Zeb's coughing some, and the last of his fur is falling out. He moves very slowly and sometimes has trouble remembering simple tasks. When the show was up in St. Paul six months ago, a Como Zoo zoologist came to visit the monkeys, complimented her on their general health and well-being, and at her request looked Zeb over.

"How old is he?" the zoologist, Gina, asked.

"I don't know," Aimee said. The man she bought the show from hadn't known either.

"*I'll* tell you then," Gina said. "He's old. I mean, seriously old."

Senile dementia, arthritis, a heart murmur. No telling when, Gina said. "He's a happy monkey," she said. "He'll go when he goes."

13.

Aimee thinks a lot about this. What happens to the act when Zeb's dead? Through each show he sits calm and poised on his bright stool. She feels he is somehow at the heart of the monkeys' amiability and cleverness. She keeps thinking that he is the reason the monkeys all vanish and return.

Because there's always a reason for everything, isn't there? Because if there isn't a reason for even *one* thing, like how you can get sick, or your husband stop loving you, or people you love die—then there's no reason for anything. So there must be reasons. Zeb's as good a guess as any.

14.

What Aimee likes about this life:

It doesn't mean anything. She doesn't live anywhere. Her world is thirty-eight feet and 127 shows long and currently twenty-six monkeys deep. This is manageable.

Fairs don't mean anything, either. Her tiny world travels within a slightly larger world, the identical, interchangeable fairs. Sometimes the only things that cue Aimee to the town she's in are the nighttime temperatures and the shape of the horizon: badlands, mountains, plains, or skyline.

Fairs are as artificial as titanium knees: the carnival, the animal barns, the stock-car races, the concerts, the smell of burnt sugar and funnel cakes and animal bedding. Everything is an overly bright symbol for something real, food or pets or hanging out with friends. None of this has anything to do with the world Aimee used to live in, the world from which these people visit.

She has decided that Geof is like the rest of it: temporary, meaningless. Not for loving.

15.

These are some ways Aimee's life might have come apart:

1. She might have broken her ankle a few years ago, and gotten a bone infection that left her on crutches for ten months, and in pain for longer.

2. Her husband might have fallen in love with his admin and left her.

3. She might have been fired from her job in the same week she found out her sister had colon cancer.

4. She might have gone insane for a time and made a series of questionable choices that left her alone in a furnished apartment in a city she picked out of the atlas.

Nothing is certain. You can lose everything. Eventually, even at your luckiest, you will die and then you *will* lose it all. When you are a certain age or when you have lost certain things and people, Aimee's crippling grief will make a terrible poisoned dark sense.

16.

Aimee has read up a lot, so she knows how strange all this is.

There aren't any locks on the cages. The monkeys use them as bedrooms, places to store their special possessions and get away from the others when they want some privacy. Much of the time, however, they are loose in the bus or poking around in the worn grass around it.

Right now, three monkeys are sitting on the bed playing a game where they match colored balls. Others are pulling at skeins of woolen yarn, or rolling around on the floor, or poking at a piece of wood with a screwdriver, or climbing on Aimee and Geof and the sofa. Some of the monkeys are crowded around the computer watching kitten videos on YouTube.

The black colobus is stacking children's wooden blocks on the kitchenette table. He brought them back one night a couple of weeks ago, and since then he's been trying to make an arch. After two weeks and Aimee's showing him repeatedly how a keystone works, he still hasn't figured it out, but he keeps trying.

Geof's reading a novel aloud to the capuchin Pango, who watches the pages as though she's reading along. Sometimes she points to a word and looks up at him with her bright eyes, and he repeats it to her, smiling, and then spells it out.

Zeb is sleeping in his cage: he crept in there at dusk, fluffed up his toys and his blanket, and pulled the door closed behind him. He does this a lot lately.

17.

Aimee's going to lose Zeb and then what? What happens to the other monkeys? Twenty-six monkeys is a lot of monkeys, but they all like each other. No one except maybe a zoo or a circus can keep that many, and she doesn't think anyone else will let them sleep wherever they like or watch kitten videos. And if Zeb's not there, where will they go, those nights when they can no longer drop through the bathtub and into their mystery? And she doesn't even know whether it *is* Zeb, whether he is the cause of this or that's just her flailing for reasons again.

And Aimee? She'll lose her safe artificial world: the bus, the identical fairs, the meaningless boyfriend. The monkeys. And then what?

18.

A few months after she bought the act, when she didn't care much whether she lived or died, she followed the monkeys up the ladder in the closing act. Zeb raced up the ladder, stepped into the bathtub and stood, lungs filling for his great call. And she ran up after him. She glimpsed the bathtub's interior, the monkeys tidily sardined in, scrambling to get out of her way as they realized what she was doing. She hopped into the hole they made for her, curled up tight.

This only took an instant. Zeb finished his breath, boomed it out. There was a flash of light, she heard the chains release and felt the bathtub swing down, monkeys shifting around her.

She fell the ten feet alone. Her ankle twisted when she hit the stage but she managed to stay upright. The monkeys were gone.

There was an awkward silence. It wasn't one of her successful performances.

19.

Aimee and Geof walk through the midway at the Salina Fair. She's hungry and they don't want to cook, so they're looking for somewhere that sells $4.50 hotdogs and $3.25 Cokes, and Geof turns to Aimee and says, "This is bullshit. Why don't we go into town? Have real food. Act like normal people."

So they do, pasta and wine at a place called Irina's Villa. "You're always asking why they go," Geof says, a bottle and a half in. His eyes are a cloudy blue-gray, but in this light they look black and very warm. "See, I don't think we're ever going to find out what happens. But I don't think that's the real question anyway. Maybe the question is, why do they come back?"

Aimee thinks about the foreign coins, the wood blocks, the wonderful things they bring back. "I don't know," she says. "Why *do* they come back?"

Later that night, back at the bus, Geof says, "Wherever they go, yeah, it's cool. But see, here's my theory." He gestures to the crowded bus with its clutter of toys and tools. The two tamarins have just come in, and they're sitting on the kitchenette table, heads close as they examine some new small thing. "They like visiting wherever it is, sure. But this is their home. Everyone likes to come home sooner or later."

"If they have a home," Aimee says.

"Everyone has a home, even if they don't believe it," Geof says.

20.

That night, when Geof's asleep curled up around one of the macaques, Aimee kneels by Zeb's cage. "Can you at least show me?" she asks. "Please? Before you go?"

Zeb is an indeterminate lump under his baby-blue blanket, but he gives a little sigh and climbs slowly out of his cage. He takes her hand with his own hot leathery paw, and they walk out the door into the night.

The back lot where all the trailers and buses are parked is quiet, only the buzz of the generators, a few voices still audible from behind curtained windows. The sky is blue-black and scattered with stars. The moon shines straight down on them, leaving Zeb's face shadowed. His eyes when he looks up seem bottomless.

The bathtub is backstage, already on its wheeled dais waiting for the next show. The space is nearly pitch-dark, lit by some red EXIT signs and a single sodium-vapor lamp off to one side. Zeb walks her up to the tub, lets her run her hands along its cold curves and the lions' paws, and shows her the dimly lit interior.

And then he heaves himself onto the dais and over the tub lip. She stands beside him, looking down. He lifts himself upright and gives his great boom. And then he drops flat and the bathtub is empty.

She saw it, him vanishing. He was there and then he was gone. But there was nothing to see, no gate, no flickering reality or soft pop as air snapped in to fill the vacated space. It still doesn't make sense, but it's the answer that Zeb has.

He's already back at the bus when she gets there, already buried under his blanket and wheezing in his sleep.

21.

Then one day:

Everyone is backstage. Aimee is finishing her makeup and Geof is double-checking everything. The monkeys are sitting neatly in a circle in the dressing room, as if trying to keep their bright vests and skirts from creasing. Zeb sits in the middle, beside Pango in her little green sequined outfit. They grunt a bit, then lean back. One after the other, the rest of the monkeys crawl forward and shake his hand and then hers. She nods, like a small queen at a flower show.

That night, Zeb doesn't run up the ladder. He stays on his stool and it's Pango who is the last monkey up the ladder, who climbs into the bathtub and gives a screech. Aimee has been wrong that it is Zeb who is the heart of what is happening with the monkeys, but she was so sure of it that she missed all the cues. But Geof didn't miss a thing, so when Pango screeches, he hits the flash powder. The flash, the empty bathtub.

Afterward, Zeb stands on his stool, bowing like an impresario called onstage for the curtain call. When the curtain drops for the last time, he reaches up to be lifted. Aimee cuddles him as they walk back to the bus. Geof's arm is around them both.

Zeb falls asleep with them that night, between them in the bed. When she gets up in the morning, he's back in his cage with his favorite toys. He doesn't wake up. The monkeys cluster at the bars peeking in.

Aimee cries all day. "It's okay," Geof says.

"It's not about Zeb," she sobs.

"I know," he says.

22.

Here's the trick to the bathtub trick. There is no trick. The monkeys pour across the stage and up the ladder and into the bathtub and they settle in and then they vanish. The world is full of strange things, things that make no sense, and maybe this is one of them. Maybe the monkeys choose not to share, that's cool, who can blame them.

Maybe this is the monkeys' mystery, how they found other monkeys that ask questions and try things, and figured out a way to all be together to share it. Maybe Aimee and Geof are really just houseguests in the monkeys' world: they are there for a while and then they leave.

23.

Six weeks later, a man walks up to Aimee as she and Geof kiss after a show. He's short, pale, balding. He has the shell-shocked look of a man eaten hollow from the inside. "I need to buy this," he says.

Aimee nods. "I know you do." She sells it to him for a dollar.

24.

Three months later, Aimee and Geof get their first houseguest in their new apartment in Bellingham. They hear the refrigerator close and come out to the kitchen to find Pango pouring orange juice from a carton. They send her home with a pinochle deck.

COURTING THE QUEEN OF SHEBA

AMANDA C. DAVIS

We were still setting up for the matinee when Billy came tearing into the grassy back lot, face aglow. He strode right past me and stopped before Arthur Whitman, our minstrel. "You got to see this," he panted. "There's a new outside show, and it's got a dead girl."

Mr. Whitman and I passed back and forth a look of weary tolerance, as would a set of overtaxed parents. As a lady rider I had been with Prince's Hippodramatic Show for three years; Mr. Whitman, for two. We knew better than to fuss over the games and exhibitions that poached our customers and took advantage of our advertising for their own profit. But Billy was the newest rider in the show. He had yet to learn.

"A dead girl?" said Mr. Whitman, who had the voice of a droll Easterner when not corked up in blackface. "Waxworks, more like."

Billy shook his head vehemently. "Not *new* dead—*old* dead. And it's real as Alice's—uh—" Luckily at that moment he noticed me nearby, and he stammered into silence. Mr. Whitman's eyebrows piqued (whether at Billy's claim or the evaded vulgarism) and he agreed to join Billy for a closer look. I, not yet in my costume and therefore properly attired for a public appearance, followed.

The "dead girl" was housed in a canvas tent not far across the inn yard from our own. The proprietor sat on a collapsible chair near the entrance, beside a wooden marquee: **SEE THE QUEEN OF SHEBA, FIVE CENTS.** A fair price if she was as advertised, but outside shows never are, so Mr. Whitman offered the proprietor a free ticket to our matinee in exchange for entry, and the man relented. Had he made it to the circus, it would have made him a splendid bargain: seats could be had for a quarter. With all parties thinking they had made a shrewd deal, we slipped inside the tent to pay homage to the Queen of Sheba.

The tent was small; the Queen fit it snugly. She lay in a box with a glass top, barely five feet from head to toe, and every inch of her had shriveled to paper. Most of her body was wrapped in brittle cloth the color of sand that looked as if it might break at a touch, although I could see part of her shrunken hand and much of her skull, to which still clung several wisps of light-colored hair.

"The Queen of Sheba," said Billy, in a satisfied tone. "She ain't the looker she's made out to be."

Mr. Whitman bent over the case, deep in scrutiny. "Sheba or not, she has been very classically preserved. The weave of the linen is remarkably like those I have seen abroad—" Whether Mr. Whitman had ever been abroad was unconfirmed, but he listed several cities in Africa and Europe. I thought the linen remarkably like the ones we saw every day in cheap hotels. "Look at the narrowness of her torso below the rib cage. The internal organs have undoubtedly been removed. Billing her as the Queen of Sheba—a typical humbug. But she may well be a genuine Egyptian mummy."

When we had seen our fill, we filed into the bright summer sun.

"It's remarkable," I said, as we were leaving, "that the proprietor let us stay as long as he did. Most men would have called us out long ago."

"He knows we're fellow showmen," said Billy confidently. "Did right by us, didn't you, friend?" He delivered the proprietor a friendly blow to the arm.

The proprietor tipped to one side, slid from the chair, and fell to the ground, stone dead.

Billy's face went white as bone. Mr. Whitman had more sense. In a flash, he took the proprietor under the shoulders and dragged him into the tent to lay beside the box with the Queen of Sheba. He nearly didn't fit. We picked up the sign (so as to discourage others from disturbing us) and stuffed ourselves into the tent: three living souls, and two dead ones.

Billy had his hand over his mouth. I suppose it was all he could do to keep from gibbering like a monkey. Mr. Whitman fetched him a box on the ear.

"Hold your mettle," Mr. Whitman said to him. "No man dies of a bruised arm. Obviously, our friend perished quite naturally while we were within his exhibit. See, his face bears the signs of some heart trouble."

I avoided the face of the proprietor, instead gazing into the desiccated face of the Queen. "I wonder, was he alone?"

"Alone?" barked Mr. Whitman. "He traveled with the Queen!"

"Heart trouble," said Billy. He still looked quite pale. "I thought I was a murderer."

"Only a fool," said Mr. Whitman. "Come. We will leave this unlucky man with his display and alert Mr. Prince. He is our employer, after all, and to be frank, dealing with corpses is far beyond my level of pay."

At the word "pay" Billy roused slightly. "Hang on," he said. You could see the mossy water-wheel of his brain slowly churn up his thoughts. "This poor old coot was chargin' a half-dime a person just to come in an' look. Say we got a thousand people here and everyone wanted to see. That's—that's—"

"Quite a sum," said Mr. Whitman.

I saw what they were aiming at, and felt obliged to intervene. "We cannot claim this man's property just because he died in our presence."

To our eventual detriment, Mr. Prince did not agree.

I must say this in our defense: we saved the proprietor from the potter's field. In between the matinee and the evening show we managed to bribe the local Methodists into laying him out in preparation for burial in their churchyard the following Sunday. It cost a small fortune, but Mr. Prince was happy to pay it—we were, after all, expecting to rake in thirty to forty dollars per day showing the Queen. I think the arrangements slaked his conscience. They did not slake mine.

A paper inside the proprietor's jacket told us his name had been Harold Collins. Billy went quite overboard in pretending to mourn "dear old Harry." I didn't speak to him all day. The situation turned my stomach. We had made Collins's death into profit, his funeral into a play. Then again, he was—as Billy had noted—a showman. Perhaps he would have wanted to participate in one last spectacle.

The circus put on an impressive show that night. We riders performed tricks and tableaux, saddled and bareback, that left the audience gasping. Mr. Whitman capered beautifully. Our acrobats were Mercury; our strongman, Atlas. Quite simply, we astounded them.

We retired to our hotel, boarded the horses, ate late, and claimed our rooms. As a rule I boarded with another rider called Kathleen. Our habits suited one another. We turned in early. I am sure I fell asleep first. It must have been hours, but it seemed to be mere minutes before I awoke to the sound of Kathleen turning restlessly beside me in bed, whispering to herself.

This disturbance being rare, I murmured into my pillow: "Hush, dear." When she did not cease, I raised my head a little, hoping to rouse her by my own movements. "Wake up, Kathleen." My voice must have been weak—I sleep soundly and wake with difficulty—for the tossing and the whispering did not stop.

I had resolved to bear it out when her whispers grew clearer. "Gone and gone and gone . . . days and days . . . will it never end? Oh will it never end?"

"Kathleen," I said, still not quite willing to open my eyes, "please . . . "

Fingers like dead grape vines brushed my shoulder. "*I'm so hungry.*"

Without warning, the fingers dug hard and deep into the dent at the corner of my collarbone. I cried out. Now fully awakened, I rolled to confront Kathleen—

—only to see the corpse of the Queen of Sheba lying beside me in her place, staring at me through long-dried eye sockets and grinning with long yellow teeth!

Needless to say, I screamed—from the depths of my chest, with all my breath. Before I knew it, half a dozen performers crowded into my room, some with candles, most in bedclothes . . . and myself, in bed in my nightgown with the sheets to my chin, with no corpse beside me and no explanation for why I had awoken nearly the entire hotel.

To my equal shame and relief, Mr. Prince pushed through the gathering crowd, all bombast and authority; and when he asked what disturbed me, and I sheepishly admitted it was naught but a dream, he cleared out the room as efficiently as he might have cleared out sneak-ins from beneath the tiered seating. Soon we were alone.

"See here," he said, "you're sensible, Alice, and a good rider. I'll forgive a night terror or two. Only don't make a habit of it." As he closed the door he added, so that only the two of us could hear, "And when Kathleen comes back, tell her for God's sake to be more discreet. Our reputation is poor enough as it is."

He had spoken of what I had noticed but dared not acknowledge: Kathleen was not here. I had never heard her voice, never felt her touch. Yet I was never alone.

I lit a candle, and lay on my back for the rest of the night, cruelly and inescapably awake.

Well before dawn we were roused for the journey to the next town. (Kathleen was back by then, indecently tousled and wholly immune to my cold shoulder.) We dressed mechanically and met in the dining room for breakfast—more sleep-dogged than usual. Before I sat Mr. Whitman approached me privately.

"I hear," he said, "that you had some trouble this past night."

"A very little," I said. The long night and terrible shock must have worn on my nerves, because I added, "I suppose you rushed to my aid only to find a silly girl having a bad dream."

He cleared his throat. "I did not, in fact," he said. "At the moment you—ah—alarmed the troupe, I was suffering some alarm of my own."

"Speak plainly," I snapped.

He licked his lips. "You saw her too?"

I did not answer. I did not need to.

Billy entered the dining room. His eyes were sunken in his face. The chandelier man called to him: "Hi! Billy! Are you hungry?"

Billy skittered like a foal. "What'd you say? G—d—, I never want to hear that word again!" He took his place at the table looking sullen.

"H'm," said Mr. Whitman.

"Hungry," I said, raising a hand to my mouth. "She said—"

"'I'm so hungry,'" he finished.

My own appetite vanished. I saw the same sentiment reflected in Arthur Whitman's face. "Oh, what have we done?"

He said nothing; and between his troubled silence and Billy's sullenness, breakfast was solemn indeed.

As always, the crewsmen had gone on hours before to set up the new site—leaving us to a long drive in the dim morning. We stopped at the town borders to clean the wagons and change into our costumes. Then the band played, the wagons aligned, and we made the grand entree.

Nowadays you may find entertainment on any corner, but then we offered the brightest a country farmer might hope to see. Sleek showhorses; painted carts; gay music from the bandwagon; sequins shining on our costumes. Mr. Whitman, already "corked," gamboled along, a living caricature. There were many difficulties in circus life, many inconveniences. But so few people know the heaven of wholehearted applause.

We rode through town to the lot and directly to the tent. The audience followed. While Jones the treasurer sold tickets and we prepared for the performance, Mr. Prince had several of the workers set up the tent and coffin of the Queen of Sheba.

It was to be our first day to display her, and Mr. Prince fairly bounced with anticipation. After much agonizing, he assigned Jones the treasurer to sit outside her tent collecting dues in between shows. Shame upon us all! We even used poor Harry Collins's sign, and charged the price he had set.

We all took turns sneaking to visit Jones outside his tent, and by the end of the day it was clear: the Queen of Sheba was a tremendous money-maker. The town may not have been a wealthy one, but curiosity is a powerful force against financial discretion. Hundreds paid their half-dime to see the Queen. "No wonder those penny-showmen are so keen to follow us!" Mr. Prince cackled, when Jones had counted the take. "If this keeps up she'll earn us an elephant."

Despite my weariness, I dreaded the setting sun. As Kathleen and I settled into our hotel I begged her to stay the night. She agreed, in her own fashion ("Sure I'll be stayin' the night, what do you take me for?"). Small comfort, but I took it to heart.

Dark fell. Sleep hovered over me. The Queen of Sheba seemed further away, less clear in my memory. I let my eyes flicker shut, relaxed into steady breath . . .

. . . and woke—in a terrible turnabout—to the sound of a piercing shriek from not so far away.

Almost before Kathleen and I were dressed enough to investigate, Mr. Prince came knocking with the news. I had rarely seen him so serious. "Jones is dead," he said. "His poor wife woke to find him—" He broke off, whether for propriety or the sake of his nerves.

"Was't his heart that killed him?" asked Kathleen.

"Ah . . . " said Mr. Prince. "The cause of death is not . . . immediately obvious. That is to say . . . "

"Poor coot was dried up like a winter potato," said Billy.

He sat across from us in the wagon, bouncing with every rut in the road, and though the sun had yet to rise, for once none of us tried to sleep.

"How'd ye get in see him?" said Kathleen, eyes bright.

"Don't be prurient, dear," I said. It was no use, of course. I gave Billy a look from beneath my eyelashes to let him know I didn't truly want him to stop telling his tale.

"Got there first," Billy bragged to Kathleen. "So's no one could keep me out. There was Mrs. Jones in her night-cap and Jones laying there—and I about half didn't know him—because Jones never was *that* thin!"

"*Thin,*" I said.

"Skin and bone," said Billy. The grin faded from his face. I suppose that was the moment the realization truly struck him. "Skin and bone."

Kathleen shivered and leaned on my shoulder. "Will we be havin' another funeral?"

"Play out the play," said Mr. Whitman, in his deep glum voice. He sat not too far from Billy but I had not thought he was listening. "Jones and the new widow have been left behind pending their journey home. I believe Mr. Prince has arranged for a casket and transport. We, of course, will do as we do."

"Can't even take a day off when your treasurer dies," said Billy in disgust.

But missing a day off did not trouble me as much as did Billy's description of Jones's corpse. I could not shake from my mind the memory of my nightmare—or else vision.

I had heard the pleas of the Queen of Sheba.

And Jones died looking very hungry.

The treasurer managed a thousand vital tasks, but none of them to do with the performance itself, so his absence did not prevent us from putting on our usual show. (It did, however, make us mutter to one another about when and whether we would have our pay.) Mr. Prince himself sold tickets. He ordered the chandelier man, who managed our lighting, to sell showings to the Queen of Sheba.

I would like to tell you that we outdid ourselves with every show, but in truth every day brought a fresh audience—so our acts rarely varied. The audience left; the take was counted; the tent was dissembled, the center pole discarded. One variation tonight: the next day being Sunday, the crew did not leave immediately for the next town, but stayed the night. We did not perform on Sundays. Public opinion did not allow it.

We woke early intending to go to church (a matter of piety for some, a matter of appearance for others). At breakfast, however, I noticed that one of our number was staring at his plate rather than emptying it: the chandelier man, who had spent the previous day with the Queen of Sheba. Mr. Whitman caught my gaze. He had noticed too. As soon as possible he took the man aside. I carried on gay conversation with the others, ever watching from the corner of my eye. When Mr. Whitman came to beg my company, I excused myself immediately and followed him to a quiet corner.

It had cost Mr. Whitman much patience and some of his whiskey before the chandelier man gave up his story, but when he did, it went like this:

He (the chandelier man) boarded with one of the drivers. The driver, we all knew, was a stout little man fond of drink and food, a chewer of tobacco, and he liked to carry some bread or an age-wrinkled apple with him, as he said, "to carry him to breakfast." This he kept beside the bed. Both men fell asleep quickly. (Circus folk always did; sleep we found more scarce than gold.) Sometime during the night, the chandelier man woke to the sound of weeping.

("I heard no weeping," I said. "I did," said Mr. Whitman.)

In the dim light the chandelier man saw a slim figure by the bed. He would not reveal who he thought it might be, but he was not alarmed until it laid a hand on his arm. The fingers, he said, were tough as wood, rough as bark. It leaned its face down and whispered—

"I'm so hungry," I said, at the same time Mr. Whitman did. He nodded gravely.

Only then did the chandelier man begin to see the face—or understand whose it was. He said his heart went mad in his ribs. He told Mr. Whitman of a gaping mouth, eyes sunk so deep they might not remain in their sockets, hollow cheeks, flaking skin. They stared at one another for some moments. Then the chandelier man—rigid with fear—cried: "Hungry, are you? Why—have a bite!"

And he lunged across the sleeping driver, snatched up the age-wrinkled apple, and hurled it at the Queen's gawping face.

The Queen's mouth closed with a hard snap. Like the last wisp of smoke from a dead candle slipping through a window, she vanished.

The chandelier man barely had time to recover before the driver, who had seen nothing and knew only that he had been lunged upon in the middle of the night, started a large quarrel over what was going on and why they were both unpleasantly awake. To compound matters, the driver's apple could not be found. As of breakfast it did not seem that the chandelier man had been forgiven.

Mr. Whitman and I regarded each other for a somber moment. Then he said—as a barbecue-goer remarking on the mild weather—"I'm beginning to believe we have a problem on our hands."

He startled a laugh from me; then, a scowl. "You're suggesting—"

"I am," he said quietly.

"It's preposterous."

"Perhaps," he said. "Miss Monroe, please listen. For all my songs and japes in the ring, I am a scientist at heart. To link these recent events to our new acquisition . . . I admit it is preposterous. But I fear that not to do so may be far worse."

I stared at him: Mr. Whitman, the droll Easterner; Mr. Whitman, the blackface jester. "I won't be made a fool, Mr. Whitman."

Again he grew quiet. "I would never presume."

I have known a man or two who thought they might slide the wool over a pretty girl's eyes; I have also been fortunate to know sincerity. Mr. Whitman radiated it. And something else: something far more convincing. In his sincerity I detected restrained but genuine fear.

"You sound as if you may have a plan," I said.

"I do," he said, his countenance clearing to hear me come to his side. He nodded his head toward the others in their Sunday best. "I'm afraid it will make heathens of us for a day."

I tossed my head. "I am a lady rider with a traveling circus," I said, in a haughty voice that, following my intent, made him laugh. "I can hardly be worse."

In the space of ten minutes we became both heathens and criminals: ignoring the church bell in order to hitch two horses to our smallest wagon and abandon our employer with the corpse of a Queen hidden beneath a quilt. I, who traveled almost without ceasing, felt the old thrill of the road rise anew. It must have been the illicit aspect that excited my sensibilities; that, or the freedom. I traveled daily. But I always traveled where someone else demanded I go.

Mr. Whitman explained himself as we drove. The Queen's nocturnal appearances, he said, had too much in common to come from our individual imaginations. He and I had only discussed the phrase "I'm so hungry" among ourselves; Billy, as far as he could ascertain, never admitted hearing it to anyone, though he reacted strongly enough to the word that morning. The chandelier man, then, had not heard it from us. Either we four had invented the phrase independently or it had a common source.

"As for poor Jones," he added, "who can say what he might have seen or heard?"

"Billy said he looked thin."

"Thin as a starveling," he said.

So Mr. Whitman determined the validity of his—our—visions. Jones' death, and the chandelier man's apparent near miss, convinced him of the danger. Those performers who spent time near the Queen became the objects of her wrath. To him the course seemed clear. The Queen of Sheba must be gotten rid of. And who would know how to do so but the original proprietor?

"But," I said, coloring, "the proprietor—Mr. Collins—is dead."

"So is the Queen," he said. "The fact has failed to quiet her. And Mr. Collins is not yet in his grave."

We had an appointment with a dead man. And we were bringing a dead woman to meet him.

The journey took most of the morning. Not far from town we heard the pealing of church bells.

"I do feel heathen," remarked Mr. Whitman.

Something in the character of the anthem gave me pause. "No," I said slowly, recalling hundreds of church bells in hundreds of towns across America. "Those are funeral bells."

"Collins," we said together, and he urged the horses toward the sound of the bells.

We reached the church just in time to see a procession from the church, with six men bearing the coffin toward its final resting place. I could not imagine that so many people had turned out for a funeral for a man none of them had properly met, but then I remembered—our business thrived upon the scarcity of spectacle. Surely the funeral of a stranger counted as a spectacle worth seeing.

Mr. Whitman pulled the horses to a halt. I leapt down nimbly enough to turn a few heads; he followed less prettily, and hurried around the cart. "Stop!" I cried, running toward the funeral party.

The men bearing pall stopped, as one does when hearing the word "Stop" cried in a high woman's voice; at once I was the center of attention. I sought the preacher. His eyes lit up at the sight of me, and I knew he recognized me—from the show or from our prior delivery of the body, I could not guess. "Do not bury this man yet," I pleaded, with the whole town looking on. "We—we must add something to the coffin."

There were looks all around. The preacher took me around the shoulders. "It would not do to open the coffin now," he said, under his breath. "Give his effects to the poor. We should carry on."

"No," said Mr. Whitman, coming up behind us. The pastor turned—and he let out a start: for Mr. Whitman had laid the glass coffin containing the Queen of Sheba at his feet.

No performance of ours could have commanded the utter attention that did this simple act. *Oh*, I thought; *if Mr. Prince knew the show we were giving for free!* But I did not speak. The preacher drew away from me, and he bent low over the coffin. "Is this—is this—a *girl*?"

"Please open the coffin," I said again.

He stood, with a face like he had been smacked by an iron. "Let the coffin down," he said, in a hoarse voice, to the pallbearers. "Gentlemen, please take your ladies home." No one moved. "Then—please—open the coffin."

The six bemused men obeyed. Someone procured a hammer, and the nails were pried free; the coffin lid came open with a stench and a grisly sight, though not so much as I had feared for a man three days dead. Mr. Whitman took up the Queen under his arm—that is how small she was—and brought her coffin alongside Collins's in the thick churchyard grass. He found the latch upon the glass and, gently as a mother peeling back a blanket from her child, laid open the casket so that the two dead souls lay side by side under the blue sky.

Then—with a hiss of a kettle left too long on the fire—the Queen of Sheba *rose*.

She lurched up in her coffin, shroud tearing at her mouth so that it gaped wide as a scream, turning her head from side to side blindly. The air filled with cries of horror. We could not have planned a better show! Her bone-thin wrists arched as she scrabbled to take hold of her coffin walls; then her groping fingers fell upon the coffin nearby, and further still she crawled, until the brittle hands took hold of Collins within his coffin.

She hissed, wordlessly. Her voice was like dry wind. By spasms she jerked her way to join him in the coffin.

The mouth-rent in her shroud opened wider. Like spiders the dry fingers clutched his jaws. Then she drew herself down, down, to his face, and her tiny teeth showed and then—the teeth tore into his dead flesh, over and over, and the hiss of her voice became a gurgle, a terrible glugging, and her breath bubbled with gore.

I screamed; we all screamed, I am sure. Heedless of us, the dead Queen feasted.

"Bury them!" I shrieked. "Bury them both!"

Mr. Whitman leapt forward to Collins's coffin. Laying his shoulder to it he shoved the box along the grass until it came to the hole that had been laid open for it. "Help me!" he roared. One brave soul came to his side. Together they hurled the coffin, and the pair joined within in awful union, six feet deep.

Mr. Whitman scrambled for the shovel, and began throwing dirt over the Queen and her prey; I dashed to his side and did the same with my hands. Before I knew it, others had joined. We rained grave dirt upon them until we could see them no longer, then until the dirt stopped moving, then until the earthen mound beside the stone was unexpectedly gone.

I fell back and felt Mr. Whitman's arms catch me. "She is gone," he said. His hands shook, but they held mine firmly nonetheless. "I suspect she is hungry no more."

"Then let us leave her here," I whispered.

And while the crowd of good Christians made mob among themselves, trying to understand what we or they had done, we left behind the buried dead, the empty coffin, and the best audience of our lives.

That was our adventure. Of course we had trouble from Mr. Prince when at last we returned, late that evening, as all prepared to move along to our next engagement the following day. Mr. Whitman took him aside and made the argument that by disposing of the Queen we had in fact preserved the entire circus. He did not go so far as to call us heroes. But we did it privately to one another.

His argument worked; we kept our jobs. Mercifully, we had no more deaths or nightmares. Mr. Prince did take some revenge from our salaries, but this did us little harm in the long run: we extorted much of the difference from Billy, whose life we insisted that we had saved. And as Mr. Whitman and I learned soon enough, while we wintered between traveling seasons and I took his name as my own, the old adage is true: Two may live as cheaply as one.

And for that happy discovery, I can thank no one but the Queen of Sheba!

CIRCUS CIRCUS

ERIC M. WITCHEY

When the circus was very small, it believed it would grow up to have many multi-colored big tops with banners on the support poles and three rings in each tent. It lived in Mexico then, and its smaller tents were brand new—the Bottle Throw, the Wheel of Fortune, and especially the Palmist and Mystic—because she loved the circus most; and love was, after all, the food that made the circus grow.

The circus worked hard and won the favor of many. It grew, and one day it came across an old circus that was dying. On its last day, the old circus gave up its three big tops. One became a temporary shelter for refugees from a country farther south than Mexico. One became a cover over a produce market in a large village in the Yucatan. The third was given as a gift to the younger, growing circus.

Like other circuses, it went north in the summer, to the land of white people and hard languages. Always, though, it returned to Mexico for the winters. There, like the other wintering circuses, it traveled from village to village. At each village, the circus would find a small, clear area, an area nobody wanted or cared about, a place to dig in its poles and stakes and lift its canvas and lay out its midway and wait for the laughter and love of the children.

At each village, it sent out its people—the stilt walker, the acrobat (because it was still a young circus and only had one acrobat), the fat lady who was also the bearded lady, and the many clowns because anyone could be painted up and sent out to hang fliers and talk to children.

Children.

The circus grew strong on the love of children. It sent out its people to call to the children and bring them from far and wide to spend their pesos and to toss the balls and spin the wheels and have their fortunes told.

Many years passed, and finally a year came when the circus pushed farther south than it had ever gone before—far into steaming highlands and jungles. There, it came on a village, and it settled into a clearing among the trees and called to the people all around, and they came, as they always did. Even though it was in the dark forest, the village was the same as so many villages, and the circus was happy. It had given up the idea that it would one day have many big tops. It had given up the idea that its tents and banners would always be bright. It had grown enough to have two acrobats and to take delight in giving delight.

The children came. They came and played in the midway and laughed.

One boy, a boy who hoped to grow up and join the circus—there was always such a boy in every village, and the circus was careful to pay attention to them—came on the last night before it was time for the circus to move on.

He was a smallish boy who might one day make a good acrobat. Unlike the other boys of his village, this boy had red hair and freckles on bronze skin. The boy had only five centavos, and the circus wondered how he would spend them. At the big top, certainly. Or watching the Geek.

But the boy had purpose in his stride, and he went along the midway straight to the fortune teller. He walked in and sat down on one side of her round table. He stared into her crystal like he might see for himself the things that only a gifted seer like the circus' Señora Bruja could see.

Señora Bruja, her real name was Maria, swished her skirts and flipped her gray hair and flashed her many rings before she sat down.

The circus liked that. It liked Maria more than most of the others. In its earliest memories, she was there. Sometimes at night she would talk to the circus, and the circus would listen, and it made the circus happy.

The boy watched all.

Señora Bruja settled in her chair. She held out her hand, palm up, and said, "Show the spirits that you value their advice."

The boy stared into the crystal and ignored her.

"Cross my palm with gold," she said.

The boy looked up. "This is all I have." He put his centavos on her palm. "Is it enough?"

Señora Bruja closed her long fingers around the coins. She looked up toward the top of her tent, which was not so new as it had once been, and she said, "Spirit of the circus, this boy begs our advice. Is it enough?"

Of course it was.

No circus could turn down a boy who might one day run away to join it.

The circus rustled its canvas and flapped its tent flaps and tugged on the ropes and stakes just enough to answer.

"It is enough," she said.

The boy's eyes went wide and his mouth opened.

"Ask your question, then, my son," Señora Bruja said. She slipped the coins into a pouch at her waist and closed her eyes to wait for the boy to compose himself and offer his question.

After some time, she opened her eyes to see why the boy was silent. From time to time, boys would get scared and run away without ever asking their questions.

He was still there, sitting and staring.

"Well?" she said.

"The circus can answer you." He said it like he knew it was true.

Now, normally Señora Bruja would have said something mystical and scary, but this boy wasn't pretending. He wasn't being silly. He was just saying that the circus could answer, and since it could, Señora Bruja just said, "Yes."

"Wow," the boy said.

"Yes," Señora Bruja said.

"Will you ask the circus something for me?"

Neither the circus nor Señora Bruja, in all her years as a fortune teller, had ever met such a boy as this. She leaned forward, put her elbows on her table, and slid her crystal out of the way so she could see the boy better. "What is your name, boy?" she asked.

"Manolo," he said. "And I want to grow up and be a circus."

"You mean join the circus?"

"No," Manolo said. "I want to be a circus. I want to have tents and acrobats and animals, and I want all the children from all the villages to love me."

Señora Bruja sat back. "Ah," she said. "I see."

For a while, the two people sat and just looked at each other. The circus is patient in the way that things are and people are not, but even a circus can't wait forever. Finally, it flapped and tugged and reminded the two that they were not alone.

"Yes," Señora Bruja said to the circus. "I will ask again."

"The circus," the boy said.

"It wants to know your questions."

The boy sat up straight. He looked all around him.

"Just ask," Señora Bruja said. "It will hear you."

"How can I become a circus?"

Neither Señora Bruja nor the circus had ever heard such a question, and neither of them had any idea how to answer. They sat for a while. A line formed outside Señora Bruja's tent. The circus thought and thought. Finally, it opened tent flaps and tugged on ropes and whispered, "Be a boy who loves to smile and laugh."

Señora Bruja spoke the words for the boy.

The words seemed to make the boy sad. Finally, his green eyes narrowed and his freckled cheeks colored like a golden-red rose, and he smiled broad and wide. "I will," he said. "I want to be a circus, so I will!"

He left and others came to sit in the chair. Others came to ask about lovers and money and children and people long ago gone to other lives and worlds.

No other child came. No other question caught the circus' attention or surprised Señora Bruja.

That night, lying in the stillness and darkness before sleep, Señora Bruja spoke. "The boy," she said.

The circus knew the one.

"He is very sad."

"Why?" the circus asked.

"He is not like the other children here."

"So he is special?" the circus asked.

"So he is, but he is also hurt deep in his heart—alone. Perhaps he should come with us."

"He wants to become a circus," the circus said. "He is a boy."

"Circuses come from somewhere," Señora Bruja said, "as do boys. Perhaps they are not so different."

"Tomorrow," the circus said, "when it is time to leave, we will ask him to come along."

Señora Bruja smiled, nodded, and slept.

The circus did not.

During the deepest part of the night, the weather in the forest changed. Clouds came to cover the stars. Breezes became winds. The smell of distant rain and dust mingled in the wind and pulled at canvas and sisal ropes.

Wakeful, the circus became very uneasy. Such signs are not to be ignored by a circus, and together with the odd boy, the circus was sure morning would bring ill omens.

Sunrise brought light, but clouds covered the sun. Even so, striking began and was well underway when Señora Bruja returned from searching for the boy. She came to her tent, tears in her eyes. She sat in her chair, knocked her crystal to the floor, and sobbed.

The circus waited and listened. She would speak when she had breath.

At last, she picked up her crystal, settled it on her table, wiped her eyes, then spoke. "He's dead."

"The boy?"

"Yes."

The crying took her again, and she sobbed a while longer. The strikers came and found her crying. The circus sent them to do other chores while it listened to Señora Bruja.

"How?" the circus asked.

"Bullies in the village. He told them that he talked to you."

"So they killed him? For that?"

"No. They only laughed. He laughed as well. One hit him, and still he laughed. They told him to stop laughing. He told them he was going to become a circus and that he would be a boy who smiled and laughed from now on."

"And?"

"They beat him to make him stop laughing. They kicked him to make him stop smiling. He laughed and smiled. One of them kicked his head. He died."

The sobs came to her again.

The circus could not cry, but it sighed long and hard. It let the damp winds come in and out of its remaining tents, and it moved the horses and bears to groan, and even the strikers paused in their work and crossed themselves for the boy, though they did not know that he was dead.

"We killed him," Señora Bruja said.

"No," the circus said. "Hatred killed him. They hated his smile, and they hated his laughter, and they killed him."

"We told him he could be a circus."

"Yes," the circus said.

The rain came at that moment. It was a powerful rain, a hard rain, and Señora Bruja's tent was the only tent left standing, so all the strikers, and Geeks, and freaks, and barkers, and even the two acrobats came and gathered in her tent.

Señora Bruja lit a lantern and placed it in the center of the table beside the crystal, which scattered shards of colored light throughout the tent.

One of the acrobats said, "This is a very strange storm. A terrible storm. The tent will not hold."

One of the strikers said, "It will hold. We set the stakes deep and the poles are strong."

The circus said, "Maria, tell them."

Señora Bruja said, "We have done wrong; we must set the wrong right."

The circus had her tell the tale of the boy, and when she was finished, the circus told her that it had a plan. It gave her instruction for all its people.

Even in the terrible storm, the strikers went out of the tent, the barkers went with them to help if they could, the acrobats climbed poles and lines to secure tents even though lightning might kill them, and Señora Bruja read in her mystical books until she was sure she knew how to do the things she needed to do in the days to come.

On dawn of the day after the circus was to have left, the big top was up again—the big top, the midway, the barkers, the Wheel of Fortune, the Bottle Toss, and Señora Bruja's tent. The acrobats cavorted in new sunlight in the early morning path to the gates of the circus, and the circus had been moved so its fences and gates surrounded the village's graveyard.

The big top stood over an open grave, a freshly dug grave, a grave at center ring that was just the right size for a boy who had smiled in the face of death.

The man on stilts, the fat lady, the acrobats, and all the strikers and barkers and animals went into the village and handed out fliers to a free show.

The acrobats, who were by far the strongest and fastest of all in the circus, took special care to find the bullies, the three boys who had beaten a smiling child. Each of those boys received a special, front-row ticket.

Now, the mother of the boy who smiled was sad, of course. While the village buzzed with excitement for the strange doings of the circus, she donned a black scarf, her black dress, and she cried while she washed her son.

Crying, she put him in a small cart. Still crying, she hitched her burro to the cart and started up the hill outside the village, started the long trudge through the jungle forest and up to the graveyard where she would say goodbye to her son.

She was so sad that she didn't notice that the circus had moved. She was so sad that she didn't notice the line of silent circus people on both sides of the path to the graveyard.

As a mother should be who must bury her son, she was so sad that she did not notice that the circus held open the flaps of the big top for her or that the sun disappeared when she, the cart, and the boy went inside, or even that the open grave was in the center of center ring.

She simply went about the business of wrapping her son in her best linens and, with the help of two strikers, laying him into the grave.

While she knelt next to her son's grave to pray his soul into the next world, the people of the town arrived for the promised, free show.

As the circus expected, they had all noticed that the circus had moved. Not one person from the entire village could resist the invitation to come to the big top in the graveyard. Such a thing had never been seen, never even been heard of.

The tiers of benches filled. The performers prepared. Señora Bruja donned the Ring Master's uniform, and the Ring Master helped harness the trick horses and helped muzzle the dancing bears.

All in silence.

The orchestra wore black. They sat with their instruments on their laps.

The crowd was silent.

The performers were silent.

The tent flaps and ropes were silent.

The only sound in all the circus-surrounded graveyard was the sound of a mother praying for the soul of her son.

When she said, "Amen," she looked up. For the first time, her grief parted enough to see that she and her son were surrounded by the villagers and that the villagers were surrounded by a circus.

Señora Bruja, wearing the top hat and tails, stepped up to her, placed a gentle hand on her shoulder, and said, "Your son loved the circus."

The boy's mother nodded.

"We wish to say goodbye in our way. May we?"

The mother looked around. She nodded again.

Two clowns came across the center ring and helped the woman to a seat. A trainer came with carrots for the burro and led him away to one side.

The seats were full. The bullies sat in a row, excited and a little confused, but clearly unrepentant.

Señora Bruja smiled and lifted her hand to her Ring Master's top hat.

The circus closed the tent flaps. Ropes tied them shut. Darkness filled the space inside the tent.

Señora Bruja began the performance. The music sounded. The clowns moved into the center ring.

People murmured in the darkness.

Someone tried the ties on the flap and found they could not undo the ties without light.

Clown horns sounded. Clown laughter filled the tent.

Señora Bruja announced each act in order, and each act performed in the darkness.

From time to time, people tried to leave by the tent flaps or by crawling under the edges of the tent, but at the edges of the tent they found tigers and lions and geeks and bearded ladies.

Finally, the acrobats had swung on their trapeze in the dark, the most dangerous and death-defying of the feats, and one that was very important to the circus' plan and the magics of Señora Bruja's books.

Señora Bruja called for lights, and the spotlights were lit, and the big top over the boy's grave filled with light, and the people of the village sighed their relief.

Señora Bruja stood before the three bullies. "This was a performance for our friend, Manolo," she said. "Forever more and after that, he will never again see a circus because of what you have done."

The bullies fidgeted and looked about.

Señora Bruja pointed to one, the smallest, "You," she said, "to prove how big you were, threw the first stone."

"He was laughing at us," the boy said.

"You," she pointed to the second boy, who was bigger and leaner and harder in jaw and arm, "to show that you were bigger and stronger and loyal to the other boys, you struck the first blow."

"He wouldn't quit smiling," the boy said.

"And you," she strode up to the largest of the boys, the boy that had the darkest eyes, the boy that hated so much that he would never smile unless someone else was hurt, the boy whose hatred infected others. "You set them to the task, and you kicked Manolo so hard that he died."

"He's different," the boy said, "His father was from the North. He deserved to die." The boy spat.

The people of the village bowed their heads in shame. The clowns frowned, filed up, and stood in a row, three on each side of Señora Bruja.

"You!" she said, pointing to the first boy, "Come down into the ring."

"No," the boy said, but two clowns had already grasped his arms. The boy screamed for help, and several men in the crowd began to get up, but the circus shook and stretched its ropes and raised such a howl that the men became afraid and sat back down.

Señora Bruja brought the boy to the grave. The clowns held him.

"Here," she said, "Is where a boy's joy ends. Here is where you put him, and here is where you will one day come."

The boy cried. He sobbed. "I'm sorry," he said. "I'm so sorry."

Señora Bruja lifted her long-fingered hand, and with a quick motion, she flicked a tear from the boy's cheek. The tear rose in the spotlight. It flashed like a trapeze artist in a sequined suit. It rose, arched, sparkled, fell, and came to rest on the linens of Manolo's shroud.

The clowns released the boy, who ran for his life. The tent flaps untied, opened, and let him run off into the bright daylight of the first day of his new life.

The tent flaps closed again.

The people murmured, but now that they had seen what the circus had in mind, they were more calm.

Señora Bruja and the clowns went to face the second boy. "You," she said, "Come down."

Braver in his cowardice than the first boy, the second stood tall and stepped into the ring. Escorted by clowns and Ring Mistress, he approached the grave. There, he made a show of crying and claiming he was sorry.

The circus laughed so all could hear.

The sound of it sent a stir of fear through the crowd.

The false sorrow of the boy ended.

Señora Bruja took up his hand. "You," she said, "drew first blood with your blow, and you shall return in kind." She crossed his palm with a long fingernail. A cut appeared in his palm.

The boy howled in earnest now, and the clowns held him.

Señora Bruja spoke, "If you have no sorrow for your actions, then you will give of your life." She shook his hand, and three drops of blood arched out, crimson and bright, and fell to the shroud—one each over Manolo's eyes and one over his mouth.

People gasped. A woman screamed.

Señora Bruja freed the boy.

Holding his injured hand, he ran. He ran, looking back over his shoulder, and he tripped on the ring, tumbled, fell, broke his neck and died.

Silence filled the tent.

The lifeless boy, still holding his hand, head bent back and to the side in an impossible posture, held the eyes of every face in the big top.

The clowns and Señora Bruja stood before the third boy. "Come down," she said.

The third boy said something very rude. He stood, turned, and headed for the aisle and the tent flaps.

A bear three times his size stood on hind legs in the aisle. Its hands came up to its muzzle and stripped away the leather cup and straps. The bear lifted its lip and growled.

A wet stain appeared on the boys pant leg.

A girl giggled, and the boy turned red.

"Come down," Señora Bruja said.

The boy, followed by the dancing bear, came into the ring. He followed Señora Bruja to the grave of Manolo.

"Manolo came to us," she said. "He wanted to be a circus."

A few foolish people laughed, still believing it was only a show. Most did not.

"That's just stupid," the boy said.

The circus laughed. The boy cringed. Silence filled the tent once more.

"You kicked his head," she said. "What gift do you offer the dead?"

The boy spit on the shroud.

Señora Bruja nodded.

The clowns grasped the boy's arms.

The boy struggled, but these clowns had striker's muscles. These clowns could lift a fifty pound mallet and bring it home on a stake. These clowns could hang upside down from a pole ring and pull on fist-thick ropes and tie them off.

The struggles of a boy, even a boy the size of a man, were nothing to them.

Señora Bruja took the boy's head between her hands. She looked deep into his eyes. "From you," she said, "The gift shall be mind. For all your days, and until you are one hundred years old, you will know that once you hurt a smiling boy. You will remember the joy in his smile and laughter, but you will never see joy in a smile or hear it in laughter again. You will remember that once your mind was clear—but you will only speak gibberish and riddles and everyone you meet will laugh at you and make fun of you."

She kissed him on the lips, took water from his mouth, then she too spit on the grave of Manolo.

The clowns released the boy. He screamed. He cried. He spoke, but only foolish noises and slobber came from his lips.

The little girl laughed again.

Señora Bruja turned to the people. She held up her top hat. The trumpet sounded three times. She thanked them for coming to the performance, and she bade them go, she bade them remember Manolo, and she bade them be kind to one another in his memory.

The tent flaps opened.

Silent, somber people filed away from the circus and back to the village.

Finally, only the circus, the people of the circus, a mother, a burro, and an open grave remained.

"Come," Señora Bruja said, "Come down."

The mother stepped into the ring.

"Together, we will bury your son," Señora Bruja said. Together, they knelt. All the people of the circus knelt with them. All took up handfuls of dirt and worked to bury the boy who had wanted to be a circus.

When the grave had been filled, Señora Bruja said, "For three days, we will stay here. I hope you will stay with us."

"My burro?" Manolo's mother asked.

The circus whispered to Señora Bruja. Señora Bruja nodded.

"Yes," Señora Bruja said. "Your burro will stay with the performing horses."

"It's true, then," the mother said. "Manolo told me you could speak to the spirit of the circus."

"The spirit of the circus can hear me and speak to me if it chooses, and it has asked me to do one more thing before we rest." She crossed the mound of the grave, and she knelt, and she placed three coins, Manolo's centavos, in a row on the mound of the grave. Then she drew a circle around the coins.

Each morning, Señora Bruja and the mother of Manolo returned to the grave in the big top. On the third morning, the mother gasped. There, where the coins had been was a tiny big top tent. The fabric was new and striped in gay, red and white. Pennants of red, and white, and green fluttered at the points of the small poles. Flaps hissed and snapped in a tiny breeze.

The tiny circus laughed, and the laugh was the laugh of Manolo.

Señora Bruja handed Manolo's mother a book of arcana, a fortune teller's book. "Now," Señora Bruja said, "We strike and move on. For a time, you will go with us. In a few years, you will go North—you and your circus."

"My son," she said.

"No. He is a circus now. He will grow. He will spread smiles and laughter, and you will be his fortune teller.

Manolo's mother nodded solemnly.

The circus sighed, and all the people in it smiled and nodded and went about the work of creating the smiles and laughter that saves souls.

PHANTASY MOSTE GROTESK

FELICITY DOWKER

The Black Eyed Kid was present at the beginning and the end. He saw everything—always had, probably always would—but it didn't do him or anyone else much good.

Josh Tarnell assumed the knock at his front door at 8:30 pm was the pizza guy delivering his pepperoni deep pan: extra cheese, easy on the sauce. He threw a robe on over his boxer briefs and pulled the door open with one hand, rummaging with the other in the bowl he kept full of change on the hall table.

"Just a sec. I know I've got enough here, won't be—"

It was not the pizza guy.

A small boy stood on the stoop, head cocked to one side, hands shoved in the pockets of his ragged denim shorts. The wan glow of the flickering streetlights revealed a network of scratches criss-crossing their way up the boy's pale legs, and a large brown stain on his lettered t-shirt (*I CHOW DOWN AT BLIMEY'S DINER!*). The boy's eyes were completely black. They gleamed with a wet, fishy coldness as Josh took an involuntary step back, heart slamming against his ribcage.

"Can I come in?" The boy's lips peeled back from his teeth in a grin, revealing a delicate train-track of braces. Josh wanted to scream and slam the door in the kid's face, but even as adrenaline spurted like battery acid in his veins, his mind insisted there was a logical explanation.

Contacts. He's wearing contacts, and one of his buddies dared him to knock on the door and spook whoever opened it. Well, mission accomplished. But don't let on. You know how boys are; you were one not so long ago.

"Nice one, kiddo. You really had me going for a moment there. I'm expecting company, though, so . . . "

"The pimply redhead on the bike with a pizza in his basket? He won't be coming along any time soon. He ran into some trouble."

What the . . .

"Hmmmn. Let me guess. You and your buddies drank his blood, right? Sucked him dry. Ooga booga!" Josh wiggled his fingers at the kid, and had the unnerving feeling that if he kept it up for a moment longer, the kid would lean forward and bite them off. *Crunch*. He recoiled, clasping his hands protectively over his heart.

"No. Can I come in?"

"No? But isn't that your deal? You're being a vampire, right? The creepy eyes, the need to be invited in. I got it, I'm down with it."

"Oh, I'm not a vampire. Can I come in?"

Josh frowned. The little brat was starting to freak him out. He was almost robotic in his persistence, and those eyes were something else.

"Look, I appreciate the effort you've gone to and all—nice job with the eyes—but I just want a quiet night in with a book and some pizza. How about you go try your trick on someone else now, huh?"

"Why don't you just shut the fuck up and let me in, Josh?" The boy's shoulders were drawn up around his ears, and he'd started moving his hands around in his pockets. They were rippling, as if he had tentacles hidden inside them.

Josh tightened his grip on the door handle.

"You kiss your mother with that mouth?" He wanted to clobber the little shit. How dare he turn up on his doorstep uninvited and scare the bejesus out of him?

And just how did he know my name?

"I never had a mother. Seriously, you've got to let me in. If you don't—"

Josh shut the door. As soon as the latch clicked into place, a volley of violent blows rained down on the other side of the wood. Josh stumbled away from the door, hand flying to his mouth, robe falling open.

"Go away," he whispered, and then, as the onslaught reached a crescendo, "Fuck off! Leave me alone! I won't let you in!"

Silence fell like a guillotine blade.

Call someone. Anyone. That kid could still be out there, and even if he's gone, he could come back. You don't want to be alone if that happens. No, not at all.

Josh was punching Erin's number into his phone before he even realized what he was doing. He thought about hanging up before she answered, but as he dangled in indecision, her concise voice spoke into his ear.

"What do you want." It wasn't a question, but a statement of inevitability. She'd known he'd call, eventually. And, as always, she'd been right—though the night's events should surely be noted as extenuating circumstances.

"Something just happened. I . . . can you come over?" The handset was suddenly slippery, sliding in his sweaty palm. He kept one eye fixed on the door, and wondered if the kid's flat black orbs were looking back at him on the other side. Fear snaked up his spine, cold and fast.

"What happened?" Erin was worried despite her better judgment; Josh heard the concern in her voice. He felt like shit for bothering her, but he was glad his welfare still mattered to her.

"Nothing. I mean . . . something . . . but it's hard to explain. Can you come over? Please."

"If this is some sort of game, I'll kick your ass, Josh. I'll be there in half an hour."

"Be careful," he blurted, but she'd already hung up.

"A kid," Erin said flatly, staring down into the steaming cup of tea she held in her hands. He'd always enjoyed her hands. Small, white, and delicate, like fine bone china.

"Not just any kid," Josh said, hearing the whine creep into his voice and hating himself for it.

"A kid with black eyes, then. But they must have been—"

"Contacts. Yeah, I know. The thing is, I'm not so sure they were. He was weird. He made me feel . . . horrified." *God. I'm wasting her time. She'll storm out in disgust any minute. And who would blame her? I'm talking crap.* "He wanted to come in. He almost smashed through the door," he added, desperate to justify his panic. It was already receding, fading into nothingness, and it left only embarrassment in its wake.

"Yeah. There's blood on it, actually," she said, still looking at her tea.

He blinked.

"On the door? Are you serious?"

" 'Fraid so. I saw it on the way in. Thought it must be yours. I assumed . . . " Erin let the words hang in the air. Across from her, Josh shifted on the couch, hugging an overstuffed cushion to his chest like a shield.

"I don't do that anymore."

"That's good, Josh. That's really good. I'm glad."

She looked at him then, and he felt like crying. So much history trembled in her gray eyes. So much love, but hate, too. Had it always been that way? Worst of all, he could see she didn't believe him. Not a single word.

"I'm better now," he murmured.

She smiled in response, but her eyes retained their glassiness. He knew the wall she'd built against him could never again be breached. Their time had been and gone. He'd fucked it up for good.

"You're seeing someone else."

"Oh, Christ, Josh. Just when I think we might be able to have a civil conversation."

"You are, aren't you? I can tell. I can smell him on you."

"Maybe all you smell is your own *bullshit*," she said, slamming her cup down on the coffee table, milky brown tea slopping over her rigid fingers. She stood up, rifling in her bag for her keys, and shoved one arm into the sleeve of her jacket.

Josh lurched to his feet, trying to ignore the buzzing that had begun in his ears. The Big Feelings were welling up, and it would feel so much better if he could just let a little trickle of them out, ease the pressure . . . but no. He'd been serious when he said he was better. He hadn't felt that hideous, wonderful release in months. He dealt with the Big Feelings in other ways now. Saner ways. Journals. Therapy. Pizza. Ways that didn't involve Seth and bubbling red blood welling up from clean, straight cuts . . .

Stop thinking about it. La la la don't think about it la la la block it out la la la.

(let me in . . . oh not by the hair on my chinny chin chin!)

Shuddering and rubbing his forehead with shaking hands, he gave Erin a sickly smile.

"Ez, I'm sorry. Please don't go. I don't . . . I've had a shock tonight. I was stupid a minute ago, and I apologize. Can we pretend I never said anything?"

She stopped her angry preparation for departure and stood staring at him, mouth ajar, coat hanging half on, half off.

"You've never apologized to me before," she said, just as he thought the silence might stretch forever. "Not once."

"I must have. Maybe not much, but I must have at least a few times in the three years you were stuck with me." He tried for a rueful chuckle, but it ended up sounding like a death rattle, and he shut up fast.

"No. Never. Not once."

"Well. I'm sorry now. Will you stay?"

"Yes," she said, letting her coat slide to the floor. A moment later, her bag followed it, landing with a soft *whump.*

"Let's go to the Long Chat Place," she said suddenly, and the Big Feelings were gone without a trace.

The memory of the kid's dark eyes sank back into his subconscious, and he felt a new sensation rush up from his feet, a sensation that swirled in his belly before shooting through his heart and reaching his brain in a starburst of brilliant intensity. What was that? Was it . . . joy?

"Ok. I'll get my keys," he smiled.

"It doesn't mean . . . "

"Don't say it, Ez. I know. You don't need to say it."

She lowered her eyes, and he hurried to get his shit together before she changed her mind.

The Long Chat Place was one of their spots; one of the random sites they'd courted, embraced, kissed, talked, and exchanged little pieces of each other's souls. It was a sporting ground, a grassy oval dotted with goalposts and white markings, sprawled at the end of Josh's street behind a barrier of willow trees. At this time on a Sunday night, it was deserted and still. The moon was a pale, bloated corpse, drifting above them in the fetid waters of the starless sky. A heavy breeze soughed through the twisted branches of the guardian trees and gusted about the open field, bringing with it the stench of something spoiled and oozing.

Josh ignored it.

Nothing could be ugly tonight. Not with Erin by his side, here in this sacred and mundane place. The Big Feelings nibbled on the insides of his mind, whispering to be let out, but he repressed them, too.

"Let's sit here. We used to sit on this exact spot, do you remember? Once, we even—"

"Josh, what's that?" Erin interrupted him, pointed into the gloom, squinting.

He found himself noting the straight length of her arm, the tilt of her hips, the way her brown curls intertwined and spun in the wind like double helixes. He wondered idly if he could overpower her, tackle her from behind and push her down on the moist grass, pin her under his weight and have her one last time. If she screamed, he could tangle his fingers in those curls and grind her face into the soil, muffling her voice as he slid in and out of her, the ghoulish moon watching.

He felt heat begin to throb in his groin, and shifted, trying to ease the pressure as he strained against his jeans.

She might even like it. She always was into the weird stuff. She pretends to be so straight, but she's got a kink in her a mile wide. What's she playing at anyway, leading you out here in the middle of the night, to this place of all places? Fucking tease.

The Big Feelings weren't nibbling anymore; they were biting and clawing, tearing their way free. He had to do something. It was her or him. Him or her. God, just a bit of relief, that's all he needed. One way or another . . .

"Josh." She was at his elbow, squeezing his arm, her lips close to his ear.

He jumped. What had he been thinking? What had he almost done?

(let me in)

"I . . . what did you say?"

She pulled back, studying him, her fingers tight on his forearm. She was anchoring him. He'd slipped away for a moment, gone surfing on the Big Feelings, and they both knew it.

"I said: what's that?"

'That' was a large circus tent, rising up out of the ground like a tumour. It was swathed in darkness, and its canvas flaps waved in the breeze like beckoning hands, inviting Erin and Josh into its gaping maw.

Squinting as Erin had a moment ago, Josh made out the figure of a man standing near the tent's opening. He was motionless.

Waiting.

"It's a tent," Josh said.

Erin sighed.

"Y'think? Wow, lucky I have you with me to explain such mysteries. I can see it's a tent, Josh, but what is a Big Top doing in the middle of the footy oval at the bottom of your street?"

"I have no idea," he said, moving forward.

Her fingers slipped away from his skin, and he felt a moment of acute loss. Nevertheless, he strode through the grass, and she had to trot to keep up with him. A jolt of perverse pleasure made his nerves sing as he heard her breathing roughen and saw her white sneakers flash in the dark, almost a blur.

Yeah, that's it. Jog. You left me, remember? So now you can hustle, bitch. Mush! Mush!

"Josh, wait! Do you think we should go near it? There's someone there. Maybe we should—"

"I bet that's where the kid came from. It's a circus. That's got to be his dad, or his boss, or something. I'm going to have a word with him about what the little jerk's been up to."

"But—"

"You don't have to come," he snapped. He cast an angry glare at her, and saw the shocked O of her mouth, the hurt tilt of her head.

"Josh?" The word bore the weight of a thousand questions and accusations. That caused the fight to go out of him, and he wondered just what the hell he thought he was doing.

Go home. See her to her car and let her drive away. Go inside, eat your cold pizza, scribble in your journal until the Big Feelings die. Go to bed. Everything will be ok.

"Good eve," the man outside the tent said as they approached. "Won't you step inside?"

"Yes," Josh said, his tongue heavy in his mouth.

God, the buzzing in his ears was deafening. He needed to sit down and have some water. Erin's hand was on his arm again, and her small nails dug into his flesh as she coughed, trying to get his attention. He liked the feeling of her hot skin against his. Even the sting of her nails was sweet.

"Hello," Erin said, nodding at the man.

Now that they were closer, Josh saw the guy was a short, round barrel, clad in a giant baby's onesie. Bright light spilled out from the tent, and as Josh's eyes adjusted, he noticed that the fabric of the man's suit was not only pink, but had little yellow rocking horses dotted all over it. An enormous dummy, easily the size of Josh's foot, hung around the man's neck on a thin chain. His head was bald, emblazoned with strange tattoos.

Freak. He's some sort of circus freak, for sure. Man, I love this shit.

"We're just out for a walk," Erin informed the man, who smiled in response. "So thank you for the invitation, but we'd better be on our way. Are you open tomorrow? Will there be a show? Maybe we can come back then."

"There's always a show," the man said, his eyes swinging back and forth between Erin and Josh. "But the best ones are on at night. Right now is a great time. The perfect time, in fact. Would you like to see?"

"Yes," Josh said again.

Erin hissed next to him, her nails gouging so deep that they must surely have drawn blood.

The man stepped aside and waved his hand in a sweeping gesture of welcome. Josh was already moving forward, Erin's nails snagging on his skin before they slid away.

"My name is Seth," the man said.

Erin let out a choked gasp, and Josh smiled.

"Of course it is." In that moment, everything inside Josh's mind was red and silver. The flash of light on surgical steel, the wet glee of gushing blood, the sharp, blessed release.

Seth.

How he'd missed Seth. This man was not *that* Seth, of course. Or perhaps, in a way, he was.

"Are you coming in, Ms. Duhammond? Mr. Tarnell seems to be quite interested."

Josh didn't turn around to see Erin's reply. He could already picture the pained look on her face, and he wasn't sure he wanted to see Seth's. He stood under the tent flaps, listening to them snap in the breeze, waiting. He kept his eyes on the yellow canvas floor beneath his feet. It wasn't time to look around yet. Whatever the signal was, it hadn't been given.

The moment stretched. Josh's breathing slowed. The sound of his heartbeat in his ears joined the rhythmic motion of the tent flaps.

Erin sighed.

"All right," she said, her voice thick and wet. "All right. I'll come in. I'll do it for Josh's sake. But you already knew that. Didn't you, *Seth*? Somehow, you know rather a lot."

"Ladies first, Ms. Duhammond."

"Oh, call me Erin, you bastard. We're getting personal, after all, aren't we?"

"Yes, Erin. You're right. Quite personal."

Erin's hand slipped into the crook of Josh's elbow once more, and his heartbeat sped up to a jackhammer cacophony.

"Let's begin our tour," Seth said softly, raising the tent flaps and gesturing them inside.

"The first question that must be answered is both delicate and mundane." Seth had hopped into a giant brass cradle positioned just inside the entrance, where he perched like an imp, his fingers fluttering to the giant dummy as if for reassurance. "That is, the question of payment."

"Payment?" Josh only had a balled up tissue and a paperclip in the pocket of his trackpants, and he doubted that would suffice. "I don't have anything on me . . . "

"I beg to differ, Mr. Tarnell—Josh, if I may. You have a great deal of value on you at all times. You too, Erin. The real question is: what are you willing to give?"

"Nothing," Erin snapped. "We're not willing to give anything. Look, you've got a quirky thing going on here. You've got the look, you've pulled some tricks, and I can appreciate that. But we've had a rough night, and I can't help but feel you're taking advantage—"

"She still has your scalpel, you know, Josh. She didn't get rid of it. She lied to you. It nestles in a bed of black velvet at the bottom of her wardrobe. She took it out and showed it to her boyfriend once—showed him the rusty stains on the blade. She told him all about how they got there. All about *you*, Josh." Seth circled the teat of the grotesque dummy with one calloused finger, caressing it like a lover's nipple. "She cried on his shoulder, and he *comforted* her all night. Over and over. Isn't that the darnedest thing?"

Josh turned his head far enough to see Erin's face. Her chin was shaking and her eyes were wide. She looked at him, hopeless, imploring. Her skin looked unnaturally pale against the vivid yellow interior of the Big Top, and the Big Feelings buzzed and chirruped in his head.

He craved steel in his hand.

"Josh, I'm leaving. I can't believe you're going along with this. I came over tonight because I was worried. Remember? I was worried about you. But this is . . . crazy. You can come with me. Now. We can still—"

"You can have her," Josh said suddenly, surprised to hear his own voice. He felt soporific, floaty. "Would that do? You can take her. But only for a little while. Only long enough for me to have a look around. Then you have to give her back. She's mine, you see."

"I quite understand. Thank you, Josh. That's an appropriate fee."

"What the fuck—are you completely insane?" Erin screamed.

Josh winced in irritation. The loud, jagged sound was all wrong in this place. He wanted it to stop.

"*Have* me? I'm *yours*? Do you even know what the hell you're talking about?"

"Not really."

"I'm *leaving*. Get that through your thick skull. I'm gone. Take care, Josh. Take a lot of care. In fact, get professional care. You need it."

Erin turned to go. Josh watched with dispassionate eyes as she paused, her back to him. Her hands—pretty, tender things—fluttered forward like timid birds and began to feel their way across the seamless canvas in front of her. They found no opening. The tent flaps had disappeared, leaving no trace of an exit. Her shoulders rose in a sharp inhalation, fell again as the breath blasted out of her. She seemed to deflate, folding in defeat. Finally, she turned, facing Josh and Seth, her eyes narrowed, her lips thin. Her quivering chin betrayed her unease.

"Ok. I don't know how you did that. I don't know how you've done any of this. I'll admit that. But it doesn't make you clever. It makes you sick. I'll say this once, and if you don't do as I say I'll scream and bring the neighborhood down here: let me out."

"Scream away, dear girl. We rather like that in here, and nobody out there will hear a thing." Seth smiled, a broad, moist expression that threatened to split his face in two. "Payment has been given and taken. You're here until Josh leaves. You can wait where you stand, or you can come with us as we journey through the show. That much is up to you."

For the first time, Josh looked around. They stood in a short, high-ceilinged corridor. Nothing but blank yellow canvas surrounded them. Aside from Seth's bizarre cradle, no furnishings broke up the dazzlingly bright space. At the far end of the hall, a red velvet curtain hung, embellished with gold writing that Josh couldn't quite make out. The air was cool and sweet. The sound of children laughing and something like the jangling of an ice cream van's music—"Greensleeves," perhaps—danced across the room to Josh's ears.

"Josh? Can you even hear me?" Erin appeared at his elbow again, niggling like a horsefly. "Just come back, ok? Come back to me. We'll leave together."

"I'm going in, Ez. This is something special. You don't have to come.

But you can't leave, either. I don't want you to, so you can't." He knew she was furious, knew that if they'd been outside this otherworldly tent, she would have given him one of her disappointed, sad looks and walked out on him. She'd always called the shots. If Josh was good, she stayed. If Josh was bad, she left. Reward and punishment. Erin giveth and Erin taketh away.

Well, not in here. And if that pissed her off? Good.

"We'll just take a *little* bit of you," Seth said, smiling impishly. "Nothing you'll miss. The curl of your hair. The shine of your eyes. The softness of your skin. Not such a bad deal, is it? Fair trade, I think."

Is he serious about those things? Will he really take them from her? How? Why? No. He's kidding.

"What does the curtain say?" Josh asked, pacing down the hall. Ever since Erin had pointed the tent out to him, his legs had moved with a mind of their own. In fact, his forward movement had almost always been out of his control. That was precisely the problem.

Nearing the thick fabric, he read the large swirls of golden stitching that looped through the velvet:

Salioso's House of Monsters, Moste Grotesk and Phantastique

"This is the sort of thing I always wished would come to town as a kid. I read about travelling freakshows, amazing monsters, all that stuff. But they're not real. They're horror movie fodder." Josh reached out and touched the curtain. It felt like molten chocolate, the burgundy folds pouring between his fingers in a rush. It was liquid, suspended in semi-solid form. It sent a honeyed golden whisper through his fingertips and into his bloodstream.

"I'll be surprised and deeply offended if you retain that sentiment once you've seen my performers, Josh," Seth said. "But enough shilly shallying. Shall we begin?"

Seth brushed past Josh and slid the curtain aside. Its brass circlets whickered along the wooden rail it dangled from, and it seemed to sigh as it opened. Now Josh could smell fairy floss, buttered popcorn, and sawdust. The children's laughter and ice cream van music was gone, replaced by a steady drumbeat and an unfamiliar shuffling noise.

The Big Feelings were blessedly silent.

Erin punched him on the bicep. Hard. For a moment the room

shimmered, fractured, and he felt enormous regret as the foul odor that had coated the Long Chat Place filled his nostrils. Then everything was solid again.

Erin pushed past him, scowling.

"If I'm here, then I'm coming with you—but I'll be damned if I'll follow you around like some captive damsel," she bit.

Again, he had the overpowering urge to grab her curls, hurt her, defile her.

"You can follow *me*."

"Our first stop will be the Hidebehind," Seth said, before Josh could act on his urges.

"What's a Hidebehind?" Josh asked.

There was no answer, and Josh walked a little faster, keeping Seth's curious onesie-clad form in his sights, along with Erin's bouncing curls.

"In answer to your previous question, Josh, *this* is a Hidebehind."

Seth motioned to the empty air in front of him with a theatrical flourish. Josh's shoulders slumped.

It's all crap, after all.

They stood in a small lounge. A red velvet couch took up most of the room, bursting with stuffing and mangled silver springs. A grandfather clock leant against the far wall. Candles sputtered in gouged-out holes around the clay chamber. A rumpled gray blanket was bunched at one end of the couch, as if someone had leapt hastily out from under it.

"There's nothing in here," Erin said.

Josh nodded, sighing.

"Yeah. This was fun for about five minutes, but now I see—"

"Ah, but you don't *see* anything, Josh. That's rather the point. Instead, what can you hear?" Seth nibbled on his foul dummy like an aperitif, grinning at Josh around the bulbous thing.

And . . . there was a sound. Followed by another. And still another.

Raspy breathing; the subtle swish of a body shifting its weight; a low snarl that rolled around the room, lingering.

"There *is* something in here," Josh murmured. Erin backed up against him in silent confirmation, her spine pressing against his belly. He felt her trembling. He didn't know whether to comfort her or crush her. He settled for wrapping his arm around her shoulders, holding her to him.

"The Hidebehind. American folklore. Never seen directly, but notorious for appearing in the corner of the eye. That couch is our Hidebehind's universe. He sleeps on it, sits on it, and most of all, hides behind it when his lair is invaded. He's really very territorial and can be quite aggressive." Seth's tone was part rote tour guide, part proud parent.

"So . . . this is a room with a monster in it, but we can't see it." Erin had regained enough composure to sound scathing.

Seth seemed delighted by her remark. "Not at all. You can see him, but only in your peripheral vision. Few people use their peripheral vision actively, but it's really very easy. If you allow your eyes to become unfocused and relaxed, fixed on nothing in particular, and, paradoxically, pay close attention to everything *not* in your line of sight . . . "

Josh tried it. The little room blurred and he felt his consciousness retreat inwards, as if pulled by invisible claws.

Then something immense and misshapen lurched out from behind the couch. It was shimmering and indistinct, swaying and changing with unseen eddies of light and air. Where its head should've been, two muscular arms sprouted. Where its arms should've been, a legion of small heads bobbled, malevolent eyes glittering. It moved forward on writhing tentacles, its gyrating torso a mass of decaying teeth. It was at least seven feet tall.

Josh jumped and blinked, his eyes swimming back into focus. The creature was gone, but a roar sounded from behind the tattered couch. Erin gasped and turned, burying her face in his chest.

"It's not real," she said. "It can't be real. It's an optical illusion. A trick of the light."

"Yes." He said. "It must be."

Try as he might, he couldn't make his eyes unfocused again. Seth sat on the couch, smiling. Finally Josh hissed in annoyance, and Seth stood as if a signal had been given.

"The shock of seeing the Hidebehind often makes your body refuse to let you see it again. Deliberately, at least. But don't worry. You'll no doubt get a final look as we leave this room."

Seth scurried to the curtain at the far end of the room, and waited for Josh and Erin to follow. Erin raised her head from Josh's chest and looked up at him with wide grey eyes.

"Are you going further in?" She didn't load the question, didn't throw in any sarcasm.

Josh traced a finger down the nape of her neck, wondering at the effect she had on him. Good Josh and Bad Josh loved her with equal passion.

"Yes," he replied, wishing he could have given her the answer she wanted.

She stiffened.

"Let's do it, then."

As they followed Seth through the curtain, the Hidebehind leapt into Josh's peripheral vision. It was fast, and it charged towards them, its countless faces contorted. It hated them, meant to destroy them. Josh looked directly at the thing, and, with a scream of frustration, it disappeared.

"Easy," he breathed. "Done."

The curtain closed behind them, and they stood in a dim hall, with yet another curtain awaiting them at the far end. Seth hitched up his onesie, which had begun to wilt down toward his fluffy feet, and regarded them sternly.

"Now, there is the matter of payment. We operate on an installment basis. The first installment—Erin staying with us—was paid as your entrance fee. Now that you've seen the first exhibit, another installment is due. Shall we say . . . "

Before Josh or Erin could react, Seth stretched out one of his flabby hands and stroked Erin's hair. Erin gasped. Seth stepped back, dipping his head in a satisfied nod.

"That is most acceptable," he said, spinning neatly on his heels and heading for the next curtain.

"What did he do to me? I feel . . . funny." Sweat stippled Erin's brow. She swayed like a tree about to topple. Her skin had developed a green tinge. Josh reached out to steady her, but recoiled with a startled exhalation.

Erin's bulging eyes implored him. "What? What's wrong with me?"

"N-nothing. I just . . . let's keep going." He wasn't lying, not really. The change she'd gone through wasn't big in the scheme of things, wasn't overtly horrific. Aside from looking ill, the only thing wrong with Erin was that her hair wasn't curly anymore. It fell in straight sheets, heavy and dull, a shroud draped over Erin's head. She struggled to hold her head up as they staggered forward, as if the weight of her tresses—somehow so horribly *reduced*—pulled her down.

"I'll look after you," Josh told her, knowing it was an empty promise.

"I know you'll try. I feel like me being here with you might be the only thing that can help you now. I'm sorry I wasn't always there in the past. I'm sorry I couldn't stay when you were—"

"That's all over now. I told you, I'm better." He didn't want to hear her talk about the time the Big Feelings ran his life, the era of steel and blood and tears. Something was wrong with him, yes. Something was very wrong with this place, sure. But it wasn't *that* wrongness. It wasn't the

(LET *me* IN)

ills of old, and that had to count for something.

He hurried after Seth, ignoring his sickened heart.

"And now to the Ferris Wheel." Seth threw the curtain aside. The sound of screeching metal drifted toward them on the rancid breeze that flowed through the Big Top. Erin grimaced and held her nose.

Josh frowned. "A Ferris Wheel is not a monster."

Seth giggled. "It is in Salioso's House of Monsters. Everything here is *moste* grotesk and phantastique, my dear friends." He ushered them in.

The room beyond the curtain was enormous. The roof was so high it couldn't be seen. The walls were hundreds of meters apart. Josh cupped his hands to his mouth and shouted wordlessly. His voice bounced again and again off the un-boundaries of the room. The vast expanse of yellow— always that cheerful yellow!—finally swallowed his yell after what felt like an eternity.

"This place has got to be ten times the size of the whole tent," Erin said.

"Yes," Seth responded. "Easily. Now, shall we ride our good friend Ferris?"

Josh looked sidelong at Seth. "You say it like the Wheel is a pers—"

Oh God.

Josh stopped marveling at the gigantic room and looked at the Wheel in the center of it.

Its red metal struts jutted up into the heavens, dotted at their ends with carriages like grossly oversized cherries. Fairy lights twinkled all over the structure, and somewhere, calliope music played as the Wheel groaned through endless rotations.

Josh moaned.

A man was crucified on the Wheel.

His torso, positioned at the center of the contraption, was pushed forward by the convex hub behind it so that he seemed to be jutting his pelvis suggestively at them. His head was slumped forward onto his chest, dark clumps of hair obscuring his face. His arms and legs were impossibly stretched, tethered to the Wheel, tapering from the center to the outer limits. The red of the struts was not paint but the man's blood, flowing in ceaseless rivulets. The metal carried the blood like mechanized veins, feeding it to the membranous carriages. The Wheel bore the blood-filled sacs around and around, and the tortured man spun with them, stretched and helpless.

"Meet Ferris," Seth said, his feet marking a jig of excitement on the canvas floor. "He's a relatively new addition to our show, but I think you'll agree he's a good 'un."

"That's the sickest thing I have ever seen. I know it's not real . . . but it's sick. You should be ashamed. Do children come through here?" Erin prodded Seth in his fuzzy chest.

Seth's mouth opened wide in a cackle, and he stroked her finger when it jabbed his sternum. Erin shuddered, swaying on her feet again. Josh moved to catch her. She felt like a bony bird in his hands, brittle and barely there at all. He turned her around gently. Her eyes rolled toward him, and he suppressed a scream.

They were pure black, gleaming flatly in her head, and the image of the boy on his doorstep earlier that night (was it the *same* night? It seemed so distant now) flashed through his mind.

"What have you done to her?" Josh reeled her in like a tiny fish, securing her in his arms, glaring over her head at Seth. The little man smiled serenely back at him.

And then Ferris began to shriek.

Josh looked back at the lengthened man on the Wheel, and saw Ferris' head rise. The man's eyes whirled in their sockets, his mouth twisting in an impossibly wide grimace. Blood spilled from his eyes, nose, mouth and ears. He struggled against his impossible bonds, causing the Wheel to shudder on its rotation, but not halt.

"Make him stop, make him stop, please, make him stop . . . " Erin whimpered into Josh's ribs. Josh's mind tilted a little more. The Big Feelings rushed forward, seizing him in his moment of weakness.

He clenched and unclenched his fists against Erin's back. The craving for a blade to be in each of them was a physical pain. He wondered how much force it would take to crush her into lifelessness; not much, given her current fragility.

If he only had a blade . . . if he had a blade, he could turn the Big Feelings on himself, release enough of his own blood to appease them and ensure he spilt none of hers . . . if she hadn't taken his Seth, his scalpel, his release . . . if . . .

"You won't hurt her, Josh. Our business is not yet done here. There are more installments to be made on the agreed payment. You'll control yourself." Seth's voice was polite, but beneath it a layer of iron lurked.

The Big Feelings receded a little, and Josh looked at the smaller man, fuming.

"You're mad. This is disgusting. We want to leave."

"Oh, I'm afraid that's quite impossible. There's only one way out of here, and that's straight ahead. We can't exit until we've been through all the exhibits. Now, we can leave this room and move on to the next if you wish, but it seems a shame to leave Ferris without enjoying the full extent of his talents . . . "

Seth darted forward and placed his hand on one of the sac carriages, his fingers splayed on the membrane. The carriage wobbled and belched under his touch, then bowed inward, giving way. Seth's arm disappeared into the thing up to the elbow.

"It's very warm inside the carriages. They have their own special heating, you might say. Quite womblike, and the filling tastes simply delicious. Ferris works so hard to keep the carriages supplied; won't you at least have one ride to show your appreciation?"

The man on the Wheel gave a final ululating cry before his head fell forward again. Then all was silent except for the perpetual dripping of his blood and the gamboling of the calliope tune in the background.

"I'm not going near that thing," Josh whispered.

Seth sighed and withdrew his hand—clean and smooth—from the blood sac with a juicy *squelch*. "As you desire. What a waste. Well, onward!" With a loud suck of his dummy, Seth was off, scampering toward the far curtain.

Erin went limp in Josh's arms. He swept her up and, carrying her like a baby, followed Seth. He kept his eyes fixed on the floor and didn't look at the profane Wheel again. Erin's eyelids fluttered. Josh glimpsed the blackness of her eyes and shivered. Yet . . . he was still excited. He wanted to see what lay on the other side of the curtain. He wanted to keep going. He was glad Erin was unconscious so that his niggling conscience could be quieted for a moment.

The Big Feelings snarled like prowling panthers and he smiled, stroking them in his mind.

I'll let you off your chain soon. I know I'll have to. But . . . not yet.

The curtain rose and fell, and they materialized in a dark corridor, in between

(worlds)

exhibits.

"I suppose you want another payment now," Josh said, his voice a dull glimmer in the gloom.

Seth raised an eyebrow at him, surprised.

"Why, no. I'm not greedy. As you saw, I took the liberty of securing the next installment while we were visiting young Ferris back there."

Contemplating Erin's half-closed gimlet eyes, Josh nodded.

"Yeah. So you did. Then why have we stopped here?"

Seth leaned forward conspiratorially.

"As I said, I'm not greedy. I don't take payment where it's not due, and what's more, I like to give back where I can. So I'm going to give you a gift. A piece of her to keep for your very own. You'd like that, wouldn't you, Josh?"

The Big Feelings drew back, and Josh clutched Erin to him, hissing.

Seth chuckled.

"Oh, not like that. I would never harm her, Josh. You're doing that all by yourself. This was your idea, remember?"

"Why, you—you—"

"Now, now. Back to my boon to you. Did you know she's thought about you every day since she left you that final time? She's driven to your house on numerous occasions, parked at the end of your street, and watched your comings and goings. Just to make sure you were alright. Isn't that the sweetest thing?"

Josh felt Erin's pulse thrumming weakly beneath his fingertips and pictured her lurking, watching him. Caring for him. Her unmoving form was an accusation in his arms.

"She watched to see if you had started cutting yourself again. She had

Seth—*your* Seth, the blade, the relief, not *me*, of course—but there are other cutting edges in the world, and she wondered if you were using them. When she was certain you were not, she stopped following you. But she still dreamt of you every night, cried into her pillow over you every morning, dug her nails into her boyfriend's back and pretended it was you every time they—"

"Stop." Wetness trickled down Josh's cheek. Tears. That was new. He'd sooner let blood than cry. It was a rare occurrence, but better to do it while Erin couldn't see, couldn't hear, couldn't look at him with worry in her eyes—although, now that they were unadulterated black, he wondered if her eyes could contain any emotion at all. The thought brought forth a choked sob, and Seth patted him on the shoulder.

"There now. Let it out. We like the release of bodily fluids here. Anyway, she still loves you. She would have taken you back in a heartbeat. Oh, she would have pretended to put up a fight, and you would have played along like the little pup you are, but she always intended to be with you in the end, Josh. You might have been completely healthy. You surely would have had a long and fruitful life together. But . . . . "

Josh's tears became a flood, pattering down on Erin's unresponsive skin.

"That'll never happen now, as I'm sure you've deduced. So there is my gift to you: the knowledge of what you had and lost. Some people never realize such mysteries for themselves. It's a great boon. Cradle it to you as you cradle her, and let's move on. You know, I think we'll only see one more exhibit. Maybe two. It's different for everyone, but you and your lover took the least time yet. Interesting."

With that, Seth skipped forward, vanishing through the next curtain.

Still shaking with sobs, clinging to Erin's stirring body like a life-raft, Josh followed.

"Don't wake up, Ez," Josh crooned into her flat hair. "Just keep sleeping, love."

But she did wake, twitching in his arms until he gently placed her on her feet. She looked at him with fathomless black eyes and his mind gave a final tilt, swinging him in earnest toward madness.

"Are we free?" she said. "Did we get out? Has it all gone away?"

"I'm afraid not, my dear. But you're lucky enough to have awoken in time to see the next exhibit." Seth sounded bored. He plopped his dummy into his mouth and gnawed at it as if it were a juicy bone, sucking and slurping with abandon.

Erin's face drooped.

Seth spoke around his dummy, the words mangled and wet. "Without further ado, may I introduce . . . Salioso's room of Doppelgangers! Of course, since you're a smaller group than we're used to, there are only two here today, but I'm sure they'll prove extremely entertaining nonetheless."

Barely bothering to complete the flourish of his hand, Seth crossed the mirrored room and sat on one of the wooden chairs on the opposite side, the only furnishings in the chamber. One of the mirrors shimmered and wavered, and two figures stepped out.

Josh gasped. Erin stared, flat-eyed.

Their precise doubles stood facing them. Erin's had her newly straight brown hair and black eyes, but, unlike Erin, throbbed with life and energy—and was completely naked. She taunted Erin, gyrating inches from her, cupping her nude breasts and leering, her pink tongue lashing over her ruby lips.

"Cold, dead fish," the thing sneered. "I'm more than you ever were. He never wanted you. He always wanted me. He saw *me* when he looked at you. I'm here now. You're as good as dead. Ugly, stupid bitch!"

The creature leant forward on the final word and spat in Erin's face. The saliva slithered down Erin's cheek as she stood motionless. Furious, Josh slapped the woman-thing open handed across the face. Far from deterred, the creature dropped into a crouch and clasped Josh's calf, rubbing herself against him, panting.

"Oh, you know I like it rough," it moaned. The thing's hands were hot and its body was slick; Josh felt his own body respond despite himself. "You were thinking about giving it to me rough, remember, in the Long Chat Place? You wanted me then. You want me now. Stay here, lover, and have me! Have me as long and as hard and as often as you want. Anything you like. I want you. She's nothing compared to me. It's me you've wanted. Take me!"

The thing reached for his belt and unbuckled it in one smooth pull. He wavered, Big Feelings flooding his brain while blood rushed to his groin. She felt amazing. Her hand made his closed zipper a distant memory and he felt the cool air on his bare legs as she tore his jeans off. He rocked back on his heels as her fingers grasped him, as her sex massaged his leg, as her lips wrapped around him . . .

Then he heard the distinctive sound of a punch next to him, followed by a muffled moan and tearing fabric.

"No! Stop! Please, Josh, don't hurt me!"

Did Erin really see that man-thing—and whatever it was trying to do to her—as being *him*?

Did *he* really see the thing kneeling before him now as *her*?

With a snarl, he shoved the female Doppelganger's head away from him and turned to Erin. The male Doppelganger—the Josh-thing—had her on the floor, one hand gripping her throat, the other yanking the remains of her skirt from her. The creature was naked like its female counterpart.

"Get away from her," Josh roared, aiming a massive kick at the creature's head. His boot connected with a jarring thud and the thing rolled over several times, coming to rest against the wall.

Sinuous, tempting arms clutched his shoulders from behind, and a velvet voice murmured in his ear. "That was gallant. I've always loved your chivalrous side. You'll slip into me like a hot knife into butter. I'll never leave you, never deny you, not like *her*. I'm soft and delicious, but I'm hard and strong, too. You can do what you like to me and I'll bounce right back—and I'll *love* it."

The thing's tongue snaked from its plump lips and lapped at Josh's earlobe. He shuddered, a jolt of white heat rocketing through his body and numbing his mind. He wanted to turn and grab the creature, throw it to the ground, and climb aboard. He wanted to say the dirtiest, vilest, evilest things to it and watch its face as he did. He wanted to hurt it and love it and own it. He wanted . . . he wanted . . . want . . .

"Josh," Erin whispered from the floor.

He wanted to *kill*.

He spun around and tore the creature's spindly arms from his shoulders. He saw surprise on the Doppelganger's face as it turned to run. Before it could get away, he reached out and caught a fistful of brown, lank hair. The creature screeched and flailed, twisting away from him.

Josh stepped forward, hooking one foot under the Doppelganger's pedaling feet and pulling them out from under the thing. The pseudo-Erin fell face-first to the floor, howling. Not hesitating, Josh dropped one knee into the creature's back and landed with the full force of his body right between its jutting shoulder blades.

As the woman-thing gave a final scream, Josh released the creature's hair and reached forward, grasping its chin in one hand and forehead in the other, and

yanked

back.

The creature's neck broke. After the loud *snap*, all was still and silent at last.

"Interesting," Seth commented from his perch. "A waste, to be sure. She was a delight. But . . . very interesting indeed."

Josh fell back from the dead creature in disgust and crawled toward Erin. She sat in the tatters of her skirt, her arms wrapped around herself, black eyes bottomless and her face slack. When he neared her, her mouth twitched, but she said nothing.

"I'm so sorry, Ez," he croaked. "I love you, and I wish I'd never brought you in here. I wish I'd been strong enough to stand up to the Big Feelings and to Seth, but you know he was always my weakness and my release, and I couldn't deny him." He was babbling gibberish now, and yet, it made sense and it was important that she hear him, where ever she'd gone.

"Heads up," Seth remarked casually.

Josh only had a moment to look up before the male Doppelganger's fist knocked him onto his back. His jaw rang with pain, and the world blurred into a hazy web of yellow.

"She's mine," snarled the Doppelganger. "Always was. Always will be. I own the bitch. What's left of her, anyway. What's left will do just fine for my purposes."

The thing's laughter was oily and low, oozing like pus.

Rage propelled Josh up and at the creature. It was waiting for him, dropped low in a fighting crouch, its appendage dangling like an added insult between its muscular thighs. It was him, of course, but . . . better, harder, stronger, and with far more hatred than he'd ever felt for anything pumping through its supernatural veins.

He hit it head-on, and it fell, crushed under his body. Without pausing to think, he made his thumb and forefinger into prongs and rammed them into the thing's eyes. He felt the membrane burst, and pushed on, through the jelly and oozing liquid, into the squiggly mush of the creature's brain.

He ground everything his fingers touched to a fine paste. The creature screamed, gurgled, and finally fell silent. Its body jerked under him. The sensation was revoltingly intimate. He rolled off and staggered to his feet, gasping for breath.

The Big Feelings were quiet, and for a moment he cruised, drifting on the blissful waves of nothingness.

"Well," Seth said, standing. "I think we're just about done. Let's adjourn for our final business, shall we? If you could help Ms. Duhammond to her feet, we'll be on our way."

Josh reached down and pulled Erin into his arms for the last time. She felt like a bag of feathers. She was almost gone. He squeezed her and it was like hugging a cloud of vapor. She was diminishing as the seconds ticked by. Whatever had been Erin Duhammond was almost extinct.

And he'd done it.

His tears formed a shimmering curtain, shrouding his eyes as Seth led him and the bundle of skin and bones he carried through the last red velvet curtain in Salioso's House of Monsters, Moste Grotesk and Phantastique.

"Don't touch her," Josh said. "No more of your payments. You've taken enough."

"Yes, I have. Payment has been made in full. I took the final one while you enjoyed your time with Ms. Duhammond's Doppelganger. You didn't even notice."

(the softness of your skin)

The life was gone from Erin. It winked out in her black eyes as Josh looked down on her, and then, without a sound, she disappeared.

"What have you done with her?" Josh fell to his knees, tears burning his cheeks like acid rain.

"I haven't done a thing. You did it all, Josh. You made choices every step of the way. You followed your desires and your impulses. You designed and delivered the payment. I merely obliged you. Erin is now part of Salioso's show. And so are you."

The room around them was bare: yellow walls, yellow floor, yellow ceiling. No furniture. Average size. But it was gravid with life; it ebbed and flowed and bent and stretched before Josh's eyes. It was almost as if it itched to take shape, but waited for direction.

"Where is she?" Josh's voice was a whisper. His tears had dried up.

"Nowhere, as far as you're concerned. Although I rather think she might form part of your exhibit. I have a sense for these things, after the time I've spent here."

Twirling his dummy on its chain, the little man broke into a whistle. He strolled to the far end of the room and pressed his hand to the wall. It melted at his touch, exposing a gaping hole. He stepped into it and threw Josh a cheery wave.

"Farewell, young Josh. I'll see you again. So many souls come to Salioso's House, and they're all eager for a show. You'll entertain a great number of them, forever and forever and forever. You and your Big Feelings, boogeying on down in the ultimate Big Top. It's a beautiful thing. Oh, look. Your exhibit is taking shape. And yes, there she is. Splendid."

"Who is Salioso?" Josh's lips were stiffening, and his brain seemed to be grinding to a halt. He forced the words out, knowing they were probably his last.

"You asked that a little late, m'boy! And it really doesn't matter. He's no one and nothing you'd understand. But he owns you. And, unlike you, Josh, he never gives up that which is his."

The wall closed with a *thud*, and Seth was gone.

Josh had been wrong. As his body snapped and cracked, driving him across the room and into a position outside his control—as his brain petrified and changed, motivating him in ways he could not override—his *real* last words slipped from between his bloodying lips.

"Ez," he sighed. "Erin."

"Step right this way, please! Keep together now, this one gets a bit messy and I wouldn't want you to get lost in the spatter. Yes, that's right, sit down there, nice and comfy. All settled? Good, we'll begin. Allow me to introduce—the Cutting Man!"

The dwarfish entertainer, now wearing a garish purple tutu and leotard, his tattooed bald head shining in the light reflected from the yellow canvas, motioned grandly to the stage at the front of the long room. A group of twenty people sat spellbound, gazing up at it, waiting for their entertainment to commence. The tutu-clad man's eyes roamed the crowd, and, unseen, he made a gun out of his thumb and forefinger and mimed shooting each person in the head. The nametag on his left breast read HI! MY NAME IS STEVE-O! Josh would have told the crowd that he'd known the man as Seth once upon a nightmare, but he was unable. It didn't matter, anyway.

Josh stood on the stage, still, quiet, waiting. In his hand, a giant scalpel—so big it was more of a sword—sparkled. Etched in large black letters on the blade was the word *Seth*. He raised the blade at a right angle to his body and paused. She wasn't here yet.

The crowd was hushed. A little boy whispered to his mother and she shushed him, not wanting to miss a moment of the coming show.

Ah. There.

Erin crossed the stage on gliding feet, her diaphanous white gown billowing behind her. Her hair was a glossy brown, plentiful with curls. Her eyes were grey and bright. Her skin was flushed with beauty and life. Her smile was wide and generous, and her hand was on her heart.

It always began this way.

"I love you," he told her. As he uttered the words, his hand swung above his head, and brought the vicious blade down on Erin. It struck with an audible *crack*, cleaving her skull in two. Her head stayed stubbornly on her body, branching off in two directions like a forked tongue. Her hand—small, pale, delicate—jerked away from her heart and fluttered to her wounded head. The gash was clean, and she smiled at him around it.

"I love you, too," she said. She felt no pain.

Josh took it all.

He felt the fountain of blood spurt from his own head, felt the searing, crippling agony. He swayed on his feet, but didn't—couldn't—fall. He would not be permitted to collapse to the ground until this was over. Until she was a twitching, unrecognizable pile of pieces on the floor, and he was a red geyser of suffering.

His love was his blade, and he scored them both with it, but he felt the pain. For that, at least, he was thankful.

"Mummy, is it real?" The little boy was crying.

His mother's voice was shocked, but calm. "Of course not, darling. It's just a show. The nice man *might* have warned us it wasn't going to be suitable for children—" she threw a shrewish look over her shoulder at "STEVE-O", who smiled disarmingly in response, "—but it's not real. You just hide your face in Mummy's shoulder here, and—"

"No," the boy said, sniffing. "I want to see."

Yes. Of course he did. They all did. And Josh would give them what they wanted. He had no choice. "I want to protect you," he told Erin, this time lopping off her right arm. She looked at the dry stump in mild bemusement, then turned her radiant smile on him.

"I'm safe as long as I'm with you," she said.

His right shoulder was an orchestra of pain. Blood gushed to the floor in torrents of bubbling claret, and he gritted his teeth. It was all he could do. The ability to scream had been taken from him. Everything had been taken from him, other than the abilities he had used most in life: the release of his own blood, and the damaging of the one he held most dear whilst hurting himself.

This was his great and secret show.

In the back row, behind the spectators and the little man in the tutu who clapped his hands in delight at each new blow, a familiar boy stood. His face was contorted with grief, and he wrung his hands in distress. Blood red tears dripped from his black eyes. His t-shirt declared to the world his preference for *BLIMEY'S DINER*.

"Should have let me in, Josh," he whispered. "I tried to warn you, to save you. I try to save them all. They never let me in."

The man in the tutu's tattooed head spun 180 degrees on his shoulders, his neck bunching in pink ridges. His eyes locked on the Black Eyed Kid, and his mouth widened in an immense snarl. The boy slipped away through the red velvet curtain.

"I really must do something about that 'un," the man said, adjusting his STEVE-O badge and turning back to the bloody onstage action. "He's a pest, to be sure. Still, he never does any real harm. There's no stopping them when they're determined to see the show."

In the background, the tune of an ancient calliope ground on and on, and the scent of popcorn and sawdust drifted on the thick, rancid air.

LEARNING TO LEAVE

CHRISTOPHER BARZAK

When I was twelve years old, my mother broke one of the ceramic elephants my father had given her as an anniversary present. I'm not sure for which anniversary it had been a gift, but it was my mother's favorite, a circus elephant, with gold braiding draped around its neck, a red fez on its head, and a brown glazed saddle on its back where an absent rider could sit if they'd wanted to. My mother used to let me play with her elephant collection whenever I took to a terrible boredom but remained well behaved, which was often. I was a good girl in those days. So often I'd found my mother crying over my father that, growing up, I tried hard not to cause her any more sadness.

The argument that led to the smashing of the anniversary elephant occurred sometime in the early hours of a Friday in late June. I woke to the sound of my mother's voice, a shriek that filled the house, followed by the smash of the elephant on the tiles of the kitchen floor.

Three days earlier we had celebrated my father's birthday by driving to a truck stop on I-90 for dinner. This was my father's favorite place to eat. At dinner, everyone had seemed pleasant and happy. I ate beans and potatoes and egg salad from the buffet. My mother settled on a small breast of chicken. My grandmother, who had lived with us for the past year, ate nothing but mashed potatoes. She said her gums were hurting her something fierce. My father ate steak with a ravishing hunger, sopping up the orange yolk of his eggs with triangles of toast. This was his favorite meal, whether it was breakfast, lunch, or dinner. Afterwards, we went home and watched television until we were so tired we fell into our beds.

When I woke the next morning to the sound of my mother smashing the elephant, I nearly turned over and fell back to sleep. But something, guilt or compassion or both of these things, made me sit up, brush my hair, and go down to see what was the matter.

My mother sat on the floor next to the elephant shards. My father was nowhere to be found. This was not a shocking scene really. Let's get that clear right off. Mine was not a happy family, even if we managed to have pleasant birthday meals together. My mother was the saddest person I'd ever met. What made her sad was my father, who was also sad, but in a different way. My father was sad for some unnamable reason. He worked in a factory that made paint can lids, just the lids, and drank at a bar called the Roanoke nearly every day, after a ten hour shift. Sometimes he came home from the bar. Sometimes he didn't. Sometimes he went home with women who drank there, too. This was disrespectful to my mother, and also to me, his adolescent daughter who needed a good male role model so that she would not grow up to fall into romances with men who were just like her father, who she thought she could change, but that is another story altogether. I say all the things my father did were disrespectful, but the most disrespectful thing was that my father did nothing to hide these things from other people, or from his family. I might have scored his bad behavior test a little easier if he'd have taken our feelings into account more often.

I didn't ask my mother what happened. The possible disasters associated with my father made a list of small but powerful things. He had either come home drunk that morning, or he had not come home at all. Instead of prying, I let her sit with her arms wrapped around her legs, her head on her knees, and sob. I took the broom from its corner, swept up the pieces of elephant, and disposed of them in the trash for her instead.

Later that day my grandmother would suck her teeth and shake her head at my mother's weakness. "I could have told you he'd do that," she'd say. My grandmother was a nasty woman and did not realize her own nastiness. She was fond of telling my mother all the bad things she knew about my father after he had just committed one of his atrocious acts. I think when my grandmother said things like, "I heard he goes round to that Sylvia Cordial's house too. Don't think he's got only one hussy," that she was intending to push a little so that my mother would finally break and throw him out. But all she managed to do with her well intended, badly reasoned, dirty laundry lists about my father was to make my mother cry.

My father didn't come home all that day or night. It was not until the next morning that we'd hear from him. Let me revise: That I'd hear from him.

I was the one who picked up the phone while my mother lay in bed to hear my father say, "Ellie, morning darlin'. Be a good girl and put your mother on the phone."

I did not immediately move to do anything. Instead I decided to ask a question. This was very bold of me, if I do say so myself. I was not one to ask questions. I believed that, for the most part, this was between him and my mother, that they needed to solve their own problems and that I shouldn't have to be involved. But I was lying to myself with that reasoning and slowly coming to the realization that I, too, suffered from their problems. It was when I realized I would have to live with them for six more years that I decided to ask my question. "What happened?" I asked. I figured when an elephant gets broken, blood badder than usual has been spilled.

"Just put your mother on the phone, Ellie," he told me.

I covered the mouthpiece with the palm of my hand and thought about this for a while. Then I uncovered the phone and said, "No. I want you to tell me what happened."

I waited for a while and my father finally said, "Ellie, God damn it! Do as you're told!"

This time I listened. I hated when my father raised his voice. It made something inside me go rubbery with fear. So I did as he said and shouted up the stairs, "Dad's on the phone!" But I didn't hear my mother stir. I uncovered the phone and said, "No dice," to my father, and he hung up from wherever he'd been calling from.

It didn't take long for my parents to make up. Since this was a regularly occurring event in our household, they had their forgiveness rituals down pat. Later that night my father came home with a handful of flowers. He handed them to my mother through the narrow space of the chain-locked door. The flowers were wilted and hopeless, with roots and dirt dangling from their stems. He had obviously picked them from someone else's yard. Still, when he begged her, she swung the door open and he thanked her by wrapping her up in his arms. My mother hated when he begged. She couldn't refuse his ability to make her feel as though she was so powerful he'd do anything to make her happy again. And maybe that was true some, because for a while, he *would* try to make her happy, and me too.

I dreaded it when my father decided to take an interest in us. He'd give me things, but they were never what I wanted, and I would accept his offerings feeling as though I had to be the worst daughter in the world. Or at least in Ohio. Or at least in our town.

Every summer a traveling carnival dragged its sorry act through our part of the state, on its way across the country. It set up red-striped tents and sideshow booths and tables filled with memorabilia to buy. It played circus music, organ pipes, as loud as possible, hoping the music would have pied-piper effects on the local kids. Usually we never went—my father said nothing but Amish would be milling around those fairgrounds—but now, suddenly, he thought it would be the perfect cure for our woes.

So we went on what had to be the hottest day of summer, in the third week of July, and saw everything the carnival offered. There was a man who swallowed swords. There was a man who walked on a bed of hot coals. There was a woman who clenched a rope in her teeth and spun on it in midair. There was a woman they stuffed in a box, who twisted her body into unbelievable positions. Her manager would pierce her box with knives but she always managed to bend around their blades. They called her the Plastic Woman, and her manager would let you slip round to the back of the box to see her for a dollar. My father and mother and I went back to see her. Her legs were up behind her ears and her arms were spread across the width of the box, her hands placed flat against its sides. She gritted her teeth in a forced smile. We stared at her for a while, gaping, and the man behind us chuckled. He told my father he wondered what else she might do for a dollar. Both of them laughed and went off to have a beer.

There were other things to see at the fair, too. There was a large blue tent where two monkeys guarded the entrance. They took the ticket you bought to get inside. Sometimes they fought over which one got to take your ticket, and all the town mothers would laugh and say, "Aren't they something?" while the kids rolled their eyes and sighed.

Inside the tent, bleachers were arranged in a circle against the walls, and pale orange sawdust covered the floor. A lion tamer stood in the center of the tent. He snapped his whip at the lions. A man on a trapeze threw women in the air to another man on another trapeze. The women's bodies floated in space for what seemed like eternity, before the men grasped their hands and swung them to safety. They didn't use a net, which my mother said was illegal, but nobody seemed to mind. There were elephants as well, which excited my mother. She said, "I haven't seen a live elephant since I was nine years old and your grandpa, God rest his soul, took me to the circus."

The elephants paraded behind their trainer, a man who made them roll over, sound their trumpets, stand on their hind legs, kneel down and pick him up for a ride, trot in circles, and finally stand on pedestals. My mother and I watched all of this in a glaze of amazement. Her own excitement excited me. She said, "Elephants are one of the smartest creatures on this here earth, Ellie," and I nodded and sighed with wonder.

After the elephants performed we went to see them in what the ringmaster called their natural environment. The natural environment happened to be behind the tent. We ran back there as if we were rock star groupies with backstage passes, only to be disappointed to find the elephants behind the lion cages, tied to posts. It ruined the moment, really, to see them standing there, chewing on hay, completely and utterly mundane. A man fed them hay and my mother warned him that the posts didn't seem strong enough to keep an elephant tied down. "Those posts," she said, waggling her finger, "why they're no bigger than saplings."

The man laughed like we were dumb. He said, "These here elephants are too stupid to pull at their posts, ma'am," and proceeded to tell us they'd been tied up since they were babies, when they weren't strong enough to pull away. "They've learned to have a rope round their necks by now," he said, grinning, reassuring us of something. "Really," he said, "they don't know the difference. They don't realize they're strong enough now to pull away."

For the rest of the day, my mother behaved strangely. She gave me caramel apples and quarters to play arcade games, she let me drink five lemon shakes. A vacant stare was all she could manage, and sometimes she'd snap suddenly awake and say something like, "Yes? Come again?"

Finally, hours later, I told my mother I wanted to go home. My mother agreed, but we couldn't find my father. We checked everywhere, and checked everywhere again, until finally one of our neighbors, Mrs. Banesville, a woman who played piano for the church choir and worked at the butcher shop cleaning carcasses, told us she'd seen him leave several hours ago. "With that Pliable Woman," she said.

My mother corrected her. "It's the Plastic Woman, Mrs. Banesville," she said. To which Mrs. Banesville replied by nodding and blinking. "The Plastic Woman," my mother repeated, as if we hadn't heard her the first time.

My mother didn't go home and cry like I expected. She didn't wait up for my father or tell me to go to bed. She ignored my grandma, who paced the hallways with her arms waving wildly as she advised my mother on exactly what she had to do to save herself from this torture, which consisted of divorcing my father or else maiming him. My mother simply sat at the kitchen table, drinking coffee. She stared into space and agreed with my grandma, but you could tell she wasn't really listening.

I went out on the porch roof that sat just below my bedroom window, thinking things would be fine even though my father wasn't home. He'd done far worse things to upset my mother in the past. I saw our neighbors, the Hendersons, return from the fair a couple of hours later, and watched as the yellow lights in their house turned off, one by one. I imagined Mrs. Henderson going from room to room, flipping off switches. I imagined her tucking her small children into bed, turning on a bedside fan. It was all very peaceful and strange, thinking about the Henderson family, and soon I fell asleep beneath the stars with the taste of caramel still in my mouth, and the organ music from the fairgrounds still piping in my ears.

It wasn't till the next morning that I learned what had happened while I slept. I got the story from a variety of sources—my nasty grandmother, who loved to talk about it, also from my father and various people in town, and even a bit from my mother, so what I relate now is partially made up, but also mostly true.

During the night, my mother left the house and slipped back into the fairgrounds. She untied all of the elephants and told them they were free to leave. "Get out of here," she told them. "This is your big break." She smacked their hindquarters to move them, and offered handfuls of peanuts as bribes. Later she told me she'd planned to get them out of there and leave things at that, but one of the elephants had suddenly knelt down and offered her a ride. My mother couldn't refuse the gesture, so she swung herself up on its back, and the pack of them rode out of town together, down Highway 88.

They made it to Pennsylvania by the next morning, when a cop spotted them crossing I-90. Negotiating the morning traffic, moving as fast as they could with the cars and semis blaring their horns around them, they were not hard to miss. They were trying to make it into the hills of the Allegheny Mountains, where they planned to hide and rest. The police rounded up the elephants with the help of their trainer, and afterwards they called my father to fill him in. My father, who'd returned in the night, who knows when, tore out of our driveway to retrieve my mother from the Pennsylvania Highway Patrol. "I hope to God they didn't film this for that police show," he muttered as he dashed out the front door.

When they arrived home several hours later, my mother wasn't speaking, and my father kept saying, "Come on, Hannah. Talk to me, baby." But she wouldn't. Not a word would come out of her for several days and nights. My father pulled out his wallet and gave me ten dollars. He asked me to go to the fairgrounds and buy my mother a new ceramic elephant to replace the one she'd smashed the previous month, which I did, taking nearly an hour to pick out just the right one.

When I gave her the new elephant later that night, my mother stroked my hair and said, "Have you been washing with my Coconut shampoo, Ellie? Your hair is so silky." I smiled and said I'd done that, even though I hadn't washed my hair for a couple of days. Really, the difference was in her hands, I thought. They were slowly becoming as rough and calloused as my grandma's, and I thought at some point, even sandpaper would feel smooth to her.

My mother's escape with the elephants had been joyous. She told me that herself. For several hours, riding on their backs, she had felt like she was an explorer, riding up into the mountains, to a place in her imagination that she had never touched. "It felt like what flying must feel like," said my mother. "Like taking off into the blue air."

I did not make much of what happened, and I tell you now I wish I had. I was too much like my mother, though, too used to everything, too ready to sweep up the pieces instead of letting them lie there and look at them for a while. If I had said something, encouraged her, told her how proud I was, that she and I should save our money and leave, then perhaps she would have felt that feeling again some day, and learned how to keep a hold of it.

Instead, two years later my father would leave us for good. One morning he didn't come back from wherever he'd been the night before and after a few weeks passed a letter arrived from California, saying he was sorry but he wouldn't be back this time. My mother tore that letter to pieces, and afterward I gathered them in the privacy of my room and taped them back together. In case my father did return one day, I wanted to be able to take his words out and say he'd retracted his position from our lives and that I had it in writing. I wanted proof to be able to tell him he could no longer return.

Leaving was probably the best thing my father could have done, and when I think about it I still thank him for finally having the courage to permanently flee whatever it was in our family that caused him to leave temporarily and so often for most of my early years. What I do not thank him for, what I am still angry with him for to this very day, is that he preempted any possibility of my mother ever learning to leave on her own.

It was some time after he left, probably a few weeks after we got the letter, that my grandmother, still caught in the idea that supporting her daughter consisted of talking badly about my father, told my mother, "I knew that man would leave you high and dry, I knew it from the start, but no. You wouldn't listen. Now if your father were alive, you'd have listened to him, but nooo—"

"Shut up," I interrupted. "Shut up, you stupid old woman. Can't you see she doesn't need your haranguing?"

My grandmother looked at me in shock. Tears filled her eyes, but she left the room and left my mother, finally, alone.

This was the first in a series of interruptions I would make as I grew older. First with my grandmother, then with my mother as I graduated and left home against her will, left Ohio altogether, to attend college. Then later, with boyfriends and two husbands, then with my own children, after they grew up and became young twenty-somethings who thought they knew better, who thought their mother was a foolish middle aged woman who didn't know how to settle down. "Shut up," I'd say, interrupting them whenever they tried to tell me who I was. "This is me," I'd say. "This is who I am," I told them all.

Whenever I did that, I'd feel some part of me learning to leave, learning how to leave people who would only bind me to what they wanted. No one, I'd think, would ever keep me to being only one woman again. Each time I said, "No," each time I said, "Shut up," or, "Get out," I'd remember

my grandmother's face from the day I first said something completely
mine. I would think of how she crumpled and withered. I would think of
the power I felt as she melted to nothing, like a green-faced witch, right
before my eyes.

GINNY SWEETHIPS' FLYING CIRCUS

NEAL BARRETT, JR.

Del drove and Ginny sat.

"They're taking their sweet time," Ginny said, "damned if they're not."

"They're itchy," Del said. "Everyone's itchy. Everyone's looking to stay alive."

"Huh!" Ginny showed disgust. "I sure don't care for sittin' out here in the sun. My price is going up by the minute. You wait and see if it doesn't."

"Don't get greedy," Del said.

Ginny curled her toes on the dash. Her legs felt warm in the sun. The stockade was a hundred yards off. Barbed wire looped above the walls. The sign over the gate read:

> **First Church of the Unleaded God**
> **& Ace High Refinery**
> WELCOME
> KEEP OUT

The refinery needed paint. It had likely been silver, but was now dull as pewter and black rust. Ginny leaned out the window and called to Possum Dark.

"What's happening, friend? Those mothers dead in there or what?"

"Thinking," Possum said. "Fixing to make a move. Considering what to do." Possum Dark sat atop the van in a steno chair bolted to the roof. Circling the chair was a swivel-ring mount sporting fine twin-fifties black as grease. Possum had a death-view clean around. Keeping out the sun was a red Cinzano umbrella faded pink. Possum studied the stockade and watched heat distort the flats. He didn't care for the effect. He was suspicious of things less than cut and dried. Apprehensive of illusions of every kind. He scratched his nose and curled his tail around his leg. The gate opened up and men started across the scrub. He teased them in his sights. He prayed they'd do something silly and grand.

Possum counted thirty-seven men. A few carried sidearms, openly or concealed. Possum spotted them all at once. He wasn't too concerned. This seemed like an easygoing bunch, more intent on fun than fracas. Still, there was always the hope that he was wrong.

The men milled about. They wore patched denim and faded shirts. Possum made them nervous. Del countered that; his appearance set them at ease. The men looked at Del, poked each other, and grinned. Del was scrawny and bald except for tufts around the ears. The dusty black coat was too big. His neck thrust out of his shirt like a newborn buzzard looking for meat. The men forgot Possum and gathered around, waiting to see what Del would do. Waiting for Del to get around to showing them what they'd come to see. The van was painted turtle-green. Gold Barnum type named the owner, and the selected vices for sale:

Ginny Sweethips' Flying Circus
SEX*TACOS*DANGEROUS DRUGS

Del puttered about with this and that. He unhitched the wagon from the van and folded out a handy little stage. It didn't take three minutes to set up, but he dragged it out to ten, then ten on top of that. The men started to whistle and clap their hands. Del looked alarmed. They liked that. He stumbled and they laughed.

"Hey, mister, you got a girl in there or not?" a man called out.

"Better be something here besides you," another said.

"Gents," Del said, raising his hands for quiet, "Ginny Sweethips herself will soon appear on this stage, and you'll be more than glad you waited. Your every wish will be fulfilled, I promise you that. I'm bringing beauty to the wastelands, gents. Lust the way you like it, passion unrestrained. Sexual crimes you never dreamed!"

"Cut the talk, mister," a man with peach-pit eyes shouted to Del. "Show us what you got."

Others joined in, stomped their feet and whistled. Del knew he had them. Anger was what he wanted. Frustration and denial. Hatred waiting for sweet release. He waved them off, but they wouldn't stop. He placed one hand on the door of the van—and brought them to silence at once.

The double doors opened. A worn red curtain was revealed, stenciled with hearts and cherubs. Del extended his hand. He seemed to search behind the curtain, one eye closed in concentration. He looked alarmed, groping for something he couldn't find. Uncertain he remembered how to do this trick at all. And then, in a sudden burst of motion, Ginny did a double forward flip, and appeared like glory on the stage.

The men broke into shouts of wild abandon. Ginny led them in a cheer. She was dressed for the occasion. Short white skirt shiny bright, white boots with tassels. White sweater with a big red G sewn on the front.

"Ginny Sweethips, gents," Del announced with a flair, "giving you her own interpretation of Barbara Jean, the Cheerleader Next Door. Innocent as snow, yet a little bit wicked and willing to learn, if Biff the Quarterback will only teach her. Now, what do you say to *that?*"

They whistled and yelled and stomped. Ginny strutted and switched, doing long-legged kicks that left them gasping with delight. Thirty-seven pairs of eyes showed their needs. Men guessed at hidden parts. Dusted off scenarios of violence and love. Then, as quickly as she'd come, Ginny was gone. Men threatened to storm the stage. Del grinned without concern. The curtain parted and Ginny was back, blond hair replaced with saucy red, costume changed in the blink of an eye. Del introduced Nurse Nora, an angel of mercy weak as soup in the hands of Patient Pete. Moments later, hair black as a raven's throat, she was Schoolteacher Sally, cold as well water, until Steve the Bad Student loosed the fury chained within.

Ginny vanished again. Applause thundered over the flats. Del urged them on, then spread his hands for quiet.

"Did I lie to you gents? Is she all you ever dreamed? Is this the love you've wanted all your life? Could you ask for sweeter limbs, for softer flesh? For whiter teeth, for brighter eyes?"

"Yeah, but is she *real?*" a man shouted, a man with a broken face sewn up like a sock. "We're religious people here. We don't fuck with no machines."

Others echoed the question with bold shouts and shaking fists.

"Now, I don't blame you, sir, at all," Del said. "I've had a few dolly droids myself. A plastic embrace at best, I'll grant you that. Not for the likes of you, for I can tell you're a man who knows his women. No, sir, Ginny's real as rain, and she's yours in the role of your choice. Seven minutes of bliss. It'll seem like a lifetime, gents, I promise you that. Your goods gladly returned if I'm a liar. And all for only a U.S. gallon of gas!"

Howls and groans at that, as Del expected.

"That's a *cheat* is what it is! Ain't a woman worth it!"

"Gas is better'n gold, and we work damn hard to get it!"

Del stood his ground. Looked grim and disappointed. "I'd be the last man alive to try to part you from your goods," Del said. "It's not my place to drive a fellow into the arms of sweet content, to make him rest his manly frame on golden thighs. Not if he thinks this lovely girl's not worth the fee, no sir. I don't do business that way and never have."

The men moved closer. Del could smell their discontent. He read sly thoughts above their heads. There was always this moment when it occurred to them there was a way Ginny's delights might be obtained for free.

"Give it some thought, friends," Del said. "A man's got to do what he's got to do. And while you're making up your minds, turn your eyes to the top of the van for a startling and absolutely free display of the slickest bit of marksmanship you're ever likely to see!"

Before Del's words were out of his mouth and on the way, before the men could scarcely comprehend, Ginny appeared again and tossed a dozen china saucers in the air.

Possum Dark moved in a blur. Turned 140 degrees in his bolted steno chair and whipped his guns on target, blasting saucers to dust. Thunder rolled across the flats. Crockery rained on the men below. Possum stood and offered a pink killer grin and a little bow. The men saw six-foot-nine and a quarter inches of happy marsupial fury and awesome speed, of black agate eyes and a snout full of icy varmint teeth. Doubts were swept aside. Fifty-calibre madness wasn't the answer. Fun today was clearly not for free.

"Gentlemen, start your engines," Del smiled. "I'll be right here to take your fee. Enjoy a hot taco while you wait your turn at glory. Have a look at our display of fine pharmaceutical wonders and mind-expanding drugs."

In moments, men were making their way back to the stockade. Soon after that, they returned toting battered tins of gas. Del sniffed each gallon, in case some buffoon thought water would get him by. Each man received a token and took his place. Del sold tacos and dangerous drugs, taking what he could get in trade. Candles and Mason jars, a rusty knife. Half a manual on full-field maintenance for the Chrysler Mark XX Urban Tank. The drugs were different colors but the same: twelve parts oregano, three parts rabbit shit, one part marijuana stems. All this under Possum's watchful eye.

"By God," said the first man out of the van. "She's worth it, I'll tell you that. Have her do the Nurse, you won't regret it!"

"The Schoolteacher's best," said the second man through. "I never seen the like. I don't care if she's real or she ain't."

"What's in these tacos?" a customer asked Del.

"Nobody you know, mister," Del said.

"It's been a long day," Ginny said. "I'm pooped, and that's the truth." She wrinkled up her nose. "First thing we hit a town, you hose 'er out good now, Del. Place smells like a sewer or maybe worse."

Del squinted at the sky and pulled up under the scant shade of mesquite. He stepped out and kicked the tires. Ginny got down, walked around, and stretched.

"It's getting late," Del said. "You want to go on or stop here?"

"You figure those boys might decide to get a rebate on this gas?"

"Hope they do," Possum said from atop the van.

"You're a pisser," Ginny laughed, "I'll say that. Hell, let's keep going. I could use a hot bath and town food. What you figure's up the road?"

"East Bad News," Del said, "if this map's worth anything at all. Ginny, night driving's no good. You don't know what's waiting down the road."

"I know what's on the roof," Ginny said. "Let's do it. I'm itchy all over with bugs and dirt and that tub keeps shinin' in my head. You want me to drive a spell, I sure will."

"Get in," Del grumbled. "Your driving's scarier than anything I'll meet."

Morning arrived in purple shadow and metal tones, copper, silver, and gold. From a distance, East Bad News looked to Ginny like garbage strewn carelessly over the flats. Closer, it looked like larger garbage. Tin shacks and tents and haphazard buildings rehashed from whatever they were before. Cookfires burned, and the locals wandered about and yawned and scratched. Three places offered food. Other places bed and a bath. Something to look forward to, at least. She spotted the sign down at the far end of town.

MORO'S REPAIRS
Armaments*Machinery*Electronic Shit of All Kinds

"Hold it!" Ginny said. "Pull 'er in right there."

Del looked alarmed. "What for?"

"Don't get excited. There's gear needs tending in back. I just want 'em to take a look."

"Didn't mention it to me," Del said.

Ginny saw the sad and droopy eyes, the tired wisps of hair sticking flat to Del's ears. "Del, there wasn't anything to mention," she said in a kindly tone. "Nothing you can really put your finger on, I mean. okay?"

"Whatever you think," Del said, clearly out of sorts.

Ginny sighed and got out. Barbed wire surrounded the yard behind the shop. The yard was ankle-deep in tangles of rope and copper cable, rusted unidentifiable parts. A battered pickup hugged the wall. Morning heat curled the tin roof of the building. More parts spilled out of the door. Possum made a funny noise, and Ginny saw the Dog step into the light. A Shepherd, maybe six-foot-two. It showed Possum Dark yellow eyes. A man appeared behind the Dog, wiping heavy grease on his pants. Bare to the waist, hair like stuffing out of a chair. Features hard as rock, flint eyes to match. Not bad looking, thought Ginny, if you cleaned him up good.

"Well now," said the man. He glanced at the van, read the legend on the side, took in Ginny from head to toe. "What can I do for *you*, little lady?"

"I'm not real little and don't guess I'm any lady," Ginny said. "Whatever you're thinking, don't. You open for business or just talk?"

The man grinned. "My name's Moro Gain. Never turn business away if I can help it."

"I need electric stuff."

"We got it. What's the problem?"

"Huh-unh." Ginny shook her head. "First, I gotta ask. You do confidential work or tell everything you know?"

"Secret's my middle name," Moro said. "Might cost a little more, but you got it."

"How much?"

Moro closed one eye. "Now, how do I know that? You got a nuclear device in there, or a broken watch? Drive it on in and we'll take a look." He aimed a greasy finger at Possum Dark. "Leave *him* outside."

"No way."

"No arms in the shop. That's a rule."

"He isn't carrying. Just the guns you see." Ginny smiled. "You can shake him down if you like. *I* wouldn't, I don't think."

"He looks imposing, all right."

"I'd say he is."

"What the hell," Moro said, "drive it in."

Dog unlocked the gate. Possum climbed down and followed with oily eyes.

"Go find us a place to stay," Ginny said to Del. "Clean, if you can find it. All the hot water in town. Christ sakes, Del, you still sulking or what?"

"Don't worry about me," Del said. "Don't concern yourself at all."

"Right." She hopped behind the wheel. Moro began kicking the door of his shop. It finally sprang free, wide enough to take the van. The supply wagon rocked along behind. Moro lifted the tarp, eyed the thirty-seven tins of unleaded with great interest.

"You get lousy mileage, or what?" he asked Ginny.

Ginny didn't answer. She stepped out of the van. Light came through broken panes of glass. The skinny windows reminded her of a church. Her eyes got used to shadow, and she saw that that's what it was. Pews sat to the side, piled high with auto parts. A 1997 Olds was jacked up before the altar.

"Nice place you got here," she said.

"It works for me," Moro told her. "Now what kind of trouble you got? Something in the wiring? You said electric stuff."

"I didn't mean the motor. Back here." She led him to the rear and opened the doors.

"God a'Mighty!" Moro said.

"Smells a little raunchy right now. Can't help that till we hose 'er down." Ginny stepped inside, looked back, and saw Moro still on the ground. "You coming up or not?"

"Just thinking."

"About what?" She'd seen him watching her move and didn't really have to ask.

"Well, *you* know . . . " Moro shuffled his feet. "How do you figure on paying? For whatever it is I got to do."

"Gas. You take a look. Tell me how many tins. I say yes or no."

"We could work something out."

"We could, huh?"

"Sure." Moro gave her a foolish grin. "Why not?"

Ginny didn't blink. "Mister, what kind of girl do you think I am?"

Moro looked puzzled and intent. "I can read good, lady, believe it or not. I figured you wasn't tacos or dangerous drugs."

"You figured wrong," Ginny said. "Sex is just software to me, and don't you forget it. I haven't got all day to watch you moonin' over my parts. I got to move or stand still. When I stand still, you look. When I move, you look more. Can't fault you for that, I'm about the prettiest thing you ever saw. Don't let it get in the way of your work."

Moro couldn't think of much to say. He took a breath and stepped into the van. There was a bed bolted flat against the floor. A red cotton spread, a worn satin pillow that said DURANGO, COLORADO and pictured chipmunks and waterfalls. An end table, a pink-shaded lamp with flamingos on the side. Red curtains on the walls. Ballet prints and a naked Minnie Mouse.

"Somethin' else," Moro said.

"Back here's the problem," Ginny said. She pulled a curtain aside at the front of the van. There was a plywood cabinet, fitted with brass screws. Ginny took a key out of her jeans and opened it up.

Moro stared a minute, then laughed aloud. "*Sensory* tapes? Well, I'll be a son of a bitch." He took a new look at Ginny, a look Ginny didn't miss. "Haven't seen a rig like this in years. Didn't know there were any still around."

"I've got three tapes," Ginny explained. "A brunette, a redhead, and a blond. Found a whole cache in Ardmore, Oklahoma. Had to look at 'bout three or four hundred to find girls that looked close enough to me. Nearly went nuts 'fore it was over. Anyway, I did it. Spliced 'em down to seven minutes each."

Moro glanced back at the bed. "How do you put 'em under?"

"Little needle comes up out the mattress. Sticks them in the ass lightnin' fast. They're out like *that*. Seven-minute dose. Headpiece is in the end table there. I get it on and off them real quick. Wires go under the floorboards back here to the rig."

"Jesus," Moro said. "They ever catch you at this, you are cooked, lady."

"That's what Possum's for," Ginny said. "Possum's pretty good at what he does. Now what's *that* look all about?"

"I wasn't sure right off if you were real."

Ginny laughed aloud. "So what do you think now?"

"I think maybe you are."

"Right," Ginny said. "It's Del who's the droid, not me. Wimp IX Series. Didn't make a whole lot. Not much demand. The customers think it's me, never think to look at him. He's a damn good barker and pretty good at tacos and drugs. A little too sensitive, you ask me. Well, nobody's perfect, so they say."

"The trouble you're having's in the rig?"

"I guess," Ginny said, "beats the hell out of me." She bit her lip and wrinkled her brow. Moro found the gestures most inviting. "Slips a little, I think. Maybe I got a short, huh?"

"Maybe." Moro fiddled with the rig, testing one of the spools with his thumb. "I'll have to get in here and see."

"It's all yours. I'll be wherever it is Del's got me staying."

"Ruby John's," Moro said. "Only place there is with a good roof. I'd like to take you out to dinner."

"Well sure you would."

"You got a real shitty attitude, friend."

"I get a whole lot of practice," Ginny said.

"And I've got a certain amount of pride," Moro told her. "I don't intend to ask you more than three or four times and that's it."

Ginny nodded. Right on the edge of approval. "You've got promise," she said. "Not a whole lot, maybe, but some."

"Does that mean dinner, or not?"

"Means not. Means if I *wanted* to have dinner with some guy, you'd maybe fit the bill."

Moro's eyes got hot. "Hell with you, lady. I don't need the company that bad."

"Fine." Ginny sniffed the air and walked out. "You have a nice day."

Moro watched her walk. Watched denims mold her legs, studied the hydraulics of her hips. Considered several unlikely acts. Considered cleaning up, searching for proper clothes. Considered finding a bottle and watching the tapes. A plastic embrace at best, or so he'd heard, but a lot less hassle in the end.

Possum Dark watched the van disappear into the shop. He felt uneasy at once. His place was on top. Keeping Ginny from harm. Sending feral prayers for murder to absent genetic gods. His eyes hadn't left Dog since he'd appeared. Primal smells, old fears and needs, assailed his senses. Dog locked the gate and turned around. Didn't come closer, just turned.

"I'm Dog Quick," he said, folding hairy arms. "I don't much care for Possums."

"I don't much care for Dogs," said Possum Dark.

Dog seemed to understand. "What did you do before the War?"

"Worked in a theme park. Our Wildlife Heritage. That kind of shit. What about you?"

"Security, what else?" Dog made a face. "Learned a little electrics. Picked up a lot more from Moro Gain. I've done worse." He nodded toward the shop. "You like to shoot people with that thing?"

"Anytime I get the chance."

"You ever play any cards?"

"Some." Possum Dark showed his teeth. "I guess I could handle myself with a Dog."

"For real goods?" Dog returned the grin.

"New deck, unbroken seal, table stakes," Possum said.

Moro showed up at Ruby John's Cot Emporium close to noon. Ginny had a semiprivate stall, covered by a blanket. She'd bathed and braided her hair and cut the legs clean off her jeans. She tugged at Moro's heart.

"It'll be tomorrow morning," Moro said. "Cost you ten gallons of gas."

"Ten gallons," Ginny said. "That's stealin', and you know it."

"Take it or leave it," Moro said. "You got a bad head in that rig. Going to come right off, you don't fix it. You wouldn't like that. Your customers wouldn't like it any at all."

Ginny appeared subdued but not much. "Four gallons. Tops."

"Eight. I got to make the parts myself."

"Five."

"Six," Moro said. "Six and I take you to dinner."

"Five and a half, and I want to be out of this sweatbox at dawn. On the road and gone when the sun starts bakin' your lovely town."

"Damn, you're fun to have around."

Ginny smiled. Sweet and disarming, an unexpected event. "I'm all right. You got to get to know me."

"Just how do I go about that?"

"You don't." The smile turned sober. "I haven't figured that one out."

It looked like rain to the north. Sunrise was dreary. Muddy, less-than-spectacular yellows and reds. Colors through a window no one had bothered to wash. Moro had the van brought out. He said he'd thrown in a lube and hosed out the back. Five and a half gallons were gone out of the wagon. Ginny had Del count while Moro watched.

"I'm honest," Moro said, "you don't have to do that."

"I know," Ginny said, glancing curiously at Dog, who was looking rather strange. He seemed out of sorts. Sulky and off his feed. Ginny followed his eyes and saw Possum atop the van. Possum showed a wet Possum grin.

"Where you headed now?" Moro asked, wanting to hold her as long as he could.

"South," Ginny said, since she was facing that direction.

"I wouldn't," Moro said, "Not real friendly folks down there."

"I'm not picky. Business is business."

"No, sir," Moro shook his head. "*Bad* business is what it is. You got the Dry Heaves south and east. Doom City after that. Straight down and you'll hit the Hackers. Might run into Fort Pru, bunch of disgruntled insurance agents out on the flats. Stay clear away from them. Isn't worth whatever you'll make."

"You've been a big help," Ginny said.

Moro gripped her door. "You ever *listen* to anyone, lady? I'm giving good advice."

"Fine," Ginny said, "I'm 'bout as grateful as I can be."

Moro watched her leave. He was consumed by her appearance. The day seemed to focus in her eyes. Nothing he said pleased her in the least. Still, her disdain was friendly enough. There was no malice at all that he could see.

There was something about the sound of Doom City she didn't like. Ginny told Del to head south and maybe west. Around noon, a yellow haze appeared on the ragged rim of the world, like someone rolling a cheap dirty rug across the flats.

"Sandstorm," Possum called from the roof. "Right out of the west. I don't like it at all. I think we better turn. Looks like trouble coming fast."

There was nothing Possum said she couldn't see. He had a habit of saying either too little or more than enough. She told him to cover his guns and get inside, that the sand would take his hide and there was nothing out there he needed to kill that wouldn't wait. Possum Dark sulked but climbed down. Hunched in back of the van, he grasped air in the shape of grips and trigger guards. Practiced rage and windage in his head.

"I'll bet I can beat that storm," Del said. "I got this feeling I can do it."

"Beat it where?" Ginny said. "We don't know where we are or what's ahead."

"That's true," Del said. "All the more reason then to get there soon as we can."

Ginny stepped out and viewed the world with disregard. "I got sand in my teeth and in my toes," she complained. "I'll bet that Moro Gain knows right where storms'll likely be. I'll bet that's what happened, all right."

"Seemed like a decent sort to me," Del said.

"That's what I mean," Ginny said. "You can't trust a man like that at all."

The storm had seemed to last a couple of days. Ginny figured maybe an hour. The sky looked bad as cabbage soup. The land looked just the way it had. She couldn't see the difference between sand recently gone or newly arrived. Del got the van going again. Ginny thought about yesterday's bath. East Bad News had its points.

Before they topped the first rise, Possum Dark began to stomp on the roof. "Vehicles to port," he called out. "Sedans and pickup trucks. Flatbeds and semis. Buses of all kinds."

"What are they doing?" Del said.

"Coming right at us, hauling timber."

"Doing *what?*" Ginny made a face. "Damn it all, Del, will you stop the car? I swear, you're a driving fool."

Del stopped. Ginny climbed up with Possum to watch. The caravan kept a straight line. Cars and trucks weren't exactly hauling timber . . . but they were. Each carried a section of a wall. Split logs bound together, sharpened at the top. The lead car turned and the others followed. The lead car turned again. In a moment, there was a wooden stockade assembled on the flats, square as if you'd drawn it with a rule. A stockade and a gate. Over the gate a wooden sign:

FORT PRU
Games of Chance & Amusement
Term*Whole Life*Half Life*Death

"I don't like it," said Possum Dark.

"You don't like anything's still alive," Ginny said.

"They've got small arms and they're a nervous-looking bunch."

"They're just horny, Possum. That's the same as nervous, or close enough." Possum pretended to understand. "Looks like they're pulled up for the night," she called to Del. "Let's do some business, friend. The overhead don't ever stop."

Five of them came out to the van. They all looked alike. Stringy, darkened by the sun. Bare to the waist except for collars and striped ties. Each carried an attaché case thin as two slices of bread without butter. Two had pistols stuck in their belts. The leader carried a fine-looking sawed-off Remington 12. It hung by a camou guitar strap to his waist. Del didn't like him at all. He had perfect white teeth and a bald head. Eyes the color of jellyfish melting on the beach. He studied the sign on the van and looked at Del.

"You got a whore inside or not?"

Del looked him straight on. "I'm a little displeased at that. It's not the way to talk."

"Hey." The man gave Del a wink. "You don't have to give us the pitch. We're show business folk ourselves."

"Is that right?"

"Wheels of chance and honest cards. Odds I *know* you'll like. I'm head actuary of this bunch. Name's Fred. That animal up there has a piss-poor attitude, friend. No reason to poke that weapon down my throat. We're friendly people here."

"No reason I can see why Possum'd spray this place with lead and diarrhetics," Del said. "Less you can think of something I can't."

Fred smiled at that. The sun made a big gold ball on his head. "I guess we'll try your girl," he told Del. " 'Course we got to see her first. What do you take in trade?"

"Goods as fine as what you're getting in return."

"I've got just the thing." The head actuary winked again. The gesture was starting to irritate Del. Fred nodded, and a friend drew clean white paper from his case. "This here is heavy bond," he told Del, shuffling the edges with his thumb. "Fifty percent linen weave, and we got it by the ream. Won't find anything like it. You can mark on it good or trade it off. Seventh Mercenary Writers came through a week ago. Whole brigade of mounted horse. Near cleaned us out, but we can spare a few reams. We got pencils too. Mirado twos and threes, unsharpened, with erasers on the end. When's the last time you saw *that?* Why, this stuff's good as gold. We got staples and legal pads. Claim forms, maim forms, forms of every sort. Deals on wheels is what we got. And *you* got gas under wraps in the wagon behind your van. I can smell it plain from here. Friend, we can sure talk some business with you there. I got seventeen rusty-ass guzzlers runnin' dry."

A gnat-whisker wire sparked hot in Del's head. He could see it in the underwriter's eyes. Gasoline greed was what it was, and he knew these men were bent on more than fleshly pleasure. He knew with androidial dread that when they could, they'd make their play.

"Well now, the gas is not for trade," he said as calmly as he could. "Sex and tacos and dangerous drugs is what we sell."

"No problem," the actuary said. "Why, no problem at all. Just an idea, is all it was. You get that little gal out here and I'll bring in my crew. How's half a ream a man sound to you?"

"Just as fair as it can be," Del said, thinking that half of that would've been fine, knowing dead certain now that Fred intended to take back whatever he gave.

"That Moro fellow was right," Del said. "These insurance boys are bad news. Best thing we can do is take off and let it go."

"Pooh," said Ginny, "that's just the way men are. They come in mad as foamin' dogs and go away like cats licking cream. That's the nature of the fornicatin' trade. You wait and see. Besides, they won't get funny with Possum Dark."

"You wouldn't pray for rain if you were afire," Del muttered. "Well, I'm not unhitching the gas. I'll set you up a stage over the tarp. You can do your number there."

"Suit yourself," Ginny said, kissing a plastic cheek and scooting him out the door. "Now get on out of here and let me start getting cute."

It seemed to be going well. Cheerleader Barbara Jean awoke forgotten wet dreams, left their mouths as dry as snakes. Set them up for Sally the Teach and Nora Nurse, secret violations of the soul. Maybe Ginny was right, Del decided. Faced with girlie delights, a man's normally shitty outlook disappeared. When he was done, he didn't want to wreck a thing for an hour or maybe two. Didn't care about killing for half a day. Del could only guess at this magic and how it worked. Data was one thing, sweet encounters something else.

He caught Possum's eye and felt secure. Forty-eight men waited their turns. Possum knew the caliber of their arms, the length of every blade. His black twin-fifties blessed them all.

Fred the actuary sidled up and grinned at Del. "We sure ought to talk about gas. That's what we ought to do."

"Look," Del said, "gas isn't for trade, I told you that. Go talk to those boys at the refinery, same as us."

"Tried to. They got no use for office supplies."

"That's not my problem," Del said.

"Maybe it is."

Del didn't miss the razor tones. "You got something to say, just say it."

"Half of your gas. We pay our way with the girl and don't give you any trouble."

"You forget about *him?*"

Fred studied Possum Dark. "I can afford losses better than you. Listen, I know what you are, friend. I know you're not a man. Had a CPA droid just like you 'fore the War."

"Maybe we can talk," Del said, trying to figure what to do.

"Say now, that's what I like to hear."

Ginny's fourth customer staggered out, wild-eyed and white around the gills. "Goddamn, try the Nurse," he bawled to the others. "Never had nothin' like it in my life!"

"Next," Del said, and started stacking bond paper. "Lust is the name of the game, gents, what did I tell you now?"

"The girl plastic, too?" Fred asked.

"Real as you," Del said. "We make some kind of deal, how do I know you'll keep your word?"

"Jesus," Fred said, "what do you think I am? You got my Life Underwriter's Oath!"

The next customer exploded through the curtain, tripped and fell on his face. Picked himself up and shook his head. He looked damaged, bleeding around the eyes.

"She's a tiger," Del announced, wondering what the hell was going on. " 'Scuse me a minute," he told Fred, and slipped inside the van. "Just what are you doing in here?" he asked Ginny. "Those boys look like they been through a thrasher."

"Beats me," Ginny said, halfway between Nora and Barbara Jean. "Last old boy jerked around like a snake having a fit. Started pulling out his hair. Somethin' isn't right here, Del. It's gotta be the tapes. I figure that Moro fellow's a cheat."

"We got trouble inside and out," Del told her. "The head of this bunch wants our gas."

"Well, he sure can't have it, by God."

"Ginny, the man's got bug-spit eyes. Says he'll take his chances with Possum. We better clear out while we can."

"Huh-unh." Ginny shook her head. "That'll rile 'em for sure. Give me a minute or two. We've done a bunch of Noras and a Sally. I'll switch them all to Barbara Jean and see."

Del slipped back outside. It seemed a dubious answer at best.

"That's some woman," said Fred.

"She's something else today. Your insurance boys have got her fired."

Fred grinned at that. "Guess I better give her a try."

"I wouldn't," Del said.

"Why not?"

"Let her calm down some. Might be more than you want to handle."

He knew at once this wasn't the thing to say. Fred turned the color of ketchup pie. "Why, you plastic piece of shit! I can handle any woman born . . . *or* put together out of a kit."

"Suit yourself," Del said, feeling the day going down the drain. "No charge at all."

"Damn right there's not." Fred jerked the next man out of line. "Get ready in there, little lady. I am going to handle *all* your policy needs!"

The men cheered. Possum Dark, who understood at least three-fifths of the trouble down below, shot Del a questioning look.

"Got any of those tacos?" someone asked.

"Not likely," Del said.

Del considered turning himself off. Android suicide seemed the answer. But in less than three minutes, unnatural howls began to come from the van. The howls turned to shrieks. Life underwriters went rigid. Then Fred emerged, shattered. He looked like a man who'd kicked a bear with boils. His joints appeared to bend the wrong way. He looked whomper-eyed at Del, dazed and out-of-synch. Everything happened then in seconds thin as wire. Del saw Fred find him, saw the oil-spill eyes catch him clean. Saw the sawed-off barrels match the eyes so fast even electric feet couldn't snatch him out of the way in time. Del's arm exploded. He let it go and ran for the van. Possum couldn't help. The actuary was below and too close. The twin-fifties opened up. Underwriters fled. Possum stitched the sand and sent them flying ragged and dead.

Del reached the driver's seat as lead peppered the van. He felt slightly silly. Sitting there with one arm, one hand on the wheel.

"Move over," Ginny said, "that isn't going to work."

"I guess not."

Ginny sent them lurching through the scrub. "Never saw anything like it in my life," she said aloud. "Turned that poor fella on, he started twisting out of his socks, bones snapping like sticks. Damndest orgasm I *ever* saw."

"Something's not working just right."

"Well, I can see that, Del. Jesus, what's that!"

Ginny twisted the wheel as a large part of the desert rose straight up in the air. Smoking sand rained down on the van.

"Rockets," Del said grimly. "That's the reason they figured that crazy-fingered Possum was a snap. Watch where you're going, girl!"

Two fiery pillars exploded ahead. Del leaned out the window and looked back. Half of Fort Pru's wall was in pursuit. Possum sprayed everything in sight, but he couldn't spot where the rockets were coming from. Underwriter assault cars split up, came at them from every side.

"Trying to flank us," Del said. A rocket burst to the right. "Ginny, I'm not real sure what to do."

"How's the stub?"

"Slight electric tingle. Like a doorbell half a mile away. Ginny, they get us in a circle, we're in very deep shit."

"They hit that gas, we won't have to worry about a thing. Oh Lord, now why did I think of that?"

Possum hit a semi clean on. It came to a stop and died, fell over like a bug. Del could see that being a truck and a wall all at once had its problems, balance being one.

"Head right at them," he told Ginny, "then veer off sharp. They can't turn quick going fast."

"Del!"

Bullets rattled the van. Something heavy made a noise. The van skewed to a halt.

Ginny took her hands off the wheel and looked grim. "It appears they got the tires. Del, we're flat dead is what we are. Let's get out of this thing."

And do *what?* Del wondered. Bearings seemed to roll about in his head. He sensed a malfunction on the way.

The Fort Pru vehicles shrieked to a stop. Crazed life agents piled out and came at them over the flats, firing small arms and hurling stones. A rocket burst nearby.

Possum's guns suddenly stopped. Ginny grimaced in disgust. "Don't you tell me we're out of ammo, Possum Dark. That stuff's plenty hard to get."

Possum started to speak. Del waved his good arm to the north. "Hey now, would you look at that!"

Suddenly there was confusion in the underwriters' ranks. A vaguely familiar pickup had appeared on the rise. The driver weaved through traffic, hurling grenades. They exploded in clusters, bright pink bouquets. He spotted the man with the rocket, lying flat atop a bus. Grenades stopped him cold. Underwriters abandoned the field and ran. Ginny saw a fairly peculiar sight. Six black Harleys had joined the truck. Chow Dogs with Uzis snaked in and out of the ranks, motors snarling and spewing horsetails of sand high in the air. They showed no mercy at all, picking off stragglers as they ran. A few underwriters made it to cover. In a moment, it was over. Fort Pru fled in sectional disarray.

"Well, if that wasn't just in the nick of time," Del said.

"I hate Chow Dogs," Possum said. "They got black tongues, and that's a fact."

"I hope you folks are all right," Moro said. "Well now, friend, looks as if you've thrown an arm."

"Nothing real serious," Del said.

"I'm grateful," Ginny said. "Guess I got to tell you that."

Moro was taken by her penetrating charm, her thankless manner. The fetching smudge of grease on her knee. He thought she was cute as a pup.

"I felt it was something I had to do. Circumstances being what they are."

"And just what circumstances are that?" Ginny asked.

"That pesky Shepherd Dog's sorta responsible for any trouble you might've had. Got a little pissed when that Possum cleaned him out. Five-card stud, I think it was. 'Course there might have been marking and crimping of cards, I couldn't say."

Ginny blew hair out of her eyes. "Mister, far as I can see, you're not making a lot of sense."

"I'm real embarrassed about this. That Dog got mad and kinda screwed up your gear."

"You let a *Dog* repair my stuff?" Ginny said.

"Perfectly good technician. Taught him mostly myself. Okay if you don't get his dander up. Those Shepherds are inbred, so I hear. What he did was set your tapes in a loop and speed 'em up. Customer'd get, say, twenty-six times his money's worth. Works out to a Mach seven fuck. Could cause bodily harm."

"Lord, I ought to shoot you in the foot," Ginny said.

"Look," Moro said, "I stand behind my work, and I got here quick as I could. Brought friends along to help, and I'm eating the cost of that."

"Damn right," Ginny said. The Chow Dogs sat their Harleys a ways off and glared at Possum. Possum Dark glared back. He secretly admired their leather gear, the Purina crests sewn on the backs.

"I'll be adding up costs," Ginny said. "I'm expecting full repairs."

"You'll get it. Of course you'll have to spend some time in Bad News. Might take a little while."

She caught his look and had to laugh. "You're a stubborn son of a bitch, I'll give you that. What'd you do with that Dog?"

"You want taco meat, I'll make you a deal."

"Yuck. I guess I'll pass."

Del began to weave about in roughly trapezoidal squares. Smoke started to curl out of his stub.

"For Christ's sake, Possum, sit on him or something," Ginny said.

"I can fix that," Moro told her.

"You've about fixed enough, seems to me."

"We're going to get along fine. You wait and see."

"You think so?" Ginny looked alarmed. "I better not get used to having you around."

"It could happen."

"It could just as easy *not*."

"I'll see about changing that tire," Moro said. "We ought to get Del out of the sun. You think about finding something nice to wear to dinner. East Bad News is kinda picky. We got a lot of pride around here . . . "

THE AARNE-THOMPSON CLASSIFICATION REVUE

HOLLY BLACK

There is a werewolf girl in the city. She sits by the phone on a Saturday night, waiting for it to ring. She paints her nails purple.

She goes to bed early.

Body curled around a pillow, fingers clawing at the bedspread, she dreams that she's on a dating show, a reality television one. She's supposed to pick one boyfriend out of a dozen strangers by eliminating one candidate each week. After eliminations, she eats the guy she's asked to leave. In her dream, the boys get more and more afraid as they overhear screams, but they can't quite believe the show is letting them be murdered one by one, so they convince each other to stay until the end. In the reunion episode, the werewolf girl eats the boy who she's picked to be her boyfriend.

That's the only way to get to do a second season, after all.

When she wakes up, she's sorry about the dream. It makes her feel guilty and a little bit hungry, which makes her feel worse. Her real-life boyfriend is a good guy, the son of a dentist from an ancestral line of dentists. Sometimes he takes her to his dad's office and they sit in the chairs and suck on nitrous oxide while watching the overhead televisions that are supposed to distract patients. When they do that, the werewolf girl feels calmer than she's felt her whole life.

She's calling herself Nadia in this city. She's called herself Laura and Liana and Dana in other places.

Despite having gone to bed early, she's woken up tired.

Nadia takes her temperature and jots it down in a little notebook by the side of the bed. Temperature is more accurate than phases of the moon in telling her when she's going to change.

She gets dressed, makes coffee and drinks it. Then goes to work. She is a waitress on a street where there are shirt shops and shops that sell used records and bandannas and studded belts. She brings out tuna salads to aged punks and cappuccinos in massive bowls to tourists who ask her why she doesn't have any tattoos.

Nadia still looks young enough that her lack of references doesn't seem strange to her employers, although she worries about the future. For now, though, she appears to be one of a certain type of girl—a girl who wants to be an actress, who's come in from the suburbs and never really worked before, a girl restaurants in the city employ a lot of. She always asks about flexibility in her interviews, citing auditions and rehearsals. Nadia is glad of the easy excuses, since she does actually need a flexible schedule.

The only problem with her lie is that the other girls ask her to go to auditions.

Sometimes Nadia goes, especially when she's lonely. Her boyfriend is busy learning about teeth and gets annoyed when she calls him. He has a lot of classes. The auditions are often dull, but she likes the part where all the girls stand in line and drink coffee while they wait. She likes the way their skin shimmers with nervous sweat and their eyes shine with the possibility of transformation. The right part will let them leave their dirty little lives behind and turn them into celebrities.

Nadia sits next to another waitress, Rhonda, as they wait to be called back for the second phase of the audition for a musical. Rhonda is fingering a cigarette that she doesn't light—because smoking is not allowed in the building and also because she's trying to quit.

Grace, a willowy girl who can never remember anyone's order at work, has already been cut.

"I hate it when people stop doing things and then they don't want to be around other people doing them," Rhonda says, flipping the cigarette over and over in her fingers. "Like people who stop drinking and then can't hang out in bars. I mean, how can you really know you're over something if you can't deal with being tempted by it?"

Nadia nods automatically, since it makes her feel better to think that letting herself be tempted is a virtue. Sometimes she thinks of the way a ribcage cracks or the way fat and sinew and offal taste when they're gulped down together, hot and raw. It doesn't bother her that she has these thoughts, except when they come at inappropriate moments, like being alone with the driver in a taxi or helping a friend clean up after a party.

A large woman with many necklaces calls Rhonda's name and she goes out onto the stage. Nadia takes another sip of her coffee and looks over at the sea of other girls on the call-back list. The girls look back at her through narrowed eyes.

Rhonda comes back quickly. "You're next," she says to Nadia.

"I saw the clipboard."

"How was it?"

Rhonda shakes her head and lights her cigarette. "Stupid. They wanted me to jump around. They didn't even care if I could sing."

"You can't smoke in here," one of the other girls says.

"Oh, shove it," says Rhonda.

When Nadia goes out onto the stage, she expects her audition to go fast. She reads monologues in a way that can only be called stilted. She's never had a voice coach. The only actual acting she ever does is when she pretends to be disappointed when the casting people don't want her. Usually she just holds the duffel bags of the other girls as they are winnowed down, cut by cut.

The stage is lit so that she can't see the three people sitting in the audience too well. It's one of those converted warehouse theaters where everyone sits at tables with tea lights and gets up a lot to go to the bar in the back. No tea lights are flickering now.

"We want to teach you a routine," one of them says. A man's voice, with an accent she can't place. "But first—a little about our musical. It's called the Aarne-Thompson Classification Revue. Have you heard of it?"

Nadia shakes her head. On the audition call, it was abbreviated ATCR. "Are you Mr. Aarne?"

He makes a small sound of disappointment. "We like to think of it as a kitchen sink of delights. Animal tales. Tales of magic. Jokes. Everything you could imagine. Perhaps the title is a bit dry, but our poster more than makes up for that. You ready to learn a dance?"

"Yes," says Nadia.

The woman with the necklaces comes out on the stage. She shows Nadia some simple steps and then points to crossed strips of black masking tape on the floor.

"You jump from here to here at the end," the woman says.

"Ready?" calls the man. One of the other people sitting with him says something under his breath.

Nadia nods, going over the steps in her head. When he gives her the signal, she twists and steps and leaps. She mostly remembers most of the moves. At the end, she leaps though the air for the final jump. Her muscles sing.

In that moment, she wishes she wasn't a fake. She wishes that she was a dancer. Or an actress. Or even a waitress. But she's a werewolf and that means she can't really be any of those other things.

"Thank you," another man says. He sounds a little odd, as though he's just woken up. Maybe they have to watch so many auditions that they take turns napping through them. "We'll let you know."

Nadia walks back to Rhonda, feeling flushed. "I didn't think this was a call for dancers."

Rhonda rolls her eyes. "It's for a musical. You have to dance in a musical."

"I know," says Nadia, because she does know. But there's supposed to be singing in musicals, too. She thought Rhonda would be annoyed at only being asked to dance; Rhonda usually likes to complain about auditions. Nadia looks down at her purple nail polish. It's starting to chip at the edges.

She puts a nail in her mouth and bites it until she bleeds.

Being a werewolf is like being Clark Kent, except that when you go into the phone booth, you can't control what comes out.

Being a werewolf is like being a detective who has to investigate his own crimes.

Being a werewolf means that when you take off your clothes, you're still not really naked. You have to take off your skin, too.

Once, when Nadia had a different name and lived in a small town outside of Toronto, she'd been a different girl. She took ballet and jazz dancing. She had a little brother who was always reading her diary. Then one day on her way home from school, a man asked her to help him find his dog. He had a leash and a van and everything.

He ate part of her leg and stomach before anyone found them.

When she woke up in the hospital, she remembered the way he'd caught her with his snout pinning her neck, the weight of his paws. She looked down at her unscarred skin and stretched her arms, ripping the IV needle out of her skin without meaning to.

She left home after she tried to turn her three best friends into werewolves, too. It didn't work. They screamed and bled. One of them died.

"Nadia," Rhonda is saying.

Nadia shakes off all her thoughts like a wet dog shaking itself dry.

The casting director is motioning to her. "We'd like to see you again," the woman with the necklaces says.

"Her?" Rhonda asks.

When Nadia goes back onstage, they tell her she has the part.

"Oh," says Nadia. She's too stunned to do more than take the packet of information on rehearsal times and tax forms. She forgets to ask them which part she got.

That night Rhonda and Grace insist on celebrating. They get a bottle of cheap champagne and drink it in the back of the restaurant with the cook and two of the dishwashers. Everyone congratulates Nadia, and Rhonda keeps telling stories about clueless things that Nadia did on other auditions and how it's a good thing that the casting people only wanted Nadia to dance because she can't act her way out of a paper bag.

Nadia says that no one can act their way out of a paper bag. You can only rip your way out of one. That makes everyone laugh and—Rhonda says—is a perfect example of how clueless Nadia can be.

"You must have done really well in that final jump," Rhonda says. "Were you a gymnast or something? How close did you get?"

"Close to what?" Nadia asks.

Rhonda laughs and takes another swig out of the champagne bottle. "Well, you couldn't have made it. No human being could jump that far without a pole vault."

Nadia's skin itches.

Later, her boyfriend comes over. She's still tipsy when she lets him in and they lie in bed together. For hours he tells her about teeth. Molars. Bicuspids. Dentures. Prosthodontics. She falls asleep to the sound of him grinding his jaw, like he's chewing through the night.

Rehearsals for the Aarne-Thompson Classification Revue happen every other afternoon. The director's name is Yves. He wears dapper suits in brown tweed and tells her, "You choose what you reveal of what you are when you're onstage."

Nadia doesn't know what that means. She does know that when she soars through the air, she wants to go higher and farther and faster. She wants her muscles to burn. She knows she could, for a moment, do something spectacular. Something that makes her shake with terror. She thinks of her boyfriend and Rhonda and the feel of the nitrous filling her with drowsy nothingness; she does the jump they tell her and no more than that.

The other actors aren't what she expects. There is a woman who plays a mermaid and whose voice is like spun gold. There is a horned boy who puts on long goat legs and prances around the stage, towering above them. And there is a magician who is supposed to keep them all as part of his menagerie in cages with glittering numbers.

"Where are you from?" the mermaid asks. "You look familiar."

"People say that a lot," Nadia says, although no one has ever said it to her. "I guess I have that kind of face."

The mermaid smiles and smoothes back gleaming black braids. "If you want, you can use my comb. It works on even the most matted fur—"

"Wow," says the goat boy, lurching past. "You must be special. She never lets anyone use her comb."

"Because you groom your ass with it," she calls after him.

The choreographer is named Marie. She is the woman with the necklaces from the first audition. When Nadia dances, and especially when she jumps, Marie watches her with eyes like chips of gravel. "Good," she says slowly, as though the word is a grave insult.

Nadia is supposed to play a princess who has been trapped in a forest of ice by four skillful brothers and a jaybird. The magician rescues her and brings her to his menagerie. And, because the princess is not onstage much during the first act, Nadia also plays a bear dancing on two legs. The magician falls in love with the bear, and the princess falls in love with the magician. Later in the play, the princess tricks the magician into killing the bear by making it look like the bear ate the jaybird. Then Nadia has to play the bear as she dies.

At first, all Nadia's mistakes are foolish. She lets her face go slack when she's not the one speaking or dancing, and the director has to remind her over and over that the audience can always see her when she's onstage. She misses cues. She sings too softly when she's singing about fish and streams and heavy fur. She sings louder when she's singing of kingdoms and crowns and dresses, but she can't seem to remember the words.

"I'm not really an actress," she tells him, after a particularly disastrous scene.

"I'm not really a director," Yves says with a shrug. "Who really is what they seem?"

"No," she says. "You don't understand. I just came to the audition because my friends were going. And they really aren't my friends. They're just people I work with. I don't know what I'm doing."

"Okay, if you're not an actress," he asks her, "then what are you?"

She doesn't answer. Yves signals for one of the golden glitter-covered cages to be moved slightly to the left.

"I probably won't even stay with the show," Nadia says. "I'll probably have to leave after opening night. I can't be trusted."

Yves throws up his hands. "Actors! Which of you can be trusted? But don't worry. We'll all be leaving. This show tours."

Nadia expects him to cut her from the cast after every rehearsal, but he never does. She nearly cries with relief.

The goat boy smiles down at her from atop his goat legs. "I have a handkerchief. I'll throw it to you if you want."

"I'm fine," Nadia says, rubbing her wet eyes.

"Lots of people weep after rehearsals."

"Weird people," she says, trying to make it a joke.

"If you don't cry, how can you make anyone else cry? Theater is the last place where fools and the mad do better than regular folks . . . well, I guess music's a little like that, too." He shrugs.

"But still."

Posters go up all over town. They show the magician in front of gleaming cages with bears and mermaids and foxes and a cat in a dress.

Nadia's boyfriend doesn't like all the time she spends away from home. Now, on Saturday nights, she doesn't wait by the phone. She pushes her milk crate coffee table and salvaged sofa against the wall and practices her steps over and over until her downstairs neighbor bangs on his ceiling.

One night her boyfriend calls and she doesn't pick up. She just lets it ring.

She has just realized that the date the musical premieres is the next time she is going to change. All she can do is stare at the little black book and her carefully noted temperatures. The ringing phone is like the ringing in her head.

I am so tired I want to die, Nadia thinks. Sometimes the thought repeats over and over and she can't stop thinking it, even though she knows she has no reason to be so tired. She gets enough sleep. She gets more than enough sleep. Some days she can barely drag herself from her bed.

Fighting the change only makes it more painful; she knows from experience.

The change cannot be stopped or reasoned with. It's inevitable. Inexorable. It is coming for her. But it can be delayed.

Once she held on two hours past dusk, her whole body knotted with cramps. Once she held out until the moon was high in the sky and her teeth were clenched so tight she thought they would shatter. She might be able to make it to the end of the show.

It shouldn't matter to her. Disappointing people is inevitable. She will eventually get tired and angry and hungry. Someone will get hurt. Her boyfriend will run the pad of his fingers over her canines and she will bite down. She will wake up covered in blood and mud by the side of some road and not be sure what she's done. Then she'll be on the run again.

Being a werewolf means devouring your past.

Being a werewolf means swallowing your future.

Methodically, Nadia tears her notebook to tiny pieces. She throws the pieces in the toilet and flushes, but the chunks of paper clog the pipes. Water spills over the side and floods her bathroom with the soggy reminder of inevitability.

On the opening night of the Aarne-Thompson Classification Revue, the cast huddles together and wish each other luck. They paint their faces. Nadia's hand shakes as she draws a new red mouth over her own. Her skin itches. She can feel the fur inside of her, can smell her sharp, feral musk.

"Are you okay?" the mermaid asks.

Nadia growls softly. She is holding on, but only barely.

Yves is yelling at everyone. The costumers are pinning and duct-taping dresses that have split. Strap tear. Beads bounce along the floor. One of the chorus is scolding a girl who plays a talking goat. A violinist is pleading with his instrument.

"Tonight you are not going to be good," Marie, the choreographer, says.

Nadia grinds her teeth together. "I'm not good."

"Good is forgettable." Marie spits. "Good is common. You are not good. You are not common. You will show everyone what you are made of."

Under her bear suit, Nadia can feel her arms beginning to ripple with the change. She swallows hard and concentrates on shrinking down into herself. She cannot explain to Marie that she's afraid of what's inside of her.

Finally, Nadia's cue comes and she dances out into a forest of wooden trees on dollies and lets the magician trap her in a gold-glitter-covered cage. Her bear costume hangs heavily on her, stinking of synthetic fur.

Performing is different with an audience. They gasp when there is a surprise. They laugh on cue. They watch her with gleaming, wet eyes. Waiting.

Her boyfriend is there, holding a bouquet of white roses. She's so surprised to see him that her hand lifts involuntarily—as though to wave. Her fingers look too long, her nails too dark, and she hides them behind her back.

Nadia dances like a bear, like a deceitful princess, and then like a bear again. This time, as the magician sings about how the jaybird will be revenged, Nadia really feels like he's talking to her. When he lifts his gleaming wand, she shrinks back with real fear.

She loves this. She doesn't want to give it up. She wants to travel with the show. She wants to stop going to bed early. She won't wait by the phone. She's not a fake.

When the jump comes, she leaps as high as she can. Higher than she has at any rehearsal. Higher than in her dreams. She jumps so high that she seems to hang in the air for a moment as her skin cracks and her jaw snaps into a snout.

It happens before she can stop it, and then she doesn't want it to stop. The change used to be the worst thing she could imagine. No more.

The bear costume sloughs off like her skin. Nadia falls into a crouch, four claws digging into the stage. She throws back her head and howls.

The goat boy nearly topples over. The magician drops his wand. On cue, the mermaid girl begins to sing. The musical goes on.

Roses slip from Nadia's dentist-boyfriend's fingers.

In the wings, she can see Marie clapping Yves on the back. Marie looks delighted.

There is a werewolf girl on the stage. It's Saturday night. The crowd is on their feet. Nadia braces herself for their applause.

MANIPULATING PAPER BIRDS

CATE GARDNER

A flyer drifted a hundred feet down into the pit where Mack Johnson leaned against a drainpipe, and where the giant Tarasov Baranowski folded paper. Mack's translucent hand plucked it from the air. He scratched a match against the rock wall and held the flyer up to it.

> **Stoker's Distorted Carnival & Sideshow.** *Do your intestines dangle outside your trousers? Have you grown a fourth breast? Do your ears pick up signals from other worlds? Then join us and see the world*.*

The small print read: **you will actually travel no further than Ohio, though we do have an excellent postcard collection.*

Mack threw the expended match into a fire that was comprised of twigs and dried leaves.

To his left, Tarasov flicked his wrists and the paper birds, attached by string to his thick fingers, danced. The birds were the giant's deviation. Mack watched them fly as Tarasov flung his arms left, right and above his head. Mack's thin lips curled back to reveal bone. A large grey disentangled from Tarasov's fingers and surged towards Mack's right eye. He flicked it aside. Blood bubbled were the paper sliced through his skin.

Mack sneered. "Careful I don't set light to you as you sleep."

"We'd both melt."

Tarasov plucked the carnival flyer from Mack's hand and began to fold it—as he did most things that fluttered down from the world.

"We should join," Mack said, as he circled the pit.

The place was too small for one let alone two men. As usual, Tarasov ignored him. It wasn't the first time Mack had threatened to leave. The clang of his boots on metal gained the giants' desired attention.

"You can't go up there," Tarasov said.

Mack looked up and met only a pinprick of light. He began to climb the ladder. Liberation did not sit easy on his shoulders.

"You'll wear yourself out," Tarasov called after him. "When you fall, I'll slice off your skin and make birds of it. It's thin enough."

It was Mack's turn to ignore the giant. The bird constructed out of the carnival flyer fluttered by his ear and crashed into the brick wall. Still he climbed. It was a long way up and he would not feel relief until it was a long way down. He'd been here too long. He had scurried down the ladder in the great earthquake of 1875 and Tarasov had persuaded him to stay.

A carrier pigeon swooped down from the world above. A further two followed its smooth course, while a fourth broke a wing against the rock walls and fell into the waiting fire. It would make a tasty supper if he proved coward. Resolved to continue on, Mack reached within ten feet of daylight when fingernails scratched at his ankle.

"We have been too long down here," Mack said, gaining another step. He should have done this many years ago.

"I agree." Tarasov's hand grasped hold of his ankle.

"You can snap the bone off, I'll hobble or crawl away from here if need be."

"Who speaks down there?" a voice thundered.

The darkness to which he was accustomed returned as a hulking figure blocked out the sun. A hand reached down.

"Joey Docherty will pull you out."

As he emerged into the day, Mack Johnson kissed the turf as his jaw slammed against the rim. Joey Docherty was not as burly as his shadow and voice hinted. As both rescuer and rescued sizzled beneath the midday sun, flat on their backs and gasping for air, shadows gathered about them. The expected exclamations were missing. There was no, *he needs meat on his bones and skin on his meat*; or why, *I can almost see his organs*.

"Is this Stoker's Distorted Carnival & Sideshow?" he asked.

Joey wiped sweat off his brow. "It is and you look as though you slipped through its bars."

Distorted figures gathered. As paper birds fluttered about them, Mack knew Tarasov had surfaced.

Candy striped tents, dulled by dust and years, and a bedraggled collection of man, beasts, and wagons circled. Canvas, stretched between stakes, declared all manner of oddities concealed within—The Exhumed Escapologist, The Terrifying Swords Man, The Electro-Shock Triplets, and so on weaving darker hells with each turn.

A short man, with a snout in place of nose, held out his right trotter for Mack to shake. "Paul Porker."

"Pleased to meet you. Pleased to meet you all."

Mack shook every hand, trotter, foot, and claw he met. Blood dripped as a sword-finger sliced through his palm.

"Apologies," the polished man said. "I got carried away with the welcome."

Tarasov coughed. The crowd looked up. The paper birds dangled silent from his fingers and offered the group no show. They turned their backs to him.

"What a marvel you are, Mack Johnson," Joey Docherty said.

"My companion, Tarasov Baranowski, is the showman. I am just a thin man with dehydrated skin and a visible network of veins, muscle and bones."

"He is a large man indeed but giants do not make for many dollars. For one, their heads tend to poke from the top of their tents. We were forced to use the last pair as tent poles."

Tarasov's fingers twitched but did not conduct, giving the impression that the birds were dying. The giant sank to his knees and caused the earth to rumble. He met this new audience eye to eye. Tarasov raised his hands.

As Mack took a step back, he pulled Joey with him.

"He is angry."

With the crook of the middle finger of Tarasov's right hand, a bird pecked the monocle from a one-eyed man, and then returned to pluck an eyelash from his startled eye.

"Bravo," a man said, clapping. He wore top hat and tails. "Bravo, bravo, I can offer ten percent of the door rate plus free tent and breakfast. Oh and give Sebastian his monocle back or the roustabouts will have an awful mess to clean up."

As Mack found himself sitting in a cage with a rickety chair and wobbly table, he declared himself almost satisfied. Having access to the key would have sealed the deal.

Joey leant against the bars with his arms folded and sweat stains on his shirt. He grumbled on about his morning spent clearing up after the Human Bear and Sebastian after they got into a fight over the last sausage.

"There was meat, fur, and blood all over the benches and tables. Stoker had me carry them, plus the Bear's carcass, over to a new tent he has set up next to your friend Tarasov's pitch. That man is sure pulling in the dollars."

Mack sighed. He needed a talent. The donation bucket that dangled from his cage contained cigarette papers, lollypop sticks, and spit. He didn't even have the clothes on his back or the shoes on his feet. All Stoker had allowed him to keep were his soiled underpants and string vest.

"Roll up, roll up," Barker called out as the crowds began to make their way over the dust-dry fields. "Grotesques galore. See the Wasting Human in his cage, visit the great Tarasov and his magical birds, witness a corpse escaping its coffin, drink with Siamese Twins in our saloon, and marvel at our Aerial Acrobats and Dancing Monkeys. Roll up, roll up."

"He's giving me a headache." Mack held his head in his hands.

"They'll give you a bigger one."

Joey ducked under the cage as a gaggle of children darted into the circle. A round boy, destined for a future tent, stuck out his tongue. Twin girls spat onto the floor of his cage. A ginger-haired boy emptied his pockets of rotten apple cores and plopped them into the bucket one by one as if playing a game. Mack heard Joey snigger.

"Come closer, children," Mack urged. "Let me tell you the secret of the . . . "

Joey rushed out from beneath the cage with a roar. The children scattered. Mack slumped off his chair and clutched his stomach. It hurt to laugh, yet he couldn't stop. Joey pulled at his lips, turning them into a frown.

"Tut."

Breath wheezed as Mack thumped his fist against the floor.

"Tut, tut"—an umbrella rattled against the bars of the cage—"tut."

"Pardon us, madam." Joey clutched hold of his side.

"You should be ashamed," she admonished.

She smacked the umbrella against Joey's arm, and then poked it through the bars to prod Mack. Recovered, Mack grabbed hold of the end of the umbrella and twisted it hard. The woman let out a gasp as she did a full revolution. Her skirts fell over her head as she turned for a second time. A crowd began to gather.

"Roll up, roll up. See the Wasted Human and the Spinning Schoolmarm. Roll up, roll up."

"Put me down."

Mack couldn't. His bucket was filling with every cent the crowd had. Pockets were emptying faster than she was spinning. A riotous applause went straight to his head. An eyeful of projectile vomit caused him to hesitate and left the Schoolmarm dangling upside down. She showered Joey's boots. A paper bird flew between the bars and stabbed him in the arm.

Tarasov towered over the crowd. He cured their laughter. The giant picked the Schoolmarm off the umbrella and placed her on the ground. A flock of birds darted above her.

"Roll up, roll up. See the Giant Tarasov revive a Vomiting Spinning Underwear Flashing Schoolmarm. Roll up."

"I'll roll up my sleeves and give them another show in a minute." Joey showed Barker his fists.

"Roll up, roll up. See the Roustabout dangle from a tent pole."

Joey backed away. He slammed his fist against Mack's cage and swatted at one of Tarasov's paper birds as it mocked him. His humor evaporated. As the crowd followed Tarasov and his birds back to his tent, emptying Mack's bucket as they departed, Joey pushed his face against the bars.

"Hey," a voice called out.

As Mack looked up and Joey turned, twin bags of flour hit them both in the face. They sputtered, the expected expletives muffled. Joey's fists and feet went into automatic pugilist stance. Mack wiped the flour from his eyes, lips and nostrils. As Joey boxed blindly at empty air, the flour-throwing child fled. Barker brought his fist up to Joey's nose with a thud!

"Ouch, what did you do that for?" Joey clutched his nose. Tears streaked down his cheeks. His voice distorted. "I'm bleeding."

"You need to remember your place, Roustabout."

Barker shoved a brush into Joey's hand. "Roll up, roll up. Watch as a couple of Fools realize their place in the Great Stoker's Distorted Carnival & Sideshow."

Joey looked at his brush.

"Hit him," Mack urged. "Knock out his teeth."

Joey sank back against the cage. His nose was a bloody red. Mack reached down and grabbed the keys from Joey's belt. The roustabout didn't complain as he jangled them in the lock. Dust billowed as he jumped down. Mack grabbed the brush and as he made a run at Barker, he glimpsed Stoker from the corner of his eye. He tripped on the brush, rolled forward and knocked Barker out cold with the end of the brush. He jumped up with a flourish, the flush to his cheeks concealed by the flour.

"Bravo, bravo," Stoker clapped. "So you're more than skin and bones, Mr. Johnson. We must get you a tent and a costume."

"The green wig is an insult," Joey sneered. "And if you want a red nose so much, I can thump you like Barker thumped me."

Joey still wore the flour, as did he, though for Mack the flour was now part of his costume. Tarasov stood in the doorway to the tent, manipulating his paper birds.

"So what are you going to do?" Tarasov asked. "In your act, I mean."

Mack looked at his sorry reflection. His lips down turned and the wig did nothing to complement his translucent skin. His sigh released a shower of dust that clouded the mirror. As his parents had long ago said, he was useless, and now he was about to prove it in front of a crowd.

"You should never have left the pit."

Tarasov was right.

"Don't listen to him, jealousy works his lips," Joey whispered. "He won't make a dime when your tent opens. I'll help you."

Joey took the wig off Mack's head and placed it on his own. His fist wiped the mirror clean. They looked like twins—the before and after photos, life and de-wigged death. A breeze slipped into the tent as Tarasov left. A single paper bird perched on the chair. Life twitched through its wings though it had been de-strung.

"He wants me back in that pit."

"He can want."

"Roll up, roll up. Groom your beards, gleam your swords, repaint your faces, for the crowd is journeying across the field. Roll up, roll up. Be at your most grotesque, I hear the dimes jangling, I see the dollars peeling back in eager fingers. Be the jester. Roll up."

Joey poked his bloodied nose out of the tent door. "They're lining up outside Tarasov's tent."

Mack crushed the bird between his fists and left it balled up in the corner. "If the crowd won't come to us, we shall go to it."

He pulled a blue nylon wig, with a DuPont label, out of his costume box. They appeared grotesque twins. They should name themselves something hideous.

Mack and Joey crept between the tents, appeared only as glimpses of evil to scare the smallest of children. They made a pit stop at Henry the Haircutter's wagon to steal scissors. Blades glinted as the snipped their way through the back of Tarasov's tent. Like naughty children, they sniggered. They crept up behind the mighty Tarasov and his erratic aerial display. The giant squawked. Mack was amused to find his old friend so enthralled before an audience. *Shove him in the pit and leave him there.* They rushed forward. The crowd guffawed as the two clowns began to snip at the strings as if liberating the birds. The crowd screamed as blood spurted. Mack had snipped off Tarasov's left thumb, Joey his right.

Joey grinned at the reaction of the audience. He stabbed the scissors into the giant's chest and then placed his fingers to his red lips in an *oh!*

"Did I do that?" He giggled.

A swarm of paper birds flapped their wings and attacked the two . . . clowns.

"Roll up, roll up. Visit us in the next town. Tell your neighbors of the Great Stoker's Distorted Carnival & Sideshow. Roll up, roll up. Follow us to Wiggonsville."

"Help me remove this grille," Joey said, perched on the top of the ladder. "Stop sulking and do something. I'll find you," he called out to the departing carnival. "I'll follow you to Wiggonsville or Columbus or wherever. Joey Docherty knows your routes. Expect to find Joey Docherty in your nightmares. You are not the only carnival in town. Joey will be famous."

"They were."

"You're not the only carnival in the country. Gentry, Davenport, Cole

Brothers, Honest Bill. They'll come looking to sign us up. Okay, maybe not Honest Bill."

"Do you like pigeon?" Mack asked.

"Pigeon pie?"

"Not quite."

"We just have to wait," Joey's eyes bulged as he peered between the bars of the grille. "Next circus that pitches, we'll be its stars."

WINTER QUARTERS

HOWARD WALDROP

Perhaps I should start "When he was twelve, he ran away from the circus."

Maybe I should begin "As circuses go, it was a small one. It only had two mammoths."

I'll just start at the beginning: The phone rang.

"Hey, Marie!" said the voice of my friend Dr. Bob the paleontologist. "Do you remember Arnaud?"

"Was the Pope Polish?" I asked.

"Well, the circus is in town, and he's in it. Susie Neruda took her nieces and nephews yesterday and recognized him. She just called me." Then he paused. "You want to go see him?"

"I didn't think you and circuses got along," I said.

"For this, I'll ignore everything in my peripheral vision."

"When would you like to go?"

"Next show's in forty-five minutes. I'll swing by and pick you up."

"Uh, sure," I said, looking at the stack of departmental memos on my desk. I threw the antimacassar from the back of my office chair over them.

He hung up.

When he was twelve, he ran away from the circus. Dr. Bob Oulijian, I mean. His father had managed two of them while Bob was trying to grow up. One day he showed up on the doorstep of his favorite aunt and said, "If I ever have to see another trapeze act or smell another zebra's butt in my life, Aunt Gracie, I'll throw up." Things were worked out; Aunt Gracie raised him, and he went on to become the fairly respected head of the paleontology department in the semi-podunk portion of the state university system where we both teach. What was, to others, a dim, misty vista of life in past geologic ages, to him was, as he once said, "a better circus than anyone could have thought up."

We whined down the highway in his Toyota Heaviside, passing the occasional Daimler-Chrysler Faraday. A noise dopplered up behind us, and a 1932 bucket-T roadster came by, piloted by a geezer in motorcycle goggles.

"Soon you'll be studying *them*," I said to Dr. Bob, pointing.

"Oh," he said. "Dinosaurs. *Très amusant.*"

Did I remember Arnaud?

It was while we were all—me, Dr. Bob, our colleague Dr. Fred Luntz the archaeologist, Susie Neruda (neé Baxter)—undergraduates *here*, at this podunk North Carolina branch of the state university, just after the turn of the millennium, that Arnaud showed up. We assumed he was French, maybe Belgian or Swiss, we didn't know, because he didn't talk. Much, anyway. He had that Jacques Tati-Marcel Marceau-Fernandel body type, tall and thin, like he'd been raised in a drainpipe. He was in the drama department; before we knew him, we knew *of* him.

About half the time we saw him, he was in some form of clown déshabille, or mime getup. We assumed it was for the acting classes, but a grad student over there said no, he just showed up like that, some days.

"Does he do anything special?" I asked Dr. Bob. "Did Susan say?"

"I don't think so, or she would have. I'm assuming he mostly puts out fires inefficiently and throws pies with accuracy, unless circuses have changed a great deal since my time."

For what do we remember Arnaud?

It was in November, his first semester, and he was out on the east mall passing out flyers, in full regalia: a polka-dot clown suit, clownwhite, bald headpiece, a hat the size of a fifty-cent flowerpot. He had a Harpo bulbhorn he honked as people came by.

The flyer said:

HITLER THE MAGNIFICENT
An Evening of Transformational Sorcery
JONES HALL 112
7 P.M. NOVEMBER 8th

Well, uh-oh.

It wasn't an evening, it was more like fourteen or fifteen minutes.

It wasn't sorcery, but it was transformative: it transformed him right out of college. To say that it wasn't well received is bending the language.

Jones 112 was the big lecture hall with multi-media capabilities, and when we got there, props and stuff littered the raised lecture platform. Some pipes, a fire extinguisher, a low platform raised about a meter off the ground on two-by-four legs; some big pieces of window glass. In true Brechtian fashion prop men sat on the stage playing cards.

By seven the place was packed, SRO.

The lights went down; there were three thumps on the floor, and lights came back up.

Out came a Chaplin-mustached Arnaud in a modified SA uniform. He wore a silk top-hat with a big silver swastika on the front. He wore a cloak fashioned after one of the ones the Nazis were going to make all truck-drivers wear, back when they were designing uniforms for each profession.

His assistants were a padded-up fat guy with medals all over his chest, and a little thin guy with a rat-nose mask.

First, Hitler hypnotized twenty-two million Germans: he gestured magically at a *découpage* of a large crowd held up by the two guys.

Then they painted Stars of David on the plate glass, and Hitler threw a brick through it.

His assistants came back with a big map of Poland, and he sawed it in half with a ripsaw.

After each trick, he said, "Abracadabra, please and *gesundheit!*"

Then they brought out three chairs, and three people came out on stage and sat down in them.

In the first, a young woman in her twenties. In the second sat a man in his forties, playing on a violin. At the end chair, an old man in his eighties.

Hitler the Magnificent took off his cloak and covered the young woman. "Abracadabra, please and *gesundheit!*" he said, and pulled away the cloak. The chair was empty except for a wisp of smoke drifting toward the ceiling. He put the cape over the violinist, repeated the incantation, and snapped it away. In the chair was the violin and a lampshade with a number on it.

He covered the old man, spoke, and raised the cloth. In the chair seat there was now a bar of soap. The thin assistant picked it up and threw it into a nearby goldfish bowl of water. "So light it floats!" he said.

Prop men lit fires along the pipes and pushed them toward Hitler the Magnificent and the two assistants. Surrounded by the closing ring of fire, with a mannequin wearing a brown-blond wig and a wedding dress in his arms, he climbed onto the two-by-four platform, miming great heights, and jumped down next to a wet Luger water pistol, while the fat and thin assistants drank green Kool-Aid from a washtub and fell to the floor.

The stagelights lowered, and the only sound was the *whoosh* of the fire extinguisher putting out the flames on the pipes.

Then the lights came back up.

You could have heard a pin drop. Then—

It wasn't quite the Paris premiere of *Le Sacre du Printemps* in 1913, but it might as well have been.

You'd think with the whole twentieth century behind us, and a few years of this one, and Mel Brooks' *The Producers*, most of the *oomph* would have gone out of things like this. But you'd be wrong.

I got out the fire exit about the time the firemen and the riot squad came in through it.

He was thrown out, of course, for violations of the University fire codes and firearms policy, for causing a riot, and for unauthorized use of Jones Hall. Plus he spent a couple of days in the city jug before he was expelled.

About a week before that performance, Arnaud had spoken to me for the first and only time. I was in the cafeteria (where we all usually were), alone, between classes, drinking the brown stuff they sell instead of coffee, actually doing some reading in Roman history.

I looked up. Arnaud was standing there, looking like a French foreign exchange student.

"Ever read any Nigidius Figulus?" he asked.

Taken aback by his speaking, I still wanted to appear cool. "Not lately," I said.

"Should," he said, and walked away.

That night I got out my handbook of Latin literature. Nigidius Figulus was a neo-Pythagorean of Cicero's time, an astrologer, a grammarian;

much concerned with Fate and the will of the gods. In other words, the usual minor Roman literary jack-of-all-trades the late Republic coughed up as regular as clepsydra-work.

The next day I spent in the Classics library, reading epitomes of his writings.

Not much there for me.

We pulled into the parking lot of the exhibition hall where the circus was, and who do we see but Dr. Fred Luntz getting out of his car with his stepson. Bob called to him. He came over. "Susan call you, too?" asked Dr. Bob.

"No. Why?" asked Fred.

"Arnaud's in this circus."

"Arnaud? Arnaud. I'll be damned." We went in and sat down on the bleachers.

As circuses got, it was a small one. It only had two mammoths.

Mammontelephants, actually, but you know what I mean.

They were second-billed in the show, too—and they didn't come in with the Grand Entry Parade. (Dr. Bob noticed immediately. "They usually don't get along with other elephants," he said.) Fred's stepson, about eight, and the product of the previous marriage of his trophy wife, was looking everywhere at once, His name was of course Jason. (In ten years you'll be able to walk into any crowded bar in America and say "Jason! Brittany!" and fifty people will turn toward you . . .)

We saw Arnaud in the Grand Entry, then in the first walkaround while riggers changed from the high-wire to the trapeze acts; we watched the tumblers, and the monkeys in the cowboy outfits riding the pigs with the strapped-on Brahma bull horns; we ate peanuts and popcorn and Cracker-Jacks and cotton candy. Halfway through, the ringmaster with his wireless microphone said: "Ladeez an Genuhmen, in the center ring [there was only one], presenting Sir Harry Tusker and His Performing Pachyderms, Tantor and Behemoth!"

There were two long low blasts from the entrance doorway, sounds lower than an elephant's, twice as loud. I felt the hair on my neck stand up.

Walking backwards came Sir Harry Tusker, dressed in pith helmet, safari jacket, jodhpurs, and shiny boots, like old pictures of Frank Buck. In came Tantor and Behemoth—big hairy mounds with tusks and trunks, and tails like hairy afterthoughts. Their trunks were up and curved back double, and each let out a blast again, lower than the first. The band was playing, of course, Lawrence Welk's "Baby Elephant Walk."

The crowd applauded them for being *them*; Jason's eyes were big as saucers.

They went to the center of the ring and you realized just how big they really were, probably not as big as mammoths got (they were both females, of course) but big, bigger than all but the largest bull African elephants. And you're not used to seeing females with tusks two meters long, either.

They did elephant stuff—standing on their hind legs, their hairy coats swaying like old bathrobes, dancing a little. In the middle of the act a clown came out—it was Arnaud—pushing a ball painted to look like a rock, acting like it weighed a ton, and Behemoth picked it up, and she and Tantor played volleyball while Sir Harry and Arnaud held the net.

It was pretty surreal, seeing hair elephants do that. It was pretty surreal seeing big shaggy elephants the size of Cleveland in the first place.

The show was over too soon for Jason.

At the souvenir booth, Dr. Fred bought him a copy of *The Shaggy Baggy Saggy Mammontelephant*, a Little Golden Book done by a grand-descendant of the author of the original elephant one. It was way below his reading level, but he didn't mind. He was in heaven while we left word and waited out back for Arnaud.

He showed up, out of makeup, looking about 40, still tall and thin. He shook hands with us like we'd seen each other yesterday.

Jason asked, "Are you really a clown?"

Arnaud looked around, pointed to himself, shook his head no.

"Let's go get something to eat besides popcorn," said Dr. Bob. "When do you have to be back?" Arnaud indicated eighteen, a couple of hours.

"Come on," said Dr. Fred Luntz. "We're buying."

Arnaud smiled a big smile.

"It's all wrong," said Dr. Fred. "They're treating them like circus elephants, only shaggy, instead of what they are. The thing with the rock is more like it, if they're going to have to perform."

Arnaud was eating from nine or ten plates—two trays—at the cafeteria a kilometer or so from the exhibition hall. The four of us had only eaten a couple of pieces of pie, jello salads, and some watermelon because we were so full of circus junk food. Arnaud's metabolism must have been like a furnace. Occasionally he would look up from eating.

"Better that, than them not being around at all," said Dr. Bob.

"Well, yes, of course. But, Sir Harry Tusker. African white-hunter archetype. All wrong for mammoths."

"Yeah, well, what do you want? Siberians? Proto-Native Americans?" asked Bob.

"I mean, there was enough grief twenty or so years ago, when they were first brought back—the Russians tried taking frozen mammoth genes from carcasses in the permafrost late last century, putting them in Indian elephants, their nearest living relatives—"

"This is your friend, Dr. Bob, the paleonologist, Fred . . . " said Dr. Bob.

"Okay. Okay. But didn't work last century. Suddenly, it works. Exact same procedure. Suddenly, we have mammontelephants, all female of course. Big outrage; you can't bring back extinct animals to a time they're not suited for; it's cruel, etc. Like the A-Bomb and physicists; geneticists *could* bring back the dead, so they *did*. Or purt-near, anyway. So we give in. They're in zoos at first, then circuses. Ten, twenty, thirty at first, now maybe one hundred, two hundred—only a few are in the game preserves in Siberia run by the World Wildlife Fund and the Jersey Zoo (and there was a big fight about *that*). Then five years ago, hey presto! There's males. Someone went into a male completely buried in the frozen ground and retrieved the whole system (and how's you like *that* for a job, huh, Bob?) and then we have viable sperm, and now there are five or six males, including the one up in Baltimore, and more on the way. What I'm saying is, turn 'em loose somewhere, don't just look at them, or make 'em act."

"Like loose where? Like do what?" asked Bob.

"Like, I don't know," said Dr. Fred.

Arnaud continued shoveling food into his face.

"What did you think about the mammoths, Jason?" I asked him.

"Neat!" he said.

"Me too," I said.

"Look, you know as well as I do what the real reason people want to shut all this down is," said Dr. Bob. "It's not that they don't want extinct animals brought back into a changed climate, that they have an inability to adapt from an Ice Age climate—you go up or down in altitude and get the climate you want. Mammoths in the high Rockies, in Alaska, in Siberia. Sure, no problem. And it ain't, like they *say*, that we should be saving things that are going extinct now first: they're still here, they'll have to be taken somewhere to live, and people will have to leave them alone—island birds, rare predators, all that. That's their big *other* argument: Fix now *now*, then fix *then*. The real reason is the same since the beginning: we're playing God, and they don't like it."

"Sure it has a religious element," said Fred. "But that doesn't mean you have to put the mammontelephants in some sort of zoo and circus limbo while you decide if there's to be more of them or not. Nobody's advocating bringing back *smilodons* (even if you could find the genetic material), or dinosaurs if you want to go the mosquito-in-amber wild goose chase. This comes down to questions of pure science—"

"If we can, we have to?"

"You're talking like the people who don't want them—or the two wooly rhinos—back," said Fred.

"No, I'm giving you their argument, like people give me. They're here because we couldn't stop ourselves from bringing them *back*, any more than we could stop ourselves from killing them *off* in the first place. Where was the religion in that?"

I was looking back and forth. I was sure they'd had this discussion before, but never in front of me. Arnaud was eating. Jason was reading his book for the tenth time.

Arnaud looked at the two docs as he finished the last of everything, including a pie crust off Fred's plate.

"Plenty religion involved," said Arnaud. "People just don't understand the *mammoths*."

Fred and Bob looked at him.

"Yeah?" asked Bob.

"They let me know," said Arnaud. He patted his stomach and nodded toward the door.

As we let him off at the circus, he reached in his shirt pocket and handed Jason six long black hairs, making a motion with his left arm hanging off his nose and his right forming a curve in front of him.

"Mammoth hair! Oh boy oh boy!" said Jason.

Then Arnaud pointed to Dr. Bob and made the signal from the sixty-year-old TV show *The Prisoner*—Be Seeing You.

That night I read about mammontelephants. The first were cloned less than thirty years ago, and there were some surprises. The normal gestation period for the Indian elephant is twenty-two months; for the mammontelephants it was closer to eighteen. The tusks of Indian elephant cows normally stick out less than twenty centimeters from their mouths; that of the mammontelephants two, two-and-a-half meters and still growing. (What the tusks of the males, all six or seven of them in the world, will be, no one knows yet, as the first is only six years old now—it's guessed they could grow as long as those of fossil true bull mammoths.) Their trumpeting, as I said, is lower, deeper, and creepier than either Indian or African elephants (a separate species). It's assumed they communicate over long distances with subsonic rumbles like their relatives. They have developed the fatty humps on their heads and above their shoulders, even though most aren't in really cold climates. Yes, they have the butt-flap that keeps the wind out in cold weather. The big black long guard hairs (like the ones Arnaud gave Jason) are scattered over the thick underfur, itself forty centimeters thick. Further clonings—with twelve- and thirteen-year-old mammontelephants carrying baby mammontelephants to term—has speeded up the process: most elephants don't reproduce until they're fifteen or so. And you get a more mammoth mammontelephant. What will happen when Mr. and Ms. Mammontelephant get together in another six or seven years? They might not like each other. That's where Science will come in again . . .

Pretty good for an old lady English prof, huh?

Everybody knew the IQRA meeting in October (hosted by the podunk portion of the University we work for) was going to have Big Trouble. The IQRA is the International Quaternary Research Association—everything prehistoric *since* the dinosaurs—and it contained multitudes, among which are people in the profession against the retrieval and propagation of extinct species. They were vocal, and because the meeting was also going to have a large bunch of paleo- and archaeogeneticists there too, the media had already started pre-coverage on it—sound bites, flashes of personalities, a fleeting glimpse of the male mammontelephant in the Baltimore Zoo.

You know. Big Trouble.

I know all this because Dr. Bob is the University's host for this Cenozoic shindig, and is calling me every day or so. Out of nowhere he says, "I got a *fax* from Arnaud. Can you imagine? His circus plays up in Raleigh the day before the conference opens, last show of the year before winter quarters." It had been two months since he'd eaten the cafeteria out of house and home.

"What did he say?"

"That's all. I guess he just wanted us to know. I sure as hell won't have time to see him. I'll be dodging brickbats, no doubt."

A week later, Dr. Bob showed up in my office.

"Uh, Marie," he said. "There've been more faxes. Lots more. Something's up. Want to be an unindicted co-conspirator?"

The news was full of the IQRA; you couldn't turn on your monitor or TV without seeing people with placards and signs, or Professor Somebody from Somewhere making speeches. I watched some of it, switched over to the Weather Shop. There was a guy yammering on about long-term climatic change, Big and Little Ice Ages; global warming, myth or legend; etc. I ran up their feed and got the forecast: overcast, maybe some mist, 15°, just cool enough for a sweater.

There was a cardboard box on the front porch with a note on it—MARIE: BRING THIS TO MY LECTURE. SIT ON 3D ROW AISLE.—and a wristbadge with **STAFF** stamped on it in deep holograms.

The place was mobbed. I mean outside. The campus cops had a metal detector outside the front door. City cops were parked a block away, just off campus.

I looked in the box. There was a double-bladed Mixmaster and a big glass bowl.

I threaded my way through the crowd and walked up to the campus cops, bold as brass.

"What's in the box, doc?" he said, recognizing me and looking at my wristbadge.

I opened it and showed him. "For the mai-tais at the social hour," I said.

He looked at it, handed it around the detector, passed it in front of the sniffer dog. The dog looked at it like it was the least interesting thing on the earth. Then the dog looked east, whined, and barked.

"That ain't his bomb bark," said the K-9 cop. "He's been acting funny all morning."

"Can I go in now?" I asked.

"Oh, sure. Sorry," said the main cop, handing me the box once I went through the metal detector with the usual nonsense.

The crowd, barred from coming in without badges, swayed back and forth and shined preprinted laser messages into any camera pointed toward them, or waved old-fashioned signs. A couple of people from my department were in there with them.

Dr. Bob's speech, "Long-Term Implications of Pleistocene Faunal Retrieval on Resuscitated Species: An Overview," was supposed to start at 1300, but by 1215 the place was full. Including plenty of people with signs, and, I saw, Professor Somebody from Somewhere I'd seen on the news. The most ominous thing: in the program, the last fifteen minutes was to be Q and A discussion.

It was a big lecture hall, with a wall to the right of the platform leading out to where I knew the building's loading dock was. The wall blocked an ugly ramp from view and destroyed most of the acoustics—it had been a local pork-barrel retrofit ten years ago. Bureaucratic history is swell, isn't it?

At 1255 Dr. Bob came in. He went up to the podium. There was mild applause and some sibilant hissing. Really.

"Thank you, thank you very much. Normally I would introduce the speaker, but hey! that's me!" There was some disturbance out at the hall doors. "I know you're all as anxious as I am for me to start. But first—a small presentation that may—or may not—shed some light on my talk. I honestly don't know what to expect any more than you do." A *boo* came from the back of the hall, loud and clear.

The lights went down, and I heard the big loading dock doors rattle up, grey daylight came up from the ramp and—

—in came something:

It was a tall thin man, bent forward at the waist, covered in a skin garment from head to foot. He had a tail like a horse, and what I hoped were fake genitals high up on the buttocks. His head was a fur mask and above it were two reindeer antlers. The face ended in a long shaggy beard from the eyes down and he had two tufted ears like an antelope's.

In the middle of the face was a red rubber nose. The feet were two enormous clown shoes, about a meter in length, the kind that let whoever's wearing them lean almost to the ground without falling over.

The hair figure walked around, looked at the audience, and went to the blackboard and, placing its right hand on it, blew red paint through a reed, and left the outline of its hand on the green panel.

Someone booed just as I remembered where I'd seen pictures of this thing before. Some cave painting. Dordogne? Lascaux? Trois Frères, that's it. The thing was usually called the Sorcerer of Trois Frères, thought to be some shaman of the hunt, among the bison and horses and rhinos drawn and scratched on the walls of the cave 25,000, 40,000 years ago . . .

Tantor and Behemoth walked in through the loading-door ramp.

It got *real* quiet, then.

The Sorcerer picked up a child's toy bow and arrow and fired a rubber-tipped arrow into Tantor, who backed down the ramp, out of sight of the audience. I could see the shadow of another man there, from where I sat. He was pulling something up over one of his arms.

The Sorcerer mimed being hot, and Behemoth swayed like she was about to faint. The man pulled down his animal skin to the waist, and fired another suction-cup arrow into Behemoth's hairy side; she backed out of the room.

The Sorcerer took off his costume (except the rubber nose and clown shoes), which left him in a diaper. He played with a small ziggurat, then took the model of a trireme from someone on the left side of the room, then a bishop's crozier from another (how had I not seen all these props and people when I came in?). Then he put on a lab coat and glasses, came down to where I sat, and took the mixer from me ("Bonjour," he whispered), and went back to the stage, where someone—Dr. Bob?—threw him a pair of Faded Glory blue jeans with double helixes painted on them (*one* person in the audience actually laughed). He plugged in the mixer, threw the jeans into the glass bowl and watched them swirl around and around, took them out, went to the right stage wall and—an elephant's trunk, a cloth puppet on the arm of the man whose shadow I watched on the loading-ramp wall, along with those of the mammontelephants—snaked around the corner and grabbed the jeans and disappeared.

The lab-coated figure waited, then Tantor and Behemoth walked back onstage again, their eyes dark as dots of tar, their small double-hand-sized ears twitching.

The man went to the blackboard, picked up the hollow reed, and blew red ocher pigment onto his right hand.

Slowly he held it up, palm toward the mammontelephants.

Tantor and Behemoth bowed down onto their front knees. They curled their trunks up in the same double-curve as those on the elephant statues in the Babylon sequence of D.W. Griffith's *Intolerance*. And then they gave the long slow loud trumpets of their kind, a sound cutting across a hundred centuries.

Every hair on my body shot straight up.

The lights went off. I saw shadows of shapes leaving, heard a truck start up. The loading door clanged down with a crash, and a spotlight slowly came up, centered on the red outline of the hand on the blackboard.

Then the houselights came back up and Dr. Bob Oulijian was alone at the lectern.

We were at the freight depot with Sir Harry Tusker and Arnaud.

They made ready to load Behemoth and Tantor onto their personal freight car. "*Everybody else*," said Sir Harry, "goes by truck to winter quarters in Florida. *We* go by train to Wisconsin, the shores of Lake Geneva. We join up with the circus again in March. The girls here get to play in the winter. Me and Arnaud get to freeze our balls off out *there*." He pointed NW.

Arnaud stood with Tantor's trunk wreathed around his right arm. He scratched her under the big hairy chin.

"Better load up," said the freightman.

"West at three hundred kilometers per hour," said Sir Harry. Then: "Girls! Hey!" he yelled. "*Umgawa!*"

They started up the concrete ramp. Then something—a change in the wind? a low rumble from far away, from the direction of Baltimore? indigestion?—caused both mammontelephants to stop. They lifted their trunks, searching the wind, and let out their long low rumbling squeals.

"*Umgawa!*" said Sir Harry Tusker, again.

Behemoth took Tantor's tail, and followed her up the ramp and onto their private car.

Sir Harry and Arnaud followed, turned, waved, closed the doors of the car, and waved again through the small windows.

In a few minutes the train was gone, and in a few more, beyond the city limits, would be a westbound blur.

Though it was October, and though this was North Carolina, that night it snowed.

PUBLICATION HISTORY

ABOUT THE AUTHORS

For the past five years, **Neal Barrett, Jr.** has written a monthly humor columm for Blue Cross' *Life Times*, a publication that reaches half a million readers. In 2007, the works of his fifty years of writing were collected in the Southwestern Collection of Texas State University Archives in San Marcos, Texas. Two of his 2008 stories appeared in *Asimov's Science Fiction*. Bill Shafer of Subterranean Press has announced plans to publish a "career-spanning" collection of "The Best of Neal Barrett, Jr." This volume will include works from 1960 through the present. In May of 2010, Barrett was honored at the Science Fiction Writers of America Annual Nebula Weekend in Coco Beach, Florida. He was named Author Emeritus, for "Lifetime Achievement."

Christopher Barzak grew up in rural Ohio, went to university in a decaying post-industrial city in Ohio, and has lived in a Southern California beach town, the capital of Michigan, and in the suburbs of Tokyo, Japan, where he taught English in rural elementary and middle schools. His stories have appeared in many venues, including *Nerve, The Year's Best Fantasy and Horror, Teeth, Asimov's,* and *Lady Churchill's Rosebud Wristlet*. His first novel, *One for Sorrow,* won the Crawford Award for Best First Fantasy. His second book, *The Love We Share Without Knowing,* is a novel-in-stories set in a magical realist modern Japan, and was a finalist for the Nebula Award for Best Novel and the James Tiptree Jr. Award. He is also the co-editor of *Interfictions 2,* and has done Japanese-English translation on *Kant: For Eternal Peace,* a peace theory book published in Japan for Japanese teens. Forthcoming in August 2012, his collection, *Birds and Birthdays,* will be published by Aqueduct Press, and in March 2013, his full length short story collection, *Before and Afterlives,* will be published by Lethe Press. Currently he lives in Youngstown, Ohio, where he teaches fiction writing in the Northeast Ohio MFA program at Youngstown State University.

Holly Black is the author of bestselling contemporary fantasy books for kids and teens. Her titles include the Spiderwick Chronicles (with Tony DiTerlizzi), the Modern Faerie Tale series, the Good Neighbors graphic novel trilogy (with Ted Naifeh), and the Curse Workers series. Holly has been a finalist for the Mythopoeic Award, a finalist for an Eisner Award, and the recipient of the Andre Norton Award. She lives in New England with her husband, Theo, in a house with a secret door.

Amanda C. Davis is a combustion engineer who loves baking, gardening, and gory low-budget slasher films. Her short fiction has appeared in *Shock Totem, Orson Scott Card's InterGalactic Medicine Show*, and others. You can follow her on Twitter (@davisac1) or read more of her work at www.amandacdavis.com.

Australian writer **Felicity Dowker** has won and/or been shortlisted for numerous awards for her writing and reviews, including the Ditmar, Chronos, Aurealis, and Australian Shadows Awards. Along with fellow writers Alan Baxter and Andrew J. McKiernan, Felicity is co-founder and contributing editor at dark fiction news and reviews site Thirteen O'Clock (www.thirteenoclock.au). Felicity's debut short story collection *Bread and Circuses* was released in June 2012 by Ticonderoga Publications. Felicity's work can be found all over the place, most recently in *The Year's Best Australian Fantasy and Horror* Volume 2. Like most writers, Felicity is currently working on a novel.

Amanda Downum lives near Austin, Texas, in a house with a spooky attic. Her day job sometimes allows her to dress up as a giant worm. She is the author of *The Drowning City, The Bone Palace, and Kingdoms of Dust*, published by Orbit Books. Her short fiction has appeared in *Ideomancer, Realms of Fantasy*, and *Weird Tales*. For more information, visit www.amandadownum.com.

Cate Gardner is a British horror and fantastical author with over a hundred stories published. Several of those stories appear in her collection, *Strange Men in Pinstripe Suits*. She is also the author of two novellas: *Theatre of Curious Acts* (Hadley Rille Books) and *Barbed Wire Hearts* (Delirium Books). You can find her on the web at www.categardner.net.

Kij Johnson writes science fiction, fantasy, and slipstream literature, and is a winner of the Nebula and World Fantasy Awards. She teaches at the University of Kansas. She splits her time between Lawrence and Seattle.

Barry B. Longyear is the first writer (and maybe the only writer) to win the Nebula Award, the Hugo Award, and the John W. Campbell Award for Best New Writer, all in the same year. In addition to his acclaimed *Enemy Mine* series, his works include numerous short stories, the *Circus World* series, the *Infinity Hold* series, and novels ranging from *Sea of Glass* to *The God Box*, as well as his much praised *Science Fiction Writer's Workshop-I*. His online writing seminar, *The Write Stuff*, is now available as a trade paperback and in Kindle format. His recent works include *Jaggers & Shad: ABC is for Artificial Beings Crimes*, the complete award-winning series that appeared in *Analog*, in addition to two previously unpublished tales; *Dark Corners*, his hardest hitting collection of stories from the dark side; and *The Enemy Papers* (all three novels of the *Enemy Mine* series, including the never-before-published *The Last Enemy* and the Drac bible, *The Talman*). A complete list of his awards, books, short stories, and other writings is available on his website, www.barrylongyear.com.

Andrew J. McKiernan is a writer and illustrator living and working on the Central Coast of NSW, Australia. First published in 2007, his stories have since been nominated for multiple Aurealis, Australian Shadows, and Ditmar Awards and been reprinted in a number of Year's Best anthologies. His work can be found here and there, like a slow sprouting fungus, www.andrewmckiernan.com.

Jessica Reisman's stories have appeared in an array of magazines and anthologies. Five Star Speculative Fiction published her first novel, *The Z Radiant*. She dreams awake, has visions asleep, and enjoys tea and artful cocktails while living in Austin, TX, with well-groomed cats. For more about her fiction, visit www.storyrain.com.

Ken Scholes is the award-winning author of over forty short stories and three novels. His epic fantasy series, the Psalms of Isaak, is being published to great critical acclaim by Tor in the US and by multiple publishers overseas. Scholes is also a winner of the Writers of the Future contest. He lives in Saint Helens, Oregon, with his wife and daughters. He invites readers to learn more about him and his writing at www.kenscholes.com.

Douglas Smith is an award-winning author of speculative fiction, with over a hundred short story sales to professional markets in thirty countries and two dozen languages. His collections include *Chimerascope* (ChiZine Publications, 2010), *Impossibilia* (PS Publishing, 2008), and *La Danse des Esprits* (Dreampress, 2011), a translated fantasy collection published in France. Doug has twice won Canada's Aurora Award, and has been a finalist for the international John W. Campbell Award, the Canadian Broadcasting Corporation's Bookies Award, Canada's juried Sunburst Award, and France's juried Prix Masterton and Prix Bob Morane. A multi-award winning short film has been made based on Doug's story "By Her Hand, She Draws You Down," and films based on other stories are also in the works. Doug's website is smithwriter.com and he tweets at twitter.com/smithwritr.

Peter Straub is the *New York Times* bestselling author of more than a dozen novels, most recently *A Dark Matter*. He has won the Bram Stoker Award for his novels, *Lost Boy Lost Girl* and *In the Night Room*, as well as for his recent collection, *5 Stories*. Straub was the editor of the two-volume Library of American anthology *The American Fantastic Tale*. He lives in New York City.

E. Catherine Tobler lives and writes in Colorado. Among others, her fiction has appeared in *SciFiction, Fantasy Magazine, Realms of Fantasy, Talebones, and Lady Churchill's Rosebud Wristlet*. She is an active member of SFWA and senior editor at *Shimmer Magazine*.

Genevieve Valentine's fiction has appeared or is forthcoming in *Clarkesworld, Strange Horizons, Journal of Mythic Arts, Fantasy, Lightspeed*, and *Apex*, and in the anthologies *Federations, The Living Dead 2, Running with the Pack, After, Teeth*, and more. Her nonfiction has appeared in *Lightspeed, Tor.com*, and *Fantasy Magazine*, and she is the co-author of *Geek Wisdom* (out from Quirk Books). Her first novel, *Mechanique: A Tale of the Circus Tresaulti*, won the 2012 Crawford Award. Her appetite for bad movies is insatiable, a tragedy she tracks on her blog, genevievevalentine.com.

Jeff VanderMeer's fiction has been published in over twenty countries. His books, including the best-selling *City of Saints and Madmen* and *Finch*, have recently made the year's best lists of the *Wall Street Journal*, the *Washington Post*, and the *San Francisco Chronicle*. VanderMeer's surreal, often fantastical fiction, has won two World Fantasy Awards and an NEA-funded Florida Individual Writers' Fellowship and Travel Grant, along being a finalist for the Hugo Award, Nebula Award, and many others. He regularly reviews books for the *New York Times Book Review*, *Los Angeles Times Book Review*, and the *Washington Post* while his short fiction has appeared in *Conjunctions*, *Black Clock*, *Arc*, *Tor.com*, among others. With his wife Ann, the Hugo Award-winning editor of *Weird Tales*, he has edited such iconic anthologies as *Steampunk*, *Steampunk Reloaded*, *The New Weird*, and *The Weird*, *The Thackery T. Lambshead Pocket Guide to Eccentric & Discredited Diseases*, and *The Thackery T. Lambshead Cabinet of Curiosities*. He is the author of the definitive *The Steampunk Bible*. VanderMeer is the assistant director for the unique teen SF/Fantasy writing camp Shared Worlds, based at Wofford College. He lives in Tallahassee, Florida.

Howard Waldrop, born in Mississippi and now living in Austin, Texas, is an American iconoclast. His highly original books include *Them Bones* and *A Dozen Tough Jobs*, and the collections *All About Strange Monsters of the Recent Past*, *Night of the Cooters*, and *Going Home Again*. He won the Nebula and World Fantasy Awards for his novelette "The Ugly Chickens."

Deborah Walker grew up in the most English town in the country, but she soon high-tailed it down to London, where she now lives with her partner, Chris, and her two young children. Find Deborah in the British Museum trawling the past for future inspiration or on her blog: http://deborahwalkersbibliography.blogspot.com. Her stories have appeared in *Nature's Futures*, *Cosmos* and *Daily Science Fiction*.

Eric Witchey has made a living as a freelance writer and communication consultant for over twenty years. In addition to many non-fiction titles, he has sold more than seventy short stories and two novels. His stories have appeared in six genres on five continents, and he has received recognition from New Century Writers, Writers of the Future, Writer's Digest, The Eric Hoffer Prose Award program, and other organizations. His How-To articles have appeared in *The Writer Magazine, Writer's Digest Magazine,* and other print and online magazines. When not teaching or writing, he spends his time fly fishing or restoring antique, model locomotives.

ABOUT THE EDITOR

Ekaterina Sedia resides in the Pinelands of New Jersey. Her critically acclaimed novels, *The Secret History of Moscow*, *The Alchemy of Stone*, *The House of Discarded Dreams*, and *Heart of Iron* were published by Prime Books. Her short stories have sold to *Analog, Baen's Universe, Subterranean*, and *Clarkesworld*, as well as numerous anthologies, including *Haunted Legends* and *Magic in the Mirrorstone*. She is also the editor of *Paper Cities* (World Fantasy Award winner), *Running with the Pack*, and *Bewere the Night*, as well as forthcoming *Bloody Fabulous* and *Willful Impropriety*. Visit her at www.ekaterinasedia.com.